THE CEMETERY BOOK

Books by Tom Weil

A Clearing in the Jungle
A Balance of Power
Last At the Fair: A Book of Travel
America's Heartland
America's South
The Cemetery Book: Graveyards, Catacombs and Other
  Travel Haunts Around the World

THE
CEMETERY BOOK

*Graveyards, Catacombs and
Other Travel Haunts
Around the World*

Tom Weil

HIPPOCRENE BOOKS
New York

For information, address:
HIPPOCRENE BOOKS, INC.
171 Madison Avenue
New York, NY 10016

ISBN 0-87052-916-1

Library of Congress Cataloging-in-Publication Data available

Printed in the United States of America

*To the memory of long-cemeteried Paul Kalter Weil (d. 1965),
with filial affection, and
To Peter and Emil, with fraternal fondness*

Contents

What is this world? what asketh men to have?
Now with his love, now in his colde grave
Allone, withouten any compaignye.

—Chaucer, *The Knightes Tale*

First Writes: By Way of Introduction

THIS book has been a labor of love, but a labor nonetheless. People frequently ask how long it takes to write a book. The only truly accurate answer is: all your life, for to a work a writer brings what he has experienced, thought, and felt ever since he gained awareness of the world. A more precise response to that question, however, is that a book requires two or three years to produce, taking into account only the time that the author is directly involved with the work. In the case of *The Cemetery Book: Graveyards, Catacombs and Other Travel Haunts Around the World* the correct answer would be

9

that I have been working on the book, off and on—with travel, research, investigation of foreign sources, drafts and revisions—for more than twenty years. Buried deep in my files repose this book's earliest versions, which originated in 1972. Ever since then I have continued to add material, recast, revise, and otherwise update the book. I do not mention this preparation period to suggest that such a lengthy gestation necessarily yields a quality result, but simply to indicate that the subject matter of this book has occupied my attention— and pleasurably so—for an unusually long period of time.

More than a quarter of a century has passed since, for reasons unknown to me, I first started to visit cemeteries during my foreign travels. It quickly became clear to me that cemeteries were fascinating places, and over the last twenty-five years I enthusiastically pursued my hobby of collecting cemeteries whenever I traveled in a foreign land. It is always interesting and perhaps baffling what, or who, attracts a person's attention in life. I am in no way a morbid or a melancholy type—rather the contrary—but somehow I always enjoyed visiting cemeteries, churchyards, catacombs, ossuaries and other such precincts of the departed. From such visits I accumulated over many years an extensive collection of first-hand impressions and information. To these on-the-spot findings I added material gleaned from years of research in libraries and overseas archives and, in time, this book took shape. But what shape?

The arrangement of this unwieldly and disparate material presented me with great vexations. What sort of connective tissue could possibly join the bare bones of all the different cemeteries scattered around the world? I finally managed to perceive certain similarities and connections between seemingly unrelated cemeteries, and out of the chaos I gradually imposed an order, but hardly an exclusive one, for virtually every cemetery covered in the text can be viewed from different perspectives and thus might well have been included in another chapter. As it is, each chapter integrates distinct and scattered cemeteries into a narrative that tells a story. Thus the cemeteries described serve as elements in a larger context, a convenience which both avoids a mere listing of the far-flung and greatly varying places included and offers the reader an over-riding point of view. A book review published in *The Economist* (in 1986, long after this book took form) of *The Railway Station: A Social History* by Jeffrey Richards and John Mackenzie noted: "The authors have used the station as a sort of tracer element to look at the history of a wide variety of social changes." Similarly, in this book the cemetery provides the underlying element which structures a cohesive narrative, one hopefully more interesting and thought-provoking than simply a disconnected account of each separate site.

By no means does this book present a complete account of important or interesting cemeteries around the world. Such a work would require many volumes, some of which I could write, for my own left-over material would serve to fill another book or two at least as long as this one. Here I have included from my cemetery collection only a relatively small selection, specimens chosen to give the flavor of graveyards and their charms and delights. Although the text includes most of the famous European cemeteries, it covers few Americans ones, for it emphasizes lesser known, if no less fascinating, burial grounds located in far lands or otherwise difficult of access. Due to space limitations I have for the most part omitted church tombs and epitaphs, especially interesting in England and France. Included, however, are some cemetery-connected subjects—especially material on cemetery history—which seemed to me to add a new dimension to the basic subject. In a very few cases I have slightly altered the wording or punctuation of an epitaph or inscription, or changed the lettering between capitals and lower case, in order to make the material clearer to the reader, but in no case have I altered the sense of the original. Translations from the European languages of epitaphs, inscriptions and published materials are, for the most part, mine. In those few cases where no date of death appears by a decedent's name, either the grave marker failed to include that information or I was otherwise unable to find it. Cemeteries are among life's most immutable elements and seldom change, except to add more graves. Very rarely, however, a latter-day visitor may find some sort of difference between my description of a particular cemetery and its present state, perhaps inevitable given the quarter century span of time it took me to assemble, organize and describe my cemetery collection in this book. For such variations I can only suggest that you take the text as a description not of how the place now appears but as how it once was.

A book like this consists of material gathered both by search—travel to the sites—and research. Over the years, as I sporadically buried myself in libraries, dusty archives, and other such collections to resurrect published material it became apparent to me that few complete bibliographies on the subject existed. For that reason I have included a list of more than 150 books, many of them somewhat obscure, which may be useful to someone who wishes to read further about cemeteries. In an attempt to restrict the bibliography to works of more general interest, studies of the sociological aspects of cemeteries, books on regional or local burial grounds, and other such specialized works are largely omitted.

Working for so many years on a subject which others might consider eccentric or even morbid never vexed me. At no time did I ever feel like the French writer Robert Sabatier, who in the preface of his 1967 *Dictionary of Death* relates that he felt compelled to hide from his friends the precise subject matter of the book he was writing. Although my subject did not embarrass me it did challenge me, particularly as to how to use dead characters to make the narrative come alive. In "Fenimore Cooper's Literary Offenses" Mark Twain lists "nineteen rules governing literary art," one of them requiring "that the personages in a tale shall be alive, except in the case of corpses, and that always the reader shall be able to tell the corpses from the others." Although everyone (except myself, for now) mentioned in this book is a corpse, hopefully it does not violate Twain's rule nor recall W. C. Fields's comment that undertakers in Philadelphia practice the world's most difficult profession because morticians there cannot always tell if they are burying a live person or a deceased one. But the fact that the people who populate the narrative happen to be among the departed does not represent the essence of this book. I want to emphasize that this work is about cemeteries, burial grounds, catacombs, and other such places: it is not a book about death.

I well realize that a cemetery collection, such as the one assembled in this volume, is not to everybody's taste. It seems to me that someone who happens to visit a few cemeteries (for other than personal reasons) either soon loses all interest in such places or becomes beguiled by them. For me, of course, the latter was the case, but others differ in their reaction. By the time John Lloyd Stephens, the famous nineteenth-century American traveler, visited the catacombs at Alexandria, Egypt, in 1835 he had seen the burial areas in Petra, Thebes and Jerusalem and was unimpressed, having "by this time lost much of my ardor for wandering among the tombs," he wrote in *Incidents of Travel in Egypt, Arabia Petraea, and the Holy Land*. I, however, never lost my enthusiasm for graveyards, and to this day I never fail to seek out and visit cemeteries and other such sights when traveling abroad. I would like to think that such a curious hobby might not seem completely without merit or interest. The great English travel writer Sacheverell Sitwell once considered the question of why one would spend years to produce a book on a somewhat eccentric and perhaps essentially useless subject. Referring in *For Want of a Golden City* to an early-nineteenth-century book by an "amateur of rose windows," Sitwell observes:

> Many a drearier holiday task can be imagined than that of travelling about collecting and comparing rose windows. Not so long ago, there were such amateurs in plenty, who spent their time in writing down the Latin inscriptions upon wall tablets and tomb stones. But that was in the age of Latinity; though I have even met in the Bapistery at Pisa an American lady and her daughter who told me that their hobby was going round such buildings collecting echoes *and* inscriptions.

The echoes I leave to others, but the inscriptions echoing from the past as found in cemeteries the world over I happily, as an amateur, collected over the years. In his *Brief Lives* John Aubrey, who also fancied graveyards and tomb inscriptions, remarked "How these curiosities would be quite forgott, did not such idle fellowes as I am putt them downe." Now I, a fellow idler, have put down my impressions of cemeteries and other travel haunts. Mortal men write books a lot in hope they won't be quite forgot.

I.

Gravestone Rambling

CEMETERIES enliven life. For years I have visited graveyards around the globe where those who came before us repose beneath the earth. Cemeteries contain not only the departed but also a rich array of artwork, gardens, writings, historical evocations, and any number of other enhancements which afford the visitor a pleasant and enlightening interlude. After Henry Wadsworth Longfellow guided a young Englishman named Henry Arthur Bright through Mt. Auburn Cemetery in Boston the visitor wrote in his diary: "Cemeteries here are all the 'rage'; people lounge in them and use them (as their tastes are inclined) for walking, making love, weeping, sentimentalizing, and every thing in short." I too have found cemeteries similarly hospitable to wide-ranging experiences, for burial grounds all around the world abound in delights that have induced me to linger for hours among the tell-tale epitaphs, artfully carved gravestones, statuary pompous and modest, park-like plantings, monuments, mausoleums and memories which haunt last resting places. Very nearly "every thing in short" eventually surfaces at cemeteries—the curious, the commonplace, the grotesque, the humorous and occasionally even the deceased. A century ago in 1896, a man named W. T. Vincent began the preface of his book *In Search of Gravestones Old and Curious:* "I am a gravestone rambler and I beg you to bear me company." Likewise, I have rambled with great pleasure through cemeteries the world over and, echoing Vincent's phrase, I invite you to revive with me some of the delights I discovered in those lively precincts of the dead.

Cemeteries are in no way morbid or gloomy, nor is this book. Quite to the contrary, burial sites—with their rich collection of monuments, epitaphs and evocations of other lives and times—offer life-enhancing experiences. Joseph Addison recorded in the *Spectator* (30 March 1711) that his visit to the tombs at Westminster Abbey in London provoked not melancholy but "rather thoughtfulness, that is not disagreeable." Addison spent the afternoon "amusing myself with the tombstones and inscriptions" at the abbey, where "I entertained myself with the digging of a grave," after which he examined at "this great magazine of mortality" the monuments "covered with such extravagant epitaphs, that, if it were possible for the dead person to be acquainted with them, he would blush at the praises which his friends have bestowed upon him." Then, "in the poetical quarter, I found there were poets who had no monuments, and monuments which had no poets." Finally Addison concludes, "I know that entertainments of this nature are apt to raise dark and dismal thoughts in timorous minds and gloomy imaginations; but for my own part, though I am always serious, I do not know what it is to be melancholy; and can therefore take a view of nature in her deep and solemn scenes, with the same pleasure as in her most gay and delightful ones." Graves may present deep and solemn scenes, but graveyards offer delightfully diverting places where, like Addison at Westminster Abbey's tombs, a visitor with an open mind, an inquisitive mentality and an attitude of amplitude can amuse and entertain himself, as have I through long years as a gravestone rambler.

So culturally, historically, biographically and scenically rich are cemeteries that people see in them many different things. In *Finnegan's Wake* James Joyce called a burial ground a "seemetery" and "hearseyard," an "underground heaven, or mole's paradise," its architect a "Mgr. Peurlachasse," a place where one finds "show coffins, winding sheets, goodbuy bierchepes, cinerary urns, liealoud blasses, snuffchests, poteen tubbs, lacrimal vases, hoodendoses, reekwaterbeckers, breakmiddles, zootzaks for eatlust." Until the early nineteenth century, masons in England used local stones for grave markers, so old burial grounds contain a record of an area's geology. When Vincent Van Gogh in Drenthe, Holland, came across "one of the most curious cemeteries I have ever seen," he describes it in colorful painterly terms—"one sees a number of graves grown with grass and heather, many of them marked with white posts bearing the name . . . [and] the dark stretch of pine wood which borders the cemetery separates a sparkling sky from the rugged earth." To the artist—who concludes, "It was not easy to paint"—the cemetery represented the subject for a picture. To the sculptor Lopez in Andre Malraux's *Hope,* cemeteries served more literally as a source for his art: "Good stone costs a heap, you know; but the cemeteries are stiff with it . . . So I looted the graveyards, nights, and all the stuff I turned out in those days was carved off R.I.P.s"—ripping off the R.I.P.s. As time went by and my own graveyard visits multiplied, I began to see cemeteries as great repositories of all sorts of curiosities—

treasure troves of artful and awful architecture, epitaphs grave and humorous, forgotten vignettes of history, odd facets of human society and culture—all relegated to relative obscurity. Somehow it became interesting to me to resurrect and preserve this long buried material which existed on the margin of life. So originated this book.

Cemeteries make good books. With their cast of characters, plots, covers, wordy epitaphs, dramatic stories, and book-shaped graves, tombs resemble tomes. In his *Autobiography* Mark Twain, referring to the many dead contemporaries he wrote about, noted that "this book is a cemetery." Contrariwise, a cemetery is a book, for at a burial ground can be read all sorts of stories, tales and dramas. A story lies behind—or beneath—each marker. Over the door of the New York Public Library reading room appears the inscription (unattributed, but from John Milton's *Areopagitica*): "A good Booke is the pretious life-blood of a master spirit, imbalm'd and treasur'd upon purpose to a life beyond life." So too, in a burial ground repose the embalmed, who still offer in their stories lively tales that transcend the grave. In *Constantinople* F. Marion Crawford complained that "there is something incongruous in treating dead men like books, to be arranged in neat order and catalogued as volumes are in a library." But graves seem more like tomes scattered at random in a second-hand book store, for the cemetery browser never knows just who or what he will find. This uncertainty, of course—and the anticipation which it inspires—is one of the great charms cemeteries offer the gravestone rambler. J. A. Piganiol de la Force, a collector of tomb inscriptions, went so far in his 1742 *Description de Paris, de Versailles, etc.* as to refer to epitaphs as "public archives." Indeed, cemeteries do serve as collections where a visitor can learn about a society's culture and history, for epitaphs document the past. A scholar named K. Hopkins studied ancient Roman tombstone inscriptions to determine two-thousand-year-old social and demographic information, recounted in "On the Probable Age Structure of the Roman Population," published in *Population Studies* (1966). I would not claim that graveyards necessarily provide an all-inclusive perspective on a civilization or people. Because burial areas prove more durable than most other remnants of the past, such funereal relics furnish only a limited view of a society. "Tombs, burial objects, mummies, temples, churches and pyramids tend to skew our view of the past," notes Daniel Boorstin. But cemeteries do tell us much about the culture which they serve, for how a society disposes of and remembers its dead says something about its way of life. "One can trace the transformations in existential values and social mores by analyzing the image of death which the cemeteries reflect," states Richard A. Etlin in *The Architecture of Death.*

So it is that one can unearth in a burial ground all sorts of evocations of a society's history and very essence. American gravestones from the period 1680 to 1810, for example, offer one of the best ways to study colonial and federal art as well as social, economic and religious conditions of the times. Dead men tell no tales but their tombstones do. Sometimes the stony stories inscribed on the markers err or exaggerate. In the United States "typographical errors" were so common in the early days that most states passed laws prohibiting tombstone information from serving as proof of birth, death or vital statistics, or as evidence in court. In France a widower successfully petitioned to remove from the monument to his late wife an epitaph, written by her father, stating that she had died "the victim of an unhappy marriage." Such postmortem digs, mistakes, and biographical hyperbole not withstanding, grave markers bear vignettes that can speak volumes about a deceased. Even the disquieting blank scroll that marks Herman Melville's grave at New York's Wood-lawn Cemetery says something while saying nothing. The famous French architect Viollet-le-Duc maintained that a history of mankind could be written from graves. "Of all monuments," he stated in the *Dictionary of French Architecture*, "tombs are those that present perhaps the broadest subject for the study of the archaeologist, historian, artist, even philosopher." It is this broad range of resources which, if you dig deep enough, graveyards offer. I gradually came to realize that breadth rather than depth characterized cemeteries. More than just a city of the dead, a necropolis—a metropolis populated by people in a state of lapsed existence—is a living settlement (very settled, to be sure), a repository of all the human dramas, comedies and tragedies. There at the graveyard survives no motion, but emotion; no motion, but moving inscriptions, descriptions and proscriptions; no motion, but the confused commotion of the past asking to be heard from beyond the grave.

Cemeteries are especially confused places, for they often consist of a largely random grouping of people who, for the most part, have only one thing in common—their non-being. Although certain graveyards include mainly departed with some affinity—religious, ethnic, institutional, geographic—most burial grounds around the world contain a chaos of characters. Cemeteries can give rise to strange grave fellows: you can never be sure who might end up lying near one another. Graveyards brim over with the unexpected, a feature which lends part of their charm. I have never visited a cemetery without being surprised. A graveyard always offers something whimsical, bemusing, unusual, unexpected, thought-provoking, past-invoking. Collecting cemeteries is like reading an encyclopedia: every page, every grave amuses, informs, instructs. Each article and each tomb appears randomly, with nothing in common but the first letter or the last rites. It seems passing strange how lifelessness draws together forever in one spot such disparate types. This is especially true of expatriate graveyards (described in Chapter III) where people from the far corners of the globe occupy their little corner of the earth surrounded by locals buried in their own homeland. How curious to find a stray traveler lying in alien soil in close proximity to utter strangers from a completely foreign culture. Just about the only curiosity I have failed to find in a cemetery is my own marker. Nathaniel Hawthorne once wrote: "I should like to find a gravestone in one of those old churchyards, with my own name on it." I quite agree: I too would like to discover such a marker—with Hawthorne's name on it, not mine.

Visiting cemeteries in no way induced in me morbid thoughts or intimations of mortality. Quite to the contrary, graveyards always deepened my interest in life. In *Algerian Chronicle* Albert Camus relates how, strolling about a burial ground at dusk, "I felt no different from these beings sheltered in the cemetery where they finally found themselves. But I would keenly feel the difference between us a few hours later when everyone would be obliged to eat something." To be sure, precincts of the dead offer much food for thought, but at the end of the day they instill an appetite for life: our thoughts turn to the next meal, the next day, the next travel adventure, all the nexts which time holds for us. The yesterdays buried in a cemetery inspire us to treasure our tomorrows.

For me, one of the greatest pleasures in visiting graveyards, especially remote or obscure ones, has been to revive— even if only in passing—the forgotten dead. There is something especially poignant about coming across the forlorn grave of an accomplished soul whose deeds and very existence have virtually vanished from human memory. Those ignored departed who struck my fancy sufficiently to record have, in a small way, been rescued from oblivion, resurrected and in these pages assembled from the far corners of the earth. Between the covers of this book they transcend their coffin cover and again join the here and now, momentarily escaping the there and then that possesses them. In "Our Old

Home" Hawthorne tells of finding a nearly illegible epitaph on a gravestone at the Lillington churchyard near Leamington Spa in England: "Poorly lived,/And poorly died/ Poorly buried/And no one cried." Hawthorne, who makes out the name of the deceased as one John Treeo (d. 1810), notes how "there is a quaint and sad kind of enjoyment in defeating (to such slight degree as the pen may do it) the probabilities of oblivion for poor John Treeo, and asking a little sympathy for him, half a century after his death." Now, more than a century and a half after his death, Treeo receives another recall from oblivion. Even poor Treeo merits preservation in our memory, for the past and all its inhabitants helped form the present just as we, in our turn, are now shaping the future. G. K. Chesterton discusses the importance of the past's influence on the present in *Orthodoxy,* arguing that our antecedents should not be disenfranchised: "Tradition means giving votes to the most obscure of all classes, our ancestors . . . All democrats object to men being disqualified by the accident of birth; tradition objects to their being disqualified by the accident of death." Chesterton pleads that we should "have the dead at our councils. The ancient Greeks voted by stones; these shall vote by tombstones. It is all quite regular and official, for most tombstones, like most ballot papers, are marked with a cross." In fact, the deceased vote whether they are on the rolls or not, for the past has legislated much of the contemporary way of life. It thus struck me as interesting to meet at their last resting places the long-gone adventurers, soldiers, explorers, travelers, scientists, inventors, politicians, clergymen, artists, authors, minor functionaries, and all the others who served to shape what to them was the future, what to us is the present, what to our descendants will be the past. Those of us who presently occupy the earth are at one with our predecessors beneath the earth and our successors, yet to materialize.

A chapter in Victor Hugo's *Les Miserables* bears the title, "Cemeteries Take What Is Given Them." In return, cemeteries give whatever a gravestone rambler wants to take from them. Epitaphs offer a graveyard's most obvious souvenirs. These incriptions range from the humorous to the pensive to the poetic: "What I expected but not so soon," "Anything for a change," "After Hollywood, nothing is a surprise" (actor Rex Bell), "Back to the silents" (Clark Gable's proposal for his own epitaph), and the anti-epitaph on the late-nineteenth-century grave of Aseneath Soule, a poor soul whose stone at Mayflower Cemetery in Duxbury, Massachusetts, laments; "The chisel can't help her any"; the thought-provoking: "Death's but a Sleepe,/and if a Sleepe,/Why Then to Bed" (William Rounsevall, d. 1659, in Cornwall, England); the poetry to Clorina Haywood at St. Bartholomew's, Edgbaston, England:

Warm summer sun shine kindly here:
Warm summer wind blow softly here:
Green sod above lie light, lie light:
Good-night, Dear Heart: good-night, good-night.

An epitaph can often evoke the decedent and, in some cases, humankind. During a church service in Suffolk, Charles Dickens's David Copperfield notices a grave inscription on the sanctuary wall: "Affliction sore long time I bore/physicians were in vain/Till death gave ease and God did please/To ease my grief and pain." These sentiments provoked David to ponder the human element underlying the words: "I look up at the monumental tablets on the wall, and try to think of Mr. Bodgers late of this parish, and what the feelings of Mrs. Bodgers must have been, when afflictions sore, long time Mr. Bodgers bore, and physicians were in vain. I wonder whether they called in Mr. Chillip, and he was in vain; and if so, how he likes to be reminded of it once a week." David's reaction to an epitaph—that attempt to expand "the little, little span/The dead are borne in mind," as Kipling put it—presents a quintessential example of a burial inscription's evocative effect on the living, for the funereal words in a certain sense brought old Bodgers, with all his aches and pains, back to life. Each time I read an epitaph anywhere in the world, I tried to visualize the person memorialized and, like David Copperfield, almost always wondered about their life, for not only ghosts of the departed but also so many unanswered questions haunt graveyards.

As time goes by only a fragment of a memory, a brief epitaph, a fading relief portrait, an effaced bust, a weather-weary statue, remains to represent a life. Those artworks give shape to the person memorialized by the inscriptions. Such statues and busts, along with a wide range of funerary architecture, lend cemeteries the aspect of a museum. The great cemeteries of Paris—Père Lachaise, Montparnasse, and Montmartre, described in Chapter II—no doubt contain more high quality works by famous artists than most provincial museums, while a well-Carrara-ed Italian necropolis, such as Genoa's Staglieno, abounds with eye-catching statuary. Necro-art includes all manner of works: "Saddened angels, crosses, broken pillars, family vaults, stone hopes praying with upcast eyes," as James Joyce's Leopold Bloom found at Dublin's Glasnevin cemetery (also discussed in Chapter II).

Some cemeteries seem more like sculpture gardens than places to inter the departed, although as poet George Herbert noted, "No Church-yard is so handsome, that a man would desire straight to be buried there." Statuary can afford the deceased a new lease on life, for the quality or novelty of artwork at a grave bears no necessary relationship to the occupant's fame. A person obscure while alive might, by the merits of his monument, attract more postmortem attention than he enjoyed while among the living. Some funerary monuments attain the status of masterworks. So striking did

the young John Ruskin find the fifteenth-century tomb sculpture at the grave of Ilaria del Carreto in Lucca, Italy, that the
work inspired him to become an art critic. Viewing the
monument, he "literally *began* the study of architecture,"
Ruskin recalled in his autobiography *Praeterita,* and ever after
that "loveliest Christian tomb" which incarnated "Breathing
womanhood" served him as a "supreme guide" in matters of
taste. Architectural as well as art treasures also embellish
some cemeteries, where mausoleums, residences that house
the departed, and other note-worthy constructions create a
veritable city of the dead which seems a peaceful analogue to
the bustling city beyond the cemetery walls. In *The Space of
Death: A Study of Funerary Architecture, Decoration and
Urbanism* Michel Ragon comments that mortality "has only
too seldom been studied from the point of view of architecture, urbanism, and decoration." These subjects represent
only a few of the many perspectives with which a visitor can
view cemeteries, for they contain virtually every element
known to life except life itself. But that the gravestone
rambler supplies.

Back in 1843, when the English were beginning to think
about modernizing their burial grounds, J. C. Louden's book
*On the Laying Out, Planting and Managing of Cemeteries and on
the Improvement of Churchyards* suggested that not only a
graveyard's architecture but also its plantings might serve as a
show-place to inspire visitors. A cemetery "properly designed, laid out, ornamented with tombs, planted with trees,
shrubs, and herbaceous plants, all named, and the whole
properly kept, might become a school of instruction in architecture, scuplture, landscape gardening, arboriculture, bot-
any, and in those important parts of general gardening, neat-
ness, order and high keeping." So botanically sublime are
some cemeteries that they seem like parks or gardens. One
Englishman, a well-known horticulturist named William
Robinson, even argued in 1880, in *God's Acre Beautiful, or the*

Cemeteries of the Future, that a burial ground "is most fittingly arranged as a garden." Some graveyards, indeed, became park-like enclaves—so-called garden cemeteries—while in a few cases old cemeteries were resurrected as gardens when the Disused Burial Grounds Act (1884) and the Open Spaces Act (1887) authorized the conversion of former London graveyards into public gardens. After noticing how Boston's famous Mt. Auburn, the first garden cemetery in America (1831), attracted thousands of visitors to its leafy precincts, landscape expert Andrew Jackson proposed the creation of the nation's first urban public garden space, and so began New York City's Central Park, a direct descendant of a certain sort of cemetery. Not only does funereal greenery offer pleasant park-like enclaves but it also symbolizes an idealized afterlife as described by King Arthur in Tennyson's *Idylls of the King.* The monarch relates that after his passing he will dwell in a lush "island valley . . . Deep meadow'd, happy, fair with orchard-lawns/And bowery hollows." Such an idyllic enclave many cemeteries I visited offered—a preview of a paradisal heaven, probably the only view of such a place that I will ever get.

Burial areas serve the living not only as outdoor museums, parks, and gardens but also for any number of other human activities. The unusual Merry Cemetery, located in Sapinta, Romania, is a kind of theme park which amuses visitors with nearly three hundred brightly painted, oak grave markers bearing witty verses about the departed. One typical inscription describes the fate of Dumitru Holdis, who died after years of imbibing *tzuica,* the local plum brandy: "*Tzuica* is a genuine pest; It brings us torture and unrest; Since it brought it to me, you see,/I kicked the bucket at forty-three." In contrast to the generally held view that death is no joking matter, the concept of the Merry Cemetery stems from the idea held by the Dacians, ancestors of today's Romanians, that mortality should occasion mirth—always leave 'em

laughing. In this spirit *National Lampoon* once published a
parody of *Playboy* entitled *Playdead* which, in a discussion of
France's Côte Funèbre—a renowned resort area very dead in
the off season—reported that the "best known of the many
cemeteries in the region is the quaint, overgrown burial
ground in St. Crapaud where Reggie Autonome des Trans-
ports Parisiens, the twenty-four-year-old heir to the French
subway fortune, was buried after he drove his Lotus Elan into
a lime tree on the Grande Corniche." The account continues:
"Best of the smaller French cemeteries is the Cimetière of
Notre Dame de l'Addition in Lavez-les-Mains, a small, pleasant village about thirty kilometers west of Cannes. The local
undertakers are Le Grand et Fils, and they have a well deserved three-shovel rating from the prestigious *Mortchelin*
Guide. Insist on trying the local embalming fluids. They tend
to be a little garlicky and quite filling, but they make up in
zest what they lack in sophistication." (Baedeker gives this
only one star.) As early as ancient times people imbibed and
dined in cemeteries—three-shovel category meals featuring
vintages superior to pungent embalming fluid. The Greeks
held funeral feasts at tombs, at which mourners also offered
food and wine to the deceased, perhaps a precursor of the
practice of adorning graves with vegetal leavings, flowers.
Residents of Beijing use the nearby Ming Tombs as a picnic
ground, while in *Seven Pillars of Wisdom* T. E. Lawrence
recalls the time he stopped in the Negev Desert near
Beersheba to eat "in the little cemetery, off a tomb, into
whose joints were cemented plaits of hair, the sacrificial
head-ornaments of mourners." Not far away at Petra in the
southern Jordanian desert, nineteenth-century American
traveler John Lloyd Stephens slept in an ancient Nabatean
tomb. "I crawled in feet first and found myself very much in
the condition of a man buried alive," he recalled in *Incidents of
Travel in Egypt, Arabia Petraea, and the Holy Land.* "But never
did a man go to his tomb with so much satisfaction as I felt

. . . The worthy old Edomite for whom the tomb was made never slept in it more quietly than I did." All these practical uses of cemeteries—amusement, eating, sleeping, and too many other activities to recount—transmute them from passive recipients of the departed into places hospitable to the living, for it is the living who most benefit from cemeteries and the related rituals. As St. Augustine observed; "Wherefore, all these last offices and ceremonies, that concern the dead, the careful funeral arrangements, and the equipment of the tomb, and the pomp of obsequies, are rather the solace of the living than the comfort of the dead."

Graves of the famous are especially alluring to the living. Such monuments become sightseeing destinations which draw even people uninterested in cemeteries. There is something irresistible about a hero's last resting place. I have on occasion detoured many miles just to visit the tomb of a famous figure I particularly respected. Other times the grave of a personage unknown to me but renowned in the country where I was traveling yielded pleasant surprises. Having grown up with the works of Mark Twain and his beloved Mississippi I for years wanted to see the author's burial site in Elmira, New York, far from his and my native Missouri. This longing was eventually rewarded when I visited the simple stone marker at Woodlawn Cemetery. Nearby rises a granite monument exactly twelve feet high—two fathoms, the depth which in the olden days leadmen on the river's paddlewheelers would signal by calling out to the pilot, "mark twain."

At the more remote town of Konya, in central Turkey, a combination mosque, museum, monastery, mausoleum, and memorial to Mevlana, founder of the Whirling Dervishes, is much venerated and visited by Turks but somehow little known to Missourians like me. But, then, I guess not too many Konyans revere Twain. Nor far from Mevlana's tomb an inscription records one of his thoughts, a delightfully open and forgiving sentiment: "Come, come, come again,/ Whoever you may be,/Come again, even though/You may be a pagan or a fire worshiper./Our center is not one of despair,/ Come again, even if you may have/Violated your vows a hundred times,/Come again."

In Chapter VIII of his famous *Ancient Funerall Monuments* (1631), the first work in English on epitaphs, John Weever discusses "the ardent desire most men have, and ever had, to visit the Tombes and Sepulchres of eminent worthy persons," observing how all men "are as greedily affected to view the sacred Sepulchres of worthie, famous personages, yea, and the very places, where such have beene interred, although no Funerall Monument at all bee there remaining, to continue their memories." Only at the grave which holds the mortal remains of a so-called immortal can we make a vague connection with what survives of his earthly being. Some deep-seated need inspires us to visit the greats: to gain inspiration, to pay homage, to dwell in the proximity of genius, but most of all, to make simple human contact with one who has left his mark on the world. When Virginia Woolf visited Shakespeare's grave at Stratford-upon-Avon in 1934 she meditated, as noted in *A Writer's Diary,* how "down there one foot from me lay the little bones that had spread over the world this vast illumination." Unlike many other towering figures, with Shakespeare "all the rest, books, furniture, pictures, etc. has completely vanished." Of course there are the plays, but of the man himself only the bones remain, and to visit them many a traveler has made the pilgrimage to Stratford. Such is the power that a few disintegrating bodily fragments can exert on people living nearly four centuries later.

When Shakespeare died in 1616 his will left money to buy so-called mourning rings—a tradition which originated in the Middle Ages—for some of his friends, including his brother actors Heminges, Burbage, and Cundell, whom he

fondly calls "my fellows." Mourning rings represent just one
of the hundreds of rituals practiced the world over in connection with mortality, funerals, burials and cemeteries. Graveyards, funeral rites and associated practices encompass all
elements of human life, and for that reason they have never
ceased to fascinate me. So rich in human interest are cemeteries that it has puzzled me why so few people appreciate
them. Perhaps no one likes to be reminded of final matters.
But for me, each cemetery I visit presents only firsts—novel
and unusual sights never before encountered. Occasionally in
my wanderings among the departed, I have come across a
few people visiting graveyards for reasons other than familial
or professional duties. Like me they wandered, strolled, and
studied, stopping here to read an epitaph, there to admire an
artful marker, elsewhere to examine an unusual monument.
It somehow pleased me to realize that at least a few other
souls (call them eccentric, if you will—I would describe them
as inquisitive and broadminded) found cemeteries sufficiently
of interest to devote a few precious living hours to the type of
place where they would eventually spend an eternity.

However, I never did become a cemetery fanatic, obsessed
with the subject like a few curious characters who spent their
lives, as well as their deaths, in burial grounds. A man named
François Roger de Gaignières began traveling through France
in 1695 to collect information on some three thousand
tombs, many illustrated by Louis Boudan. De Gaignières
delivered to the royal library in Paris thirty-one portfolios of
drawings, now housed in the Bibliothèque Nationale, apart
from a few illustrations which ended up at Oxford's Bodelian
library. More eccentric was a Scotsman named Robert Peterson, a stone mason who in the mid-eighteenth century deserted his wife and family to devote the next forty years to the
erection and repair of tombs for the Covenanters, a Protestant
group persecuted under the reign of Charles II. Peterson,
who inspired Sir Walter Scott's "Old Mortality" character,

wandered to isolated churchyards accompanied only by his white pony which lived on the grass growing at neglected graves. The solitary cemetery rambler was finally laid to rest in 1801, permanently installed in an environment which had nourished most of his waking hours.

As indicated by the bibliography at the end of this book, a certain number of people have found it a worthwhile endeavor to record information or impressions about burial grounds. Most of the listed authors produced their works for professional reasons, but a few, like myself, took to the field as amateurs: we did it for sheer pleasure. Although Rock of Ages granite monuments will never be as popular as rock groups—gravestones cannot compete with the Rolling Stones—perhaps this book will inspire a few new amateur cemetery collectors. They say that people who live together for a long time begin to resemble each other. I wonder if something similar is true for those who pursue a particular hobby or activity, like cemetery collecting. Do dog lovers get fleas? Does avarice possess coin collectors? Do gourmets suffer from a dyspeptic or a saucy disposition? Are writers wordy, travelers flightly? Then what about cemetery collectors? One day in a second-hand book shop in London, when I requested Mrs. Holmes's volume on London cemeteries the clerk asked me if I was an undertaker. My request may have prompted that inquiry but perhaps after years of visiting cemeteries, my mien and demeanor also contributed.

In a way, I have been an undertaker, undertaking to collect and collate and record my impressions of graveyards around the globe. There is no doubt that, in time, this book will be buried among the millions of other dust-laden volumes which repose on the shelves of libraries—those cemeteries of perhaps vain efforts. Such a fate disturbs me no more than the fact that one day I will repose, likewise dusty, in the last burial ground I shall ever frequent. Maybe my many visits to such places prepared me for that end. What I learned during my many years of gravestone rambling was that the ramble, rather than the gravestones—the travel, the activity, the challenge, the experiences, not the reminders of mortality—represented the essence of my hobby. How I have enjoyed it all: the quiet country graveyards, the remote and obscure burial grounds, the vast metropolitan necropolises, the gloomy catacombs and the cheery sun-lit cemeteries, the amusing epitaphs and the ridiculous ones, the artful markers and the pompous monuments, and above all, or below all, buried in their subterranean habitats, the people, famous and obscure, celebrated and forgotten, who preceded and predeceased us. Those long-gone souls were my companions over the miles and through the years. Reader: I know, as do you, that sooner or later you will get to a cemetery. In the meantime, why not join me in these pages for the fun and fascination of that lively, life-enhancing activity which I, in my time, have found so delightful—gravestone rambling?

II.

—

Cemeteries in History

ON the night of 16 February 1673 Molière, France's greatest playwright, was performing the title role in his play *Le malade imaginaire,* a character preoccupied with the treatment of his imaginary illnesses. During the show Molière collapsed on stage. Or perhaps it was the imaginary invalid who collapsed. The audience at the Palais-Royal theater in Paris was no doubt momentarily skeptical of the actor's stage illness, much as the French bureaucrat who, on being told that his wife had died, asked, "Is it official?" Attendants carried Molière to his house in the rue de Richelieu where the actor-author died within a few hours: life—or death—imitating art. Molière, it was said, did "mimick death" on the stage so well, "or rather ill," that "Death, delighted with his wond'rous art,/Snatch'd up the copy, to the grief of France,/And made it an original at once." Not having received the final sacraments or renounced the acting profession—a disreputable one in the church's eyes—Molière was buried after sunset without ceremony at St. Joseph's graveyard in Paris.

Some years later workers exhumed the body for transfer to Alexander Lenoir's museum of French monuments where the actor-author was to be once again on show. After reposing for a dozen years at Lenoir's museum, located in the present École des Beaux Arts building in Paris, Molière's remains were once again moved, this time to Père Lachaise cemetery. The famous writer's tomb helped to lend the burial ground sufficient prestige for the Parisian elite to covet being interred there.

Père Lachaise, the world's most famous and celebrity-filled cemetery, opened on 2 December 1804, the same week that Napoleon was proclaimed emperor. A lawyer named Nicolas Frochot, later executor of Napoleon's will, promoted the burial ground, the first major modern cemetery anywhere. In *The Architecture of Death: The Transformation of the Cemetery in Eighteenth-Century Paris* Richard A. Etlin asserts that Père Lachaise "actually represents a turning point in one thousand years of Western history." Although it is for the most part true that from before the Middle Ages to the early nineteenth century, there were no important free-standing, specially planned cemeteries, Père Lachaise represents less a turning point than a returning point. It was a reversion to the time of antiquity when the pyramids in Egypt, the Kerameikos cemetery in Athens, the Etruscan burial grounds in Italy (all discussed below) and other necropolises around the Mediterranean basin served as sites or even cities of the dead, with identifiable graves and, in some cases, individualized markers.

All such burial areas, ancient or more modern, become part of living history, for they form intrinsic elements of the society and culture of their civilization. Referring to his fellow French historians, the famous scholar Jules Michelet (d. 1874) observed: "Augustin Thierry calls history a narration, Guizot calls it an analysis; I considered that history should be a resurrection"—a sentiment preserved on Michelet's tomb at Père Lachaise. If history is indeed a resurrection then what better place to resurrect a society's past than in the cemeteries that form part of its cultural fabric and even its very essence? The ancient cemeteries preserve much about long gone civilizations, while latter-day graveyards reflect the city and society each serves. As Philippe Julian observed about Père Lachaise in *Le Cirque du Père-Lachaise* (1957), "the demographic distribution of the cemetery is, on a smaller scale, exactly that of Paris . . . The central areas suggest the 'grands boulevards,' and it is they which receive the most visitors, while in the picturesque side streets of the oldest part, around the aristocratic but dilapidated tombs reigns the silence of the faubourg Saint-Germain." So do cemeteries and their occupants incarnate many of the historical characteristics and characters that define a culture.

In medieval Paris bodies were literally ossified. The remains of Jean de la Fontaine, a contemporary of Molière also removed to Père Lachaise, originally reposed in the Cimetière ing the first years of the Christian era a new attitude developed toward the departed, with the devout seeking to be buried near a martyr's tomb. This practice, which originated in fourth- and fifth-century Roman Africa—at Damous el-Karita basilica at Carthage, for example, tombstone covers formed the floor—soon spread to Spain and Rome. In time, on the site of the revered tomb rose a chapel or church where important religious figures were buried over the years. So began a practice which has survived until the present day: after church officials refused to let ship-owner Aristotle Onassis bury his son Alexander (d. 1973) in a chapel on the

Greek island of Skorpios—a privilege reserved only for saints—the billionaire interred the boy next to the sanctuary and later built a chapel annex over the tomb.

The tomb of St. Germain, the bishop of Paris who consecrated the city, was originally installed adjacent to the Abbey of St. Vincent and in 755 moved beneath the high altar of the sanctuary which was renamed St. Germain and is now known as Saint-Germain-des-Près. Beneath the altar at St. Peter's in Rome reposes that saint. His sacrophagus served as the church's first altar, an arrangement of the type which no doubt led to early Christian altars being built in the shape of tombs. As churches proliferated they outnumbered the supply of saints and martyrs, so the devout began to divide holy remains into pieces, distributing the bones as relics to sanctify sanctuaries across Christendom. Priests and bishops, desiring to repose near the relics, found resting places beneath church floors, and before long kings and aristocrats sought the same privilege. In 337 at Constantinople Constantine the Great introduced the practice of church burial for a Christian monarch. At his request, he was interred in the forecourt of the Church of the Holy Apostles, which he had built. Clovis, the first Christian king of Gaul, was buried in 511 in a basilica on the site of the present-day Mont Sainte-Geneviève in Paris.

By the late thirteenth century rich commoners contributed large sums to the church to assure themselves permanent places in a sanctuary, while less exalted or monied types had to settle for being interred in the churchyard. The post-mortem arrangements reflected the stratification of society: the farther inside the church, the more prestigious one's position. A parish gravedigger named Robert Philip mocked these pretensions with his epitaph:

Here lie I at the chapel door,
Here lie I because I'm poor.

The farther in the more you'll pay,
Here lie I as warm as they.

Some self-denying souls who professed humility preferred to
repose at the church entrance where worshipers would tred
on the remains. Pepin the Short requested burial belly-up in
front of a church's main door, enabling the faithful to walk on
him in expiation of the sins of his father, Charles Martel, who
in the eighth century confiscated church property to raise
money to fight the Saracens. At Santiago church, in the
upper part of Trujillo, Spain, Diego Alfonso de Tapia, who
established the sanctuary, directed in his will that he be buried
just outside the entrance so that all who enter the church
would notice his grave. At the doorstep a slab with a relief
coat of arms bears the inscription: "Sepultura de Diego Alfonso de Tapia."

As demand grew for burial space near churches Saint
Cuthbert petitioned the pope for permission to establish
graveyards next to sanctuaries, a request granted in 752.
These burial grounds, consecrated by a bishop and enclosed
as separate parcels of hallowed terrain, were accepted as
appropriate areas for the remains of the devout. So began the
rather ossified patterns which prevailed unchanged in most of
Europe for a thousand years.

In Medieval Paris bodies were literally ossified. The remains of Jean de la Fontaine, a contemporary of Molìere also
removed to Père Lachaise, originally reposed in the Cimitière
des Innocents, the Cemetery of the Holy Innocents, which
had served for more than five hundred years as one of the
city's main burial grounds. The bone-crammed courtyard
occupied a small area between the rues Saint-Denis, de la
Ferronnerie, de la Lingerie (all of which still exist in the old
Les Halles market area) and the rue aux Fers. A fountain and
the Innocents Square, built in 1958, now stand on part of the

terrain where once huge common graves, thirty feet deep and about half as long and wide, held the remains of generations of Parisians. In the early days wolves and also grave robbers, who scavenged bones to supply to anatomy teachers, frequented the Cimetière des Innocents. So did prostitutes, derelicts and tramps, prompting one medieval visitor to remark that Paris was a good town to live in but not to die in. The earth at the cemetery fairly seethed and bubbled as the cadavers decomposed. After the flesh melted away workers removed the bones from the ground and stored them in ossuaries built around the courtyard.

No such hell-holes exist in Paris these days. But at venerable St. Severin church survives the city's only ancient ossuary, a fifteenth-century structure which once housed bones removed from the church's cemetery to make way for new bodies. A large stone plaque bearing a relief skull notes: "Here is the sepulcher of parish priests." One gallery runs to the church, while along the south edge of the tree-shaded churchyard stretch triangular-peaked galleries with vaulted ceilings. Ten dragon-like gargoyles look down from their ledges, except one independent fellow whose long neck curves gracefully to his right toward the church.

In former times, though, no charnel house compared with the gruesome Cimetière des Innocents. It was here that in 1424–25 there appeared the earliest known painting of the Dance Macabre, or Dance of Death, a grisly mural on the bone gallery along the rue de la Ferronnerie showing cadavers frolicking with lively and still fleshy figures, all doomed together. The cemetery served eighteen parishes, two hospitals and the Paris morgue, receiving some two thousand bodies a year, about one-tenth of the city's dead. In the eighteenth century the cemetery became a kind of community center with shop stalls, a children's playground, and public scribes enlivening the scene. By mid-century, city authorities grew concerned about the sanitary conditions at

the Cimetière des Innocents, which by then held the leavings
of some two million bodies, as well as the fifty or so other
crowded, festering burial grounds. In 1737 the Paris parliament took the first official step to deal with the problem by
requesting doctors to investigate the city's burial grounds.
The resulting report recommended better interment procedures and more hygienic maintenance of graves. In 1745
the Abbé Porée recommended in *Letters on Church Tombs* that,
for health reasons, cemeteries be transferred outside of
towns. After further investigations, the Paris parliament issued a decree on 12 March 1763 which, quoting the medical
community's concerns as to hygiene, proposed closing the
existing cemeteries and opening eight new ones on the outskirts of Paris.

The clergy opposed the proposal, not only for religious
reasons but also—and perhaps primarily—because the church
would lose revenue and influence if churchyard burial
grounds were shut down. Groups with a vested interest in
death often greatly influenced burial and cemetery procedures. In twelfth century France the church encouraged the
use of wills, stipulating that decedents without such a document could not be buried in a church or churchyard. In his
will the devout testator specified the number of masses to be
celebrated for the repose of his soul, a service which, of
course, exacted a fee from the estate. By the fourteenth
century many noble French families had become impoverished because of payments for such prayers. In Eliza-
bethan England the College of Arms controlled burials of the
aristocracy, an essentially political procedure supported by
the queen to demonstrate that the death of a powerful peer
would not diminish the throne, as another noble immediately
succeeded the deceased. For obvious reasons the College of
Arms—which supplied heralds who charged for garments,
the hearse, and other services—grew fond of funerals. One
blueblood, Robert, Earl of Dorset—put off by the practice—

stated in his will that he did not want a heraldic burial as "the usual solemnities of funerals such as heralds set down for noblemen are only good for heralds and drapers."

Back in France, on 10 May 1776 Louis XVI issued a "Déclaration Royale" providing for new cemeteries, a reform hastened by the noxious odors and sanitary problems at the Cimetière des Innocents, a bone pit seething with festering bodies. A contemporary (1775) visitor to France named Philip Thicknesse—a rather eccentric fellow, patron of the painter Thomas Gainsborough, who wrote such off-beat books as *An Account of Four Persons Starved to Death at Ditchworth* and a work on an automated chess machine—described in *A Year's Journey Through France and Part of Spain* the gruesome cemeteries that then disfigured and endangered Paris: "There are several burial pits in Paris, of a prodigous size and depth, in which the dead bodies are laid, side by side, without any earth being put over them till the ground tier is full; then, and not till then, a small layer of earth covers them, and another layer of dead comes on, till by layer upon layer, and dead upon dead, the hole is filled with a mass of human corruption enough to breed a plague."

In late 1779 putrid odors from the Cimetière des Innocents wafted into houses along the adjacent rue de la Lingerie, and by the summer of 1780 the noxious fumes spread to nearby areas. In an attempt to reduce the stench, workers opened a fifty-foot-deep common grave adding limestone as a disinfectant, but the odors persisted. Later in 1780 the authorities closed the Cimetière des Innocents, and within seven years they had shut down all the other Paris cemeteries. In 1785 the Cimetière des Innocents became a park, "silent and sinister," according to a contemporary account, at last free of the millions of bones which had been removed from the site for installation in the Paris catacombs (described in Chapter IV). Thus was transformed the ground which itself had transformed so many corpses. For half a millenium the dead of

Paris had mouldered in medieval era conditions. Now the city was ready to modernize its burial customs, instituting in the late eighteenth century procedures and practices which still prevail.

After authorities closed down the Cimetière des Innocents it became necessary to invent a new and modern way to dispose of the dead. Proposals submitted to the city swept away medieval cobwebs by suggesting practical, functional solutions. In 1801 forty entries responded to an essay contest held by the Institut de France on the subject: "What ceremonies should be performed at funerals and what regulations should be adopted regarding burial?" After much discussion the city issued a decree on 12 June 1804 setting forth rules for cemeteries and funerals in Paris, regulations which for the most part remain in effect today. The main innovations included provisions that bodies lie only side by side, not atop one another; that cemeteries should be made park-like places, garnished with greenery; that families could buy plots in perpetuity; and that survivors could erect monuments for specific decedents. The latter two provisions proved extremely popular. In effect they individualized death, personalizing it in contrast to the anonymous mass mortality common at such medieval cemeteries as the Cimetière des Innocents. By the end of the nineteenth century grants in perpetuity occupied fully three-fourths of the terrain at Paris burial grounds, while the use of tombstones at Père Lachaise, the city's first new-style cemetery, rose from fourteen in 1805, the first full year of operation, to seventy-six in 1810, 635 in 1815, and then an average of nearly two thousand a year for more than a century.

The idea for Père Lachaise began at the turn of the century when the above-mentioned Nicolas Frochot thought of locating a burial ground on Mont-Louis, the seventeen-acre hill-top estate of Baron Desfontaines, northeast of Paris. As prefect of the Seine, Frochot encountered little difficulty acquiring the property for 160,000 francs, about one franc per square meter, a small sum for such a prime parcel. It was perhaps not by chance that Alexandre-Théodore Brongniart, the architect who designed the bourse (stock exchange)—that citadel of bourgeois, monied Paris society—received the commission to create plans for the new necropolis which would be the final resting place for members of that society.

Contemporaries in England asserted that modern cemeteries should remain free of boorish, bourse-like, market touches. In *Picturesque Sketches of London Past and Present* published in 1852, Thomas Miller, arguing for solemnity in cemeteries, opined that "the price of corn, the state of the money-market, or the rising and falling of the funds are matters which ought to be discussed far away from those [departed] we followed, and wept over, and consigned to their silent chambers, there to sleep till the last trumpet sounds." But when London stockbroker Timothy Scrip of Change Alley in Cornhill died leaving a fortune of six thousand pounds an observer noted that, the exchange "being shut at the time of his death, he was not able to make a transfer, or carry any part of it to his account in the other world."

Frochot marketed Père Lachaise as a place where, in effect, the wealthy could, unlike the expired Scrip, transfer evidences of their bank accounts to the other world in the form of expensive monuments bearing inscriptions rich with praise. Père Lachaise soon served as the ultimate exchange: sinking funds, expired warrants, called securities, restructuring, going short against the box, and the like found their analogues at the cemetery, where epitaphs offered the final quotes.

When Nicolas Frochot acquired Molière's remains in 1817 for reinterment at Père Lachaise he also obtained from Alexander Lenoir's museum of French monuments the bones of another renowned French writer, Jean de la Fontaine (d.

1695), whose *Fables,* featuring animal characters, have delighted generations of readers. Like Molière, La Fontaine was reburied at Père Lachaise in an effort to improve the graveyard's standing among important Parisians. Earlier, in 1806, Frochot tried to lend the cemetery a regal air by arranging the transfer of the remains of Louise de Lorraine (d. 1589), queen of Henry III. Frochot later upgraded his collection of famous corpses by trading Queen Louise for the bodies of Heloise and Abelard. Louise moved on to the Cathedral of St. Denis near Paris, where other French royalty repose. The legendary twelfth-century lovers came to rest in a Gothic-style tomb designed by Lenoir (described below), in Père Lachaise. By such promotional techniques did Frochot gradually shape the cemetery into a fashionable quarter of Paris where the city's bourgeoisie not only sought to be buried but also competed to construct the most notable monuments. Père Lachaise offered real estate beyond the grave and a postmortem status for those unwilling to let death diminish their place in the world. It gave "absolute selfhood to those fearful of losing it," as Frederick Brown put it in *Père-Lachaise: Elysium as Real Estate,* for in the city of the dead there existed an "ossified social hierarchy," much as the one which defined a person's standing in the city of the living.

Paris socialites and leading lights gradually began moving from the city's swanky west side, where the upper crust lived, to the Cemetery of the East (Père Lachaise's official name) where they reposed. Even Parisian land speculations and profiteering reached the cemetery, for in March 1822, when the now dead Baron Desfontaines returned to the estate he had previously sold for interment, his widow was forced to pay about 250 francs a square meter for his new quarters, a rise of 24,500% in eighteen years. The cemetery had truly made a killing.

By 1825 Père Lachaise, the only Paris cemetery named for

a person—Jesuit friar François d'Aix de la Chaize, confessor to Louis XIV from 1675 to 1709 and sometime resident of Mont-Louis—had become not only a coveted final resting place but also a popular tourist attraction. Several guidebooks to the cemetery appeared, and early visitors waxed enthusiastic about the new stop on the sightseeing circuit. An English visitor commented in 1818 that "nothing can be more striking and more affecting to the imagination, than this place of burial," while an American visitor named Nathaniel Carter observed in 1825: "In all respects it very far surpasses anything of the kind I have ever seen, and the design strongly recommends itself to the imitation of all great cities." Indeed, the innovative Parisian graveyard served as inspiration and model for the new American park-like cemeteries developed in the 1830s such as Mt. Auburn in Boston, Philadelphia's Laurel Hill, and Green-Wood in Brooklyn.

Père Lachaise continues as one of Paris's great tourist attractions. An estimated eight hundred thousand visitors a year wander the winding paths—garnished by twelve thousand trees and populated by some four hundred cats—where more than a million Parisians repose. I have spent many a diverting day among the tombs there, sepulchers which house the famous, the infamous, the obscure, the remembered and, mostly, the forgotten. Although the nearby tavern called "Mieux ici qu'en face" (better here than across the way), once frequented by cemetery visitors, no longer exists, on the streets around Père Lachaise stand florists, monument shops and stores selling funeral items, places of the type that prompted French writer Villiers de l'Isle-Adam to remark: "Those are the people who invented death." The metro stop Père-Lachaise takes you near the cemetery's main entrance, by the evocatively named rue du Repos at the bottom of the hilly enclave, while from the Gambetta stop, visitors can start at the top and proceed down hill. The bookstore Éditions Vermet, located at 10 avenue du Père-Lachaise near the Gambetta stop, sells guidebooks and other publications relating to the cemetery, which is divided into nearly a hundred *divisions* comprised of smaller areas called *secteurs*.

Like chefs who eat their own cooking, the cemetery's founding father, Frochot, and architect, Brongniart, lie amidst their splendid creation. The necropolis also contains a huge cast of characters who recall much of France's history and culture over the last two centuries, and even earlier. Perhaps the most venerable inhabitants are Heloise and Abelard. A Gothic canopy constructed of stone fragments from Heloise's convent of the Paraclete shelters the couple, whose love affair scandalized the church and led to the castration of Peter Abelard by Heloise's uncle. Not every cemetery can boast such dramatic history: this has real marketing potential. Here, as with so many cemetery sites, the monument's evocations rather than the tomb itself is what beguiles the visitor. One of the secrets of enjoying cemeteries is to approach them with a certain free-spirited imagination and an openness to their powers of suggestion. Flaubert endorsed this way of viewing graveyards with his comment: "The grave of Abelard and Heloise: if someone tells you it is apocryphal, exclaim: 'You rob me of my illusions!'" So at this tomb we can cast our illusion-filled minds back five hundred years to the fifteenth-century French poet and rowdy François Villon, who in "The Ballad of Ladies of Yesteryear" answers the question, "where is good Heloise/ For whom Abelard lost his manhood and became a priest?" with the poem's famous haunting refrain: "Where are the snows of yesteryear?" It is part of the charm of cemeteries that they are yesteryear places which still today provide pleasure, enlightenment, inspiration, or perhaps just a pleasant outing. Melted are the snows of yesteryear, but at a cemetery the past still reigns.

Stories, anecdotes and historical vignettes abound among the stones of Père Lachaise—so many that a cemetery connoisseur can find intimations of the full range of human activity. The legendary lovers Heloise and Abelard represent a category of inhabitants designated by actress Cornelia Otis Skinner as the "grand horizontals," a phrase referring to their habitual position in life rather than their entombed posture. At least two of Napoleon's mistresses recline at Père Lachaise: Marie Walewski (d. 1817), who gave birth to the emperor's son in 1810; and Marguerite Saqui (d. 1866), whom he called "my madwoman," and who once danced on a tightrope strung between the towers of Notre Dame. On the tomb of Marie d'Agoult (d. 1876) appears a small head of Goethe who was her lover, but her most famous affair involved Franz Liszt, a liason which produced three children including Cosima who married composer Richard Wagner. Jeanne Herbuterne (d. 1920) lies in her accustomed position next to her long time lover, artist Amodeo Modigliani (d. 1920). The day after the artist died of tubercular meningitis she killed herself, but only ten years later did Jeanne's scandalized parents permit her to be buried beside her paramour. Legend has it that la Comtesse de Castiglione, Napoleon III's mistress, asked to be interred in the nightgown she had worn the first night she spent with the emperor. The remarkably lifelike reclining bronze figure of Victor Noir (d. 1870), a journalist and man about town shot in a duel by Pierre Bonaparte, Napoleon III's cousin, attracts women seeking virility or fertility. Females who desire to become pregnant or more passionate (or both) stroke Noir's privates, by now polished a shiny brightness. Some women supposedly hoist their skirts and mount the statue for even closer contact, a truly lusty performance in the normally laid-back and dispassionate precincts of Père Lachaise.

Creative as well as procreative types populate the great cemetery. On the monument to Balzac (d. 1850) appears a reduced copy of the large bust of the author created by David d'Angers (d. 1856), who occupies his own unembellished

tomb at Père Lachaise, rather an irony since the artist contributed more funerary sculptures to that cemetery—which art
critic Marcel Le Clere estimated offered fully a thousand
"interesting pieces of sculpture"—and to the Montparnasse
burial ground, than any sculptor. In *Choses Vues* Victor Hugo
records Balzac's rather dramatic funeral, perhaps typical of
the ceremonies afforded the greats of the era:

> The procession crossed Paris, and went by way of the boule-
> vards to Père-Lachaise. Rain was falling as we left the church,
> and when we reached the cemetery. It was one of those days
> when the heavens seemed to weep. We walked the whole
> distance. I was at the head of the coffin on the right, holding
> one of the silver tassels of the pall. Alexandre Dumas was on
> the other side . . . The coffin was lowered into the grave . . .
> The priest said a last prayer and I a few words—while I was
> speaking the sun went down. All Paris lay before me, afar off,
> in the splendid mists of the sinking orb, the glow of which
> seemed to fall into the grave at my feet, as the dull sounds of
> the sods dropping on the coffin broke in upon my last words.

Marcel Proust (d. 1922) and his parents, along with his
brother Robert and Robert's wife, occupy a small plot
marked by a simple black granite stone. Not far away rises
the large mausoleum which houses the Dominican Republic
dictator Rafael Trujillo (d. 1961), whose grandiose grave, a
cemetery attendant told me, receives considerably more attention than that of Proust, whose true monument is his
writing. In May 1961, after thirty-one years of dominance
over the Dominican non-Republic, Trujillo met his end as
assassins gunned him down and then cut off his head, which
they kept. A striking, Egyptian-style, stone figure sculpted
by Jacob Epstein rears its head over the nearby grave of Oscar
Wilde (d. 1900). When the Irish writer died in Paris at age
forty-six he was laid to rest in the unfashionable Bagneaux
cemetery outside the city. After a time an anonymous En-

glish woman provided money to remove Wilde's remains to the more elegant Père Lachaise. Perhaps the writer would have preferred to be left in peace, for he once remarked to his lifelong friend Robert Ross: "When the Last Trumpet sounds, and we are couched in our porphyry tombs, I shall turn and whisper to you, 'Robbie, Robbie, let us pretend we do not hear it.'" But up Wilde came, exhumed in an operation recalled years later by an English funeral director named Harold Nicholson:

> I never saw Oscar Wilde during his lifetime, but I very nearly saw him ten years after he was dead . . . The ceremony at Bagneaux had been a macabre fiasco. On the previous night the sextons had dug up the grave, leaving the coffin exposed with two ropes underneath it. The soil had been placed on each side of the grave and, since it had been raining during the night, the sextons thought it wise to put three tombstones on the top of the earth so as to hold it down. There were many official representatives and journalists present at Bagneaux cemetery, and as they pressed forward to gaze into the grave one of the heavy stones became dislodged and fell upon the coffin, splitting the lid open. For a few seconds the face of Wilde could be seen, peaceful and white. Then the earth followed and in a few seconds his face was obliterated by mud.

After his brief reappearance, Wilde was transferred to another coffin, then taken to Père Lachaise where in 1914 admirers unveiled Epstein's statue, suggested by the writer's poem "The Sphinx." In time, other more ardent admirers hacked away the fig leaf along with the figure's private parts beneath the leaf. The severed testicles found a place in the cemetery conservator's office where they supposedly served as paperweights.

When the young William Faulkner visited Paris in August 1925 he wrote his mother back in Mississippi about a visit "to

Père Lachaise, an old cemetery. Alfred de Musset is buried there, and all the French notables and royalty, as well as many foreigners. I went particularly to see Oscar Wilde's tomb, with a bas-relief by Jacob Epstein." Not all that many foreigners repose in Père Lachaise, but a scattering of aliens serve to internationalize that very French burial ground. One of the graveyard's rare English inscriptions appears on the tomb of British admiral William Sidney Smith (d. 1840) and his wife Caroline Mary (d. 1826) who settled in Paris after the Napoleonic Wars. Another English epitaph, on a triangular stone obelisk topped by a metal torch cradled between the heads of three lions, reads: "Tomb of Frederic Albert Winsor. Originator of public gas lighting."

The remains of Judah P. Benjamin (d. 1884), Confederate secretary of state, who died in exile in Paris, rest at Père Lachaise, far from his beloved South. Two American dancers lie there: Isadora Duncan (d. 1927), whose neck was snapped when her long scarf snagged on the rear wheel of her open car; and Loie Fuller (d. 1928), famed for her "skirt dance," featuring a diaphanous garment which she twirled into billowing folds while performing on a sheet of glass lit from below. Richard Wright (d. 1960), the black American novelist, reposes at Père Lachaise, as do Gertrude Stein and her companion, Alice B. Toklas, now truly members of the "lost generation." Stein's misspelled inscription, indicating that she was born in "Allfghany, Pennsylvania," recalls the sometimes torturously original prose of the avant-garde author.

Quite the oddest foreign grave at Père Lachaise belongs to the American rock singer and songwriter Jim Morrison (d. 1971), whose famous lyric "No one here gets out alive" could well describe both cemeteries and the world of the living. Graffiti referring to the cult personality disfigures nearby tombs, while his bust bears garish colors painted by idolaters. Flower-filled beer and liquor bottles perch on Morrison's tombstone, by which pot-smoking admirers often party. Such festive behavior seldom enlivens other graves at solemn old Père Lachaise. The cemetery boasts another cult figure, one Allan Kardec (d. 1868), a spiritualist (he preferred to call his doctrine "spiritism") who attracts a steady stream of acolytes making pilgrimages to his tomb, there to pray and to attempt to communicate with the dead. From time to time believers remain at the grave through the night, a period when the lines of communication supposedly function more efficiently, or perhaps rates are lower then.

The less other-worldly and more earthy tomb of writer Alfred de Musset (d. 1857), referred to by William Faulkner in his letter home, bears lines from the French author's poem "Lucie" instructing his survivors as to the garnishment for his grave:

> My dear friends, when I am dead
> Plant a willow at the cemetery,
> I love its weeping foliage,
> Its pallor is sweet and dear to me,
> And its shadow will be light
> Upon the earth where I shall sleep.

As the poet wished, a willow rises above his final resting place. The dead man's request, however, continues to vex the living, for the scrawny specimen—the latest in a series of trees planted there—seems not long for this world. Of the never-ending challenge to honor de Musset's wish for a willow Willa Cather observed: "This willow requested by the poet has become a subject of mirth even among Parisians, whose sense of the ridiculous is almost entirely lacking. Ever since 1857 gardener after gardener has tried to make a willow tree grow over the tearful singer's grave, but the soil of Père-Lachaise is high and sandy, and the result of fifty years of effort is a spindly yellow seedling." Tombs encompass not only bodily remains but also, sometimes, the deceased's essence—his spirit as well as his body. Cather viewed the straggly, struggling tree as a symbol of the writer's earthly existence: "De Musset certainly never got anything that he wanted in life, and it seems a sort of fine-drawn irony that he should not have the one poor willow he wanted for his grave."

Poetry and artworks on cemetery monuments lend burial grounds touches of the library or museum. Just as de Musset's own verse enhances his wordy tombstone, the monument of painter Théodore Géricault (d. 1824), who died after being thrown from a horse, bears a museum-quality, bas-relief copy of the artist's famous canvas *The Raft of the Medusa* housed at the Louvre. This work portrays the dramatic incident when the frigate *Medusa* foundered on the way to Senegal, forcing 149 passengers to put to sea on a raft which drifted in the Atlantic's open waters. The few survivors related the disaster's horrors to Géricault, who hired the *Medusa's* carpenter to build a model of the raft. Seeking to bring even more detailed realism to his work, the painter lived for a time near a hospital in which he could observe dying men. Géricault finally carried this study to its extreme by locking himself in a room with corpses from the morgue. The artist's efforts yielded a painting direct from life, or perhaps the work should be called a still-life—now, represented on his grave, very still.

In contrast to Géricault, whose most renowned work decorates his burial monument, the artist Eugène Delacroix (d. 1863) renounced such embellishment, directing in his will: "My tomb will be in the cemetery of Père-Lachaise, on the heights, in a place somewhat removed. There will be neither emblem, bust nor statue." This modesty conforms to Delacroix's image of a cemetery as a place of oblivion, as described by him after a visit in September 1854 to a small burial ground at Dieppe: "Entered the cemetery, less forbidding than that frightful Père-Lachaise, less silly, less limited, less bourgeois. Forgotten graves overgrown with grass, clumps of rosebushes and clematis perfuming the air in this sojourn of death; perfect solitude, moreover, ultimate conformity with the object of the place and with the necessary purpose of what is there, which is to say silence and forgetfulness." So magnetic was the pull of Père Lachaise for Paris's elite, however, that Delacroix asked to be buried there. It just would not do for a prominent Parisian to repose elsewhere: better frightful Père Lachaise to lie in than a delightful place with no standing.

Most inhabitants of the prestigious Paris cemetery sought there not oblivion, like Delacroix, but remembrance and even better, continuing fame. During my wanderings through the graveyard I once came across a remarkable inscription on the tomb of one Claude Bouand (d. 1840). Deeply cut in authoritative capital letters, there for all the world to see and admire forever, appears the deceased's monetary bequest: "I leave for charitable purposes, for the sick, infirm and old, (1) My house rue St. Georges 26, (2) 15,000 francs 5% bonds, (3) Interest amounting to 5,500 francs on 5% bonds, (4) 250,000 francs in cash for buildings, furnishings and a pharmacy." Hardly less modest was a man named Félix de Beaujour (d. 1828), whose nearly three-hundred-foot, lighthouse-like monument towers over the lower tombs of lesser mortals although, alas, the nature of his importance remains obscure. Fearing that trees might eventually block his name, Beaujour ordered it carved halfway up the monument, Père Lachaise's tallest.

The cemetery's largest memorial, and one of the oldest, is the three-story mausoleum built for Elizabeth Demidoff (d. 1818), a Russian princess. Wolf heads, along with miners' hammers which recall the origin of the family's fortune in gold and silver mines, decorate the huge structure at the top of which the princess reposes in a white marble sarcophagus beneath an Ionic-style temple. According to tradition, anyone who dwells in the building for a year will receive a reward of two million rubles—probably worth about seven dollars at present exchange rates.

Noteworthy also is the very first family chapel in all of Paris, built in 1815 for the Greffulhe clan, an innovation which brought to the cemetery a new type of memorial. In addition to monuments honoring individuals, there now developed structures devoted to dynasties. An entire clan could enjoy the prestige of burial at Paris's best postmortem address without regard to individual distinction, an honor described by Victor Hugo as conferring a status craved by the bourgeoisie: "Père Lachaise is very fine! To be buried in Père Lachaise is like having mahogany furniture—a mark of respectability." Perhaps the cemetery's most impressive family mausoleum houses the Rothschilds. Over the door an "R" device symbolizes the occupants while inside, beyond a corridor illuminated by four skylights, lies a room whose walls bear plaques filled with names of family members.

The presence of the Rothschilds at Père Lachaise evidences that Paris's most exclusive cemetery is ecumenical—open to all without regard to religion, politics, race or other aberrations from the norm of society. Only obscurity or poverty has barred the way to the eternal prestige of a place at Père Lachaise. To be sure, you are permitted to die in Paris even if you don't have money but you cannot rub mouldering shoulders with the elites: being buried certainly does not let you go up in the world. Dead men tell no tales, but money talks (it speaks especially good French) and for those with sufficient funds or fame the cemetery has opened its arms, or graves, and furnished the coveted respectability granted by the postmortem equivalent of mahogany furniture. So it is that the burial ground occupied by the Rothschilds also claims Communist leader Maurice Thorez (d. 1964), memorialized by a spiffy bright black stone incised with gold (why not red?) letters, no less.

Much of Père Lachaise's charm, in fact, stems from its unusually wide variety of monuments and inhabitants, characters from all eras and ways of life, drawn together—some improbably—at their final resting places. Random wanderings through that fabled cemetery unearth all sorts of curious and beguiling finds. The many pleasant hours I have spent idling away the day among those for whom time no longer counts, introduced me to a large cast of colorful, if fading, characters. One of my favorites was a geographer whose rather withdrawn name, Onésime Reclus, belies his worldly profession. Perhaps Napoleon grouched about Marshal Grouchy, whose failure to appear at the outset of the Battle of Waterloo supposedly led to the emperor's defeat. The basrelief on the tomb of Napoleonic loyalist Count Lavallette (d. 1850) shows him putting on his wife's clothing, a disguise which enabled him to escape from confinement under sentence of death.

One martial section of Père Lachaise—which on 30 March 1814 during the Napoleonic Wars became a battlefield when a skirmish broke out between Russian troops and cadets of two French military schools—consists almost entirely of tombs occupied by Napoleon's generals. The emperor himself expressed a desire to be buried at Père Lachaise, even commissioning the cemetery's architect Brogniart to design a pyramid tomb visible from any point in Paris, but the only Bonaparte whose bones repose in the graveyard is Napoleon's sister Caroline, buried in the Murat family tomb which she shares with her husband Joachim Murat, King of Naples.

Some monuments artfully evoke the deceased's profession or background. Crystal designer Rene Lalique (d. 1945) boasts a tomb which bears a crystal cross, while Mayan writing on the marker for Nobel Prize-winning writer Miguel Asturias (d. 1974) recalls his Guatemalan heritage. The grave of an animal trainer named Jean Pezon shows him riding Brutus, the lion which devoured him—presumably not only Pezon but also Brutus reposes there. Atop the marker for Claude Chappe (d. 1805) appears a replica of the semaphore signal device he invented, a dynamo that for the first time generated a continuous electrical current. A stone relief showing a woven basket heaped with potatoes reminds visitors that Antoine Parmentier (d. 1813) promoted the cultivation of that vegetable in France. On a stone relief at the monument for dramatist Eugène Scribe (d. 1861) appear representations of a quill pen, along with the masks of comedy and tragedy and sheets of music, while the marker of Georges Bizet (d. 1875), composer of *Carmen,* includes a bronze relief harp. On the night of 2 June 1875, during the thirty-first performance of the original production of *Carmen,* Celestine Galli-Marié, playing the title role, was suddenly overcome with a strange foreboding while reading her fortune in the cards: "First I, then him, for both of us death." The singer burst into tears and, on leaving the stage, fainted. It was that evening, perhaps at that very moment, that Bizet died. (A similarly curious coincidence occurred in 1893 when three floors of Ford's Theatre in Washington, D.C.—scene of John Wilkes Booth's assassination of President Lincoln—collapsed just as the coffin of Edwin Booth, John's brother, was being transported from a New York church to Mt. Auburn cemetery in Boston, Massachusetts.) Music played at Bizet's service included the funeral march by Chopin (d. 1849), who reposes (minus his heart which is housed at Warsaw's Church of the Holy Cross in his native Poland) in Père Lachaise beneath a marble statue of a seated woman, head bowed in grief and a lyre on her lap.

Other noteworthy musical figures and performers inhabit Père Lachaise. Although the tomb of Gioacchino Rossini (d. 1868), composer of *The Barber of Seville,* lies empty since admirers repatriated his remains to Florence in 1887, Edith Piaf (d. 1963) continues to attract a never-ending parade of fans who garnish the grave with flowers: "La Vie en Rose" transmuted into *la mort en roses*. A touch of piety in the form of a bronze Christ figure perches somewhat incongruously atop the tomb of the famous singer raised in a brothel, addicted to morphine, dependent on alcohol, bedded by a stream of easy-come easy-go lovers. On the tomb of Luigi Cherubini (d. 1842) appears a bust of the opera composer being crowned by a muse with a laurel wreath, while nearby lies André Grétry (d. 1813), another opera composer. When Napoleon again asked his name after having been introduced to him on many previous occasions the composer responded, "Sir, I am still Grétry." Another theater figure at Père Lachaise, actress Sarah Bernhardt (d. 1923), for years slept in her satin-lined rosewood coffin, the better to become accustomed to her final resting place. Although the famous performer wanted to be buried on Belle Isle off the Brittany coast, she ended up in Paris's Père Lachaise in a tomb inscribed with her motto, "Quand même" (in spite of everything), a phrase her stationery also bore. The actress Rachel (d. 1858), who began her career by singing for bread on the streets of Lyon, also lies in Père Lachaise, as does her contemporary, Mlle. George (d. 1867), for whom Napoleon invented a special type of elastic garter during his affair with her.

A rather more substantial achievement in the way of a connecting device originated with Ferdinand de Lesseps (d. 1894), father of the Suez Canal, whose pyramid-shaped tomb recalls his connection with Egypt. Another great French builder, Baron Haussmann (d. 1891), also reposes at Père Lachaise. Like de Lesseps, Haussmann rearranged things on a grand scale in the mid-nineteenth century, creating the major boulevards, sweeping perspectives and sense of order which still typify Paris today. Haussmann's tomb, with its fluted square columns, classical balance and perspective up Père Lachaise's avenue Principale, seems to reflect the famous city planner's urban vision.

Haussmann also proposed an innovative plan to abolish the capital's cemeteries and remove their inhabitants to a new burial ground at Méry-sur-Oise, fourteen miles north of Paris. The plan included a funeral rail service to link the new necropolis with the city. "The transport of coffins would be made in special trains," Haussmann wrote, noting that "the train trip would require less time and be less tiring to those attending the funeral than a procession on foot." In 1869 after the baron announced his idea an opponent of the proposal named Victor Fournel delivered a famous polemic against Haussmann's grandiose cemetery concept, attacking it as "the mathematical and industrial burial plan. A few more years," Fournel added tartly, "and you will see a worthy completion of the system with the invention of steam engines for burying people." Opponents of the plan who visited London to inspect a suburban cemetery at Woking, based on concepts similar to Haussmann's, reported that the burial ground was inconveniently located and, even worse, suffered from a low social standing. "Not a single gentleman is buried at Woking," they noted haughtily.

Although nothing came of Haussmann's suggestion, it was well founded in demographics—or perhaps the study of mortality trends should be called necrographics. Haussmann's contemporaries ridiculed his prediction that Paris's population of 1.8 million in 1865 would reach three million during the next half-century, but by 1910 the city boasted 2.8 million inhabitants. The baron's projections suggested to him the need for new cemeteries, especially since not only Père Lachaise (opened in 1804) but also the more recent cemeteries of Montparnasse (1824) and Montmartre (1825) had all become overcrowded by 1853, mainly because the early-nineteenth-century interest in large and permanent grave monuments quickly depleted the available space. In 1859 Paris annexed the suburban communes to form the present city of twenty *arrondissements,* a development which incorporated the new cemeteries (those established in the early 1800s) into the metropolis, just as in the eighteenth century the expanding city had absorbed the Cimetière des Innocents and burial grounds in churchyards. Today the celebrity-filled cemeteries of Montmartre and Montparnasse survive as smaller versions of Père Lachaise, enclaves of monuments and memories surrounded by the lively streets of central Paris.

Neither of those two cemeteries enjoys the leafy spaciousness or pleasant irregularity offered by Père Lachaise. "The geometrical rigor and simplicity of the plan of Montparnasse may suggest a dryness and a monotony to the layout," notes Richard A. Etlin in *The Architecture of Death*. But Montparnasse does boast an especially good collection of statuary which lends the cemetery the appearance of a gallery. In one corner of the stony graveyard stands *The Kiss* by Constantin Brancusi (d. 1957), whose nearby grave, lacking a statue, is marked only by a simple stone slab. At the tomb of Pierre Loeb, Brancusi's dealer, rises a work by Hans Arp, a lumpy and granular grey stone punctured by a fish-shaped cut-out. A more elaborate monument decorates the tomb of Gustave Jundt (d. 1884)—a realistic likeness showing the painter in a wrinkled vest, bow tie, and sporting a T-shaped moustache and beard. It is the work of Auguste Bartholdi (d. 1904), whose nearby tomb embellished by a red marble obelise and a bronze angel of his own making, recalls that his most famous creation, the *Statue of Liberty,* "illuminates the world." On the grave of César Franck (d. 1890) appears a relief bust by Rodin portraying the composer with a short musical scale on his shirt, while a statue by the deceased entitled *Grief* tops the tomb of sculptor Henri Laurens, that work a puffy female bronze figure with banana-sized toes. On the tomb of François Rude (d. 1855) appears a copy of his bas-relief *Départ de 1792* which decorates the east side of the Arch of Triumph, while the sculptor's bronze bust is by Rude's protege Cabet. Montparnasse sports no works of art from the hands of sculptors Antoine Bourdelle (d. 1906) or Jean-Antoine Houdon (d. 1828), who contributed to the burial ground only their remains.

Two odd-looking works by a lesser-known sculptor named José de Charmoy decorate—or at least stand in—Montparnasse cemetery. Atop a column over the grave of Sainte-Beuve (d. 1869) scowls an unflattering bust of the literary critic, his puffy slightly lop-sided face emerging from a swirling cloth that winds its way down the pillar and onto the tombstone. A similarly clothy figure, a gauze-swathed statue, reposes on a slab beneath a brooding bust of poet Charles Baudelaire, also a work by de Charmoy. In *Pantomime* American writer Wallace Fowlie, who encountered Baudelaire's monument while visiting the cemetery as a student in 1928, describes these strange and somewhat disquieting figures in graphic terms: "A thin column of stone rises up from the ground, at the top of which the head of a man, typifying the spirit of evil, rests in the cupped shape of two hands. The features, cast in a malicious grin, are almost hidden under stone locks of hair. Underneath this devil's face . . . extends a large slab of stone supporting the life-sized body of the poet wrapped in funeral cloth. Only his face is revealed . . . But the mask of death has been placed over the face and softens the expression and the features of suffering." Fowlie relates that when he mentioned the sculptor's name, which appears on the monument, to the proprietor of the pension where he was staying, she replied that de Charmoy had once resided at that pension, occupying the very room assigned to Fowlie.

Baudelaire (d. 1867) reposes not at the de Charmoy monument, which serves only as a cenotaph, but at the burial site of his mother Caroline (d. 1871) and stepfather, Jacques Aupick (d. 1857), a diplomat, politician and army officer. Around 1840 Baudelaire composed his own epitaph, at about the time he contracted the venereal disease which killed him a quarter of a century later: "Here lies, for having too much dwelled in street girls' holes/A young fellow who now inhabits the kingdom of moles. " The couplet recalls the epitaph of English playwright Sir William Davenant (d. 1668) who, as Aubrey recounts in *Brief Lives,* "gott a terrible clap of a Black handsome wench":

Such were his virtues, that they could command
A general applause from ev'ry hand;
His exit then this on record shall have,
A clap did usher D'Avenant to his grave.

No epitaph, however, commemorates Baudelaire. The famous writer is remembered only with the curt notation that he "died in Paris at the age of 46 on 31 August 1867." There is no poetic justice: while the great poet is denied a laudatory epitaph an obscure writer with the redoubtable name Hegesippe Moreau (d. 1836), author of something called *Myosotis,* enjoys a delightful remembrance at Montparnasse in a verse that reads: "Passer-by, on the stone that's used/ When rain and wind their kisses throw,/Read a name dear to the Muse:/Hegesippe Moreau!"

Although Père Lachaise seems to out-do Montparnasse in graves of women involved in amorous affairs, the latter boasts a number of tombs housing men of affairs. Automobile tycoon André Citroën (d. 1935) reposes beneath a simple grey marble marker, while the tombs of Julien Arpels (d. 1964) and Esther Van Cleef (née Arpels; d. 1960) recall the famous jewelry emporium, and the founder of Bon Marché department store, a man named Boucicaut, also endures the final markdown at Montparnasse. The well-known French publisher Hachette, as well as Littré and Larousse, compilers of two famous dictionaries, reached their final pages at the cemetery, as did Nicolas Conté who on Napoleon's expedition in Egypt melted down bullets and inserted the lead into

Nile River reeds, thus inventing the pencil. Charles Pigeon, inventor of a non-explodable gas lamp widely used before electricity, boasts one of the most noteworthy monuments at Montparnasse. Near the cemetery entrance stands a stone double bed on which repose, both fully clothed, Madame Pigeon—at least one supposes that the reclining female is she—and next to her, propped up on his left elbow with a pencil in his left hand and a notebook in his right in case posthumous inspiration strikes, Monsieur Pigeon. Perched on the headboard overlooking the two, stands a torch-bearing angel. A scholar named Honoré Champion (d. 1913) also enjoys a grave-side touch of home, for his sculpted figure sits at a desk by curtains and shelves of books, forever comfortable in his study. The monument of another scholar, astronomer Joseph le Verrier (d. 1877) who discovered the planet Neptune in 1846, bears signs of the zodiac and a frieze of stars.

More worldly than these heavenly observations were the far-flung explorations of Dumont d'Urville (d. 1842), an admiral who three times sailed around the world. The explorer's monument, its relief panels a veritable essay in geography, illustrates in detail his various exploits. The admiral explored such places as South America, Antarctica, New Guinea, and New Zealand, but it was in the Old World rather than those two "News" where news of d'Urville's most memorable discovery surfaced. During an expedition to the Mediterranean he happened on a mutilated white marble statue recently found in a field by a Greek peasant. D'Urville told the Marquis Séré de Rivières, the French ambassador to Constantinople, about the find, which the French government subsequently purchased. The statue became known as the Venus de Milo and now graces Paris's Louvre Museum. As for d'Urville, he died on 8 May 1842 in a train fire at Versailles, only a few miles from the home he had so often left to travel, without mishap, to the corners of the earth. On his monument appears a relief showing the flame-filled railway car in which he, his wife Adele, and son Jules (also portrayed on the monument) perished.

Other celebrities buried at Montparnasse include short story writer Guy de Maupassant, whose grave, if not his life, is an open book, the stony pages bearing his birth (1850) and death (1893) dates; Tristan Tzara (d. 1963), a founder of Dada, the 1920s literary and artistic nonsense movement; American film actress Jean Seberg (d. 1979), whose expatriate burial far from her native Iowa recalls American poet Stephen Vincent Benét's vow that "I shall not rest quiet in Montparnasse," so "bury my heart in Wounded Knee"; World War II French premier Pierre Laval (d. 1945), a German collaborator; Alfred Dreyfus (d. 1935), the central figure in the famous Dreyfus Affair a century ago, in which authorities accused the French army officer of being a German spy and sentenced him to solitary confinement on Devil's Island where the prisoner languished until cleared of the charges in 1906; François Coli, who disappeared 8 May 1927 "attempting the first air connection Paris-New York," and another pilot, Adolphe Pégoud (d. 1915), the first aviator to perform what the French call *le looping*. His bust portrays him with a spiffy curved-tip moustache and a stern expression, more Prussian than Gallic, and his epitaph states that "France has lost in Pégoud the pioneer of aerial maneuvers who will never be replaced." At Montparnasse also repose Édouard de Max (d. 1924), who played opposite Sarah Bernhardt and gave his final performance at his own funeral when he wore the make-up and costume for his favorite role of Nero; Alexandre Alekhine (d. 1946), "chess genius for Russia and France," whose monument, erected in 1956 by the International Chess Federation, includes a stone chessboard above which looms a relief of the champion player pondering his next move—perhaps resurrection; and Camille François Raspail (d. 1893), a doctor, politician and military figure memorialized by the Boulevard Raspail, which runs alongside Montparnasse cemetery.

For many years Jean-Paul Sartre (d. 1980), the most recently buried celebrity at Montparnasse, lived in an apartment on the Boulevard Raspail overlooking the cemetery. While living in Paris in 1970 I came to know Sartre, who would habitually install himself at La Coupole cafe on nearby Boulevard Montparnasse in the middle of the afternoon. There the savant, who could hardly see, was read to by an attendant, and the author would also write. I occasionally dropped by to chat with the famous intellectual. In contrast to his rather forbidding and, to me, often incomprehensible philosophic writings, Sartre himself was friendly and open. On one occasion the great man asked my advice on whether he should visit the United States not long after heavy American bombings during the Vietnamese war. Encouraging him to go, I observed that in no way would anyone consider his trip an endorsement of, or even indifference to the air raids which he vehemently opposed. The next time we met he informed me that he had cancelled his trip. So ended at the beginning my budding career as Sartre's resident advisor on the burning ethical issues of the day.

In Sartre's time, after World War II, the intellectual community of Paris centered on the Saint Germain quarter of the Left Bank, not far from Montparnasse. The artists of the previous generation, active in the 1920s, gravitated to Montmartre, the Right Bank quarter on the opposite side of Paris, where lies Montmartre cemetery, the third of the city's three major burial grounds. Henry de Montherlant, who described the graveyard in his novel *The Bachelors,* referred to the fresh air which lent the area a touch of life: "Crossing the Avenue Rachel, one was struck by a breath of tree-borne air from the cemetery of Montmartre, as though the only life among these living beings came to them from the dead." But

I found it was the noise rather than the breeze which most enlivens the cemetery, quite the noisiest I have ever come across. Not only do car-laden streets surround the cemetery but the sounds of traffic from an overhead viaduct, carrying the rue Caulaincourt, also disturb the burial ground. Those speedsters whizzing overhead and the dead who lie silently underfoot create a curious juxtaposition of energy and entropy. If anything this side of the Judgment Day could wake the departed it would be the din of Paris traffic which pervades Montmartre cemetery. Poet Alfred de Vigny (d. 1863), who once complained of "the eternal silence of the Divinity," now inhabits a tomb there, surrounded by the eternal noise of the city. Other well known authors populate the terrain. Although Stendhal (d. 1842) preferred to repose in Rome's expatriate English cemetery (described in Chapter III), the French novelist ended up at Montmartre, at first in an obscure corner under the viaduct and, since 1962 in a prominent location more appropriate to his literary reputation. The white marble monument to German poet Heinrich Heine (d. 1856) quotes the writer's musings on his final resting place: "Tired from roaming, where will I come to rest?" Heine wondered. Atop a pillar decorated with carved reliefs—a lyre, a butterfly, feather-like wings or perhaps wing-like feathers—perches a bust of the poet, eyes closed, the gaunt bearded face bearing a serene expression, as if Heine was content finally to discover where in the world he had found repose.

More musings decorate the monument of Alexandre Dumas (d. 1895)—son of the author of *The Three Musketeers* and *The Count of Monte Cristo*—whose tomb relates that "death interests me much more than life for life belongs to time while death forms part of eternity." Dumas most famous book was *La Dame aux Camélias,* a sentimental portrait of a courtesan based on the life of Alphonsine Plessis (d.1847), whose dramatic life story also inspired Verdi's *La*

Traviata. On her tomb at Montmartre appears a cluster of rather garish, enamel-covered objects including a violet cushion, red flowers, and a white card, one edge turned up, bearing the single word: "Regrets." At one time admirers established a special fund to care for her grave and to erase the graffiti scrawled by the camellia lady's would-be lovers. On hearing of Plessis's final illness Dumas rushed to her house, where he found that the camellias in her garden had turned black. Camille, as she was called, died clinging to the hand of a hired nurse, a dramatic end described by poet Théophile Gautier: "That hand she quitted only for the hand of death." Gautier (d. 1872) reposes at Montmartre beneath an elaborate monument bearing the toga-clad muse of poetry and the lines,

> The bird is on the wing, the leaf falls,
> Love dies, for it's winter,
> Little bird, light upon my tomb
> And sing when spring returns.

Other noteworthy musical types, apart from Gautier's singing bird, suffer through a noisy eternity. Jacques Offenbach (d. 1880), whose mutton chop beard on his bronze bust matches his coat's fur collar; Léo Delibes (d. 1891), composer of the ballet *Coppélia;* music teacher Nadia Boulanger (d. 1979); and Hector Berlioz (d. 1869) repose there, along with Antoine (known as Adolphe) Sax (1894), inventor of the saxophone. Ballet dancer Vaslav Nijinsky (d. 1950) arrived there in 1953 after resting a while in London's Marylebone cemetery. The tomb of Henry Storks (d. 1860), another interloper from across the channel, bears perhaps the cemetery's only English inscription: "Serjeant at law, late Chief Justice of Ely and recorder of Cambridge."

Artists include J. B. Greuze (d. 1805), whose "soul breathes through his canvases"; Jean-Honoré Fragonard (d.

1806); and Edgar Degas (d. 1917), who unceremoniously emptied the family vault of a cousin's remains to make room for himself. It is perhaps only in France that an artist in food would merit a special memorial, but there—his final sauce blended, his last pastry confected, his ultimate goose cooked—lies Marie Antoine Carême (d. 1833) beneath a tapered stone monument restored in 1936 by the Organization of French Chefs, the Restaurant Association, the Bakers' Organization, the Wine Stewards Association, and other culinary groups. Now enjoying his just desserts Carême, who served as chef to the Rothschild family, codified the delights of French cuisine in a classic twelve volume work.

Other pioneering Frenchmen at Montmartre include physicist André Ampère (d. 1836), commemorated by the amp, an electrical unit, and Jean Foucault (d. 1868), who gave his name to Foucault's Pendulum, a device which demonstrates the earth's rotation. A father-son grave houses Martin Charcot (d. 1893), whose studies on hysteria and hypnotism influenced Sigmund Freud; and Jean-Baptiste Charcot (d. 1936), a polar explorer who sailed a ship pluckily dubbed *Pourquoi Pas?* (Why Not?) Unfortunately, this defiant question received an all too harsh answer in September 1936 when the turbulent waters of the North Atlantic wrecked it on the Icelandic coast, leaving a sole survivor. Just a few days earlier Charcot had amused himself in Reykjavik, where the ship had put in for repairs, by reading Shakespeare's *The Tempest.*

In complete contrast to noisy Montmartre cemetery, tucked away nearby on the rear slope of the hill which dominates the Montmartre quarter, nestles tranquil St. Vincent. That quiet little cemetery seems like a village graveyard far removed from the big city. At a vineyard just across the way, serried rows of grapevines serve as visual echoes to the regular aisles of tombs which terrace the cemetery's slope. At the entrance a rough-surfaced granite slab marks the tomb of Swiss composer Arthur Honegger (d. 1955), while farther on lies the curious grave of Platon and Papuoe Argyriades, a miniature house with a large window from which their painted figures peer. St. Vincent's most famous inhabitant, Maurice Utrillo (d. 1955), painted scenes and vignettes of Montmartre, the like of which can still be found just a few blocks from his grave. Utrillo reposes with his wife Lucie beneath a simple pink granite slab by which a cloth-draped stone figure stands, holding a palette. Above the cemetery peeks the steeple of Sacre Coeur, a church which the painter who now lies within its shadow often included on his canvases.

St. Vincent is one of Paris's fourteen *intra-muros* cemeteries—those which lie within the city and occupy a total of fifteen hundred acres in the crowded metropolis. The capital also boasts three thousand acres of *extra-muros* cemeteries, suburban burial grounds such as Pantin, Bagneux, Saint-Ouen, La Plaine-St. Denis, Ivry, and Thiais. At Ivry and Thiais repose those who died in prison. The remote fifteenth *division* at Thiais is devoted to convicts executed by the guillotine—a few so executed as recently as the 1960s repose there—with the head neatly rejoined to the body for burial. France abolished capital punishment in 1981. The ultimate in *sang-froid* was exhibited by the Duke de Charost who read a book while being escorted to the guillotine and then, just before the blade fell, marked his place by turning down the corner of the page.

Paris's *intra-muros* cemeteries offer a scattering of celebrated occupants and noteworthy monuments. Right in the middle of the city, just across the Seine from the Eiffel tower, lies the attractive Passy cemetery which occupies valuable terrain near some of Paris's most elegant areas. Painter Édouard Manet (d. 1883) almost seems alive and enjoying those surrounding as a bronze bust with a spritely, twinkling expression and curly moustache, his two-sectioned beard dangling like small sacks. Fernand Constantine, the popular

French comedian known as Fernandel (d. 1971), occupies a simple tomb, as does playwright Jean Giraudoux (d. 1944). Near the author a monument to Henry Farman (d. 1958) includes a lifesize stone relief of the aviator pulling a lever, and the inscription: "Forerunner and pioneer of the air, first in the world to have officially completed a measured flight of one kilometer, 13 January 1908 at Issy-les-Moulineaux. Henry Farman gave wings to the world." Another world-class inscription informs the monument of Jacques Carlu, architect of two notable structures nearby, the former NATO headquarters building and Chaillot Palace, home of the Museum of Man whose entrance inscription the tomb repeats: "Things rare or beautiful artfully assembled here instruct the eye to see as never before everything which fills the world." A marker at Passy commemorates the thoroughly French Édouard Louis Béjot (d. 1885) with a thoroughly English inscription: "Not gone from memory./Not gone from love./ But gone to a father's home above." Claude Debussy (d. 1918) lies in a curved tomb bearing a stylized metal device which suggests both the composer's initials and a bent musical note.

Debussy set to music some of the poems of poet Paul Verlaine (d. 1896), who reposes at the Batignolles cemetery, just beyond port de Clichy. Other notables buried there include André Breton (d. 1966), founder of surrealism; Russian singer Feodor Chaliapin (d. 1938); a man named Benjamin Peret (d. 1959), whose marker bears the quotation: "Here I eat no bread"; and *Le Figaro's* editor Gaston Calmette, shot dead in his office by Madame Caillaux, wife of former French premier Joseph Caillaux, whose early love letters to his mistress the newspaper had published in a smear campaign.

At the Vaugirard cemetery—hidden away at 318–322 rue Vaugirard in the center of Paris—reposes another assassination victim, Paul Doumer (d. 1932), president of the French

Republic, killed by a deranged Russian. The Doumer monument also memorializes André (d. 1914), killed in World War I, and René (d. 1917) Doumer, who perished in aerial combat: "The Germans had written on his tomb at Asfeld (Ardennes): 'Died as a hero.'" Across from the Doumers stretch rows of painted white metal crosses devoted to the fallen of World War I. Usually such burial grounds occupy spacious rural quarters by the battlefields where the honored dead fell.

Hemmed in by buildings, tiny Vaugirard resembles Belleville, another vest-pocket burial ground located in a far corner of Paris beyond Père Lachaise. Belleville cemetery boasts such characters as pop singer Jean Marcopoulos (d. 1953) who died of leukemia, recalled with greasy wavy hair and thick lips above a cleft chin in a sepia hued pin-up photo. Also the Yonc-Cony family, whose monument bears a relief mask of comedy and a quotation by Gaston Cony: "Marionettes are philosophers. The worst catastrophes have never extinguished their happiness. They remain when we leave them to make the great leap into eternity." Belleville cemetery occupies one of Paris's highest points. The Télégraph metro stop recalls the so-called aerial telegraph erected on the heights by Claude Chappe (d. 1805) in 1793 to communicate news of military victories to the city. (Word regarding defeats was presumably not announced.) On Chappe's tomb appears a model of his device.

On the opposite side of Paris, beyond the Seine, lies another constricted cemetery, Auteuil, a small square burial ground overshadowed by surrounding highrises. Buried there are two Charleses—the composer Gounod (d. 1896) and the sculptor Carpeaux (d. 1875), whose lively statues decorate the facade of the old Paris opera house. Against the right wall stands a slab to painter Hubert Robert (d. 1808), remembered with the succinct but delightful inscription: "His reputation as a man of good will flatters him even more than his fame as an artist." A Yankee presence haunts this cemetery in the person of Benjamin Thompson (d. 1814), born "at Woburn near Boston in America." The epitaph recalls that Thompson, who died at Auteuil, was a well known physician and scientist, and discovered principles relating to light and heat. Twice, in 1876 and in 1923, Harvard University and the American Academy of Arts and Sciences restored the tomb of that American in Paris.

Of the many graveyards in and around Paris, I found Charonne cemetery, probably one of the least-visited, the most picturesque and among the most tranquil. Here the dead truly rest in peace. The cemetery nestles by the photogenic church of St. Germain de Charonne, whose towers recall similar ones at its namesake, the similarly named Église Saint-Germain-des-Près on boulevard St. Germain in the middle of the city. Unlike Père Lachaise (which lies only a few blocks away) and the other great Paris cemeteries, Charonne boasts no renowned inhabitants or especially striking tombs. The only noteworthy monument is a bronze statue to one François Bègue (d. 1837) which portrays him clad in a long coat, ruffled shirt and Napoleon-style hat, cane in his right hand and gloves in the left. This rather dapper image of the painter who specialized in decorating buildings was designed by Bègue himself and erected three years before his death. A heavy drinker, Bègue was buried with a bottle of liquor, proof—perhaps eighty proof—that tombs can contain spirits of the departed.

Charonne Cemetery, which closed in 1860, survives as one of the only two Paris burial grounds of the type that served the city before the Revolution and establishment soon thereafter, in the early nineteenth century, of modern-style burial grounds. The other such cemetery is the one by St. Pierre de Montmarte church. With the advent of Père Lachaise, Montparnasse, Montmartre, and the other modern cemeteries featuring individualized graves and elaborate monuments reciting the deceased's achievements, arose the need for corresponding funeral procedures which could personalize death. So developed an industry which commercialized and ritualized postmortem arrangements. John Sanderson, who visited Paris in the 1830s, described the area near Père Lachaise where "a whole street of marble yards . . . near a mile long" purveyed their wares. "Tombstones, urns, bronze gates, iron railings, crosses, pillars, pyramids, statues, and all the furniture of the grave, are laid out and exhibited here, as the merchandise of the shops and bazaars, of the latest and newest fashions," he wrote in *The American in Paris*. Competition prevailed: "By trying to under-bury one another, they have reduced funeral expenses in every branch to their minimum—there is, perhaps, no place in the world where one can die and be buried so moderately as in Paris." The area even included a sort of Dow Jones of death, a market place which dealt not in underwritings but in undertaking: "They have here, too, a kind of Exchange, where they meet to see the state of the market—to see the newest fashions or inventions of urns and crosses, and other sepulchral images, and to read over the bills of mortality, as elsewhere one reads the price current. The joy of a death is, of course, proportional to the worth, fashion and distinction of the individual who has died. When General Mortier was killed, on the 28th, stock rose one and a quarter." It is, in fact, possible to buy stock in a French funeral firm today. The shares of Pompes Funèbres Générales, which enjoys the exclusive right to burial in twenty-eight hundred graveyards around France, are traded on the stock exchange.

Another organization, Pompes funèbres municipales de la Ville de Paris, the municipal funeral office, publishes two booklets which explain everything one ever wanted to know about Paris funerals and cemeteries but was afraid to ask. The twenty-eight page *Tarifs* sets forth a detailed listing of the services and equipment provided for each of the four classes of funerals, for cremation, for the handling of corpses, and for other post mortem necessities. A first class funeral, which includes a chauffered limousine, porters and a fancy hearse, costs roughly a hundred times the fourth class service, which entitles the deceased to one attendant and a virtually unembellished hearse. For first class ceremonies all sorts of optional enhancements tempt customers—decorations for the room where the departed is laid out, a velvet cushion to hold a crucifix, sixteen glittering chandeliers, and top of the line coffins. The booklet entitled *Règlement concernant les cimetières de la ville de Paris* states that anyone who dies in the city, who is domiciled there, or whose family tomb is located there can be interred in one of Paris's twenty municipal burial grounds. The dead remain in their plots for thirty or fifty years or in perpetuity, their tenure determined by the sum paid. True to the real estate rule that location is all, plots along walkways cost more than remote sites. Special permission is needed for burial in terrain where the trees are more than twenty years old. All Paris cremations take place at Père Lachaise, with a special fee payable if organ music accompanies the procedure. Article seventy-seven forbids "drunks, street vendors, nonaccompanied children, dogs or other pets, and anyone not decently dressed" access to cemeteries, nor is "singing or music of any type" allowed. No inscription can be placed on a monument without prior approval of the authorities. And so on, for 121 paragraphs regulating every last detail of cemetery life.

At least one Anglo-Saxon observer—Donald Culross Peattie, commenting in *Green Laurels* on the burial at Montparnasse of the naturalist Lamarck in 1829—found French funerals especially funereal. The deceased was carried "through the slush and damp of a Paris December. It was the last day of the year but one—a season of graveyard weather in northern France—and in all the world there is nothing so final, so mortal, so purple and black and oppressive as a French funeral . . . at those appalling cemeteries, so ancient, so densely inhabited, the first clash of December sod on the coffin—how they all proclaim: Dead and gone! Dead and gone!" French writer Michel Vovelle referred in *Mourir Autrefois* to these elegiac French funerals as death "intensely lived"—an intensity perhaps lacking in Anglo-Saxon lands. When Frances Trollope visited Paris in the 1830s she found the attitude to death strikingly different than that which prevailed in her native England. In a chapter on Père Lachaise in *Paris and the Parisians in 1835* she commented: "Is it not wonderful what a difference twenty-one miles of salt-water can make in the ways and manners of people?" Mrs. Trollope observed how "many groups in deep mourning were wandering among the tombs . . . This manner of lamenting in public seems so strange to us!"

Even if private—though no less deeply felt—mourning characterizes the English, their cemeteries are as revealing and the epitaphs as outspoken as those in France. Kensal Green, the first major modern London cemetery, laid out in 1832, was in fact modelled after the patriarch of modern cemeteries, Père Lachaise. And like its French counterpart, which became fashionable only when royals and other celebrities arrived, Kensal Green began to gain a leading place in the life, or death, of London when a blue-blood appeared—George III's daughter Princess Sophia (d. 1848). By 1851 William Gaspey observed in *Tallis's "Illustrated London"* that a list of nobles buried there would appear "like a funereal court guide if we were to include therein the names of the duchesses, marchionesses, countesses, ladies, marquises, earls, bishops, baronets, knights and others of rank and distinction, who compose this grim levee of the dead." Additional leading Londoners of literary, scientific or other distinction gravitated to Kensal Green, in time filling its green precincts with a collection of distinguished extinguished citizens.

Although patterned after Père Lachaise, Kensal Green lacks the Paris cemetery's elegance and sense of authority, or even its well-maintained appearance. In *A Celebration of Death* James Stevens Curl observes that "the Parisian cemeteries are still impeccably kept, and are even more delightful now than when they were first laid out, for the planting has matured and the monuments have acquired the patina of age." At unkempt Kensal Green, which huddles by the bulbous tanks of a gasworks, unwieldly foliage proliferates and many of the tombs enjoy no patina but suffer from decades of decay. In *London* E. V. Lucas justifiably states: "After the order and legibility of Pere-la-Chaise, Kensal Green is rather a shock. It is a forlorn necropolis indeed." But it is precisely this natural wildness and the peeling but appealing tombs that lend Kensal Green a pleasant melancholy quite lacking at the overly organized and somewhat too civilized Père Lachaise. If the Paris cemetery resembles a library, with all the contents catalogued and arranged, the London burial ground suggests a Dickensian second-hand book store, its dusty tomes scattered every which way. Do these variances reflect underlying differences between French and English society?

Epitaphs at Kensal Green range from the exotic to the sentimental. Near the back gate reposes Frank Linsly James (d. 1890), "killed while elephant shooting at San Benito on the west coast of Africa." Farther on lies Mary Scott Hogarth, Charles Dickens' sister-in-law, greatly adored by the author. In a letter to his friend Thomas Beard the grieving novelist wrote: "I solemnly believe that so perfect a creature never breathed. I knew her inmost heart, and her real worth and value. She had not a fault." Dickens composed the epitaph for his beloved Mary: "Mary Scott Hogarth/died 7th May 1837/Young, beautiful and good/God in his mercy numbered her with his angels/at the early age of/seventeen."

Literary figures buried at Kensal Green include William Makepeace Thackeray (d. 1863), who reposes along with Anne Carmichael-Smyth (d. 1864), "his mother by her first marriage," while nearby stands a stone to Richmond Edward

Makepeace Thackeray (d. 1944), his third name mocked by the information that he died in Normandy during the war (he lies at Bayeux, France). On the simple, pink stone, box-like tomb which contains the remains of novelist Anthony Trollope (d. 1882) appears the epitaph: "He was a loving husband, a loving father, and a true friend." Not far away lies Wilkie Collins (d. 1889), one of the first mystery writers, "Author of 'The Woman In White' and other works of fiction." Members of Lord Byron's circle buried at Kensal Green include John Murray (d. 1843), publisher of the poet's work and of travel books famous in their time, poet Leigh Hunt (d. 1859), and John Cam Hobhouse (d. 1869), best man at Byron's wedding in 1815 and executor of his will. Charles Babbage (d. 1871) is indirectly connected with Byron for Lady Ada Lovelace, the poet's daughter, gave a detailed account of the Analytical Engine he invented. With its *store* (memory) and *mill* (calculating function), the engine established concepts used to devise the world's first computer. Thus reposes in obscurity at Kensal Green the man who, in the nineteenth century, created the underlying theories and ideas which revolutionized the twentieth century. The epitaph of London *Times* editor Thomas Barnes (d. 1841) describes him as "a mind familiar with our native manners and institutions and acquainted through every grade with the vast fabric of our social system," while caricaturist George Cruikshank (d. 1878) merits recollection for his temperance: "For 30 years a total abstainer and ardent pioneer and champion by pencil, word and pen, of universal abstinence from intoxicating drinks."

Among the pleasures of wandering through cemeteries—especially ones as unwieldy and unkempt as Kensal Green—is the random discovery of odd names or nuances. During my ambles I noticed such inhabitants as Octavius Toogood (d. 1892), George Stiff (d. 1874), and John Skull (d. 1934), Lightly Simpson (d. 1883), Dwarkanath Tagore of Calcutta

(d. 1846), and Rose Williams (d. 1972), memorialized by the succinct but eloquent "Goodnight Mum . . . God bless." This reminded me of the whimsical inscriptions I came across at the Sant'Anna cemetery at Asolo in northern Italy where the famous actress Eleonora Duce (d. 1924) is buried. A nearby marker to Gian Giacomo Miozzi, who died at the age of two, bears the notation (in English) "Momma's coming, darling" below which the name of Lillian Young Miozzi (d. 1929) appears with the inscription "Momma's here, darling."

Dr. "James" Barry (d. 1865), another Kensal Green character, served manfully for forty-six years in the British Army, including duty as Inspector General of Hospitals. Only when Barry died was it discovered that the officer was a woman, a fact she managed to disguise during her entire career. On the grave of acrobat Charles Blondin (d. 1897), who crossed Niagara Falls on a tightrope, stands a stone female figure, right hand on her heart and her face clouded with a serious expression as if watching his death-defying feet. A column to Thomas Hancock (d. 1865) commemorates him as "the inventor and founder of the India rubber manufacture," while other technical types include Marc Isambard Brunel (d. 1849), builder of the Thames tunnel, and his son Isambard Kingdom Brunel (d. 1859), also a famous engineer. The widely known silver-tongued auctioneer George Robins, who apparently could coax even a Scotsman to bid, ended up at Kensal Green when the final gavel fell. Robins inspired a poem which described him as a man who "warm'd his discourse till ear ne'er heard the like./'Who is that eloquent man?' I ask one near./'That, sir? that's Mr. Robins, auctioneer.'" Another commercial figure buried there is John St. John Long, who invented a patent remedy for consumption. When Long contracted the malady, however, he refused to take his own medicine and died at thirty-six, of a truly conspicuous consumption (or non-consumption).

Kensal Green and the other nineteenth-century garden

cemeteries of London were inspired by the same hygienic concerns as the new Parisian burial grounds. Both cities were polluted by overcrowded and unhealthy graveyards. Back in 1721 the Reverend Thomas Lewis wrote a tract relating his *Seasonable Considerations on the Indecent and Dangerous Custom of Burying in Churches and Churchyards,* a polemic which warned of the dangers of infection and attacked church burial as based on superstition promoted by the ecclesiastical authorities for "gain and lucre." Even earlier, rebuilding London after the great fire of 1666, Christopher Wren proposed a cemetery on the outskirts of town, a burial ground sufficiently spacious to contain attractive monuments. "I could wish all burials in churches and churchyards might be disallowed." Wren's wish—granted only much later—was echoed by Samuel Pepys, who complained in his *Diary* on 18 March 1664 about the chaotic burial conditions at his church: "To church, and with the gravemaker chose a place for my brother to lie in, just under my mother's pew. But to see how a man's tombs are at the mercy of such a fellow, that for sixpence he would (as his own words were), 'I will jostle them together but I will make room for him;' speaking of the fullness of the middle aisle, where he was to lie."

The practice of burials outside the church did come about at one place in London during the time Pepys and Wren were complaining about body-stuffed sanctuaries. In 1665 nonbelievers began using a new burial ground at Bunhill, named for the Bone Hill where in the sixteenth century more than a thousand cartloads of bones from charnel houses had been dumped. The Bunhill Fields cemetery, also known as the Dissenters' burial ground, provided a place where free thinkers could escape the fee-grabbing clergy and their costly consecrated terrain in favor of less expensive, secular real estate. Some observers later incorrectly believed that Bunhill Fields served as the site for burial of victims of the plague epidemic which struck London in the mid-1660s. Such interments were described by Daniel Defoe, best known for *Robinson Crusoe,* in *A Journal of the Plague Year:* "I have heard that in a great pit in Finsbury, in the parish of Cripplegate,— it lying open to the fields, for it was not then walled about,— many who were infected and near their end, and delirious also, ran, wrapt in blankets or rags, and threw themselves in and expired there, before any earth could be thrown upon them. When they came to bury others and found them, they were quite dead though not cold."

Among those interred at Bunhill Fields is Defoe himself (d. 1731). In his 1722 account of the earlier plague he stated by way of anticipation: "N. B.—The Author of this Journal lies buried in that very Ground, being at his own desire, his sister having been buried there three or four years before." In fact, it was nearly a century and a half before the author of *Robinson Crusoe* received proper recognition. His obelisk marker now bears a notice: "This monument is the result of an appeal in the 'Christian World' newspaper: to the boys and girls of England, for funds to place a suitable memorial upon the grave of Daniel De-Foe. It represents the united contributions of seventeen hundred persons. Septr. 1870." Next to Defoe's monument a soot-blackened stone commemorates mystical poet William Blake (d. 1827), while nearby stands the box-like tomb of John Bunyan (d. 1688). The recumbent effigy atop it for some years lacked a nose, supposedly shot off by a bullet from the neighboring artillery ground. The side of the monument bears a relief figure of a man with backpack and staff symbolizing *The Pilgrim's Progress,* Bunyan's famous religious allegory.

Because Bunhill Fields served as the Dissenters' burial ground, ghosts of figures involved in the mid-seventeenth-century Puritan revolution haunt the cemetery. The Cromwell family is represented by Henry (d. 1711), Oliver's grandson, along with his widow and offspring, and Charles Fleetwood (d. 1692), Oliver's son-in-law. In a box tomb with a broken slab reposes Thomas Goodwin (d. 1679), the independent preacher who attended Oliver Cromwell on his death bed. Another nonconformist clergyman, David Williams (d. 1716), merits a long Latin eulogy which includes the comment that "he was a lively, pungent, grave, copious, and indefatigable preacher": his parishioners might well have preferred a more fatigable preacher. In a corner by busy City Road near the cemetery entrance—where a notice warns: "No gipsy, hawker, beggar, rogue or vagabond shall enter or remain in the Burial Ground"—rests in peace Presbyterian minister Richard Price (d. 1791), credited with devising the principles that govern life insurance. Dr. Price's 1789 sermon "On the Love of Country" inspired Edmund Burke's *Reflections on the Revolution in France*. Dame Mary Page (d. 1728) enjoyed—or suffered from—the distinction of being an unwell human well: "In 67 months she was tap'd 66 times, Had taken away 240 gallons of water without ever repinning at her case or ever fearing the operation." The output of Susanne Wesley (d. 1742) proved even more substantial and important than Dame Mary's: "She was the Mother of nineteen Children of whom the most eminent were the Revs. John and Charles Wesley."

Methodism's founder John Wesley (d. 1791) reposes in the scruffy little cemetery behind the Wesley Chapel, just across City Road from Bunhill Fields. An urn atop the monument bears the inscription, "This great light." Methodists erased an earlier description of Wesley as "The patron of lay-preachers" when the sect began to consider itself equal to other religious groups.

On nearby Roscoe Street nestles yet another enclave of religious graves, the Friends Burial Ground, formerly a Quaker grave enclave in Bunhill Fields. A notice explains: "This garden is on the site of Bunhill Fields burial ground which was acquired by the Society of Friends (Quakers) in 1661. The remains of many thousands of Friends lie buried here including George Fox the founder of the Society of Friends who died 13th January 1691."

Bunhill Fields, which opened in 1665 after the plague epidemic began and just before the great fire the following year, developed as the first of London's independent burial grounds, detached from a church. As in Paris, virtually all the graveyards of the time were in churchyards crammed with corpses "one above the other, to the very top of the walls, and some above the walls," while so jammed with bodies were the churches themselves that they had become "charnelhouses . . . prejudicial to the health of the living," complained John Evelyn, who had submitted a plan for rebuilding London to Charles II. Both Evelyn and Christopher Wren, whose proposals the king accepted, suggested a new city with the helter-skelter maze of sinuous streets straightened to form long perspectives punctuated by angular parks and squares. This rearrangement would have eliminated pleasant and sometimes eccentric irregularities, converting the capital into a more geometrically balanced artifact. When Parliament considered the plans "many spoke for them, but more against" and after the House of Commons urged "some speedy way of rebuilding," Charles concluded that the old plan should be retained. Evelyn deplored the missed opportunity lamenting, in regard to the overcrowded cemeteries, that "the churchyards had not been banished to the north walls of the City, where a grated inclosure, of competent breadth, for a mile in length, might have served for an universal cemetery to all the parishes, distinguished by the like separations, and with ample walks of trees; the walks adorned with monuments, inscriptions, and titles, apt for contemplation and memory of the defunct." With this vision the forward-looking Evelyn described the modern type of necropolis exemplified by Kensal Green and Père Lachaise a century and a half later.

In contrast to Paris where only two churchyard burial

grounds survive, London boasts a number of the pre-modern cemeteries, many filled with renowned inhabitants or noteworthy monuments. It is one of the more delightful diversions of a stay in London to visit the venerable church graveyards, lingering a time to enjoy the pleasant confluence of the past and the lively present, as personified by Londoners who often use the enclaves as parks. One of my favorite such corners nestles by St. Giles-in-the-Fields, just a bone's throw from the New Oxford Street–Charing Cross Road intersection. This paved, fenced-off area, brightened with flower beds, actually serves as a children's playground, with hobby horses, seesaws and a mini-carousel incongruously installed among the boxy tombs. One inscription commands: "Hold, passenger, here's shrouded in this hearse/Unparalled Pendrell." Duly held, I continued reading about this character (d. 1671) supposedly without parallel and definitely no longer perpendicular:

A pilot to her [Britain's] royal sovereign came [and now] in
   heaven's eternal sphere
He is advanced for his just steerage here
Whilst Albion's chronicler with matchless fame
Embalm the story of great Pendrell's name.

Thus frolicking children—should they pause from their play—can learn about one Richard Penderell (spelled bi-"e" on his tomb) who in 1651 acted as guide to Charles II on the monarch's famous flight after the disastrous Battle of Worcester.

A similarly felicitous combination of the now and the then enhances St. George's Garden, an irregularly shaped park tucked behind Coram's Fields, near Russell Square, which once served as the churchyard for the now-vanished St. George's Church. Tombs scattered around the park and grave markers propped up against its brick walls have suffered from time, their eloquent inscriptions effaced and silent. One legible epitaph from 1727 reads: "Anna 6th Daughter of Richard Cromwell [Oliver's son] The Protector." Around a few tablelike tombs stand rusting picket fences entwined with thin vines, while a thick-armed, terra-cotta figure of Euterpe, muse of instrumental music, which embellished the facade of the Apollo Inn until it was demolished in 1961, now graces the park.

Another phantom cemetery survives at St. John's Garden on Horseferry Road near Westminster Hospital. The park once served St. John the Evangelist Church and a wall plaque erected in 1937 remembers those "whose bodies rest in this place formerly the burial ground of the parish . . . the names on the original memorials having become illegible through lapse of time." An 1892 book by J. E. Smith quotes an earlier source "that the burial ground contains the ashes of an Indian Chief who, having been brought to England in 1734 by James Oglethorpe [founder of Georgia], died of small-pox, and was buried in the presence of the 'emperor Toma,' after the custom of the Karakee Creeks, sewn up in two blankets, between two deal boards, with his clothes, some silver coins and a few glass beads."

Half a century later smallpox also felled a "savage" from a far country, one Prince Lee-Boo who reposes in the family grave of sea captain Henry Wilson at the old churchyard, now a children's playground, by the St. Mary Rotherhithe Church, south of the Thames. A marker inside the church tells the tale of the ill-fated fellow: "In the adjacent churchyard lies the body of Prince Lee-Boo son of Abba Thulle, Rupack or king of the island of Coorooraa, one of the Pelew or Palos islands, who departed this life at the house of Captain Henry Wilson in Paradise Row in this parish on the 27th day of December 1784 aged 20 years. This tablet is erected by the Secretary of State for India to keep alive the memory of the humane treatment shewn by the natives to the crew of the honourable East India Company's ship 'Antelope' which was wrecked off the island of Coorooraa on the 9th of August 1783. 'The barbarous people showed us no little kindness.' Acts xxviii, 2."

In the churchyard of another St. Mary's, also located south of the Thames—St. Mary's Lambeth, up-river from Westminster Bridge—reposes a famous figure from another nautical adventure, the mutiny on the *Bounty*. An inscription on the boxy tomb in the cemetery behind the church reads: "Sacred to the Memory of William Bligh, Esquire, vice Admiral of the Blue; the celebrated navigator who first transplanted the bread fruit tree from Otaheite to the West Indies, bravely fought the battles of his country, and died beloved, respected and lamented, on the 7th day of December, 1817, aged 64." His wife Elizabeth (d. 1812), their sons William and Henry (both d. 1795) and their grandchild William Bligh Barker (d. 1805) also lie there.

The next tomb houses John Tradescant (d. 1638), his son John (d. 1662), and grandson John (d. 1652). The collections of the first John, gardener to Charles I, and of his son John led to the founding of Oxford's famous Ashmolean Museum. The family patriarch established Tradescant's Ark in South Lambeth, England's earliest museum containing a collection of "rarities"—mainly natural history items. When his son died the collection passed to Elias Ashmole, who presented it to Oxford University along with his own assemblage of coins and other objects. In May 1683 the objects were put on display in the original Ashmolean building (now the Museum of the History of Science), Britain's oldest museum structure and one of the earliest in Europe. The loquacious epitaph on the tri-Tradescant tomb relates:

Know, stranger, ere thou pass, beneath this stone
Lye John Tradescant, grandsire, father, son;
The last dy'd in his spring: the other two

Liv'd till they had travell'd Art and Nature through; As by
   their choice Collections may appear,
Of what is rare, in land, in sea, in air;
Whilst they (as Homer's *Iliad* in a nut)
A world of wonders in one closet shut.
These famous Antiquarians that had been
Both Gardiners to the Rose and Lily Queen,
Transplanted now themselves, sleep here; and when
Angels shall with their trumpets waken men,
And fire shall purge the world, these hence shall rise,
And change this Garden for a Paradise.

The busy tomb bears relief panels with motifs which suggest
the range and richness of the Tradescant collection: reptiles,
snails and curious fish; obelisks, columns, capitals, cornices,
and other architectural features; thick foliage above tree
trunks; a seven-headed dragon, its lower two heads looking
down at a skull. The Founders Room at the Ashmolean
houses objects from the Tradescants' "closet of rarities," including such disparate items described in *Musaeum Tradescan-
tianum,* the 1656 catalog of the collection, as a tiny "hand of
jet usually given to children in Turkey to preserve them from
witchcraft," "divers sorts of ivory-balls turned one within
another, some 6, some 12 folds," and (not on display) a "flea
chain of silver and gold with 300 links a piece and yet but an
inch long," "a Deske of one entire piece of wood rarely
carved," and "figures and stories neatly carved upon Plum-
stones, Apricock-stones, etc." What a curious collection the
Tradescants assembled—almost as odd as, say, a cemetery
collection. The Tradescants must have been quite eccentric
fellows indeed.

One of London's most unusual collections of posthumous
markers enhances the churchyard next to St. Botolph's which
once served that congregation as well as those of St.
Leonard's and Christ Church, all located around Aldersgate

and Newgate, not far from St. Paul's Cathedral. The former St. Botolph Aldersgate churchyard, now called Postman's Park because it stretches beneath the looming buildings of the General Post Office, boasts a group of tile plaques which commemorate worthies who perished heroically, a memorial display conceived in 1887 by painter G. F Watts. Deaths remembered there include fiery mishaps suffered by Joseph Andrew Ford (d. 1871) of the Metropolitan Fire Brigade who "saved six persons from fire in Gray's Inn Road but in his last heroic act he was scorched to death"; Thomas Griffith (d. 1899), a laborer who "in a boiler explosion at a Battersea sugar refinery was fatally scalded in returning to search for his mate"; and Sarah Smith (d. 1863), "pantomime artiste at Prince's Theatre [who] died of terrible injuries received when attempting in her flammable dress to extinguish the flames which had enveloped her companion." Death by water took William Donald (d. 1876), a railway clerk "drowned in the sea trying to save a lad from a dangerous entanglement of weed"; ten year old Harry Sisley (d. 1878) "drowned in attempting to save his brother after he himself had just been rescued"; Ernest Benning (d. 1883) who "upset from a boat one dark night off Pimlico Pier grasped an oar with one hand supporting a woman with the other but sank as she was rescued"; and John Cranmer (d. 1901) "drowned near Ostend whilst saving the life of a stranger and a foreigner." Liquid also did in four men (d. 1895) trying "to save a comrade at the sewage pumping works East Ham," and Arthur Strange and Mark Tom Linson (d. 1902) who "on a desperate venture to save two girls from a quicksand in Lincolnshire were themselves engulfed." Frederick Alfred Croft (d. 1878) "saved a lunatic woman from suicide at Woolwich Arsenal Station but was himself run over by the train," Percy Edwin Cook (d. 1927) was "overcome by poisonous gas" in a high tension chamber at Kensington," and William Drake (d. 1869) "lost his life in averting a serious accident to a lady in Hyde Park whose horses were unmanageable through the breaking of the carriage pole."

Out of sight, out of mind, out of place (far from home) but somewhere in St. Botolph's churchyard repose the exotic remains of Hodges Shaughsware (d. 1626), a Persian merchant. The revised 1633 edition of John Stow's famous *A Survey of London* relates that Shaughsware "with his son came over with the Persian ambassador, and was buried by his own son, who read certain prayers, and used other ceremonies, according to the custom of their own country, morning and evening, for a whole month after the burial; for whom is set up, at the charge of his son, a tomb of stone with certain Persian characters thereon, the exposition thus:—This grave is made for Hodges Shaughsware, the chiefest servant to the King of Persia for the space of twenty years, who came from the King of Persia, and died in his service. If any Persian cometh out of that country, let him read this and a prayer for him. The Lord receive his soul, for here lieth Maghmote Shaughsware, who was born in the town of Novoy, in Persia."

Someone else who once lived in the East, and who escaped a hero's death of the kind commemorated at St. Botolph's, was John Mixxs (d. 1811): "He was the last survivor of the few persons who came out of the Black Hole at Calcutta in Bengal in the Year 1756." Mixxs reposes in the yard at St. Pancras Old Church, one of London's more interesting and lesser-known early burial grounds. The cemetery lies on St. Pancras Road behind the spooky buildings of St. Pancras railroad station which tower in the distance. Like the Charonne church in Paris, St. Pancras survives to recall another era. The picturesque sanctuary, built in a rustic style with rough brown stones and a steeple of half-timber construction, seems more suited to an English village than to the

London metropolis. The setting thus evokes burial practices which predate the nineteenth-century cemeteries.

On the church wall a well-worn stone bears the name of William Woollett (d. 1785), an engraver whose epitaph read: "Here Woollett rests, expecting to be sav'd; He gravèd well, but is not well engraved." John Soane (d. 1837), architect of the Bank of England, reposes in a vault. A simple stone marks the grave of Johann Christian Bach (d. 1782), composer son of the famous Johann Sebastian Bach. A pink granite box erected in 1890 by Africa's colonizer Cecil Rhodes to replace two decayed family tombs bears names of the Rhodes family back to the mid-eighteenth century. John Walker (d. 1807) "author of the pronouncing Dictionary of the English language" lies at St. Pancras, as does Mary Wollstonecraft Godwin (d. 1797) "author of A Vindication of the rights of Woman" and also of the more famous *Frankenstein,* not mentioned here. According to tradition the poet Shelley met Mary Godwin, his second wife, at St. Pancras when she came to visit her mother's grave there. A nearby soot-stained stone recalls William Jones (d. 1836), Charles Dickens's schoolmaster at Wellington House Academy on Hampstead Road—the inspiration for Creakle's School in *David Copperfield.*

Dickens's Dictionary of London, published by the novelist in 1879, notes: "The prohibition of intramural interments closed Bunhill-fields, as it closed many other places of burial, and the ground is now planted and open to the public as a place of recreation." St. Pancras has also become a place of recreation, for part of the venerable churchyard now serves as a children's playground, with sandbox, seesaw and other such diversions. Formerly festering graveyards now checker the metropolis with pleasant patches of green, lending a sense of openness and space. In *London In the Nineteenth Century* Sir Walter Besant remarks on the many burial grounds converted into parks. In place of the old churchyards "we have hundreds of pretty gardens with walks, and seats, and shrubs, and flowers; we have asphalted spaces on which the old men walk and the children play . . . we may see the children playing over the spot which was once foul with every kind of abomination."

Those abominable old burial grounds had long attracted criticism. Back in the mid-sixteenth century, after twenty-three London parishes abandoned their own cemeteries to use St. Paul's churchyard, Archbishop Latimer complained that the cathedral's overpopulated yard produced "much sickness and disease" as well as an overpowering stench. Three centuries later the *Cambridge Camden Society Tracts* described how graveyards had inadvertently become grisly playgrounds with "corrupted humanity left to reek under an August sun" while rowdies sported with "skulls set up for a mark at which boys may throw their stones." The most influential attack on the deplorable state of London cemeteries, George Alfred Walker's *Gatherings from Grave-Yards,* sported a long sub-title which promised (in part) "a Detail of dangerous and Fatal Results produced by the unwise and revolting Custom of inhuming the Dead in the midst of the living." Published in 1839, seven years after Kensal Green was laid out, the book complained of "the pestiferous exhalations of the dead" and helped promote the mid-nineteenth century cemetery reform movement. As in France, the church opposed any change, fearing loss of revenue, reverence, and influence. The bishop of London argued that of the hundreds of lead coffins he had seen, not one had deteriorated. In July 1842 appeared the *Sanitary Report* by Edwin Chadwick, formerly secretary to social reformer Jeremy Bentham. Notwithstanding its less-than-catchy title, the work sold more copies than any previous government publication. A supplementary report calculated that in London's 218 acres of burial grounds twenty thousand adults and nearly thirty thousand youths and children came to rest every year, a mortality rate equal to one and a half million bodies in a generation. Meanwhile "Walker of the Graveyards," as Dr. George Alfred Walker came to be called, expounded his pythogenic theory that exhalations of decaying bodies could spread disease by entering a person's system through the lungs or cuts in the skin. In June 1852 Parliament passed a bill empowering the London Necropolis and National Mausoleum Company to purchase two thousand acres in the suburb of Woking. Two years later the firm opened Brookwood, now the largest of all London cemeteries and still owned by a profit-making private company, whose telegraphic address used to be "Tenebratio, London." Located thirty miles outside the city, Brookwood once boasted its own funeral train terminal—a rather sinister designation, under the circumstances—adjoining Waterloo station. During World War II bombs destroyed these facilities and funerals now proceed to Woking by road. But the destination is no less terminal than before.

As is the case with many of London's fifty or so modern cemeteries, Brookwood lacks that patina of age and hint of hidden treasures which typify the area's more historic and picturesque burial grounds. Highgate, however, is an exception to this rule. The most alluring of the city's cemeteries, it is an overgrown, ultra-romantic enclave which nestles on the side of a slope in north London from where the view over the great metropolis in the distance "is suggestive to a meditative mind," John Timbs noted in *Curiosities of London,* published in 1885. The far city with its bristling skyscrapers, bustling crowds, worldly concerns, somehow seems distant in spirit as well as space from the decaying tombs which crowd the foliage-filled field. At Highgate the rather mournful necropolis dominates the scene, inspiring the contemplative mind to meditate on—one's dinner that evening, or what play to attend, or kings and cabbages and sealing wax and ships and shoes, for nothing but nothing evokes so vividly thoughts of daily life and mundane matters as a forlorn and gloomy cemetery. Why visit cemeteries, if not all the more to appreciate life? Another reason is to encounter such profundities as: "The philosophers have only interpreted the world in various ways. The point however is to change it." This sentiment decorates the monument to Highgate's most famous inhabitant, Karl Marx (d. 1883), whose squat bronze bust perches atop a stone block inscribed with the immortal words: "Workers of all lands unite." With Marx repose his wife Jenny (d. 1881), daughter Eleanor (d. 1898) and other relatives, while just across the way lies social reformer Herbert Spencer (d. 1903), thus creating a Marx and Spencer duo, not to be confused with the Marks and Spencer department store chain, perhaps one of the chains Marx claimed workers might lose by uniting. A simple grey stone obelisk marks the grave of Mary Ann Cross (d. 1880), a *nom-de-femme* less known than her *nom-de-plume* George Eliot. Next to Mary/George stands a stone commemorating Elma Stuart "whom for 8½ blessed years George Eliot called by the sweet name of daughter. She was pioneer in England of the Salisbury System of prevention and cure of diseases and author of 'What must I do to get well? And how can I keep so?' " Such a book title would these days certainly be a best-seller. The epitaph of Richard Smith (d. 1900) recalls another healthy achievement: "After years of patient investigation he patented on the 6th Oct 1887 his improved treatment of the wheat germ and broken wheat which made the manufacture of Hows' bread possible." A steeple-like, white marker commemorates William Friese Greene (d. 1921), "the inventor of kinematography. His genius bestowed upon humanity the boon of commercial kinematography of which he was the first inventor and patentee (June 21st 1889, No. 10301)." This must be the world's only tombstone with a patent number on it.

Symbols and signs of various other professions adorn

tombs at Highgate. On the monument to William Richard
Foyle (d. 1957) and William Alfred Westropp Foyle (d. 1963),
owners of the famous bookstore, appear large, stone open
books, while a half-life-sized stone grand piano decorates the
grave of pianist Harry Thornton, "a genius who died Oct.
19th 1918." Exercising the privilege the present enjoys of
interpreting the past, a cemetery attendant stated that Thornton was in fact only a mediocre performer, adding that someone had once warned the musician that he practiced so much
he would die at the keyboard. The prediction came true and
inspired his monument. A famous cricket player named Frederick William Lillywhite (d. 1854) reposes under a marker
showing a wicket struck by a ball to indicate that the cricketer
has finally been bowled out; on the tomb of menagerie im-
pressario George Wombwell (d. 1850) reclines a sleeping lion;
and on the marker of Atcheler, a knacker (horse slaughterer)
to the queen, perches a roughly carved horse.

Scientist Michael Faraday (d. 1867), painter John Singleton
Copley (d. 1815), and the parents (father d. 1851, mother d.
1863) and one daughter (d. 1851) of Charles Dickens rest at
Highgate, as does George Holyoake (d. 1906), the last man to
be imprisoned for atheism in England. But the most storied
tomb belongs to Elizabeth Eleanor Siddal (d.1861), wife of
poet and pre-Raphaelite painter Dante Gabriel Rossetti.
When the undertaker arrived to close the coffin lid Rossetti
put beneath her hair a manuscript poem he had been writing,
explaining, "I have often been working at these poems when
she was ill and suffering and I might have been attending to
her and now they shall go." Into Elizabeth's Highgate grave
descended the verses, there to season for eight years until, in
October 1869, Rossetti experienced a change of heart: he now
wanted to uncover his poems. The writer obtained from the
Home Office a permit to disinter the coffin which held his
wife and the manuscript. Rossetti proceeded to Highgate
along with a solicitor named Henry Virtue Tebbs, a physician

by the name of Williams, and one Charles Augustus Howell, a colorful but shadowy character who had served as John Ruskin's secretary, claimed to be Portuguese, and to have been the chief engineer of Spain's Badajoz railroad, a page to the pope, a painter, a horse dealer and a gold digger. The flickering light of a bonfire illuminated the autumnal scene that October evening when the four men gathered to resurrect Rossetti's manuscript. Howell reported that Elizabeth's hair had continued to grow after her death, and the flames played over the woman's rich red tresses, making them glow with a brilliant tone. Howell, the first to look into the coffin, removed the book, which Dr. Williams disinfected. On 13 October 1869 Rossetti wrote his brother William (d. 1919) who also reposes in Highgate: "All in the coffin was found quite perfect; but the book, though not in any way destroyed, is soaked through and through and had to be still further saturated with disinfectants . . . [The disinterment] was a service I could not ask you to perform for me, nor do I know anyone except Howell who could well have been entrusted with such a trying task." Two weeks later Rossetti, seeking to justify his violation of Elizabeth's tomb in the name of art, wrote his fellow poet Swinburne: "I hope you will think none the worse of my feeling for the memory of one for whom I know you had a true regard. The truth is, that no one so much as herself would have approved of my doing this. Art was the only thing for which she felt very seriously." On 28 October Swinburne replied that he "rejoiced" at the news and affirmed "the question whether we are all to be the richer or the poorer by one more treasure of art." So Rossetti's poems returned from the grave, perhaps the only volume of verse ever to suffer from premature burial.

Highgate opened in 1839 as one of the earlier new-style London cemeteries, the first being Kensal Green, established in 1832. Low Hill General Cemetery, however, also called the Liverpool Necropolis, began operations in 1825 as the very first modern cemetery in England. Four years later another graveyard opened in the city, installed in a disused stone quarry. Huge ramps descended dramatically to the quarry floor to give access to the catacombs and tunnels which punctured the stone walls, above which towered Liverpool's huge Gothic-style Anglican cathedral. The large number of Dissenters (non-Anglicans) in Liverpool no doubt encouraged the early establishment of a cemetery independent of the church.

In 1832 a similar cemetery opened at Glasgow—with the graves, or *lairs* as the Scots call them, cut into solid rock—on a rocky perch two hundred and twenty-five feet above the Clyde River, reached by crossing over a ravine on The Bridge of Sighs. A chaos of varied monuments bristles from the heights occupied by the Glasgow Necropolis. Modelled after Père Lachaise, the Scottish graveyard was adjudged a "grand and melancholy" place by John Loudon, who in 1843 published *On the Laying Out, Planting, and Managing of Cemeteries.*

The same year the Glasgow Necropolis opened the Dubliners, not to be outdone, established Glasnevin Cemetery. This must be one of the world's most nationalistic cemeteries, for here repose all the great Irish patriots, their remains inspiring not resurrection but insurrection. By the grave of Jeremiah O'Donovan Rossa (d. 1915) patriot Patrick Pearse delivered the famous eulogy warning the British of the power dead Irish heroes exert over the living: "The fools, the fools, the fools!—They have left us our Fenian dead, and while Ireland holds these graves, Ireland unfree shall never be at peace." The first patriot to arrive at Glasnevin was Daniel O'Connell (d. 1847), founder in 1823 of the Catholic Association and agitator for secession from Great Britain. Over his grave rises a tall, thin tower which dominates the cemetery. On the tomb of James Stephens, a Fenian Brotherhood founder, appears the sentiment: "A day, an hour, of virtuous liberty, is worth a whole eternity in bondage." Adjacent reposes Fenian leader John O'Leary (d. 1907), buried "amidst the grief of thousands of his countrymen who vowed to perpetuate the work of his life." On the right side of O'Leary's monument appears an extract from his 1905 speech at the centenary for the Irish patriot Emmet: "Emmet desired that his epitaph should not be written until his country was free . . . Strive with might and main to bring about the hour when his epitaph can be written. I have nothing more to say: but I and all of you have very much to do." Yeats's poem "September 1913" laments: "Romantic Ireland's dead and gone,/It's with O'Leary in the grave." In the well-named Republic Plot lie six early Sinn Fein members who plotted against England, "all outlaws and felons according to English law, but true soldiers of Irish liberty; representatives of successive movements for Irish Independence, their lives thus prove that every generation produces patriots who were willing to face the gibbet, the cell and exile to procure the liberty of their nation and afford perpetual proof that in the Irish heart faith in Irish nationality is indestructible." Just behind the plot a monument to John Keegan Casey (d. 1870), who died on St. Patrick's Day, remembers him as the author of "many soul stirring national ballads and songs." On the marker appear representations of a harp, shamrocks, and a scroll listing Casey's works, the last being "Decking the Graves."

Completely unbedecked is the forlorn last resting place of Irish author Brendan Behan, a slight mound of dirt vaguely indicating his whereabouts, or nowhereabouts. Almost all the other inhabitants of Glasnevin boast some sort of marker—"saddened angels, crosses, broken pillars," as James Joyce's Bloom found when he walked through the cemetery to attend Patrick Dignam's funeral. In *Ulysses* Joyce tells the story of two drunks who staggered through Glasnevin one foggy evening to look for a friend's grave. Gazing at a statue of Christ which rose above their chum's plot one of the drunks blurted out that they must be at the wrong tomb, for the figure did not look "a bloody bit like the man" buried there. Joyce, ever the exile, reposes in Zurich, Switzerland, (his grave is described later in this chapter) but his parents lie in Glasnevin, the grey stone slab at their grave inscribed: "In loving memory of John Stanislaus Joyce of Cork, Born 4th July 1849, Died 29th Decmeber 1931. And of his wife Mary Jane of Dublin, Born 15th May 1855, Died 13th August 1903."

At Paddy Dignam's funeral Leopold Bloom wonders why Dublin does not "have municipal funeral trains like they have in Milan, you know. Run the line out to the cemetery gates and have special trams, hearse and carriage and all." Trams in Milan still run out to the Cimitero Monumentale just beyond the Porta Volta, but these days the streetcars do not haul the dead in that lively northern Italian town. Doubly true to its name, the burial ground encompasses a monumentally-sized collection of monuments. When I last visited, I found at the entrance a sign of a kind I have never seen at a cemetery: a list of *anniversari del mese,* and the location of the graves featured that month. With its attention to otherwise obscure departed and their whereabouts Milan's Monumentale is a cemetery after my own heart. The first name on the list that June was Umberto Campanari (d. 1931), not entirely obscure as he was Verdi's lawyer and friend. He also served as the composer's executor and as secretary of the Casa di reposo dei musicisti, the musicians' retirement home. A few expired musicians reside in the Toscannini family plot with its mausoleum, including pianist Vladimir Horowitz (d. 1989), who married Toscannini's daughter.

Just beyond the cemetery entrance I came to the tomb of Quintili Luciano (d. 1946), a pilot whose marker incorporates a real airplane propeller. On the grave which holds three Rancati sits a tired-looking grim reaper, as if fatigued by cutting down the Rancati trio. Complete with scythe and wings, a long beard but bald head, the death figure contrasts with the nearby bronze on Tadini Mino's (d. 1946) tomb depicting a happy youth clad in an open-neck shirt, short pants, and boots sitting on a boulder with a smile on his face. In the center of the cemetery stands the so called Famedio, opened in the 1960s, a kind of hall of fame which houses monuments to some of Milan's former leading lights, among them author Alessandro Manzoni (d. 1873) and Giuseppe Verdi (d. 1901: Joe Green in plain English) commemorated by a bronze statue.

Toward the back lies the crematorium, presented to Milan in 1876 by a Swiss resident. It was in Italy that the first serious experiments in modern cremation techniques were carried out by Brunetti in 1869. An exhibition in Vienna in 1873 included a cremation apparatus bearing his name. The following year a man named Alberto Keller expired in Milan. Dying to try out the new technique, Keller remained embalmed in storage for two years as he patiently awaited permission. Finally, in 1876, he enjoyed the honor of being the very first person ashed in the new crematorium.

The most striking characteristic of the Cimitero Monumentale is the large number of family mausoleums, lending it the appearance of a city comprised of boxy mini-houses. Perhaps no other burial ground in the world contains as many. Only the Recoleta cemetery in Buenos Aires, with more than fifty-five hundred mausoleums crowded into twelve acres, can match Milan's in magnificence and quantity. Among the many mausoleums at Recoleta I came across only one conventional grave, set in a cramped plot. Its headstone was also an exception as it bore a French inscription: "Ici repose Alphone Huppé, Ne le 5 7bre 1820, décedé le 15 Août 1858, Priez pour lui." The famous Argentine author Jorge Luis Borges captured the graveyard's lapidary tone in poetry: "Lovely are the tombs, the latin bareness and the tongue-tied fatal dates, the conjunction of marble and flowers and the small squares with a patio's calmness and history's yesterdays today stayed and staid." When I met Borges in Buenos Aires in the national library, which he served as director, the writer spoke of his deep roots in Argentina. He once wrote, "I never pass by the Recoleta without remembering that my father, grandparents, and great-grandparents are buried there, just as I, too, will be." His grandfather, a cavalry officer (d. 1874) is recalled in the author's short poem "Allusion to the Death of Colonel Francisco Borges." Although Borges told me that he no longer wished to travel and felt little nostalgia for Europe, when a doctor told him in 1986 that he suffered from incurable liver cancer Borges uprooted himself and moved to Geneva, expiring in the Swiss city where he had attended high school.

Like the modern cemeteries of Europe, Recoleta was established in the early nineteenth century. Until the beginning of that century only the Franciscan order of the Recoletos occupied the district just north of downtown, overlooking the Plata River. The friars built Our Lady of the Pilar Church near their orchard which in 1821 became Buenos Aires' central cemetery, administered by the Franciscans. Sixty years later the city took control of the graveyard, remodeled it and converted it into a nonsectarian facility. By the side of the cemetery still stands the delightful Pilar church, a colonial-style structure with graceful arches, old-fashioned lanterns, topped by a tiled steeple on one side and a bell tower on the other. An attractive white-columned marble portico leads into the cemetery, which serves as Buenos Aires' Père Lachaise, the social center of the departed where fashionable citizens repose in mausoleums—the "small squares" of Borges's poem—larger than the dwellings occupied by many of the city's poor. You really have to be born into the right family to be dead at Recoleta. Some less wealthy folks with postmortem social pretensions, however, rent space on a short term lease in a Recoleta mausoleum so that their families will, for a time at least, enjoy an appropriate status. By going underground lesser citizens can rise in the world. Those fortunate enough to own land at Recoleta, one of Buenos Aires' most exclusive neighborhoods, will occasionally raze the family mausoleum, subdivide the property, sell off lots, and then build a smaller structure for themselves on part of the plot. This strikes me as an especially attractive business, for dead occupants never complain about noisy neighbors, plumbing problems or other such inconveniences. And with just a little spadework a gravelord could easily evict a tenant. On the other hand, how could a property owner ever induce a Recoleta resident to help pay for redecorating?

One of the largest mausoleums, built to house Manuel M. Ibañez, resembles in size and style a small Greek temple with four columns and steps rising the width of the building. A man named Lappas inspired another elaborate mausoleum, its plate glass door and greyish polished marble suggesting the entrance to a fancy jewelry store. A rigid iron soldier, forever at attention and holding a long saber across his chest, guards the last post of General Juan Lavalle. Near the cemetery entrance, beneath a marble statue portraying his grief-striken widow, lies Facundo Quiroga, early-nineteenth-century strong-man of La Rioja province. The statue of a sad-looking young girl clad in flowing robes at the tomb of Rufina Cambacerés recalls the legend that she was buried alive at age nineteen while suffering an attack of catalepsy. Eva Peron (d. 1952), second wife of Argentinian president Juan Peron, reposes at Recoleta in a glass-topped coffin installed in a supposedly secure steel-walled room nearly twenty feet underground, built by a firm that specializes in banks and safes. Another famous international figure buried at Recoleta is boxer Luis Angel Firpo (d. 1960), the so-called Wild Bull of the Pampas, who lost to Jack Dempsey in a world heavyweight boxing bout in 1923. In front of Firpo's mausoleum stands a twice-life-sized statue showing the pugilist clad in boxing shoes and a robe, open to reveal his powerful metal-hard chest. On the tomb-house appears a private message made public: "Luis, my love, thank you for having loved me so much, may almighty God bless your silence with light and peace. Lourdes."

Recoleta seems to have inspired similar cemeteries in Latin America, much as Père Lachaise set the pattern in Europe. The central cemetery in Guayquil, Ecuador, La Ciudad Blanca, contains dozens of mausoleums which comprise the "white city" of the dead. Some of the tomb-houses dot a hillside profuse with tropical vegetation, the green contrasting with the bright white structures, until at the top the foliage dominates the mausoleums. Up there, raw nature tries to resist man's intrusions. A caretaker cautioned me to remain below in the civilized section because robbers lurked in the overgrowth to ambush unsuspecting visitors to the isolated graves on the heights. Strolling through the white city I soon discovered that, unlike Recoleta, the mausoleums in Guayaquil house not just one family but dozens of occupants, shoe-horned into little niches. One such structure contained defunct members of the Sindicate de Choferes Professionales del Guayas—an excellent fringe benefit enjoyed by the Guayaquil taxi drivers union.

In his *Journals* French painter Paul Gauguin referred to another South American cemetery packed with mausoleums, a burial ground in Lima, Peru, where the artist lived as a child. "A French businessman, M. Maury, took it into his head to look up the rich families and suggest that they should have tombs of sculptured marble. It succeeded marvelously . . . He had armed himself for the undertaking with several photographs of sculptured tombs in Italy. It was a dazzling success. For several years ships kept arriving filled with marbles sculptured in Italy for a very low price and which made a very good effect. If you go to Lima now you will see a cemetery that is unlike any other." With its fine statuary and

Old World flavor, the Lima cemetery must resemble the burial grounds of Italy, a country which can be considered the mother of modern cemeteries much as Père Lachaise is their father.

During the millenium or more when burials in Europe customarily took place in and around churches the Campo Santo in Pisa, Italy, enjoyed a unique status as the only major, internationally known cemetery. Built in the late thirteenth century, the Campo Santo was literally a holy field, for it consisted of some fifty freightloads of earth shipped from the Holy Land where Crusaders had excavated the sacred dirt from Jerusalem's Calvary mount. The Campo Santo thus became not only Europe's first free-standing burial ground but also—its ground originating far afield—the world's most peripatetic cemetery and, in addition, it also served as the original of the so-called museum cemetery. Artworks embellish the Tuscan-Gothic cloisters delicately laced with tracery-webbed windows, and the three chapels which surround the rectangular, green field. This felicitous combination led James Stevens Curl, in *A Celebration of Death,* to adjudge Campo Santo "the most serene and beautiful cemetery in the world, and, architecturally, the finest by far. It is perfection." After Giovanni Pisano confected the white marble enclosure in 1280, artists decorated its sixty-two bays with frescoes, including the famous depiction of three hunters who come upon their own decaying corpses. The Gothic galleries are paved with six hundred tombstones of those who repose at Campo Santo and adorned with sculptures, decorated tombs, and ancient coffins. During the Renaissance tourists frequented the Campo Santo, much as Père Lachaise and other show cemeteries now attract visitors interested in tomb statuary. In his *Autobiography* Benvenuto Cellini, the sixteenth-century Florentine goldsmith, tells of a visit to the exhibits: "While I stayed at Pisa, I went to see the Campo Santo, and there I found many beautiful fragments of antiquity, that is to say marble sarcophagi." There in the shadow of the Leaning Tower of Pisa lay the forerunner of those green and serene cemetery sculpture parks now common in Europe and America.

The most striking latter-day Italian version of that first museum cemetery is Genoa's Cimitero di Staglieno. Curl, quoted above, held that "with its classical architecture, dramatic site, and essential urbaneness, [Staglieno] is unquestionably the grandest of all the cemeteries in Europe. Many connoisseurs consider it to be the most splendid cemetery in the world because of the excellence and quality of sculpture in its galleries." Those sculpture-laden galleries fan out from a central square, paved with marble grave markers just as at Pisa's Campo Santo. Thousands of statues populate the four hundred acres occupied by Staglieno, Italy's largest cemetery, established in 1844 in the suburbs between the Verlino and Bisagno rivers. At first an insignificant burial ground, Staglieno soon became a favorite haunt of Genoa's wealthy merchants, who enriched themselves in the nineteenth century through the city's maritime trade. Money, insubstantial but potent, demands tangible evidence, so Staglieno soon evolved as an avatar of posthumous consumerism.

Dead and gone they were but not forgotten, for realistic images of the departed form a veritable grave conclave of Genoa's deceased citizens. Many of the funerary figures were commissioned in advance, thus affording those still alive the chance to design the monument by which the family's standing and merit would be remembered. This naturally resulted in grandiose monuments. All manner of pomp, pretense and poses can be found at Staglieno. Even a peddler, one Caterina Campodonic (d. 1881), felt impelled to preserve her place in Genoa's society: "By selling my wares . . . [and] defying wind, sun and rain in order to provide an honest loaf for my old age I have also saved enough to have myself placed, later on, with my monument which I . . . have erected while still alive." Caterina's life-like statue shows her clad in a fringed shawl and a lace-decorated apron, an oversized rosary clasped in both hands. It was the realistic statues of Staglieno which inspired William Dean Howells to comment in *Roman Holidays* that American "millionaires have an unrivalled opportunity of immortality . . . [for they] could easily afford to give a hundred thousand dollars, or fifty, or twenty to their native or adoptive place and so enter upon a new life in bronze or marble." Howell's contemporary Mark Twain waxed less pecuniary and more poetic about Staglieno after his 1867 visit: "On either side, as one walks down the middle of the passage, are monuments, tombs, and sculptural figures that are exquisitely wrought and are full of grace and beauty. They are new, and snowy; every outline is perfect, every feature guiltless of mutilation, flaw or blemish." Such marmoreal perfection, however, makes Staglieno just too contrived and pompous, too bright and life-like, characteristics which seem to belie the sinister inscription beneath the statue of Adam perched in a niche at the cemetery's church: "It is only because of my fault that death reigns here." Back during the time of the Roman Empire, rulers would engage in *Damnatio memoriae*—the removal of all trace of political opponents by destroying their effigies. At Staglieno the opposite phenomenon prevails. The statues there remain self-assured and seemingly immune to oblivion. Staglieno, in short, seems too worldly and insufficiently underworldly.

By way of contrast is the moribund and funereal cemetery in Venice which spreads over the island of San Michele. Apart from the mournful black gondolas that seem to set a mood of mortality—Shelley calls the boat "that funeral bark"—perhaps it is the graveyard's island location which lends it such a somber tone. Death being the ultimate isolation, San Michele, possibly the only major insular cemetery in the world, is the quintessential cemetery. There the deceased repose cut off from life on the mainland, there the departed are relegated to a true back water. Death in Venice: San Michele is its domicile. Although an early edition of *Baedeker* dismissed San Michele with the comment that "the general effect of the cemetery is not stimulating," Horatio F. Brown, writing in *Life on the Lagoons* at about the same time, asserted that it was a "grim . . . terrible and sinister [place] . . . where the dead lie buried in the ooze of the lagoon-island." I found San Michele benignly grim, more forlorn than sinister. Burials began there in the early nineteenth century after Napoleon closed Venice's churchyards, a hygienic measure of the sort which had occurred in France not long before. The authorities transferred bodies from Venice to San Cristoforo, and in 1810 this islet was joined to adjacent San Michele by filling in a canal that divided the two. In its newly expanded form, San Michele became the city's burial ground and still serves as Venice's only cemetery.

For some six centuries before, the island had been home to the order of the Camaldolesi. On the site of the monastery today stands Venice's first Renaissance church. A marker in the floor just inside the door indicates the last resting place of Paolo Sarpi (d. 1623), a famous scholar and advisor to the doges, who became a symbol of the political, religious and cultural conflict that divided Venice and the Vatican. It is no idle phrase to describe Sarpi's grave as his last resting place, for his remains suffered unusually labyrinthine peregrinations before finally settling at the San Michele church. The story began in 1606 when Pope Paul V, unable to capture the dissident Fra Paolo and burn him, decided to burn his books and excommunicate the priest. When Sarpi finally died his remains were interred at the altar of the Servite church in Venice, but Pope Urban VIII blocked attempts by the Venetian Republic to erect a monument. Emboldened by this success, the pope plotted to desecrate the tomb and abduct the corpse. The Servite monks, getting wind of the plot, dug up the body and hid it in a wall inside the monastery. The following October they retrieved the remains and reburied them at the altar where they rested for about a century. In 1722 they were transferred to an urn when the Servites began restoration work on the altar. Twenty years later, after the reconstruction was complete, the pope again tried to grab Sarpi's remains, which were once again removed to safety and later returned to the altar. When the Servite church fell into ruin and demolition proceedings began in 1828, the pope plotted to obtain Fra Paolo's bones and disperse them but the Venetians took the urn, locked it in a box secured with three seals, and deposited the treasure in, of all places, the papal seminary next to the church of Santa Maria della Salute. The rescuers quickly agreed that the seminary was not a safe place so they removed the box at night and carried it in a gondola to a private house. There the container remained a time before the Venetians decided to transfer the bones to the library of St. Mark's, whose director agreed to receive the chest only if the consignment document omitted its contents. After obtaining government approval to bury Fra Paolo on San Michele, his bones were put into a new stone coffin and on 15 November 1828 interred in the church on the island, beneath an appropriate marker.

It so happened that in 1841 a book entitled *Venetian Inscriptions* fell into the hands of Pope Gregory XVI, who had lived as a monk on San Michele. On reading about Sarpi's burial in the church atrium Gregory became enraged, shouting, "They have profaned my church." When Venetians visited San Michele on the Day of the Dead (1 November) in 1846 they found that the marble slab marking Sarpi's grave had disappeared and the pavement restored to its original condition. It seemed that Pope Gregory, who by then had died, had ordered the patriarch of Venice to have the monks at San Michele remove the offending marker. But by 19 November the angry Venetians had found the missing slab and replaced it in the church floor where it, and Paolo Sarpi, remain to this day: the first grave encountered by visitors to San Michele. As recently as 1892 the Vatican protested when Venetians erected a large bronze statue of Sarpi in the Campo di Santa Fosca. The square—through which Fra Paolo used to pass on his way from the adjacent monastery to the doge's palace— lies not far from the bridge where one night in 1607 he was knifed by papal assassins and left for dead, only to survive for another sixteen years. Should that statue someday suddenly disappear, no prizes will be awarded for guessing who-done-it.

By the church on San Michele stands the fifteenth-century cloister, its floors and walls lined by stone grave markers, and beyond the sanctuary stretches the cemetery, garnished with cypress trees. The sense of space presented by the park-like enclave seems to confirm a local woman's comment, recorded by William Dean Howells: "Here we poor Venetians become landowners at last." In fact, however, the Venetian dead enjoy no such post mortem tenure, for they reside in tiny marble compartments, there to remain not for an eternity but for a mere twelve years before being evicted, their bones dumped into a common grave elsewhere on the island to make room for newcomers. On one obscure niche (the top row in the ninth unit to the left in Section VII) a marker recalls "Frederick William Rolfe, 22 July 1860–25 Oct. 1913, R.I.P." An eccentric expatriate who called himself Baron Corvo, Rolfe lived a dissolute life in Venice while writing such books as *Hadrian the Seventh* and *The Desire and Pursuit of the Whole,* a title perhaps emblematic of the Venetian locals, who lead insular lives on fragments of land riven by canals.

In contrast to the cemetery's neatly kept main area, the foreigners' section—the Reparto Evangelico—remains unkempt, with tall grass and unpruned foliage. A simple white slab inscribed "Ezra Pound" (d. 1972) marks the poet's grave. A stone box decorated with images of a palette, three brushes and a profile portrait in bronze appear on the tomb of French painter Léopold Robert (d. 1835), who committed suicide exactly ten years after his brother. His rather unflattering epitaph, composed by French poet Alphone de Lamartine, notes that he killed himself in a fit of weakness, and that "whereas Michelangelo would have overcome it, Léopold Robert succumbed." The tomb of an Englishman named Frank Stainer also bears a damning epitaph, no doubt inadvertant: "left us in peace, Febry 2nd, 1910." Defunct diplomats represent their various nations at San Michele: consuls such as Christian Nadig (d. 1913) of Switzerland; Germany's D. W. Breitling (d. 1956); Johan Mowinckel (d. 1906) from Norway; Sir William Perry (d. 1874), British consul general; and Sir Thomas Stephen Sorell (d. 1846), "Knight commander of the Royal and Military Order of San Benito de Avis in Portugal, Knight of the Royal Guelphic Order of Hanover, Lieutenant Colonel in Her British Majesty's Service and Her Majesty's Consul General for the Lombard Venetian Kingdom and the Austrian States on the Adriatic." A relief coat of arms with a pair of medals hanging from a ribbon decorate the tomb, the most impressive in the Evangelico section. Other foreigners there include travelers who never expected to end up in Venice, visitors who did not make it back home, such as Janet and Sarah McLean Drake "who perished in the steamer disaster near the Lido, Venice, 19th March 1914," and Johanna Fearon of Frognal, Hampstead, London who expired in Venice in 1887 "on the eve of her return to England."

The posted sign "Greco" which designates the area next to the Evangelico refers to the cemetery's Orthodox section. At the rear wall to the right of the chapel a translucent white marble slab bordered by pink granite bears the name Igor Stravinsky inset in blue stone above a gold-colored metal cross embedded in the marker. After the famous composer died in New York in 1971 his body was taken to Venice where thousands attended the Russian Orthodox funeral. Just off to the left reposes Russian ballet impresario Sergei Diaghilev (d. 1929), whose dancers included Pavlova and Nijinsky. Diaghilev and Stravinsky worked together on such productions as *Petrouchka* and *The Firebird*. A Byzantine-style monument marks the grave of Diaghilev, who before World War I orchestrated the removal of the Ballet Russe from Imperial Russia. Two days after he died of a diabetes attack a procession of four gondolas carried his coffin—covered with tea roses and carnations—across the lagoon to San Michele. A Russian Orthodox priest and a small choir from San Georgio dei Greci chanted the Slavic funeral service as the procession floated to the cemetery. At what was perhaps the greatest production ever inspired by the impresario, dancer Sergei Lifar, overwrought by the service, leapt into the open grave. Diaghilev died in Venice at the Hotel des Bains on the Lido where, in 1912, Stravinsky had played for him the beginnings of *The Rites of Spring*. The Hotel des Bains also serves as the setting for much of Thomas Mann's famous novella *Death in Venice*. The story opens on an appropriately funereal note with author Gustave Aschenbach, who lives (or dies) the book's title, strolling through an area near Munich's North Cemetery where he finds a stonemason's yard whose "crosses, monuments, and commemorative tablets made a supernumerary and untenanted graveyard opposite the real one"—a cemetery ghost town.

Mann himself reposes not in his native Germany but in an isolated and utterly peaceful cemetery next to a church at Kilchberg near Zurich, Switzerland. The author left the United States in 1954, and spent his last years in the house at Alte Landstrasse 39, part way down the hill from the burial ground. In his *Diary* Mann noted that he wanted his gravestone to stand in a land where German-language poets reposed. A rough-surfaced, grey stone cube in the neat little graveyard bears only the novelist's name and dates (d. 1955). On the marker also appears the name and dates of his wife

Katia (d. 1980) while adjacent reposes their eldest daughter Erika (d. 1969). By the side of the church a black marble obelisk marks the grave of Swiss writer Conrad Ferdinand Meyer (d. 1898). From the cemetery stretches a vista that includes the snow-capped Alps, green tree-filled hills studded with snug houses, and a fragment of Lake Zurich.

In Zurich lies the park-like Fluntern cemetery, which boasts the grave of another renowned twentieth-century novelist, commemorated with a simple inscription reading: "James Joyce, geboren 2 Februar 1882 in Dublin, gestorben 13 Januar 1941 in Zurich," beneath which appears an inscription for his wife Nora (d. 1951), also buried there. Due to lack of space at Joyce's original grave Nora and James for a time reposed at separate sites, but their bodies were later exhumed and reburied together, and the monument was erected in 1966 on 16 June, Bloomsday, the day on which all the events of *Ulysses* take place. At the grave appears one of the most delightful and vivid tomb statues anywhere, a life-size bronze of Joyce, slightly hunched forward and gazing off to his left, with a cane resting against his right thigh, right leg draped over the left knee. It seemed so candid that I half expected Joyce to turn to me and speak.

Fluntern is tucked into a green swatch by a birch forest on Zurichburg, one of the hills overlooking Zurich. Other departed reposing there include a man named Paul Karl Marx (d. 1968), not a convenient name in the gilt-edged Swiss banking capital; Egon Zeller (d. 1970), inventor of the *Telefongrafen,* portrayed on his marker as a writing device attached to a telephone; Rudolf Wenig (d. 1970), whose monument for some reason bears a two-foot-tall bronze Indian figure; and Ernst (d. 1941) and Margrit (d. 1973) Waser, remembered with a sentiment by the poet Rilke: "O Lord, may each die in his own way and may each life find love, meaning and need." Fluntern's meticulously clipped grass, neat but restrained flowerbeds, subdued monuments, trimmed trees and precise rows of graves reflect the order which pervades Swiss society. Even the birdhouses attached to the trees which garnish the cemetery bear numbers.

A similarly ultra-orderly burial ground and one of the most severely regular graveyards anywhere is Johannis cemetery in Nuremberg, Germany. It consists of row after row of precisely aligned, identical stone boxes, as if to suggest that in death all men are equal. Begun in 1518 after the city council prohibited interments inside the walls, Johannis developed around an earlier graveyard by a church. Flat sandstone slabs cover the tombs, enlivened only by writings and motifs on bronze relief plaques, inscriptions that recount much local history. The Latin epitaph for Johannis' most famous inhabitant, native son artist Albert Dürer (grave number 149), reads: "What was mortal of Albert Dürer lies under this tomb. He went hence the 7th of the Ides of April, 1548."

Although not as rigidly arranged as Nuremberg's Johannis, Vienna's Zentralfriedhof also projects a strong sense of order. The rather ponderous monuments and straight streets might well reflect the structured, top-heavy society that existed in the Hapsburg capital when the graveyard opened in the 1870s. Graham Greene's film script for *The Third Man* describes both the appearance and the tone of Vienna's Zentralfriedhof: "Avenues of graves, each avenue numbered and lettered stretching out like spokes of an enormous wheel. On some gravestones are the photographs of the occupants. Respectable faces with waxed moustaches and morning coats. A huge figure in armor on the family vault of a steel manufacturer; the bust of a dandified gentleman with hair parted in the middle; the master of a dancing school. The statue of a woman in an attitude of despair who raises her arms towards the portrait in relief of her husband." The movie begins with Harry Lime's supposed interment at the Zentralfriedhof and it ends with his second, definitive, burial there. After the grave-side service Lime's one-time lover Anna, draped in a bulky coat and topped by a floppy hat, hurries down a shadow-strewn path between two long rows of trees shedding their leaves as the zither music loudens and then, suddenly, the screen goes blank.

That indelible scene was projected on the screen of memory as I searched in vain for Lime's grave at the Zentralfriedhof. But the cemetery boasts other celebrities, many of them musicians no longer composing but decomposing. Both Schubert and Beethoven originally reposed in the old Währing cemetery (now a park) not far from the university. Their monuments remain there but their remains were transferred in 1888 to the relatively new Zentralfriedhof. The grave of Schubert, who died of typhus in 1828 at age thirty-one, sports two columns flanking a relief tableau showing the muse of music about to crown the composer with a laurel wreath, while the epitaph by Austrian dramatist Franz Grillparzer states: "The art of music here interred a rich possession/But hopes for fairer still." Above the grave of Beethoven (d. 1827) rises an obelisk decorated with a leaf-bordered relief lyre. The more lively monument to Brahms (d. 1897) includes mourning figures shown in relief on a stone backdrop behind a bust of the bearded composer. His right hand is pressed to his head as if puzzling over the next notes to enter in the composition book he holds open in his left. On the tomb of thick-haired Johann Strauss the Younger (d. 1899) appears a stone medallion relief portrait below which an angelic figure plays the violin and a rather solemn gowned woman fingers a harp. Strauss the Elder (d. 1849) and his other musical sons Josef (d. 1870) and Eduard (d. 1916) also repose at the Zentralfriedhof, the former in a gloomy, black stone tomb on which leans a white marble mourning figure holding a lyre.

Between the graves of Beethoven and Schubert stands a memorial to Mozart (d. 1791), who actually lies in a grave, originally unmarked, somewhere at Vienna's St. Mark's cemetery. The famous composer died impoverished and suffered "a pauper's funeral in the rain," as W. H. Auden put it in his poem "Metalogue to the Magic Flute." Mozart was taken to St. Mark's, accompanied by a few mourners, for a third class funeral. Not even his widow Constanze commemorated his grave with a marker. In 1859, however, a gravedigger decided that Mozart deserved a better fate and assembled a monument out of pieces salvaged from other tombs at the graveyard. The makeshift memorial—a broken-off column with a dyspeptic angel figure at the base—stands on the spot where the composer supposedly reposes. In fact, no one knows exactly where Mozart lies. His widow let seventeen years elapse before asking the location of her husband's tomb. More than half a century later, when the city of Vienna attempted to find the grave, the grandson of the musician Albrechtsberger, a friend of Mozart, claimed that during his childhood someone had shown him the burial site. Based on this rather time-worn recollection the city erected the marker where it now stands on Mozart's official last resting place.

Other composers at the Zentralfriedhof include Christoph Gluck (d. 1787), first of the great musicians based in Vienna; Franz von Suppé (d. 1895), author of the *Poet and Peasant* overture; Karl Millocker (d. 1899), whose musical *The Dubarry* played on Broadway; Hugo Wolf (d. 1903), composer of more than three hundred *lieder;* and latter-day Viennese waltz king Robert Stolz (d. 1975), winner of two Academy Awards, whose twenty-five hundred songs include "Two Hearts in Three-Quarter Time." (Vienna's most unusual and original grave—that of Ludwig Boltzmann, the renowned Austrian physicist who committed suicide—lies not in the Zentralfriedhof but in a cypress grove outside the city. On the stone which supports a bust of the scientist appears the simple inscription "$S = k \log w$," the formula for Boltzmann's famous theory of entropy which, appropriately enough for an epitaph, holds that every activity results in an irrevocable loss of energy, thus gradually forcing the world to run down.)

The Vienna Zentralfriedhof is the German-speaking world's most impressive cemetery and no doubt its largest as well. More than a million-and-a-half souls repose there, a number very nearly equal to the city's live population. The first stirring of cemetery reform began in 1784 when Joseph II issued a decree regulating funerals and interments. Concerned about hygiene in Vienna's overcrowded churchyards and also about the scarcity of cloth and lumber, the emperor prohibited burials which used clothes and a coffin. Each parish stocked a communal coffin, used only to transport bodies to the graveyard. There a corpse would be removed from the container, wrapped in a shroud, put into a common grave, and covered with limestone. But this callous and unpopular decree was retracted before long, apart from the provision that all burials were to take place in graveyards outside the city. Nearly a century later the city purchased some farmland for use as a central cemetery to replace Heitzing, Meidling, Währing, and other small and antiquated burial grounds. At first some Viennese burghers feared that bodies interred in the new cemetery might pollute the underground springs which supplied water to a nearby brewery. Nevertheless the first burial took place in 1874 on 1 November, All Saints' Day, celebrated annually at the Zentralfriedhof with thousands of grave-side candles that flicker like a stage effect from some romantic Viennese light opera production. Other dramas unfolded there, for the Zentralfriedhof no doubt remains unique as a cemetery which has also served as a hunting ground. Small game—rabbits, pheasants, partridges and even occasionally a deer—which proliferated in the park-like burial ground damaged graves, destroyed flowers, and at times toppled tombstones. In the late 1960s the Vienna City Council decided to deal with the problem by permitting hunting in the area. One out-doorsman, a retired grocer named Ludwig Siehs, formed a cemetery hunting club whose members were allowed to shoot small game from sunset to sunrise, when the cemetery is closed, during the designated November to mid-April season.

Vienna's Zentralfriedhof—with its park-like atmosphere, monuments that form a museum of mortality, and its care-fully planned layout—conforms to the modern cemetery typical of Paris, London and other cities of Western Europe. Its square blocks and straight streets also reflect the ultra-rational plan used to rebuild Vienna during the same period. In 1858 the municipal authorities issued an invitation for suggestions relating to the expansion and rebuilding of the Imperial capital. By 1865 the Ringstrasse was completed; then in 1869 opened the opera house, the first of the new public edifices, followed in 1883 by the city hall and the parliament buildings. Like Paris under the hand of Baron Haussmann, Vienna became a geometrically arranged city of precisely placed buildings and contrived vistas. Edward Crankshaw once wrote of Vienna's "rationalized ground plan (looking from the air like a slightly wind-blown spider's web with the Ringstrasse for a hub)," a description which might well apply to the Zentralfriedhof, completed in 1873. In this way, the cemetery expresses the *Zeitgeist* and *Weltanschauung* of Vienna in the late nineteenth century.

If a cemetery epitomizes a society then—to switch from the ordered precisions of the Germanic West to the colorful confusions of the East—Istanbul's chaotic Eyup seems to reflect that city's vibrant irregularities. Cacophony rather than geometry governs, or rather, fails to govern, both Istanbul and its burial area. Eyup's exotic precincts well typify cosmopolitan Istanbul, where Europe gives way to the East. Eyup lies along the Golden Horn, these days disfigured with baser metals such as rusty iron, shabby shipyards, gangly cranes and other eye-sores which line the dingy inlet. A picturesque alleyway lined with venerable tree trunks and antique wooden houses that recall old Istanbul leads to Eyup, truly a tombtown, its graveyards scattered all about as jumbled as the merchandise in the city's famous covered bazaar. Centuries ago Eyup became the favorite burial place for devout Muslims who wanted to repose near Eyup Ensari, standard-bearer to Mohammed himself, supposedly killed by an arrow about 674 A.D. during the first Arab siege of Constantinople. In the inner courtyard of the mosque stands the tile- and script-decorated mausoleum holding Eyup's remains, which were found and entombed in the mid-fifteenth century by Sultan Mehmet II, Turkish conqueror of the Byzantine Empire and herald of the Ottoman Empire. Since then thousands of Ottoman worthies have come to rest at Eyup, where the tombs spread in unwieldy proliferation across the landscape to form one of the world's largest burial areas. It is hard to say whether the tombs at Eyup outnumber the pigeons, for hundreds of the birds—less disciplined than those in the numbered birdhouses at Fluntern cemetery in Zurich—whirr through the air and send down a rain of droppings. These make Eyup one of the most hazardous cemeteries to visit, and perhaps the only graveyard where it is important to note what is overhead as well as underfoot.

Near the Eyup mosque stands Sokullu Mehmet Pasha's (d. 1579) türbe, one of those tomb towers seen throughout the Near East, devised by the Seljuks, a Turkish tribe which dominated Persia and the nearby regions for more than two centuries before the early 1300s. This exotic corner of Istanbul so smacks of the East that one can readily agree with Sacheverell Sitwell's observation that Eyup is "more Turkish than anything in Turkey." From the mosque I continued up a narrow brick road through a graveyard. Some of the stones bore both Islamic and Christian dates which, in tandem, seemed to lend the deceased a longevity far beyond possibility: 1336–1975. Atop many of the stone markers, about the height of a person, appeared symbols of the occupant's profession or standing: turban, fez, grapes, anchor, crossed cannons. I walked on along a rustic path that rose to a venerable wooden tea house, frequented a century or so ago when it was a coffee house by the French writer Pierre Loti. Preserved as it was in Loti's time, it commands a panorama down onto the Golden Horn and the grey domes of the türbes which dot the landscape between the hill and the Horn. The dead were everywhere. Tombs threatened to engulf all evidences of human life. Cairo's City of the Dead cemetery, discussed below, has been over-run by squatters; at Istanbul's Eyup quarter the dead have taken over the city of the living.

Eyup in Turkey survives as one of those burial grounds of great antiquity found around the Mediterranean basin in the region where very early civilizations flourished. Across that historic sea sailed the conquerors and adventures of ancient times, and on the Mediterranean's shores remain age-old cemeteries, monuments and mausoleums which still today evidence those early eras. Turkey boasted the world's first mausoleum—at least the earliest such structure so designated. After King Mausoleus of Caria died in 353 B.C. his widow Artemisia built at Halicarnassus, on the southwest coast of present-day Turkey, an imposing structure to house the monarch's remains and perpetuate his memory. Artemisia was so devoted to her husband that she supposedly dissolved some of his ashes in a potion which she drank, thus becoming one with him. When the Romans conquered Caria a century and a half later they called the tomb a *mausoleum*. The king's name survives but not his tomb. When the Turks invaded the area in the early 1400s they carried away great chunks of the building, one of the seven wonders of the ancient world. The Knights Hospitallers of St. John later constructed Petronium Castle at Bodrum, originally Halicarnassus, using the remains of the mausoleum as building materials. In the nineteenth century an English archaeological expedition salvaged from that first mausoleum some fragments now on display at the British Museum in London. These splendid pieces include panels from action-packed marble friezes depicting Greeks and Amazons in battle, crammed with lean and lithe but well-muscled figures, as well as two over-sized marble statues thought to portray Mausoleus and Artemisia, the monarch's sandled right foot extending some three feet. That first mausoleum inspired a number of imitations, most recently the civil courts building in St. Louis, Missouri, with its many-columned arcade and stair-step roof: St. Louis' trial lawyers practice in a tomb.

At Assos on the coast of Asia Minor, north of Bodrum and not far south of Troy, the ancients excavated stone for carving coffins. Because the stone's caustic property caused bodies to disintegrate a coffin came to be called a sarcophagus—*sarkos* the Greek for "flesh," and *phago* meaning "I eat," or "I consume."

It is in Greece rather than Turkey that Heinrich Schliemann (d.1890), the German archaeologist who discovered Troy, reposes. I was amused when an attendant at the Proto Nekrotafio, Athens' main cemetery located not far from the Acropolis, greeted me with the one-word question: "Schliemann?" Not many Heinrichs—perhaps just one—but any number of Georges, Constantines, and Nicholases repose at Proto Nekrotafio, attractively garnished with flowers and pine trees. Near a small Byzantine chapel toward the center of the cemetery sat two black-garbed Orthodox priests wearing those distinctive rectangular hats that look like the Greek letter *pi*. The base of Schliemann's tomb is decorated with a detailed relief frieze showing scenes related to his archaeological career. The front tableau portrays men with a long saw cutting stones while workers move building blocks, perhaps a representation of the building of Troy, while on the right side appears a classical battle scene. The most delightful frieze fills the left side, a vignette of men excavating with hoes and shovels, supervised by Schliemann clad in a kind of pith helmet, vest, and long coat, a book in his left hand and his right arm raised in command, while his wife Sophia stands nearby. Above the frieze rises a small classical Greek temple fronted by a stone bust of Schliemann.

In the classical era an area northwest of the Acropolis, across town from the Proto Nekrotafio, served as the main cemetery of the Greek metropolis. Kerameikos, as Athenians called the burial ground, took its name from the ceramic workshops located around Kerameikos Road which ran past Plato's Academy. Another road from the potters' quarter— the Sacred Way, still called the Iera Odos by the Greeks— connected Athens with the holy city of Eleusis, fourteen miles west. At the end of the fifth century B.C. it became fashionable for Athenians to bury their dead along this processional route to Eleusis and in time monuments, temples and tombs flanked the Sacred Way. The classical writer Pausanias singled out as "the most notable of all the ancient tombs of the Greeks" a mausoleum built here by a love-sick deserter from Alexander's army to honor his wife Pythionike, a former Athenian prostitute. Perhaps she wore a shoe like that once used by an ancient Athens streetwalker sporting nails that imprinted "follow me," in the ground as she strolled around the city. (One of ancient Rome's five grades of prostitutes, the Bustuariae, plied their trade in graveyards by night, while by day they occasionally served as paid mourners at funerals.)

The Persians destroyed many of the tombs around the Sacred Way when they occupied Athens in 479 B.C., and the Athenians themselves dismantled the mausoleums for materials to build fortifications agianst the enemy. Thucydides writes that the citizens used "stones of all kinds, and in some places not wrought or filled, but placed just in the order in which they were brought by the different hands; and many columns, too, from tombs and sculptured stones were put in with the rest." Part of the wall still stands in the ancient Kerameikos cemetery near the site of the Diplyon—the "double gate," ancient Athens' largest—through which Kerameikos Road passed. On the route that the road formerly followed stands the only surviving public tomb, a low, solidly built memorial once covered with marble slabs bearing the names of the Lacedaemonian warrior dead. From that corner of the cemetery I enjoyed a view down the old Kerameikos road, past the former site of the Dipylon, and across the buildings of present-day Athens and on to the Parthenon which crowns the Acropolis, the smooth bone-white remains of the ancient temple looking like the skeleton of some sort of great beast.

Kerameikos, where so many Athenians were buried, was itself gradually buried when the townspeople began using the cemetery as a rubbish dump in the late fourth century B.C. In modern times this potter's field has yielded a trove of pottery from periods extending over some five hundred years. The cemetery now serves as an outdoor museum of classical statuary, bas-reliefs, and other grave markers. Excavations in the nineteenth century unearthed the ancient graveyard and resurrected monuments which afford visitors a vivid idea of how Kerameikos appeared in the old days. Near the cemetery's main entrance—no longer the impressive Dipylon but a small gate on Hermes Street—stand some curious mushroom-like grave markers, columnar stones ringed with ridges near the top. Close by those toadstool tombs—perhaps examples of the columns mentioned by Thucydides—rise monuments from the post-classical period which started about 317 B.C. when expensive memorials were banned by law, as recalled by Cicero in *De Legibus:* "On account of the size of the tombs which we see in the Kerameikos, it was decreed that no one should make a tomb which required the work of more than ten men in three days, and that no tomb should be decorated with plaster or have the so-called *herms* [images] set on it."

Below the post-classical monuments runs the Western Road, lined with family tombs from the classical period (fourth century B.C.). One of the most striking monuments, the Dionysios, consists of a pillar which supports a large bull, curly hair matting his lowered head, powerful hind legs tensed to charge. On an elevated area between the Western Road and the Sacred Way stands the tumulus of Eukoline, which bears an endearing relief scene with three adult figures in a protective semi-circle around a child. His chin is chucked by the left hand of the woman on the left and her right hand touches the boy on his waist, while the man on the right touches the lad's shoulder. The cemetery's most famous gravestone scene appears on the funeral stele of Hegeso, a copy of the original marker from the late fifth century B.C., now in the National Archeological Museum of Athens. The relief pictures the deceased woman sitting on a chair gazing wistfully at a jewel she holds between her thumb and fore-finger. Before Hegeso stands her servant, clutching the jewel box and also looking at the gem. The attendant wears a serene expression, as if patiently awaiting the demise of her mistress: the servant perhaps covets the jewel for herself, one of the four things which, according to Proverbs, the earth "cannot bear": a "handmaid that is heir to her mistress." Another stele not far from this shows the dead Mika sitting on a stool holding a mirror in her left hand while with the other hand she waves farewell to her husband who stands next to her. Into that ancient, cold stone one can read any number of warm-blooded human emotions: vanity, love, remorse, loyalty, mourning.

The monuments at Kerameikos, along with the dozens of similar relief-decorated gravestones housed in the National Archeological Museum of Athens, vividly depict daily life during classical times. On some Greek gravestones there is a disparity between the scene and the inscription which probably arose because many Athenians purchased markers off the shelf and then added the epitaph, not necessarily connected with the vignette shown. These lapidary scenes perhaps comprised the world's first cartoons. Art historian Erwin Panofsky points out how Greek funerary monuments emphasize life, not death, noting in *Tomb Sculpture* that "from the sixth century B.C. down to the beginning of the Christian Era, Attic funerary sculpture . . . commemorates [life] rather than provides for the dead. These steles . . . show the life that had been lived in all its aspects." Designating these memorials "retrospective" because they look back on life, Panofsky observes that "we are at times unable to distinguish the departed from the survivors."

The Etruscan cemeteries in central Italy represent the most extreme example of graves intended to recall daily life and the society left behind by the departed. As Michel Ragon observes in *The Space of Death*, the "idea of the tomb continuing the house in the familiarity of everyday life was perhaps carried to its furthest limit among the Etruscans." About 1000 B.C. bands of invaders from the north entered Italy and settled around Tarquinia and Cerveteri on the west coast, not far from Rome. The newcomers disposed of their dead by cremation, placing the remains in cinerary urns and burying them in pits along with objects intended for the afterlife. While in modern times expensive monuments above ground incarnate the standing and wealth of a deceased, ancient cultures often concealed a deceased's wealth or prominence by burying the dead person's treasures along with the corpse. We seek status among our survivors; they sought solace in the afterlife. The Chaldeans of Ur, the earliest known urban civilization, entombed their royal dead with large amounts of food, drink, clothing, personal effects, and even people: Queen Shubad was put away along with her attendants, buried alive. Similarly, in the fourteenth century B.C. Chinese rulers were interred with their wives and concubines, while in other early societies, such as Egypt, surrogates—wood models of their attendants—accompanied royalty to the tomb.

As for the Etruscans, in the eighth century B.C. they abandoned cremation and switched to interment of the entire body. At first the departed reposed in simple ditch graves, but soon the bodies occupied stone mausoleums underground filled with bronze objects, as in Ur, Egypt and other ancient societies. This concern for the welfare of the dead soon inspired even more elaborate tombs—rooms designed to resemble houses, their walls decorated with frescoes showing everyday scenes and with reliefs of common objects that the departed might need in the afterlife. Only at the Etruscan burial grounds, and Egypt's famous tomb rooms at Luxor, do you enter the abode of the dead rather than simply standing outside as a detached observer.

Meeting them on their own home ground affords the visitor a vivid communion with the dead and their vanished way of life. Only rarely do cemeteries offer this nexus between the now and the then in such a striking way. When you step down to enter an Etruscan tomb you step back in time, returning to an ancient abode seemingly still occupied. In the central niche at the Tomb of the Reliefs in Cervetari stretches an empty bed-sized space with two stone pillows. The missing sleeper has perhaps just risen to raid the Etruscan equivalent of the refrigerator, or maybe to walk off insomnia—is the sleep of the dead ever so disturbed?—or to deal with other nighttime necessities. I knew that he or she would soon return, for on a bedside bench below the vacated niche lay a pair of sandles. Around the tomb appear stucco reliefs of other homey objects—furniture, a knife, a hatchet, pliers, a club, a jug, a jar, rope hanging on a hook, a ladle. At floor level the family pets, a dog and a cat, hold for an eternal moment a frozen pose which seems about to melt into motion. The tomb's most lively and delightful relief, a goose, swells out into a football-sized feathery body from which gracefully extends its neck and head, peering at the floor as if about to peck up a crumb. Did that nosy Etruscan goose just wander into the house to sniff around for food? I gazed at the bird, waiting for it to peck, but the goose failed to move so I moved on, leaving it to stare at the floor for the next thirty centuries.

In contrast to the reliefs which characterize the Cervetari tombs, the graves at the Tarquinian necropolis feature frescoes which, although one-dimensional, present vivid and colorful scenes of contemporary Etruscan life. About one quarter of the more than six thousand Etruscan tombs discovered in the Tarquinian cemetery house paintings. The mural in the Tomb of the Fortune Tellers portrays two naked gladiators wrestling in front of a pair of priests, while overhead flutter birds. The artist individualized the combatants: the man on the left appears less hefty than his bearded opponent. But another touch lent that ancient fresco a human dimension even more striking than the lifelike fighting figures: just by the shoulder of the bearded wrestler faint black lines evidence the artist's attempts to paint a difficult anatomical curve. How long did the artist struggle with that tricky turn where the shoulder falls away into the arm before he finally accepted the awkward result left to us? Other Tarquinian tombs house lively scenes of banquets, dancers, musicians, sporting events, hunters, battles, wildlife, and graphic sex activity. "This profound belief in life, acceptance of life, seems characteristic of the Etruscans," observed D. H. Lawrence about Tarquinia in *Etruscan Places*. "It is still vivid in the painted tombs . . . and is somehow beyond art. You cannot think of art, but only life itself." Paradoxically, however, those Etruscan tombs which many visitors have found so full of life yielded few human remains. In 1823, when a man named Avvolta chanced upon the Tarquinian necropolis as he cut into a tumulus while digging for stones to repair a road, he suddenly saw "a warrior stretched on a couch of rock, and in a few minutes I saw him vanish, as it were, under my eyes; for, as the atmosphere entered the sepulcher, the armour, thoroughly oxidized, crumbled away into the most minute particles; so that in a short time scarcely a vestige of what I had seen was left on the couch." Thus nearly three thousand years disintegrated into dust, leaving in the tomb only murals and reliefs to evidence the long vanished civilization.

Sometimes historic cemeteries, like the Etruscan necropolises at Cevetari and Tarquinia, survive as virtually the sole evidences of their civilizations. Thanks to a reluctance to disturb the dead, the habitations of the departed enjoy a stability, continuity and permanence which settlements of the living lack. "In most civilizations the houses of the dead are more magnificent than the houses of the living," notes Michel Ragon in *The Space of Death*. "Indeed we often know of civilizations that have disappeared, when the houses of the living have been reduced to dust, only through the houses of the dead, which have survived intact." Nowhere is this more pronounced than in Egypt where, as Pierre Montet observes in *Eternal Egypt,* "we know the [ancient] country chiefly though its tombs." That country boasts the earth's most famous monuments to the dead, the only surviving example of the seven wonders of the ancient world, structures so familiar that one sometimes forgets that the pyramids in fact served as mausoleums. The pyramids were already ancient when Herodotus—born about 484 B.C. in Halicarnassus, site of Mausoleus' mausoleum—described them and noted their dimensions, carefully adding, "I am certain, for I measured them myself." The pyramids were already old at the time of King Tut, who died about 1350 B.C., and when Tut's predecessor Tuthmosis, about 1415 B.C., excavated the Sphinx, buried over the centuries by the drifting desert sands. And although the famous pyramids at Giza—the three constructions marking the last resting places of Cheops, Chephren and Mykerinos—claim great antiquity, some of the other eighty or so ancient Egyptian pyramids even predate these.

Originally the Egyptians buried their honored dead along with various of their worldly possessions in rectangular mud brick tombs. In the Third Dynasty, about 2686 B.C., the architect Imhotep, regarded as the inventor of hewn stone construction, designed a two-hundred-foot-high, stepped structure which was built at Saqqara to mark the grave of King Zoser. Not long after that innovative monument, a pyramid was erected at Meidum near the Faiyum oasis in the western desert. It, too, began as a stepped construction but eventually the eight steps were filled with masonry and casing blocks to form the first known true pyramid. At the beginning of the Fourth Dynasty, about 2600 B.C., a monument to King Seneferu was built at Dahshur. Known as the Bent Pyramid, its lower and upper sections slope at different angles because the designers altered their alignment after discovering cracks in the gypsum mortar in the lower areas. It was Cheops, son and survivor of Seneferu, who constructed the Great Pyramid at Giza. So evolved the world's best known grave markers.

Thousands of travelers flock to Giza and many sightseers visit the Step Pyramid at Saqqara, but most of the other pyramids remain in solitude, ignored by tourists and seen only from a distance. It is somehow poignant to catch glimpses of those stately structures, haze-shrouded and remote, out in the deserted desert, as you drive through the Egyptian countryside. The magnificent but abandoned monuments—forgotten but not gone—seem to epitomize the observation on the futility of death monuments, even spectacular ones, in the "Dialogue of a Man Tired of Life," an Egyptian text from about 1000 B.C.: "Those who have built in granite, constructed chambers within the pyramid, and achieved great works, have become gods, yet their offering-tables are as empty as the tables of those who died on the river-bank without survivors to maintain their cult."

So old are the pyramids, and also the renowned relief- and fresco-embellished tombs at Luxor and elsewhere along the Nile, that little new remains to be said about them. But new things can be done to them. Since the burial facilities and their contents serve as virtually the only sources of information about the Pharaonic era, new techniques can tease from these much studied sites additional insights. In late 1987 an American team inserted a mini-camera into an underground pit by Giza's Great Pyramid to photograph a forty-six-hundred-year-old royal boat believed used to transport Cheops' soul to the underworld. To prevent the oxidation and disintegration of the ancient wood, a sealing device kept out any modern air. In their search for hidden burial chambers scientists have probed the pyramids with such devices as cosmic ray detectors, ultra sound, electromagnetic sound wave scanners (a type of underground radar), a gravity meter of the type used to detect cracks in large constructions, proton precision magnetometers able to locate hidden metallic elements, x-rays, and endoscopy, a process used by medical doctors to examine internal organs. In the 1980s physicians x-rayed fifteen mummies and more than a hundred mummified animals from the Boston Museum of Fine Arts, which boasts the world's largest collection of Old Kingdom items outside Cairo. Many of those objects came from excavations conducted at the Giza cemeteries by George A. Reisner, Harvard's last Egyptologist (d. 1942), who playfully trained his local diggers to greet visiting American scholars with the phrase: "To hell with Yale!" Mummies were first x-rayed in 1898, not long after Roentgen developed the technique, which enables latter day observers to peer into the past. The ancient Egyptians left a great legacy to posterity. From mummies, ancient tombs, and burial grounds archeologists—and more recently, scientists—have resurrected a fairly full portrait of a five-thousand-year-old civilization, a haunting and perhaps even spooky achievement. In Egypt the past is not dead and buried but alive and disinterred, a strange time warp Thomas Bailey Aldrich captured in his poem "At the Funeral of a Minor Poet":

'Tis said the seeds wrapped up among the balms
And hieroglyphics of Egyptian kings
Hold strange vitality, and, planted, grow
After the lapse of thrice a thousand years.

On display in the Egyptian gallery at the Metropolitan Museum of Art in New York are samples of such seeds, which retained their fertility over the millenia. These living remnants from ancient times symbolize the resurrection of a long-buried, age-old civilization: the tombs in Egypt encapsulated not only death but life.

Cemeteries not only help to define ancient Egyptian civilization but they also play a role in Egypt's modern life. Cairo is perhaps the world's only city where a necropolis has become a metropolis. Certain sections of central Cairo bulge with a population three times more dense than the most crowded slums of Calcutta. Built for two-and-a-half million people, greater Cairo now strains under the pressure of thirteen million inhabitants, twice as many as a decade ago. Fully a million Cairenes dwell in the City of the Dead, a vast cemetery that stretches along the capital's eastern flank, crammed with hundreds of tombs, mausoleums, and graves. There repose caliphs, Mamelukes and countless other departed, now joined by squatters who share the venerable tombs. Stark is the contrast between the cemetery's architectural gems—now somewhat dusty and unpolished—and the impoverished conditions suffered by those living in the City of the Dead, a scene described by Alan Moorehead in *The Blue Nile:* "The huge domed and minaretted tombs of the Mameluke beys, standing in the desert outside the walls of Cairo, are also an architectural triumph of their kind, and not even the dust and squalor of the slums that now surround them, or the hordes of ragged children who haunt this city of the dead, can quite obscure the revelation that there was a vision here that rose above a barbarous and material life." Like the rest of Cairo, the cemetery is densely populated and, just as the desert hems in the city to the west, so do the Mokattam hills crowd the burial ground at its eastern edge. Thus does the City of the Dead mimic the city of the living. The cemetery's northern section, commonly called the Tombs of the Caliphs, extends northeast of the Citadel, the former seat of government, while the southern area, site of the Tombs of the Mamelukes, stretches south from the Citadel toward the mausoleum of el-Imam el-Shafi, erected in 1211 to memorialize the founder of one of Islam's orthodox sects whose system of jurisprudence is dominant in Egypt. The necropolis now extends about five miles from north to south, perhaps making the City of the Dead the world's largest cemetery.

My explorations of the vast necropolis began in the southern section. Few noteworthy monuments rise in that area, apparently little-visited. My appearance inspired snarls from dogs, stares from adults, and from children persistent cries of "money" or "baksheesh," begging relentlessly as I wandered through the dusty streets. Harassed thus, I soon began to long for the less lively cemeteries common elsewhere, populated by the tongue-tied dead who speak to you only through their epitaphs. I made my way to the Tombs of the Mamelukes, at the northern edge of the section. Those mausoleums memorialize the *Mamelukes* (one owned by another person) descendants of warriors of Turkish origin enslaved and then sold to the Sultan of Egypt in the early thirteenth century.

The Mamelukes soon gained power and ruled Egypt until the Ottoman Turks conquered the country in 1517. The small, mosque-like, Mameluke mausoleums, plain and unpretentious, hardly evoke the distinguished occupants who repose there. Continuing south, ever deeper into the scruffy cemetery, I passed a maze of mausoleums and small yards filled with graves marked by brown stone boxes with upright slabs at each end. Decay had claimed many of the tombs which lay cracked, tumbled, and quite ignored by the cemetery's busy living inhabitants. Near the center of the cemetery city I noticed some women stringing laundry atop a small, domed mausoleum. A family had made itself at home in the tomb, a not-uncomfortable house, more spacious than those occupied by many Cairenes: there is something to be said for life with the dead. From the roof I gained a view across the flat square roofs that filled the graveyard, the pervasive angularity relieved only by a scattering of rounded domes, and minarets which indicated a mausoleum mosque. It was impossible to tell which structures housed the living and which the dead, and as I headed on south toward el-Imam el-Shafi's tomb mosque I crossed some rail tracks and suddenly found myself in the land of the alive, a bustling corner of contemporary Cairo: as everywhere in the world, a very thin line separates the city of the living from the city of the dead.

North of the Citadel the Mameluke sultans repose in an area called the Tombs of the Caliphs. Some historians suggest that the rulers wanted to lie in a remote area away from the tumult of the Citadel, seat of their power, so that in death they could escape the sort of violence that characterized their reigns. The late-fifteenth-century Mameluke sultan Qait Bey occupies one of Cairo's most elegant buildings, a cube-shaped mausoleum mosque well endowed with windows, and crowned by a delicate dome laced with an intricate arabesque design. Inside, space and form flow smoothly into one another to produce a seamless, well-proportioned whole.

Sacheverell Sitwell in *Arabesque and Honeycomb* adjudges the
Qait Bey mausoleum "perfection," adding that as he entered
the structure Egyptians "in their striped night gowns" emit-
ted "roars and yells for *bakshish*": some things never change.
In the mausoleum's tomb room a large, severe stone box
contains the sultan's remains, while a smaller duplicate holds
his son. The room also houses two black stones, one bearing
the outline of two shoes and the other, a footprint, supposedly tracks left by Mohammed himself. Not far away
from the Qait Bey memorial stands the mausoleum for Sultan Barkuk, a slave who fought Tamerlane and then battled
his way to become Egypt's first Circassian Mameluke. His
fortress-like tomb seems to symbolize his martial life. Big
brick blocks form the solid structure which is topped by a
crenellated fringe. Above the roof rise twin spires, more like
a castle's watch towers than minarets. Smaller mausoleums,
crumbling and abandoned, alternate with inhabited tombs in
the area near Barkuk's monument. Farther north lies an enclosed graveyard, still free of squatters at the time of my
visit—only the dead slept there—and beyond, adjacent
mausoleums for Emir Kurkmas, surrounded by rubble and
boarded up, and for Sultan Ainal. The sultan's structure
boasts an elaborately decorated minaret which overshadows
that of its neighbor, while the emir's building sports a dome
more bulky than the sultan's. The two structures comple-
ment one another, the dome-minaret-minaret-dome progression serving to unify the pair with a kind of interlocking
facade. Perhaps by now these dwellings fit for a king hold
Cairenes who reside there in the City of the Dead with the
departed emir and sultan.

The City of the Dead somewhat resembles the Zawiyet el-
Mayyiteen, (corner of the dead) at el-Minya, a Nile River city
150 miles south of Cairo. This huge cemetery occupies a
long, narrow area tucked between arid hills and a road which
parallels the Nile about a quarter of a mile west of the river,

and apparently has gradually expanded to absorb the hamlets which lie within its boundaries. A few churches and crosses evidence the cemetery's Christian section (a large Coptic community lives at el-Minya) beyond which stretches an area crammed with hundreds of domed, red brick mausoleums, beehive-like constructions which give the curious effect of the earth's surface erupting with some sort of skin disease. Farther on I found a tumbled stairway with scattered stones bearing hieroglyphic symbols, perhaps the remains of a small, ancient temple. From a rise above the steps I gained a view over the burial ground, whose round-topped mausoleums seemed to form a great field of huge brown eggs. Entering the maze of graves that comprised the heart of the necropolis, I found the city of the dead criss-crossed by streets, complete with signs and electricity poles: a well-equipped cemetery indeed. A few people haunted the quiet lanes, and before long there appeared the inevitable cluster of children, this time asking for a *baksheesh* of pens and candy. The neat streets lined with mausoleums stretched far into the distance. For a time I wandered around the inert city, every now and then peeking into the small compounds where the tombs stood. Most of them seemed similar, if not identical, like houses in a suburb developed by an unimaginative or cost-conscious builder always working from the same plan: the Zawiyet el-Mayyiteen must be the Levittown of cemeteries. The mausoleums gradually gave way to occupied houses, dwellings tucked into fringes of the cemetery. Here the El-Minyans reside in close proximity to their departed ancestors. At night this must be a very quiet neighborhood.

Back in Cairo I visited one of the latest versions of Egyptian tomb architecture. A Cairene to whom I mentioned my interest in cemeteries suggested I might like to see Nasser's tomb, a showplace where "all large visitors to Cairo" are taken, he said. Guards organize and channel visitors into the modernistic and relatively unembellished mosque, approached along a red cloth leading to the grave which is flanked by two spear-carrying soldiers clad in dress uniforms. A flourish of Arabic script at the top of the gold-decorated white marble monument proclaims, "Allah is one." On the front of the marker appear Nasser's name and his dates, "1970–1918." This arrangement of time immediately disquieted me: those of us nurtured in the Western tradition are led to believe that one lives in a left to right progression. But after lingering there a time, gazing at Nasser's reversed years, I came to accept the startling truth that you can live your life, so to speak, from right to left just as easily.

Although societies may vary in many ways Giambattista Vico maintains in the *New Science* (1725), perhaps the first general sociological study, that "all nations, barbarians as well as civilized, though separately founded because remote from each other in time and space, keep these three human customs: all have some religion, all contract solemn marriages, all bury their dead." Burial customs and cemeteries in various parts of the world, however, differ greatly, and these differences reveal how a society views its dead and their post mortem fate. In *Pilgrimage to Al-Madinah & Meccah* the famous nineteenth-century English traveler Richard Burton commented in regard to the cloth-wrapped bodies buried on the road from Mecca to Taif in Arabia: "We bury our dead, to preserve them as it were; the Moslem tries to secure rapid decomposition, and makes the graveyard a dangerous as well as a disagreeable place." Burton's contemporary, the American traveler John Lloyd Stephens, recorded in *Incidents of Travel in Egypt, Arabia Petraea, and the Holy Land* that, while perched on a tombstone at a Turkish graveyard in Jerusalem during his 1835–6 trip, he realized that Turks, unlike Europeans, visited cemeteries in a light-hearted way: "Few things strike a traveler in the East more than this, and few are to us more inexplicable. We seldom go into a graveyard except to pay the last offices to a departed friend, and for years after-

ward we seldom find ourselves in the same place again without a shade of melancholy coming over us. Not so in the East
. . . the grave is not clothed with the same terror. It is not so
dark and gloomy as to us." Part of the pleasure in visiting
burial grounds around the world is to discern in them some
of the traits which characterize the society they serve.

One world-wide burial invariable is the homage accorded
tombs of great men. Nasser's tomb in Cairo, for example,
brings us into proximity with the mighty. A certain energy
seems to emanate from tombs where history's strong men
repose. Such was the commanding authority of some leaders
that an almost palpable aura of power lingers, whether at
oversized and forbidding monuments like Ataturk's
mausoleum in Ankara, Turkey, and Napoleon's last resting
place at Les Invalides in Paris, or the simple markers to
Franklin Roosevelt at Hyde Park, New York, and to Winston
Churchill at Bladon in England. Although contact with the
mere remains of a ruler who once exercised great authority
produces awe, one's main reaction is not a feeling of proximity to power but, rather, the opposite: a sense of one's own
power. Compared to the once mighty but now fallen, the live
visitor is all-powerful. Seeing the tomb of Napoleon em-
powers you when you realize that you presently enjoy an
infinitely greater authority than does the former emperor.
So, for a time at least, you gain the next to last laugh on the
once high and mighty, now low and crumbly. The last laugh,
of course, is reserved to invincible Father Time, whose expired moments make the past one vast cemetery.

Such were my musings after a visit to the grave of Haitian
dictator François Duvalier. The once fearsome tyrant now
reposes benignly in the main cemetery at Port-au-Prince, the
capital city which trembled under his rule. Making my way
through the burial ground I passed a tomb on which two
boys played cards, the lads idling the day away shuffling kings
and queens around. Farther on stood a tombstone for a
certain Mme. Excellent Arnoux—did she live up to her

name?—and then the marker for James Muir McGuffie (d.1936) who died far from his native Scotland but apparently among family, for with him repose "Oncle Frédé" and "Tante Alice." Nearby rises the severely modern monument to President Duvalier, a shiny tile mausoleum marked only with his name and the dates "14 avril 1907–21 avril 1971." In the open space around the structure stand metal flower wreaths and metal books on which appear expressions of mourning. The metallic fixtures reminded me that Duvalier ruled his land with an iron hand, controlling Haiti even more completely than did Napoleon or Ataturk their domains. A disheveled band of men dressed in civilian clothes and armed with rifles guarded the small enclave. Unsure what they were protecting, I asked why they remained there. One man pointed to the tomb and replied, "Il est le président." Such was the almost mesmeric power exerted by the departed Duvalier on his henchman that they deemed him still in authority, ruling from beyond the grave. But their hero was not the president, not any longer, and even the most abject urchin in the slums of Port-au-Prince enjoyed infinitely more power than the great Duvalier. Visiting the tombs of the departed great, famous, or powerful is truly a life-enhancing experience.

For every Cheops, Napoleon, or Duvalier commemorated with mausoleums or other monuments, there are many defunct purveyors of power whose graves remain unknown. After Alexander the Great died of malaria in Babylon in 323 B.C., not yet thirty-three, his body, preserved in honey, was returned to Macedonia for burial. But where does the leader lie? No one knows: the greatest conqueror in history reposes in a grave as obscure as that of his most menial subject. The Sarcophagus of Alexander—housed (at the time of my visit) in the National Museum at Beirut in Lebanon—was so named not because it held the conqueror but for a scene on the box depicting an episode from one of his battles.

Similar decorated caskets survive at Tyre's ancient Greek

necropolis, a burial ground which recalls but one phase of the storied past of the island city off the coast of modern Lebanon. Mausoleums and sarcophaguses imported from Greece and later used during the Byzantine period fill the cemetery. Many of the monuments bear finely carved reliefs showing events from *The Iliad* and other classical and mythological scenes. On the second century A.D. Manead Sarcophagus, which stands at the beginning of the Byzantine road running through the necropolis, appear three gracefully posed women, their stony dresses and marble tresses fairly flowing in the breeze. Two of the figures carry a *thyrus,* the staff of Bacchus, indicating they are *maneads* (wine-frenzied women), from which the coffin takes its name. The fourth-century A.D. Sarcophagus of Helen sports two delightful carved cupids, complete with skin folds and subtly shaped kneecaps. The figure on the left has the hint of a pot belly and thick unruly hair while his companion's curly hair is neater, his chin narrower. In contrast to the pleasant simplicities of these two tombs are the coffins which depict martial events, typified by the second-century A.D. Battle Scene Sarcophagus which shows an episode from *The Iliad.* The figures crowd together in a tangle of muscular bodies and even curve around the corners of the sarcophagus, preserving the continuity and flow of the action.

Almost directly across from the Battle Scene Sarcophagus rises the tower-like Tomb with Stories, not a memorial with carved marble panels that tell a story but a two-story-high mausoleum with niches built into its walls to receive bodies. Dating from the second century A.D., the structure might well have influenced, or been influenced by, the Tower Tombs in Palmyra, a Roman city in the eastern Syrian desert. Both political and commercial matters connected Palmyra and Tyre from that time on. At the end of the second century Emperor Septimius Severus both rebuilt Tyre, burned by his rival for the Roman throne, and developed Palmyra, which he raised to the status of a Roman colony. After the two cities established commercial relations, silks carried by caravan from the East to Palmyra were sent on to Tyre where merchants dyed the cloth with the famous royal purple. The color was derived from the murex marine snails found locally, and purple garments tinted in Tyre clothed many Mediterranean bluebloods back in classical times. Palmyra's Roman cemetery includes two types of tomb—house-like structures which the city's inhabitants often transmuted into dwellings (much like Cairo's City of the Dead) after the original dead occupants had been evicted; and undergound chambers, of which the Three Brothers is the best preserved, whose frescoes recall the subterranean tombs at Luxor and Tarquinia. But Palmyra's oldest and most curious cemetery structures, apparently unique in the world, are the Tower Tombs which dot the Valley of the Tombs a short distance from the main ruins of the ancient Roman city.

Among the most striking characteristics of the ruined city out there in the desert are its isolation and its integrity as a pure relic of Roman times. Those characteristics make Palmyra truly a magnificent site, one of the world's great residues of antiquity. The Tower Tomb of Elahbel, built in 103 A.D., is typical of the structures in the cemetery valley. Built with stone blocks that diminish in size as the tower rises, the square tomb stands four stories above the desert and burrows one floor below. Inside extend multi-tiered burial niches which held three hundred members of one family, nine bodies per niche. Limestone busts of the deceased decorated the stone slabs which sealed the recesses. On the wall remain a few examples of the distinctive and unforgettable Palmyra sculpture: rounded, rather chubby heads, wide eyes, serene expressions. Two rows of figures portray four men and five women (one man married twice), while the stucco ceiling sports portraits of four brothers and their spouses, along with a design of blue flowers and square medallions. I climbed to the tomb's roof, passing the levels where the stacks of dead were stored, and from the top surveyed the litter of lintels, carved stones, building blocks and other architectural debris—remnants of nearby tombs tumbled by time, desert winds, and perhaps the hand of man—which lay scattered about on the sands. It was odd to imagine that beneath my feet three hundred bodies long ago reposed in their high-rise dwelling for the dead.

If the sepulchral scupltures of Palmyra rank among the world's most distinctive funerary figures, some of the most striking post mortem decorative writings in my cemetery collection embellish gravestones just outside the old city walls at Sada in northern Yemen. Inscribed with graceful calligraphy, the markers at Sada's Zaydi cemetery contrast with Palmyra's artful busts: at the Arab cemetery words alone memorialize the departed, while at the tongue-tied Roman graveyard silent figures commemorate the dead. At the end of the ninth century warring Hamdan tribes in the northern part of Yemen summoned a mediator to settle their differences. After al-Hadi Yahia, a descendant of Mohammed, brought peace to the region he returned to Sada and established the Zaydi dynasty, ruling there until 911. So incorruptible was Yahia, known as the Leader of the Clearly Perceived Truth, that he refused to dry himself with a towel after being told it belonged to the state. Although no longer a political force, the Zaydis remain as the only dynasty in Yemen to have survived until present times. Yahia reposes at the great mosque in the center of Sada, a medieval-type walled city with twisty alleys, an antique ambiance, and a bazaar where Maria Theresa *Thalers*—coins which originated in the Austro-Hungarian Empire in the late eighteenth century and are now favored in Yemen for their silver content—still circulate.

The *ulama* (learned men) and other leading lights of the Zaydi dynasty lie in the graveyard which stretches for some six city blocks beside the town walls. The necropolis was perhaps the most alien cemetery I ever visited. Nowhere did there appear the merest fragment of a phrase in a European language. Only Zaydis reposed here, not even one foreign figure I might recognize—no obscure but at least cognizable assistant consul, second rank artist or third rate politician, no minor scientist or major general, no stray English traveler or other expatriate soul, no one at all of my culture. I was a complete stranger there. So, for me the burial ground seemed less a cemetery than an outdoor museum of lapidary displays. In the sandy soil of the cemetery, Yemen's largest and oldest, small sections delineated by low, flat stones contain four or six graves marked by delicately cut relief or engraved inscriptions. Since the messages meant nothing to me, I contented myself with appreciating the flowing, curving calligraphy which arabesqued its way across the markers. In contrast to some of the flowery Blarney Stone-style epitaphs I had read in Western cemeteries, the script, to my eye, was enigmatic and thus emblematic of the silenced dead. In those two Middle Eastern cemeteries, at Sada and Palmyra, the artful texts and figures, elegant but not eloquent, remained as silent as the departed they memorialized.

The crossroads Mediterranean town of Tyre spread its influence not only east to Palmyra but also west along the historic sea's southern shores. In the early ninth century B.C. a Phoenician princess named Elissa sailed from Tyre to modern Tunisia to establish on the coast a city she called *qart* (city) *hadasht* (new): Carthage. Tunisia's presidential palace stands at Carthage, site of the country's governing residence since the Phoenician era, but nothing survives from ancient times to evidence the age-old continuity of what was once the world's largest city. The very absence of ruins lends the Carthage of today an especially evocative ambiance. Even its ancient burial ground lies buried somewhere beneath the empty terrain. But at Sidi-Bou-Saïd—a hilltop village on the coast a few miles beyond Carthage—lies a small Arab cemetery with

fifty or sixty graves. A mystic healer named Abou Saïd el-
Beji, who supposedly possessed magic powers, founded the
town and now reposes in a mosque built over his residence.
For the last eight hundred years, so it is said, a flame has
burned on the saint's tomb. Blue shutters and wooden trim
bring touches of color to the bright white, cube-like houses
at Sidi-Bou-Saïd, a picturesque place of the sort artists paint.
I climbed a lighthouse and gained a splendid panorama over
the Mediterranean, along the coast to Carthage, and beyond
to the fringes of Tunis some ten miles away. In the other
direction the thickly wooded hillside dropped sharply down
to the sea. Nearby stretched the cemetery, whose slabs held
scattered crumbs and water-filled indentations where birds
dined and drank.

Somewhere at Carthage reposes King Louis IX, the famous St. Louis. At least, some of his bones moulder there,
with the rest of the royal remains parcelled out among his
admirers and buried elsewhere. The Crusader king died in
the city in 1270 on one of his expeditions to wrest the area
from the Arabs, who in the late seventh century swept west
across the Maghreb. Under the Arabs the first New City lost
its importance to the new city of Kairouan, inland south of
Carthage, where the newcomers interred a saint named Abu
Jama el-Balaoui, the Prophet's Barber, so-called because he
plucked from the beard of Mohammed himself three hairs
which were placed in a pouch and later buried along with the
barber. Near his grave in Kairouan rises the famous Djama
el-Kebir (Great Mosque) founded about 670. Considered the
world's oldest university, the mosque houses a school where
clerics teach Islamic law and doctrine. After the mosques at
Mecca, Medina, and Jerusalem, Kairouan's Djama el-Kebir—
with columns pillaged from ancient Carthage—is the Muslim
world's most hallowed sanctuary. Three pilgrimages there
(some say, seven) serve as the equivalent of one *hadj* to Mecca.
Until 1881, when the French established their protectorate

over Tunisia, no infidel could enter Kairouan, but now non-Muslims visit the holy precincts at will. Many of the 128 steps which form the stairway to the mosque's minaret are ancient tombstones taken from Christian cemeteries. On some religious inscriptions survive, now separated from the deceased they once celebrated. Just outside the city wall not far from the Great Mosque stretches one of the world's most unusual cemeteries. Every person who reposes there belongs to the same clan, a family which for centuries has ministered to the needs of pilgrims who journey to Kairouan. The field of virtually identical white-washed slabs sport white head-stones that seem to form a troop of ghosts, haunting the graveyard nestling in the shadow of the square, stout minaret.

At the same time as Islam was spreading west along the Mediterranean's southern shores, Muslim traders and armies were venturing east, reaching the Indian sub-continent and beyond. In the sixteenth century the Moghuls invaded north-ern India from Central Asia, overthrowing the sultanate of Delhi and establishing a dominion which would last 250 years. The early Muslims left behind monumental evidence of their presence in the form of mausoleums, including the world's most famous burial building—the Taj Mahal.

The Taj and other earlier mausoleums mark the rise, peak, and decline of Muslim influence in India. That influence swelled when the scattered early Muslim empires in India drew together under the sultanate of Delhi. Established in 1206, the sultanate lasted through five dynasties but attained its greatest power under Mohammed ibn-Tughluq, "the Bloody King," the second ruler in the Tughluq line (1320–1413). Prince Jauna, as ibn-Tughluq was called before he took the throne, was a parricide: in 1325 he murdered his father, Ghias-ud-Din, by luring the monarch to a wooden structure rigged to collapse when nudged by elephants, a lethal feature Prince Jauna supposedly persuaded the royal architect,

Ahmad, to include. When the structure fell in and killed Ghias-ud-Din as planned, Jauna succeeded to his father's throne. Although generally an excellent administrator, scholar, and innovative economist—in 1329 he devised a coinage system using copper rather than precious metals— the new king made the mistake of moving the capital from Tughlaqabad to Daulatabad in 1327. The hard times which followed were only made worse when he subsequently removed the capital again, this time to Delhi. Mohammed ibn Tughluq also mounted a series of costly military expeditions which depleted the treasury and weakened the regime. When he died in 1351 he was buried next to his murdered father at the royal mausoleum in Tughlaqabad, not far from Delhi. Feeling a certain sense of remorse, the Bloody King had previously purchased acquittals from those he had wronged. He placed the pardons in a chest installed at the head of his tomb so that he could present them in expatiation when Allah called him to judgment in the kingdom of heaven.

The Tughlaqabad mausoleum, one of India's most attractive tomb buildings, is a leading forerunner of the distinctive Moghul style of funerary architecture. Thick, slanted walls surround the mausoleum, a squat but well proportioned red sandstone structure in the shape of a truncated pyramid. It is topped by a graceful marble dome, the very first such feature built of that material in India. White marble strips, and lofty arched doorways beneath marble lattice screens enhance the flanks of the mausoleum. The restrained appearance, regular proportions, the contrast between red stone and white marble, the dome, the terrace-like substructure, the enclosed compound—all represent techniques which would be used in later Moghul memorials.

The mausoleum survives as the only complete structure in the fourteenth-century city of Tughlaqabad, the rest of which lies in ruins. After a contemporary saint named Nizam-ud-din Aulia quarrelled with King Ghias-ud-Din, the holy one placed a cruse on the city: "May it be inhabited by Gujars or may it remain desolate." The curse worked doubly, for today not only is Tughlaqabad desolate but traces of invaders from Gujarat—an area in western India which bitterly fought the Tughlaq dynasty—have been found at the settlement, located outside New Delhi. The quarrel between saint and king broke out when the monarch requisitioned workers, employed by the holy man to build a water tank, for the royal fortress at Tughlaqabad. The tank which precipitated the disagreement still stands in New Delhi near the tomb of Nizam-ud-din Aulia, who died in 1324, aged ninety-two. His grave lies in a small and quite exotic Muslim enclave surrounded by a Hindu neighborhood.

The feisty saint rests in a flower-strewn marble tomb beneath an inlaid mother-of-pearl canopy, inside a small building crowned by a marble dome strung with electric lights. Other long, low stone slab tombs inscribed with Arabic script lay scattered around the compound, which recalled Cairo as much as New Delhi. Emperor Jahangir who reposes there, succeeded his famous father Akbar, architect of the Moghul empire, patron of arts, and ruler for almost half a century. Jahangir's son Shah Jahan built the Taj Mahal. Also there lies Jahanara Begam, sister of Emperor Aurangzeb who presided over the dynasty's end. Beyond the main courtyard reposes Amir Khusru, a contemporary of saint Nizam-ud-din Aulia and a poet, whose literary powers a nearby wall inscription praises, referring to him as a "sweet-tongued parrot."

In a New Delhi park, not far from the Muslim cemetery where Nizam-ud-din Aulia reposes, stand the tombs of the Lodi dynasty (1451–1526). An Afghan clan, the Lodis governed autocratically, alienating their subjects and paving the way for the Moghul conquest. The tombs, solid-looking structures of red and grey stone, bear blue- and green-tinted tiles above their arches, deep blue glazed wall tiles, as well as elaborate stucco decor. The Moghul dynasty was established in India in 1526 by Babur—a descendant through his mother of Ghenghis Khan and through his father of Tamerlane—after Alam Khan, uncle of Ibrahim Lodi (d. 1526), asked him for assistance in a campaign against his nephew. The death of Babur's son, Humayun, in 1556 inspired the first monumental Moghul mausoleum, which stands in New Delhi across the street from the grave of Nizam-ud-din Aulia and not far from the Lodi tombs.

Comfortably settled in his library, Sher Mandal, south of Delhi, Humayun suddenly heard the muezzin's call to prayer. Rushing to attend the service, the king fell down the stairway and suffered fatal injuries. His Persian wife, Haji Begum—mother of Akbar—built the mausoleum about 1560, hiring an architect from Persia named Mirza Ghiyas. The Muslim-Persian features—the dome, the minarets, the arches, calligraphic rather than sculpted decor, the spacious garden—make the mausoleum seem an apparition out of Arabian nights rather than Delhi days. Beneath the white marble dome, which dominates the building, opens a large alcove cut into the facade. More arches, niches, and windows puncture the wings, above which stand gazebo-like structures incorporating short marble minarets. These playful features, and the intermingling of hard white marble with soft red sandstone, lend Humayun's tomb a pleasantly varied appearance.

Humayun was succeeded by his son Akbar, called by Europeans the Great Moghul, who ruled until 1605 when he died at Agra. At Sikandra, six miles north of Agra, stands Akbar's mausoleum, completed by his son Jahangir. The impressive entrance-way, a substantial structure completely inlaid with intricate designs of colored marble and topped by a quartet of graceful white minarets, is much grander than the tomb area itself. But the palatial structure in front of the tomb area—a four-tiered construction whose three lower levels sport arched, sandstone porticos that create a light, open effect—provides an impressive enhancement to the mausoleum.

Jahangir, Akbar's heir, ruled in a less dominating manner than his father. Into his adminstration Jahangir brought his wife, Nur Jahan (Light of the World), her brother Asaf Khan, and her father, Itimad-ud-Daula. Queen Nur Jahan ordered construction (1622–28) of a mausoleum for her father, a building known as the Baby Taj. This baby seems an especially precocious child. A *pietra dura* inlay—precious stones set into marble tiles—covers most of the building, decorating its surface with delicate chromatic designs that are almost distracting in their intricacy. Inside the mausoleum the decor is no less refined. An elaborate marble mosaic floor perhaps represents a Persian carpet, and the walls are decorated with floral motifs and snake-handled wine flasks. Here stands an all-too-perfectly balanced and impeccably decorated tomb structure of the type which culminated with the Taj Mahal.

As with the pyramids, there is nothing new to be said about the Taj Mahal: one only agrees or disagrees with what has already been said. The severely regular proportions and overly controlled manner of this much praised mausoleum ultimately make the Taj a boring building. After first impressions, there are no second ones. Lying on her death bed in 1630, Empress Mumtaz Mahal made two requests of her husband, Shah Jahan, Jahangir's son: first, that he refrain from remarrying, and second, that he build for her the most magnificent tomb the world had ever known. Some twenty years later the Taj was completed, an up-dated version, a century onward, of the mausoleum which housed Humayun, Shah Jahan's great-grandfather. In only three substantial ways do the two tombs differ: the Taj is built all of marble rather than marble and sandstone; four minarets stand at the corners of the Taj's platform; and atop its onionshaped dome rests an inverted lotus motif which adds an all-too-rare touch of whimsy. Only the eccentric position of the graves of Mumtaz Mahal and Shah Jahan, located toward one side of the tomb room, breach the Taj's otherwise invariable symmetry. The sole relief to that ultimately forbidding regularity and perfection arose when I retreated to a far corner of the compound near the front gate, from where I could watch the procession of visitors who had come from all over the world to lay eyes on the famous sugary white marble confection. Patterned against the fixed facade, those colorfully clad visitors added some transient warmth and motion to the immutable, iceberg-like stone cube that stood before me.

Ever since the Taj materialized on the banks of the Jumna River visitors have made the journey to Agra. The Frenchman Jean Baptiste Tavernier, one of the first Europeans to see the building, compared it to a supposed masterpiece back in his homeland: "There is a dome above, which is scarcely less magnificent than that of Val de Grace at Paris." Commenting on the fortune lavished on the Taj, Tavernier notes in his *Travels in India*, published in 1676: "It is said that the scaffoldings alone cost more than the entire work, because, from want of wood, they had all to be made of brick." According to the Frenchman the Taj exerted a compelling influence on lesser court figures, who sought to build similar funerary memorials for themselves: "As for the tombs which are in Agra and its environs, there are some which are very beautiful, and there is not one of the eunuchs in the king's harem who is not ambitious to have a magnificent tomb built for himself. When they have amassed large sums they earnestly desire to go to Mecca, and to take with them rich presents; but the Great Mogul, who does not wish the money to leave his country, very seldom grants them permission, and consequently, not knowing what to do with their wealth, they spend the greater part of it in those burying-places, in order to leave some monument to their names."

After the Taj, however, such conspicuous consumption

through funerary monuments ended. Shah Jahan died in 1666, succeeded by his son Aurangzeb who had declared himself emperor eight years earlier after imprisoning his father in Agra's fort. Although Aurangzeb tried to expand the Moghul Empire it was plagued by domestic problems and by the time he died in 1707, aged ninety, rebellions had torn the regime apart. With his final breath Aurangzeb pleaded, "Bury me bareheaded, for they say that all who come bareheaded into God's presence will receive His mercy." It is perhaps due to Aurangzeb's self-abnegation, at least at death's door, that his followers gave his wife a memorial much more elaborate than the ruler himself received. She reposes in the Bibi-ka-Maqbara in the outskirts of Aurangabad, an inland city east of Bombay. Her mausoleum very nearly duplicates, on a much smaller scale, the Taj Mahal. As for Aurangzeb, his body lies in the village of Khuldabad, near Aurangabad, in a simple dirt grave bordered by a low marble screen provided by Lord Curzon, British viceroy of India from 1899 to 1905. Across the rectangular plot of dirt stretched, at the time of my visit, a clean, white cloth like a shroud with a small hole cut to permit a plant rooted in the ground there to grow—hardly a Taj-like tomb. In that small patch of earth reposes the last king of the great Moghul Empire.

When the Moghul Empire began to crumble away after Aurangzeb's demise the British took advantage of the confusion to obtain from the king's weak successors a series of territorial concessions in Bengal and Madras. Those permissions, or *firmans,* served—so one historian put it—as the Magna Carta of the East India Company, for the decrees formalized the British presence in the country and allowed the company to develop its commercial interests there. The next chapter includes the story of the European settlements in Asia where the burial grounds of the English, French, Dutch, Portuguese and other such foreigners evidence history in cemeteries—remains of the early expatriate adventurers, soldiers of fortune and misfortune, tradesmen and settlers who ventured from the West to far places in the East.

Twentieth-century India has memorialized its deceased leaders in ways quite different than did the Moghuls. No monumental mausoleums mark the last resting places of such modern day heroes as Gandhi or Nehru. In contrast to the Muslim Moghuls, the Hindus seek not immortality in mausoleums but oblivion in cremation. At Varanasi (Benares) on the river Ganges burn the fires of the Manikarnike and Harishchandra *ghats* where each year the bodies of more than thirty thousand people disappear into thin air. In a plush mansion overlooking the Ganga Ma (Mother Ganges) dwells the *dom raja,* leader of the low-caste *doms* who for centuries have supervised cremations in India. Ecology conflicts with necrology at the Varanasi funeral pyres, which annually burn wood from twenty-two thousand trees. Since India suffers from deforestation, an electric crematorium at the Harishchandra *ghat* will replace some of the log fires along the Ganges' shores. Without those smouldering pyres—an unforgettable sight long recalled by any visitor—the cremation ceremony will surely lose its drama. Virtually nowhere else in the world can you watch the disappearance of human remains. Smoke veils the smouldering body as the flames consume the corpse, one moment swathed in a white shroud and the next moment spirited away. We are, at the *ghats* of Varanasi, far removed from the solemn monuments and post mortem pretentions found at Paris's Père Lachaise and other such show cemeteries of the Western world.

A simple marker at Rajghat in New Delhi indicates the spot where Gandhi was cremated after his assassination on 30 January 1948. The monument impresses by its dignified simplicity. The marker stands in a large grassy space maintained as meticulously as a golf green, a welcome contrast to Delhi's dusty streets. Inside a circular compound whose walls bear plaques quoting Gandhi's words, four waist-high marble partitions enclose a square black, flower-strewn monument brightened by a large white wreath. On the side of the monument appears the inscription, written in gold letters in Hindi, "Eh Ram" (Oh God), the phrase Gandhi uttered just after the assassin Godse shot him. When attendants cremated Gandhi's body they found Godse's third bullet in the ashes. Some of the leader's friends received a few grains of ash, remains of what had once been Gandhi's body. The Gandhi World Peace Memorial at the Self-Realization Fellowship Lake Shrine in Pacific Palisades, near where Sunset Boulevard meets the Pacific Ocean in Los Angeles, also houses a portion. Most of his ashes, however, were taken to Allahabad, where Gandhi once lived, there to be cast into India's great mother river, the Ganga Ma.

Hindus, of whatever station in life, are always—in life or death—drawn back to the holy Ganges, a waterway of mystical and almost mythological character which exerts a certain incantatory power. After Prime Minister Indira Gandhi—no relation to the famous Gandhi but daughter of the previous prime minister, Nehru—was assassinated in October 1984 she underwent cremation and, as she had requested, the ashes were entrusted to the Great Lord of the Snow, scattered over the glaciers where the Ganges begins its descent to the Bay of Benegal. In late May 1991 Rajiv Gandhi, her assassinated son, was cremated at the same place on the banks of the Jumna River in New Delhi, then his ashes were scattered into the waters at the junction of the Ganges and Jumna Rivers, a site sacred to Hindus in Allahabad. Rajiv's grandfather Nehru also opted for part of his ashes to mingle with the great Ganges. His memorial at Shantivana, a half-mile or so from the original Gandhi's (d. 1948), consists of an ugly concrete platform with a grass mound bulging in its middle, marking the spot where the prime minister was cremated. For twenty-eight years Nehru had preserved the ashes of his wife, Kamala, and together their remains were, like Gandhi's and Rajiv's, thrown into the Ganges at Allahabad. Nehru's will, read in part on All India Radio by his sister Madame Pandit, explained with magnificent eloquence how to dispose of his ashes:

> When I die, I should like my body to be cremated. If I die in a foreign country, my body should be cremated there and my ashes sent to Allahabad. A small handful of these ashes should be thrown into the Ganga and the major portion of them disposed of in the manner indicated below. No part of these ashes should be retained or preserved.
>
> My desire to have a handful of my ashes thrown into the Ganga at Allahabad has no religious significance, so far as I am concerned. I have no religious sentiment in the matter. I have been attached to the Ganga and the Jumna rivers in Allahabad ever since my childhood and, as I have grown older, this attachment has also grown. I have watched their varying moods as the seasons changed, and have often thought of the history and myth and tradition and song and story that have become attached to them through the long ages and become part of their flowing waters.
>
> The Ganga, especially, is the river of India, beloved of her people, round which are intertwined her racial memories, her hopes and fears, her songs of triumph, her victories and her defeats. She has been a symbol of India's age-long culture and civilization, ever-changing, ever-flowing, and yet ever the same Ganga. She reminds me of the snow-covered peaks and the deep valleys of the Himalayas, which I have loved so much, and of the rich and vast plains below, where my life and work have been cast. Smiling and dancing in the morning sunlight, and dark and gloomy and full of mystery as the evening shadows fall; a narrow, slow and graceful stream in winter, and a vast roaring thing during the monsoon, broad-bosomed almost as the sea, and with something of the sea's power to destroy the Ganga has been to me a symbol and memory of the past of India, running into the present, and flowing on to the great ocean of the future. And though I have

discarded much of past tradition and custom, and am anxious that India should rid herself of all shackles that bind and constrain her and divide her people, and suppress vast numbers of them, and prevent the free development of the body and the spirit; though I seek all this, yet I do not wish to cut myself off from the past completely. I am proud of that great inheritance that has been and is ours, and I am conscious that I too, like all of us, am a link in that unbroken chain which goes back to the dawn of history in the immemorial past of India. That chain I would not break, for I treasure it and seek inspiration from it. And as witness of this desire of mine and as my last homage to India's cultural inheritance, I am making this request that a handful of my ashes be thrown into the Ganga at Allahabad to be carried to the great ocean that washes India's shore.

The major portion of my ashes should, however, be disposed of otherwise. I want these to be carried high up into the air in an aeroplane and scattered from that height over the fields where the peasants of India toil, so that they might mingle with the dust and soil of India and become an indistinguishable part of India.

So ended Nehru, his life now suspended in endless time, his remains returning to the earth, the cradle and cemetery of us all, for Mother Earth is truly the ultimate cemetery in history.

III

History in Cemeteries

IN an obscure corner of Paris not far from Père Lachaise cemetery five barrels of soil from far off Boston Common in New England form part of a small burial ground. This expatriate patch of earth lies tucked away behind the Sisters of the Sacred Heart convent near the Place de la Nation. During the French Revolution Parisians dubbed that square, previously called the Square of the Throne, the Square of the Throne Overthrown. The revolutionaries set up there a guillotine which, between 14 June and 27 July 1794, executed some thirty people a day, more than thirteen hundred victims in all. Still bleeding, the naked, headless bodies were thrown into pits in the grounds of the former Picpus convent nearby. A Hohenzollern princess whose brother fell victim to the guillotine later acquired the land, walled it, and converted the enclave into a cemetery for use by families and descendants of the martyrs. Among those executed at the blue-blood splattered square were family members of Adrienne de Noaille, daughter of the Duc d'Ayen. Adrienne requested that upon her death she be buried near her noble relatives at Picpus, and her husband, in turn, asked that he repose beside her. So came to rest at that quiet little Parisian enclave none other than the famous French American, Marquis de Lafayette (d. 1834), Adrienne's spouse and hero of the American Revolution. In appreciation for his help during the colony's struggle against the British, the United States Congress granted the marquis American citizenship, the only person—apart from Winston Churchill, already half American through his mother—ever to receive that honor.

Lafayette reposes in a truly Yankee setting in the French capital: his coffin nestles in Massachusetts soil, overhead hangs an American flag, nearby lies his son George-Washington de Lafayette. Although, as a plaque in the convent's Chapel of the Adoration recalls, many members of prominent French families repose at Picpus—among them such illustrious clans as Chateaubriand, Noailles, and La Rochfoucauld—the caretaker immediately takes anyone who seems to be American, by looks or accent, directly to the marquis' tomb. Yanks far from their native land can get a touch of home at the grave over which flies the American flag and where on 4 July 1917 Colonel C. E. Stanton snapped to attention and saluted while uttering the famous phrase, "Lafayette, we are here"

Although expatriates all around the world repose in foreign soil far from their homelands, Lafayette—that great American patriot—is perhaps the only person who occupies terrain from his own (honorary) land. Earth transported from the Holy Land contains the dead at Pisa's Campo Santo (as noted in the previous chapter) and such sanctified soil also (as related in the next chapter) fills the Capuchin cemetery in

Santa Maria della Concezione in Rome, but in both cases the terrain remains alien to those who repose in it.

Lafayette, like many other expatriates interred in foreign graveyards far from their native terrain, represents the history in cemeteries. It was abroad, in the country of the soil where he reposes, that Lafayette made his reputation and played his part in history. Decedents serve to revive the past, making it come alive to visitors, at burial grounds around the world. Much history reposes in cemeteries in the persons of foreigners who traveled to far corners of the earth for purposes of trade, war, religion, glory, exploration, migration, adventure, escape, science, curiosity, conquest, colonization, and any number of other reasons. Their stories—why they traveled, where they ventured, what they found, how they died abroad—abound with tales of derring-do, daring adventures, curiosities of history, amusing anecdotes, and colorful characters.

Burial abroad, far from home and all its familiarities, seems especially terminal. The deceased finds himself not only cut off from life but also from his or her native land—a double exile. Lafayette's contemporary countryman Napoleon died in exile far from France at St. Helena Island in the remote reaches of the Atlantic Ocean on 5 May 1821. British grenadiers accompanied the emperor's body to the grave: British soldiers conscripted to inter the great Napoleon, a procedure which added insult to exile. They marked the grave with a huge stone, impressive but hardly appropriate for the famous Frenchman's exalted station. There reposed Napoleon—clad in his uniform, including the famous three-cornered hat—until 1840 when his exile finally ended. The frigate *Belle Poule* carried the renowned remains, embalmed and well preserved, home to France where some six hundred thousand admirers gathered in the streets to cheer as the expatriate's body arrived in Paris on the bitterly cold day of 15 December 1840. Napoleon always wanted to repose at home, either at prestigeous Père Lachaise or better, as he ordered in a 20 February 1806 decree, in a special vault to be built for himself and his descendants in the royal basilica at St. Denis, the mausoleum church near Paris which houses all but three of the kings of France. In the end, Napoleon was awarded even more exclusive quarters. After lying in wait for twenty years in the Chapel of St. Jerome, the emperor finally came to rest at the stately Hôtel des Invalides where, at home in his native country, Napoleon enjoys spacious quarters in the middle of the French capital.

A certain atavistic drive often induces survivors or descendants of an exiled person to return their relative's remains to home terrain, or otherwise to memorialize one who died abroad. Fully one-third of the *Iliad* concerns the struggle between the Greeks and the Trojans to claim and bury the bodies of Patroclos and Hector, their respective heroes. In England during the nineteenth century it was common to erect a marker in the home parish of a person worthy of note who died away from his birthplace, while in Romania the practice of token burial survives. Those who die and are buried outside Romania merit a symbolic interment in the cemetery of their hometown, complete with a grave and a cross draped with clothes, later given to charity, to symbolize the deceased.

In earlier times, a famous expatriate's remains, or part of them, would often be repatriated. When Henry I of England died at Lyons-la-Forêt near Rouen in 1135 attendants buried his entrails, brains, and eyes there, then embalmed his body for transfer from France to Reading, in England, where he had founded an abbey. The surgeon who prepared the king's corpse died from an infection contracted during the procedure, "the last of many whom Henry destroyed," observed a chronicler. Henry's posthumous fate typifies that of famous medieval figures who died abroad. The corpses would be boiled to remove the flesh, which attendants buried at the place of death, after which the bones were returned home for interment. This repatriation both positioned the deceased on familiar ground for the final resurrection and also served the more worldly purpose of strengthening territorial claims asserted by the great man's survivors. If the bones derived from a saint, the devout coveted them as holy relics, and the church parcelled out the precious souvenirs to the faithful.

Although travelers abroad risk final exile from all the comforting familiarities of home, this possible fate hardly represents an argument against venturing into the great wide world: it simply implies that the traveler should refrain from giving up the ghost before returning home. Ghosts deserve home spooking. After relating the many benefits of travel in "On Going On A Journey," the famous English essayist William Hazlitt concludes that "we can be said only to fulfil our destiny in the place that gave us birth." Death and burial at home, snug in one's native soil, seems so much cozier than reposing in some far land. The enfolding sod and clods of familiar earth coddle us more than can any alien terrain. Burial where born lends to life a certain symmetry: there, where you began, you end, so becoming a permanent part of the corner of the earth where you started. "There is something so seducing in that spot in which we first had existence," notes Oliver Goldsmith in *The Citizen of the World,* "that nothing but it can please; whatever vicissitudes we experience in life, however we toil, or wheresoever we wander, our fatigued wishes still recur to home for tranquility, we long to die in that spot which gave us birth, and in that pleasing expectation opiate every calamity." Perhaps the very purpose of funeral services and burial rituals is to introduce the deceased to his new quarters. These procedures serve as a celebratory send-off and also as a house-warming party so that he will happily occupy the tomb room without spooking survivors. In *Death Customs* E. Bendann maintains that "the great importance attached to the disposal of the body seems to be universal. We may state that the principal is invariably the same—the dead would 'walk' unless the body is disposed of with appropriate ceremony. The natural tendency of the deceased, then, was to find his way back to the place which had been his haunt in life."

For mortals live or dead, home beckons. After American Federation of Labor leader Samuel Gompers collapsed in Mexico City in 1924 he managed to gasp, "I wish to live until I arrive in my own country; if I die, I prefer to die at home." Gompers held out until he crossed the border, expiring in San Antonio, Texas, and he reposes in Sleepy Hollow cemetery at Tarrytown, New York, along with Washington Irving and, incongruously for a union man, such capitalists and captains of industry as Andrew Carnegie, Walter P. Chrysler, William Rockefeller, and IBM founder Thomas J. Watson. Radical labor leader Bill Haywood (d. 1928) occupies more appropriate quarters in the Kremlin Wall in Moscow, where he settled in 1921, but even this Soviet devotee shunned complete severence from his native land, for the other half of his ashes resides at at Forest Home cemetery, in Forest Park, Illinois, near the graves of radicals hanged for inciting violence during Chicago's 1886 Haymarket Square labor riots. When an American named John Howard Payne, a sometime lyricist, died in Tunis, where he had served as United States consul, he was buried in North Africa far from home. Although Payne's musical play *Clari, or, The Maid of Milan* failed after twelve performances at Covent Garden, London, in 1823, a stanza from the one song that survived served as an epitaph when the Yankee's body was repatriated in 1883 and reburied at Oak Hill cemetery in Washington, D.C.:

Sure, when thy gentle spirit fled
To realms beyond the azure dome,
With arms outstretched God's angels said
Welcome to Heaven's home, sweet home.

So finally returned home the author of "Home, Sweet Home."

The epitaph for John Patterson, the first white child born in Arkansas, seemingly recalls him as a great wanderer, but he experienced a less roundabout route to his homeside grave than did John Payne. On the marker for the well-companioned Patterson (d. 1886), who reposes along with his six wives and twenty children behind their cabin home near Marianna, Arkansas, appears the epitaph: "I was born in a kingdom/Reared in an empire/Attained manhood in a territory/And now a citizen of a state/And have never been 100 miles from where I now live." This apparently peripatetic life was the result not of changing his domicile but of the changing status of his native land: Arkansas evolved from a possession of the Kingdom of Spain and then of the French Empire, to the Louisiana Territory, and finally, a state.

A curious grave marker commemorates the final resting place of Harriet Ruggles Loomis, wife of a West African missionary, in her home country. Her stone bears an engraved scene of the remote tropical harbor—shown with a ship, and palm trees towering over rows of huts—at Corisco, the island off the coast of Rio Muni in Equatorial Africa where she died. Below the picture appears the epitaph: "Ebe bobe ome, Ebe njuke na ngeb e/Oyenck'o buhua; O ka bange vake." Loomis, who lies in Oxbow cemetery in Newbury, Vermont, boasts what is no doubt the state's most foreign epitaph, but not its most exotic, for a marker at Middlebury bears an inscription reading: "Ashes of Amun-Her-Khepesh-Ef Aged 2 Years, Son of Sen Woset 3rd King of Egypt and His Wife Hathor-Hotpe 1883 B.C." Amun represents not only an expatriate burial but an extemporal one as well, for he lies far in time as well as place from the Pharaonic land of his birth. In the mid-nineteenth century A.D. the nineteenth-century B.C. child mummy was spirited away from the ancient Egyptian tomb where he had reposed for nearly four thousand years. Later, in 1886 Henry Sheldon, a collector of oddities who lived in Middlebury, bought the ancient mummy. After Sheldon's death in 1907 Amun's remains found their way to the Sheldon Museum attic where they remained until a curator discovered them in 1945. Museum officials decided to give Amun a decent burial, so they cremated the mummy and interred the remains in the family plot of George Mead, head of the Sheldon Museum, who erected a headstone to the Egyptian who had died some thirty-eight centuries before.

As Amun demonstrates, some souls are fated to lie in foreign soil. Unlike Harriet Ruggles Loomis, who found her way home to Vermont after expiring in Equatorial Africa, Amun, originally buried at home, ended up far from his native land. At Richmond cemetery in Richmond, Maine, an ordinary nineteenth-century New England graveyard includes a group of stones with Cyrillic inscriptions, markers for emigrés who lived in a local White Russian colony. There is something especially poignant about the graves of those who repose far from home. An 1847 visitor to a cemetery in Melbourne, Australia, captured the mood when he observed: "It is impossible not to feel sorry for the untoward fate of many who have laid their bones in this wild spot . . . far from fatherland, from friends, from home . . . Many who reached here, perhaps, little expected to die so far from home and be buried in the Australian forest." To come to rest in Australia, literally the ends of the earth, was a sad outcome. If, as the French say, to leave is to die a little, then to leave and never return—to succumb and repose in a foreign land—is to die a lot. A certain ineluctable destiny must determine one's final resting place. In the room at Moray Street in Edinburgh occupied by young Thomas Carlyle when he was a student, the historian-to-be scratched on a window pane an oddly haunting fragment which suggests the play of chance that controls our life and its end:

Little did my mother think
That day she cradled me
What land I was to travel in,
Or what death I should die.

So it is that the Frenchman Lafayette reposes in American soil
in Paris, while the American Quentin Roosevelt, Theodore
Roosevelt's son killed in action during World War I, was
buried near Chaméry in France where his plane crashed, the
marker bearing a line from Shelley's "Adonais": "He has out-
soared the shadow of our night."

Military dead represent a large component of the deceased
expatriate population. While the tomb for United States
Army general Lafayette merits an American flag, the cathedral at Orléans, France, boasts a seal of the United States and
a text in English commemorating the half a million American
soldiers who fought in France during two world wars "and of
whom 67,581 remain in the soil of France." Most military
cemeteries, large and rather cold places with severe and even
forbidding architecture, contain rows of identical mind- and
eye-numbing markers bearing only cursory information
about the deceased. At Belgium's Flanders Field American
Cemetery, made famous by John McCrae's poem of 1915—
"In Flanders Field the poppies blow/Between the crosses,
row on row"—Charles A. Lindbergh scattered poppies from
the *Spirit of St. Louis* on Memorial Day 1927, nine days after
his solo flight across the Atlantic.

A grave at Oise-Aisne American Cemetery at Seringes-
sur-Nesles, France, recalls another famous poem, for there
reposes sergeant Joyce Kilmer (d. 1918), author of "Trees."
For a time the body of First Lieutenant Quentin Roosevelt (d.
1918) rested at Oise-Aisne after being removed from its original grave, mentioned above. In September 1955 his remains
traveled again, this time to the Normandy American Cemetery overlooking Omaha Beach, for reburial beside his

brother, Brigadier General Theodore Roosevelt, Jr. (d. 1944), who died in World War II. History truly reposes at that burial ground in the form of a time capsule scheduled to be opened one century after the American invasion of Europe. A bronze plaque on the slab over the container states: "In memory of General Dwight D. Eisenhower and the forces under his command this sealed capsule containing news reports of the June 6, 1944, Normandy landings is placed here by newsmen who were there. June 6, 1969."

Although ancient Carthage at Tunis lacks the remains of a cemetery, the North Africa American Cemetery abuts the precincts of the classical coastal city. Thus recent dead, from twentieth-century wars, repose near the now crumbled remains of those killed in 146 B.C. when the Romans destroyed old Carthage. Most of the 2,840 American dead there perished during campaigns to occupy Morocco, Algeria, and Tunisia, while the rest succumbed elsewhere in North Africa or while serving in the Persian Gulf Command in Iran. In the cemetery chapel appears the same sentiment from Shelley's "Adonais" that adorned Quentin Roosevelt's first grave near Chaméry.

In contrast to those monumental American military cemeteries, which occupy large expanses of foreign terrain and include rather ponderous funerary structures, a burial ground for Canadian soldiers at Holten near Deventer, Holland, hides modestly. Accompanied by Dutch friends I walked from Holten to the simple graveyard a mile or two away, passing through cornfields and then a wooded area to Eekhornweg (squirrel path) which took us toward the cemetery. Heather purpled the landscape and a few early autumn leaves dappled the ground. Finally we reached the burial ground, a small enclave carved out of the woods that surround it on three sides. It is one of the most immaculate cemeteries that I have ever seen, with each blade of grass precisely cut, each flower nurtured to perfect shape and color.

At the entrance stands a simple monument bearing the inscription, "Their name liveth forevermore." A little farther on lie the graves, a thousand or so identical stone markers creating a stark symmetry of the dead. On each simple slab appear a delicately veined relief maple leaf, a carved cross (or, rarely, a Star of David) and a brief inscription revealing only name, rank, unit, date of death, and age. A few of the monuments also bear a brief sentiment which slightly personalizes the otherwise unpraised dead Canadian soldiers in that remote corner of Holland far from home. The French inscription for V. B. Pare (d. 1945) reads: "Your death gave peace to the world, Victory to your country, Glory to your family." F. P. F Cope (d. 1944) raises the question, "Is it as nothing to you,/All ye that pass by?" while L. K. Butterick (d. 1945) offers the more comforting, "In memory's garden we meet every day." Another inscription, referring to the survivors who "mourn far o'er the sea," emphasizes the expatriate nature of the tomb, while the one for A. R. L. Mylles (d. 1945) underlines another sort of distance, the space separating the living and the dead, removed to his ultimate exile: "You're like a haunting echo of sweet music, my dear. Far away but ever near."

The first expatriate American military cemetery lay not in Europe, that twentieth-century sinkhole for American youth, but closer to home in Mexico City. In 1850 Congress appropriated $10,000 to buy two acres to bury Americans killed in the battles of Chapultepec and Churusbusco during the Mexican War of 1846–47, instigated by the United States' annexation of Texas in 1845. In 1851 the remains of 750 soldiers were exhumed and reinterred at the burial ground, located at 31 Calzada Melchoir Ocampo a few miles west of the cathedral in Mexico City. A monument commemorates the troops, who entered the Mexican capital on 14 September 1847. Another 724 Americans, military veterans and others, also repose in the cemetery. During the Civil War, Congress decided to establish national cemeteries at sites where major battles had occurred, and in 1864 the government created the first Graves Registration Unit to handle the dead killed in Jubel Early's attack on the nation's capital. At the end of the century the newly organized Quartermaster Burial Corps exhumed bodies of American soldiers killed and buried in Cuba during the Spanish-American War and returned the remains to the States. This set the pattern followed after both world wars when most families opted for the repatriation of loved ones' remains, those not returned being buried in national military cemeteries abroad.

Honored treatment of war dead is an ancient tradition. Although the rulers of Sparta rather curtly told their warriors to return home either with their shields or on them, Athenians treated their departed soldiers more ceremoniously. Thucydides describes the funeral ceremonies at Athens in 431 B.C. when the first bodies were brought back from the Peloponnesian War. The Athenians gave "a funeral at the public cost to those who had first fallen in this war," placing the heroes "in the public sepulcher in the most beautiful suburb of the city, in which those who fell in war are always buried." Mourners carried in the procession "one empty bier decked for the missing,"—a symbol of those whose remains had stayed abroad. As to burial in foreign terrain Pericles, on the occasion of his famous funeral oration delivered then, noted that "heroes have the whole earth for their tomb; and in lands far from their own, where the column with its epitaph declares it, there is enshrined in every breast a record unwritten with no tablet to preserve it, except that of the heart."

In some cases, however, a tablet abroad does record the deeds of departed heroes—departed from their homeland and from life—confined to alien soil. In addition to the Yankees remembered at the American Military Cemetery in Mexico City a plaque in the capital preserves the memory of other foreigners who fell far from home during the 1847 Mexican-

American War. The marker, located at 15 Plaza Jacinto in the picturesque San Angel quarter, commemorates Irish mercenaries—adventurers such as James Kelly, Thomas Riley and Andrew Nolan—who died fighting American troops, some of them buried at the military cemetery. Mercenaries seldom garner final honors for their homeland ignores the martial efforts they exert for others, while their employer recognizes such efforts with cold cash rather than warm praise.

One exception is the quasi-mercenary Foreign Legion, an eighty-five-hundred-man agglomeration of many nationalities (other than French) melded into the fabled French fighting force. Departed members of the unit repose either in an overseas cemetery at Sidi-bel-Abbès in Algeria, fifty miles southwest of Oran, or in their substitute homeland at Puyloubier in southern France, west of Saint Maximim where the dead lie in a gravel-covered compound with rectangular grave slabs and a memorial wall bearing a long list of names. Until October 1962 the Legion's headquarters occupied facilities in the Sahara at Sidi-bel-Abbès, a tiny Berber community established around the tomb of the Muslim wise man whose name designates the village. In early 1863 two batallions departed from Sidi-bel-Abbès for Mexico. Sent to help Archduke Maximilian, the puppet ruler installed by Napoleon III, hold the throne in Mexico, the legionnaires engaged the enemy on 30 April 1863 at the village of Camerone where some sixty mercenaries fought to the death (only four survived) against two thousand Mexican soldiers. Every year legionnaires celebrate Camerone Day, the anniversary of one of the corps' most legendary encounters, with a parade and other ceremonies. On the battle site in Mexico stands a monument, installed in 1892, with a Latin inscription: "Here stood fewer than sixty men against an entire army. Its weight overwhelmed them. Life, sooner than courage, forsook these soldiers of France."

Perhaps no less famous than the French Foreign Legion,

and certainly more photographed, are another band of mercenaries—the Swiss Guards who brighten the Vatican City
with their colorful Renaissance uniforms. A guardsman who
serves five years can keep his red-and-gold uniform, customarily worn one last time when the former papal mercenary is
finally laid out in his coffin. The Vatican enlists the hundred
or so guards from all the Swiss cantons except Italian-speak-
ing Ticino, with German-speaking recruits preferred. In pro-
portion to its area and its resident population, which numbers
about nine hundred people, the Vatican City—with the Swiss
Guards, 150 *gendarmes,* fifty guards of honor, and about five
hundred Palatine guards—boasts more extensive armed
forces than any other state in the world. A little expatriate
German cemetery lies tucked into a corner of the mini-city-
state, occupying a garden-like courtyard crawling with cats.
Above this foreign enclave within the Vatican enclave in Italy
towers St. Peters' left flank. Around the cemetery wall colorful ceramic tile niches portray scenes from the stations of the
cross, described by notices in German. The deceased represent a cross-section of German society. Franz Nadorp (d.
1876), a historian and painter born in Westphalia, reposes
there as does Karl Johannes Bayer, secretary-general of European charity funds (presumably for the Catholic church).
Other nationalities also claim space in the German cemetery:
"To the memory of her highness Princess Charlotte de Nidda
[d. 1862] née Török Szendrä, Hungarian," and Louis de Paul
(d. 1880), Dutch ambassador to the Vatican, recalled (in
French) as "loyal, diplomatic, skillful son, spouse, father," a
strikingly succinct six word *tour d'horizon* of Louis's life.
Seven members of the Rohden family (d. 1863 to 1944) lie
there commemorated by three Dürer-like engravings on the
gravestone. Louis Stölzle (d. 1902), a painter, died "expatriate
from his German homeland, taken via Rome to his heavenly
home."

The expatriate Stölzle and his compatriots buried in Rome

represent a relatively rare example of Germans interred abroad. A few individual Germans, commemorated for their accomplishments, lie in foreign soil. As described in the previous chapter, the famous archeologist Heinrich Schliemann reposes in Athens, and at Permagon in Turkey, not far from ancient Troy which Schliemann discovered, lies Karl Humann, appropriately buried at the Altar of Zeus which he found in 1864. The only former colonial German territory I have ever come across lies in Lome, Togo's capital on the west coast of Africa. It is a curiosity of history that the powerful and energetic German nation accomplished virtually no overseas conquests. That little German cemetery in Lome survives as a relic of Germany's very minor role in the late-nineteenth-century colonization of the African continent.

The graveyard, located not far beyond the American embassy, occupies a shady enclave whose gnarled tree trunks suggest a certain antiquity. The section reserved for locals lacks the greenery and shade afforded by trees which only the German colonialists merit. Markers at the tombs—most of them elevated, white-washed rectangles—include those commemorating Ernst Baumgart (d. 1903), Ludwig Wolf (d. 1889), Otto Fries (d. 1908), a colonel, and Wilhelm Müller (d. 1906) who "reposes in God far from his homeland." The inscription for Beethold Hammerling (d. 1910), who "died in true service during the building of the railroad," typifies such other track builders as Max Kuchenthal (d. 1910), Reinhold Scharff (d. 1907), and Herman Schwarz (d. 1904). Walter Vehlow (d. 1909) served with the German-West African Bank, while a simply inscribed black obelisk recalls "Köhler, Gouverneur von Togo" (d. 1902). These few remnants of the century-old German presence in Togo conjure an entire era of European territorial possessions in the Black Continent, symbolized by Conrad's quintessential colonial character Kurtz, the enigmatic European in charge of an interior ivory trading post in "the heart of darkness." In his *Congo Diary*

Conrad mentions coming across a forlorn residue of the European presence in Africa, in a remote part of the back country: "On the road today passed a . . . white man's grave—no name. Heap of stones in the form of a cross." So ended some of those European adventurers who left the comforts of their homeland for the rigors of an unknown land.

Although the burial ground at the Vatican serves as a rare example of an expatriate German graveyard, Rome's Protestant Cemetery also contains Germans, and occupies both a larger space on earth and a bigger place in history. The Protestant Cemetery, established for non-Catholic foreigners, seems a United Nations of the afterlife, for there gather nearly four thousand dead from such far-flung lands as the United States of America, Greece, Russia, England, the Scandinavian countries, Germany, and even China and other Asian countries. The well-kept graveyard ranks as the finest cemetery for foreigners, both for its many interesting monuments and because it boasts "the most extraordinary collection of exiles ever assembled in one place," so H. V. Morton noted in *A Traveller in Rome.* The first foreigner known to have been interred at the *cimitero acattolico,* as Romans called the burial ground in its earliest days, was an Oxford University graduate named Werpup (d. 1715), who died after falling from his carriage on the Via Flaminia not far from the Piazza Flaminia, near which stood Rome's other secular cemetery, for prostitutes. The very first grave in the area now occupied by the Protestant Cemetery belongs to Caius Cestius, a Roman official who died in 12 B.C. and reposes in the distinctive low pyramid that rises near the Porta San Paolo in the Aurelian wall.

The Protestant Cemetery developed in the early nineteenth century in concession for a favor received by the Holy See from Protestants a few years before. In 1799, during the Napoleonic Wars, English naval officer Thomas Troubridge

captured several French ships loaded with Vatican art treasures. The British government promptly returned these to
the pope, who granted Troubridge the right to include on his
coat of arms the device of the keys of St. Peter. When the
time later came to formalize the foreigners' cemetery in
Rome, the Vatican granted the necessary permissions. The
church, however, continued to exert its control over the
burial ground. In 1817 Cardinal Consalvi refused a request by
diplomatic representatives from Russia, Prussia, and Hannover to fence in the open ten-acre plot on the grounds that the
proposed barrier would obstruct the view of Cestius' pyramid. For much of the nineteenth century the Vatican also
forebade tombstone inscriptions which could be taken to
suggest that those dying outside the Catholic religion might
gain eternal salvation: *extra ecclesiam nulla salus* (there is no
salvation outside the church). For nearly a century, from 1822
to 1916, the cemetery was maintained by three generations of
the Trucchi family. The cemetery now operates under the
jurisdiction of a committee, established in 1921, comprised of
ambassadors from the countries whose citizens repose in the
graveyard. During the early part of the 1900s directors of the
American, British, and German academies in Rome had to
approve designs for all major monuments, but few new
markers have been erected in recent years, for only especially
prominent people now receive space in the cemetery.

One latter-day celebrity interred at the Protestant Cemetery is the famous entrepreneur Charles "Lucky" Luciano,
now truly an underworld figure, who in January 1962 rode
there in an elaborate, silver-embellished black hearse pulled
by eight black horses. Later removed, he now reposes at St.
John's Cemetery in Queens, New York City.

I have spent many an intriguing hour wandering through
the pleasant tree-garnished garden cemetery which affords
welcome relief from Rome's noise and traffic. History
abounds there for the Protestant graveyard, with its rich array

of foreigners, comprises a cosmopolitan collection of characters who once enlivened Rome's daily life. A random sampling of inhabitants reveals the wide variety of nationalities and personalities interred at the cemetery, according to H. V. Morton, "the most beautiful cemetery in the world and . . . certainly the best tended." Near the entrance I found Augustus Kestner (d. 1853), minister from Hannover, Germany, at the court of Rome, and Benjamin Gibson (d. 1851), member of the British Archeological Association of London, who died "at the baths of Lucia." For an archeologist it must be wonderfully exciting to expire at a ruin such as Lucia's baths—or maybe she was his lady friend: even more exciting. The more recently expired Charles Turner (d. 1964) "loved much and was much loved." Near him reposes Shakspere Wood (d. 1886), and not far beyond rises a largish construction labelled, "Entrance to family tomb of Edwin J. Hulbert descendant of Middletown, Conn. Family U.S.A. 1630." On a slab inscribed "Faithfulness" lies a stone dog, while by a bust of Hulbert appears the inscription: "This life of mortal breath is but a suburb of the life elysian, whose portal we call death." Along the way I met George Blunt Page (d. 1930), "Christian American gentleman," and Thomas Jefferson Page (d. 1864) from Virginia, a Confederate army artillery major. Germans, English, Scots, Irish, Swedes, Norwegians, Danes, Canadians, Finns, Dutch, Russians, and even Italians (married to foreigners) lay along my erratic path. A large upright slab bore a relief profile bronze medallion labelled "Goethe Filius" (d. 1830)—the German poet's son, August, who died of smallpox three weeks after arriving in Rome. Virginia Hollis (d. 1914) of New York lies next to Principessa Emilia Ouroussof (d. 1958): the New World meets the Old. Nearby reposes Frank Fairbanks (d. 1939) of Boston, professor at the American Academy in Rome; Aeneas Macbean (d. 1864), "late banker in Rome"; Robert Brown (d. 1823), an Englishman who at the age of twenty-one "unhappily lost his life at Tivoli by his foot slipping in coming out of Neptune's Grotto," a mishap which inspired the cautionary inscription: "Reader Beware: By this fatal accident a virtuous and amiable youth has been suddenly snatched away in the bloom of health and pride of life." On the rear wall a plaque recalls Dewan Ram Lall (d. 1949), India's first ambassador to Italy "whose ashes were immersed in the Ganga River at Sangam, Allahabad." By the wall stands a statue of Psyche divesting herself of mortality, erected by Richard S. Greenough (d. 1904) of Boston, interred there far from his wife Sarah whose "mortal remains are buried in Franzensbad, Austria. Her spirit is with those she loves. Her loss was as that of the key-stone of an arch." A stone relief panel on the monument depicts a book turned to a page which reads: "The End."

Of all the expatriates who repose at the Protestant Cemetery, Thomas Dessoulavy (d. 1869) boasts perhaps the most piquant epitaph: "during 53 years [he] painted the classic scenes of Rome with truth and beauty and never ceased to be an Englishman." The inscription for Caroline Carson (d. 1892) of Charleston, South Carolina, recalls her as the daughter of James Louis Petigru, "the Union man of South Carolina." On and on I ambled, making my way through a bewildering maze of dates, names, professions, origins, a crazy-quilt of people, places, past: Hugh Caldwell (d. 1882), a colonel in the Bengal Army; John Nodes Dickinson (d. 1882), born in Grenada, West Indies, judge of the New South Wales Supreme Court in Sydney, Australia, died in Rome; Tarou Kawase (d. 1874), whose epitaph appears in Chinese; Channing Williams Cooper (d. 1878), born in Edo, Japan; John Blakeney De Mille (d. 1950), with an Arabic epitaph describing him as "beloved servant of Baha A'llah"; the Taylors, George (d. 1907) and Mary (d. 1930), of Virginia; Charles Martyne Boswell (d. 1885), of the Royal Munster Fusiliers, born in Calcutta; Jane Gray Davidson (d. 1882), widow of a major in the Bombay army; a trio of Japanese; a French chef: "Ici repose en Dieu Alfred Herzog cuisinier," died 1885 and remembered by "ses colleges de l'Hôtel du Quirnal"; surgeon-general James Macbeth (d. 1899), "a veteran of the wars of the Punjab"; Jim Dolen (d. 1965), an actor "now starring in 'Eternity'"; Mary Ellen Gerbi (d. 1882, aged eighty-eight), "our mother, granny and greatgranny, God bless her!"; and a vault built to house Charles King (d. 1867) of New York: "He was placed here until taken to his own country." Perhaps only King and crime lord Lucky Luciano, also removed from Rome to New York, of all the expatriates whose fate led them in the end to that Roman cemetery, escaped eternity in a foreign land.

It is odd to meditate on the varied lives and backgrounds of all these people. What a mixed tapestry of the past their stony stories weave. The histories of the deceased at the Protestant Cemetery summarize all manner of human endeavors, emotions, accomplishments, long since superceded by succeeding generations. One muses on the departed's struggles, victories, defeats, the thoughts of those now vanished souls when they left their homeland, their feelings when they arrived in Rome, destined to be their permanent habitation. No pattern emerges from it all—none except that rigid conformity imposed by the circumstances of their demise. From distant lands and from eras widely separated in time they joined one another—randomly drawn together in their fixed places—in death.

Yankees dominate the *zona terza,* the third section of the storied cemetery. Americans from Ohio, New York, California, Michigan, Vermont, Connecticut, Illinois, and Maine cluster there to form a little America in that patch of Italian earth. Helen King (d. 1918) of Medina, Ohio, unlike her namesake did not return home; members of Cincinnati's Stettinius family, whose relative Edward served as United States secretary of state, repose there in Rome, as does L. J.

Clawson Primm (d. 1931) of Belleville, "Illinos." Interlopers
at this American enclave include Andrew Wallace Mackie (d.
1925) of the Indian Civil Service, and the exotic Sir Charles J.
Dudgeon, born in Dumfries, Scotland, one-time resident of
Shanghai, China, died in San Remo, Italy, in 1928. The
fourth section includes a more varied selection of nationalities: Edmund Hamond (d. 1826), fellow of Jesus College, Cambridge "who died at Rome, where he came for the
benefit of his health"—surely the cemetery's most paradox-
ical epitaph; "Ian Angus, an Australian boy of 3½ years
drowned 24–5–1956"; Major George Spinks (d. 1830),
Madras Army; and Charles Dudley Ryder (d. 1823)
"drowned with five of the crew by the upsetting of a boat at
the mouth of the Tiber." By Ryder a boxy monument bears a
relief depicting an angel comforting a young girl, and an
inscription recounting the end of Rosa Bathurst, "who was
accidentally drowned on the Tiber on the 14th of March
1824, whilst on a riding party; owing to the swollen state of
the river, and her spirited horse taking fright. She was the
daughter of Benjamin Bathurst, whose disappearance when
on a special mission to Vienna, some years since, was as
tragical as unaccountable: no positive account of his death
ever having been received by his distracted wife . . . Reader
whoever thou art, who may pause to pursue this tale of
sorrows, let this awful lesson of the instability of human
happiness sink deep in thy mind.—If thou art young and
lovely build not thereon, for she who sleeps in death under
thy feet, was the loveliest flower, ever crept in bloom."

Off to the left of the Bathurst saga reposes Constance
Fenimore Woolson (d. 1894), grandniece of novelist James
Fenimore Cooper; Anne Nicolls (d. 1844), wife of General
Sir Jasper Nicolls, who "never caused pain but by her death";
Adelaide Mitchell (d. 1957) of Rockhampton, Australia;
"William Wordsworth C.I.E., scholar and poet, grandson of
Wordsworth, born 1835, died 1917, late principal of

Elphinstone College, pioneer of Indian education, wise, magnanimous, tenderhearted"; Maria Polhemus (d. 1903), "born in Brooklyn, Long Island." By the rear wall lies the graves of Bertie Berke Mathew (d. 1844), who "died by a fall from his horse while hunting in the Campagna near Porta Salara"; nearby are travel writer Augustus William Hare (d. 1834), fellow of New College, Oxford; Michael Hosgood (d. 1954), born in Cheribou, Java; Devereux Plantagenet Cockburn (d. 1850) "of far off Britain," his now distant homeland eulogized in the Latin inscription on one side of the box bearing a reclining stone figure with a partly open book resting on the hairy dog beside him: "Britannia! my beloved land where my heart remains even if my bones you don't contain." A less dramatic and more succinct sentiment appears on the tomb of a pair of Americans, Sophia Howard (d. 1852) and Jessie Howard Tyson (d. 1863): "In a foreign land these two sleep together."

Off to one side of the cemetery, near Cestius' pyramid, stretches a grassy swath, the *parte antica,* where the oldest graves lie. A notice states: "During the levelling works at the base of the pyramid the remains of three bodies were found, one of which was under a leaden shield" bearing a Latin inscription to George Langton, an Oxford student interred in 1738. Nearby, a mottled stone in the ground serves as a memorial to William Shelley (d. 1819, aged three), "son of Percy and Mary Wollstonecraft Shelley." In a letter to his friend Thomas Love Peacock Shelley called Rome's Protestant graveyard, "the most beautiful and solemn cemetery I ever beheld." Indeed, Shelley and his contemporary John Keats are the two most famous figures interred there. That poetic pair, darlings of the Romantics, exert on Anglo-Saxon visitors to Rome a magnetic pull. When the Yankee travel writer Bayard Taylor arrived in Rome on 27 December 1844 he recorded in his journal that soon, at long last, he would make the pilgrimage enabling him "to say in after years, that I have . . . mused by the graves of Shelley [and] Keats."

True to his reputation as one of the great poets of the romantic era, Shelley died and ended up at the Protestant Cemetery in a dramatically romantic way. During a sailing trip off the Italian coast in 1822 when he was thirty, the writer disappeared. For nearly two weeks nothing was heard from Shelley's ship, but then two drowned bodies washed ashore near Viareggio, a central Italian coastal town. "The face and hands, and parts of the body not protected by the dress, were fleshless," wrote the poet's friend Edward Trelawny, who recognized Shelley's corpse only because the dead man carried in his pockets a volume of Aeschylus and a book of Keats' poems. This shows the importance of always traveling with high-class reading matter: not only does such material help others identify you, it also greatly improves your posthumous reputation. Shelley's friends temporarily buried him there on the beach while Trelawny consulted with Tuscan officials in regard to the final disposition of the body. Under Italian law, anything washed ashore from the sea had to be burned as a cautionary measure against the plague. Officials dispatched a military guard to the site to ensure that Shelley's handlers observed the regulation. Shelley's friends and the Italian officials finally agreed that the body should be disinterred and immediately cremated, so on a mid-August morning (variously recorded as the 13th, 14th, 15th, or 16th) in 1822 Trelawny, and poets Byron and Leigh Hunt—perhaps the most literate team of undertakers in history—gathered on the beach at Viareggio to perform the ritual. As workmen disinterred the poet's body they cracked the skull with an iron mattock. The flesh, Trelawny recounted, had decomposed to "a dark and ghastly indigo colour. Byron asked me to preserve the skull for him; but remembering that he had formerly used one as a drinking cup, I was determined Shelley's should not be so profaned." The fire was kindled and then "more wine poured over Shelley's dead body than he had consumed during his life." The fire roared. After the men lifted the corpse onto the funeral pyre Trelawny tossed salt and frankincense onto the flames and poured wine and oil over the cadaver. The oil and salt lent the dancing flames a shimmering, quivering tone as Shelley cooked. Hunt recalled the "inconceivable beauty" of the flickering flame-sheet as it "bore away towards heaven in vigourous amplitude . . . It seemed as though it contained the glassy essence of vitality." Presently, Trelawny wrote, "the corpse fell open and the heart was laid bare. The frontal bone of the skull, where it had been struck with the mattock, fell off; and, as the back of the head rested on the red-hot bottom bars of the furnace, the brains literally seethed, bubbled, and boiled as in a cauldron, for a very long time." Flames consumed the body, apart from a few bone fragments, "but what surprised us all," Trelawny noted, "was that the heart remained entire. In snatching this relic from the fiery furnace, my hand was severely burnt." Trelawny presented Shelley's heart to the poet's wife, Mary Godwin. When Mary died in 1851 the heart was found in her desk, dried to dust and wrapped in a copy of "Adonais." Mary had wanted to repose next to her husband in Rome, but in the end she was buried in the family vault at St. Peter's church in Bournemouth together with her husband's heart, and their son, Sir Percy Florence Shelley, and her parents, William and Mary Wollstonecraft Godwin, who were moved from Old St. Pancras in London. Although the organ salvaged was more likely Shelley's liver, the legendary heart activated imaginations for years. When Marcel Proust was translating Ruskin he somehow began to muse on Shelley's heart, so the French novelist sent his manservant to some friends in Paris to make inquiry. The servant proceeded to the Yeatman house, rang the bell and when the door opened announced, "Monsieur has sent me to ask Monsieur and Madame what became of Shelley's heart."

As for the rest of Shelley's remains, Mary decided that his ashes should be placed beside their son William, who had been buried in Rome in the Protestant Cemetery's *parte antica* three years before. The ashes, contained in an oak casket, were delivered to Freeborn, the British consul in Rome who, upon learning that the Vatican had closed the old section of the cemetery, stored the remains in his wine cellar. After Freeborn and Joseph Severn, a literary hanger-on who had befriended Keats, tried without success to obtain special permission for his burial in the *parte antica* they attempted to disinter William so as to rebury the boy with his father's ashes. But beneath the child's stone they found the skeleton of a grown man, which prompted Severn to renounce the search for it would be "a doubtful and horrible thing to disturb any more strangers' graves in a foreign land. So we proceeded very respectfully to deposit poor Shelley's ashes alone" in the graveyard's new section. A few weeks later, in February 1823, when Trelawny arrived in Rome he decided to move the remains of his friend Shelley to a more desirable location, so he purchased a better plot near the rear wall and transferred the ashes to their present resting place—"mighty meat for little guests," wrote Francis Thompson in an essay on Shelley. In the first quadrangle at Oxford's University College—from which Shelley was "sent down" in 1811, his freshman year, for publishing a tract in favor of atheism— stands a deathly pale marble statue of a nude Shelley spread supine, just washed ashore from the fatal shipwreck. Installed in 1893, this monument was meant to decorate the poet's grave at the Protestant Cemetery but Shelley's marker there remains splendidly simple, a white slab embedded in the ground bearing only his name, the words *cor cordium* (heart of hearts), the dates of his birth and death in Latin, and the haunting lines, added by Trelawny, from the poet's favorite play, *The Tempest:*

> Nothing of him that doth fade
> But doth suffer a sea-change
> Into something rich and strange.

Trelawny reposes next to his old friend. When he transferred Shelley to the plot back by the wall Trelawny installed there his own blank stone, which for years mystified tourists who made the pilgrimage to Shelley's grave. But finally the marker acquired its inscription. In the latter part of 1880 Trelawny, then eighty-eight, contacted the cemetery director, Signor Trucchi, to advise him that he would soon be in a position to use his part of the ground. In October of the next year an English lady turned up at the cemetery with a box that held Trelawny's ashes. Since she lacked the documents necessary to proceed with burial, the director sent the woman away with the box. Within two weeks, however, he was "moored at last on the stormless shore," as Swineburne wrote in "Lines on the Death of Edward John Trelawny." The inscription on Trelawny's stone echoes the heart-felt sentiments which connected him with Shelley in life and then in death:

> These are two friends whose lives were undivided;
> So let their memory be, now they have glided under the
>   grave: Let not their bones be parted,
> For their two hearts in life were single hearted.

John Keats reposes in the *parte antica* where Shelley's friends tried unsuccessfully to inter him. In the preface to his elegaic poem "Adonais," inspired by Keats' death a year before his own, Shelley described the burial ground where soon he too would repose: "The cemetery is an open space among the ruins, covered in winter with violets and daisies. It might

make me in love with death to think that one should be
buried in so sweet a place." The flowers there appealed to
Keats. As the poet lay dying he asked his friend and deathbed
companion Severn to visit the burial ground and describe it
to him. On being told about the anemones, violets, and
daisies the poet whispered that he could already feel "the
daisies growing over me." It was not long before Keats
started to push daisies. He had arrived in Rome September
1820 suffering seriously from tuberculosis. His health quickly
worsened and he took to his bed in a corner room next to the
Spanish Steps, where the constant play of water in the fountain reminded the poet of a phrase from *Philaster,* a play by
Beaumont and Fletcher: "all your better deeds shall be in
water writ." A week or two before he died on 23 February
1821, aged twenty-six, Keats told Severn that he wanted no
name engraved on his gravestone but simply the words:
"Here lies one whose name was writ in water." Lord Alfred
Douglas, the last surviving member of Oscar Wilde's circle,
told the story that Robert Ross, a wild and tempestuous
character who served as Wilde's literary executor, was once
asked what epitaph he wanted, to which he replied: "Here lies
one whose name is writ in hot water." Keats' marker bears
the date of death—shown as 24 February because he expired
after nightfall and in papal Rome the day ends with the
angelus—along with an inscription added by Severn, above
the single phrase Keats had requested, in defiance of the
deceased's desire for simplicity: "This grave contains all that
was mortal, of a young English poet, who, on his death bed,
in the bitterness of his heart, at the malicious power of his
enemies, desired these words to be engraven on his tomb
stone: 'Here lies one whose name was writ in water.'" The
grave is a true curiosity in one respect, for it lacks Keats'
name, which appears only on the adjacent one for Severn,
"devoted friend and death-bed companion of John Keats
whom he lived to see numbered among the immortal poets

of England." Severn succumbed in 1879, fifty-eight years
after Keats' demise, at the ripe old age of eighty-five. Just
behind the two tombs stands a small stone inscribed: "Here
also are interred the remains of Arthur Severn, the infant son
of Joseph Severn, who was born 22 Nov. 1836 and accidentally killed 15 July 1837. The poet Wordsworth was present at
his baptism in Rome." A wall off to the left holds a stone
relief medallion of Keats with the lines:

K—eats! if thy cherished name be "writ in water"
E—ach drop has fallen from some mourner's cheeks;
A—sacred tribute; such as heroes seek,
T—hough oft in vain for dazzling deeds of slaughter.
S—leep on! Not honoured less for Epitaph so meek!

Keats' self-composed epitaph, "writ in water," would have
better suited the drowned Shelley, transmuted from life to
death by the waters of the Mediterranean. The sea has
claimed many a traveler. Some victims lie lost in the briny
deep, truly landless men and women, while others lie not in
the sea but overseas. A few claimed by the waters returned to
earth to repose in their homeland. An epitaph to Thomas
Wordman (d. 1796) in the evocatively named Ancient Cemetery at Wiscasset, Maine, captures the expatriate flavor of old
salts brought low on the high seas: "In foreign climes, alas!
resigns his breath,/His friends far from him in the hour of
death." A square marble pillar at Old Town cemetery in
Sandwich, Massachusetts, recalls "Capt. James L. Nye of
Sandwich, who was killed by a whale in the Pacific Ocean
Dec. 29, 1852, while in command of the Bark Andrew of
New Bedford." The sea sometimes spared those who tried its
tempestuous nature. The captain of the frigate *Constitution,*
fondly known as "Old Ironsides," feared he might perish far
from home, unprepared, so while moored at a harbor in
Madagascar, Mad Jack Percival bought some mahogany

planks which the ship's carpenter used to build a fancy coffin, tailor-made for the skipper. Percival kept the box in his cabin but never needed to use it as Old Ironsides weathered every storm. When the captain finally retired in Dorchester, Massachusetts, he installed the coffin in his front yard where it served as a drinking trough for dogs and horses. A monument at Center Cemetery in Harvard, Massachusetts, records the ironic fate suffered by another sea captain who sailed unscathed: "Erected in memory of Capt. Thomas Stetson who was killed by the fall of a tree November 28, 1820 Aet. 68. Nearly 30 years he was master of a vessel and left that employment at the age of 48 for the less hazardous one of cultivating his farm."

Many who ventured across the seas never returned: they repose under seas or overseas. At Ridgefield Cemetery in Ridgefield, Connecticut, a monument recalls Elisha and Charity Hawley's four sons "whose remains lie interred in various parts of the world," while Evergreen Cemetery in Stonington, Connecticut, contains a stone in memory of Amos and Hannah Denison's four boys, one side of the marker recounting where and when each of the adventurous fellows died: Ezra (d. 1812) in the War of 1812 aboard a privateer "off the Western Islands"; Amos (d. 1816), swept from the deck of the schooner *Nancy* on a trip to the West Indies; Charles (d. 1817), who succumbed in South America at Paramaribo, Surinam; and Edward (d. 1818), who died at Balaria in India. A similar monument on a wall at Shandon church in Cork, Ireland, memorializes the four Downes boys who died at scattered points around the world—typifying the fact that Irish youth comprised one of the country's main exports. Edward Patrick died in New York; Richard in London; Henry drowned in the South Seas; and Joseph went down off the Cape of Good Hope—a misnomer for him. A plaque at St. Werburgh's church in Dublin honors an expatriate saved from the sea: "Sacred to the memory of John

Mulgrave, an African Boy, Shipwrecked on the Coast of Jamaica in the year 1833, when he was taken under the protection of the Earl of Mulgrave, then Governor of that Island, in whose family he resided till the 27 of February 1838, when it pleased God to remove him from this life by a severe attack of Small Pox. His Integrity, Fidelity, and kind and amiable qualities, has endeared him to all his Fellow Servants, at whose desire this Tablet is erected by his God-mother."

Another monument in Dublin recalls that many souls left their homelands for religious reasons. At the Carmelite convent on Aungier Street reposes the famous St. Valentine, beheaded on Valentine's Day, 290. No special connection exists between Valentine and Ireland. The saint's remains arrived there in the nineteenth century only because Father Spratt of the convent asked the pope for some holy relics, and from the inventory on hand the pontiff selected Valentine. Two brass plaques on top of the orange-crate–sized box recount the details of the transaction: "This shrine contains the sacred body of Saint Valentine the martyr, together with a small vessel tinged with his blood." In December 1835 workers unearthed the saint's remains at St. Hippalytus cemetery in Rome and "deposited them in a wooden case covered with painted paper, well closed, tied with a red silk ribbon, and sealed with our seals," says the transmittal document delivered to Father Spratt. Thus was the good saint assigned, sealed, and delivered to Dublin where he now rests.

Other foreigners also occupy Dublin soil. Protestant expatriates from France repose in a neglected patch of ground in the Irish capital. An inscription on a stone lintel over the door of a house on Merrion Row, one of the city's most elegant streets, refers to "Huguenot Cemetery 1693." Through the grill fence I saw among the litter of waste paper, beer bottles, and cans, a scattering of broken or tumbled stones with illegible inscriptions. This forlorn graveyard, flanked by sleek

office buildings, occupies expensive center city terrain, perhaps second in value only to the burial ground claimed by
Trinity Church at Broadway and Wall Street in downtown
Manhattan. Many of the Protestant Huguenots, French Cal-
vinists, fled into exile after Louis XIV revoked the 1598 Edict
of Nantes, which had given the Protestants many privileges,
in 1685. The Huguenots suffered a sort of internal exile as
well, for in their own land the government treated them as
aliens. As late as March 1751 royal troops dispersed a Protestant religious meeting.

The French Protestants at first interred their departed in
gardens, fields or woods. Some came to repose in Paris's
famous Cimetière des Innocents, described in Chapter II, but
in 1562 the authorities forced the Huguenots to disinter their
dead there. Protestant victims killed during the St. Bar-
tholemew's Eve massacre in 1572 were thrown into a mass
grave dug at the site now occupied by 30 rue des Saints-Pères.
Between 1576 and 1678 the Protestants used the yard at the
Trinité church for interments, but after the 1713 Treaty of
Utrecht, which formalized the Protestant nations' victory
over Louis XIV, the Catholic king found himself forced to
establish a cemetery for foreign Protestants. These expatriates
finally received their own burial ground in the area of the
Renaissance and Porte-Saint-Martin theaters on boulevard
Saint-Martin. That cemetery served the foreign non-Catholic
community from 1725 until 1762 when the larger Grange-
aux-Belles graveyard, near the present-day Saint-Louis hospital, opened.

When religious persecution forced the Huguenots to flee
from France, they left their scattered remains around the
earth. In Charleston, South Carolina, America's only
Huguenot church still uses French for the annual service, a
ceremony recalling the arrival of the persecuted Protestants in
the 1680s. It is often forgotten that French Huguenots—not
the Portuguese—first settled Rio de Janeiro, in 1555. Only

after their leader—a seaman named Nicholas Durand de Villegagnon, a professed Calvinist but a confessed Catholic—weakened the new colony by persecuting the Huguenots were the Portuguese able to drive the French out of Brazil in 1560.

Most of the French who ventured abroad, however, traveled not for religious reasons but for gain. Like other Europeans, they sailed to the far corners of the earth seeking colonies, commercial influence and resources. Cemeteries filled with French expatriates survive to evidence those adventurous pioneers. Even areas generally thought of as influenced only by the English boast French burial grounds. At the French (or Tiretta) cemetery on Park Street in Calcutta, not far from the larger and better-known English burial ground just up the street, repose in India's dusty soil a few French citizens far from their homeland and even distant from their motherland's former Asian colonies. Unlike the Dutch, the Portuguese, and especially, the English, the French failed miserably in their attempts to colonize countries in the Far East, so cemeteries with French expatriates remain rare in Asia. At the Calcutta burial ground decayed, tumbled, and cracked gravestones litter the weed-filled enclave. Foliage rooted in the roof of the monument to Coralie de Bast (d. 1819)—"She shone like a ray of light, but she passed away like it" (all the epitaphs are in French)—garnishes the structure, while an alcove in its crumbling walls sheltered a straw pile. Was this someone's bed? Maybe—as at the tomb houses in Cairo's City of the Dead—someone living dwelled there, sleeping a few feet above the more soundly sleeping, entombed Coralie. The epitaph for Joseph Rondo (d. 1840) claims that "his faults he tried to correct, but not to hide," while the inscription for Charles Louis Schmaltz (d. 1799) informs us that he "received from Nature the happy gift of genius."

A curious tiny French enclave and memorial in a remote corner of New Zealand also serves to evoke France's failures in the East. Surrounded and dominated by Dutch-named and English-permeated New Zealand, the cemetery survives at the lovely little seaside village of Akaroa, located in French Bay on the southern part of the Banks Peninsula, fifty miles from Christchurch. In 1838 a French whaling captain named Langlois bought thirty thousand acres of Banks Peninsula from the Maoris, after which he returned to France where he persuaded merchants in Nantes and Bordeaux to lobby the admirality for support in colonizing the area. Investors formed the Nanto-Bordelaise company to develop the property, and on 8 March 1840 the *Comte de Paris* sailed from Rochefort carrying sixty emigrants. As at other places the French tried to colonize in the Far East, they competed with the British. Heavy winds prevented the *Comte de Paris* from landing in Akaroa harbor so on 9 August the ship anchored in a bay on the other side of Banks Peninsula, a delay which allowed the *Britomat* to reach Akaroa first, on 10 August. The following day the captain landed to claim British sovereignty over the area. In 1846 France formally recognized British sovereignty over all of New Zealand, so that little band of early French settlers represented not the vanguard of a colonial empire but only a historical dead end. The memory of these French expatriates survives in the so-called Old French Cemetery in Akaroa, not a burial ground with visible graves but simply an unattractive concrete monument on the site of the phantom graveyard. On the plaque appear such names as Mesdames Libeau, Pierre David, Le Vaillant, and Etéveneaux, and Monsieurs Fleuri, Rouslot, Jendrot and Captain Le Lievre. The notice also refers to "many other early settlers who rest in this burial ground, but whose graves were not identifiable when the government effected improvements in 1925. The earliest known burial took place in May 1842." Six of the settlers who arrived on the *Comte de Paris* were German, a reminder of the small role Germany played in Europe's colonial expansion.

That unstylish concrete marker scarcely detracts from the delightful surroundings where the colonists repose, for the monument stands on L'Aube Hill surrounded by pine trees. Birds and flowers spread their wings and scents in the air while the needled tree branches frame green hills that border the soft blue waters of Akaroa harbor below. A few delightful remnants of the tenuous French presence linger in that far corner of New Zealand. The Langlois-Etéveneaux House, built about 1842 and restored and furnished as a typical French colonial dwelling, somehow seems a bit lonely there in British New Zealand. Streets labelled rue Lavaud (on which the residence stands), rue Jolie, rue Benoit, rue Balguerie, and rue Croix—also shown on a second sign as Cross Street—lend an exotic touch.

The French enjoyed greater success in West Africa than in Asia. After the Napoleonic Wars ended in 1815, French merchants expanded their business activities in the area. As a result of more than a century of conflict with Britain, France had lost most of its holdings in America and Asia, leaving Africa as one of the few opportunities for overseas expansion. Between 1838 and 1842 a French naval officer named Bouet-Willaumez concluded treaties with African chiefs along the west coast, including Grand Bassam in the Ivory Coast, where in 1843 settlers from France built a fortified trading post. Near La Paillote restaurant and beach stands a statue inscribed (in French): "To her children deceased in the Ivory Coast—France."

In Ougadougou, capital of Upper Volta (later renamed Burkina Faso) I visited the local cemetery on evocatively named rue de le Chance, so-called, no doubt, because the national lottery office stood on that street. Perhaps mere chance led the French to that burial ground in the capital of

Upper Volta. At the entrance to the cemetery stand two square pillars, one topped with a cross, the other with a Muslim star and crescent. Most of the tombs in the graveyard, which occupies a relatively well shaded city block, bear a cross, witness to the European influence in the country. Lizards scurried as I made my way along the dusty paths. Almost all the tomb inscriptions were in French. Christiane Nagot (d. 1961) and Renee Perreux (d. 1966) served as missionaries, perhaps to good effect for Léberdé Miningou (d. 1975), so his epitaph relates, became the first representative of Upper Volta to the West African Bible Society. A metal plaque recalls John William Hall, born 30 January 1937, died 24 June that year, his six month existence ending far from Europe. (Little Johnny's brief existence recalls an eight-month-old's epitaph elsewhere: "Since I have been so quickly done for,/I wonder what I was begun for.") Near the Hall marker stands a large, blue-tiled tomb which houses Dominique Y. Koboré (d. 1972), minister of labor, first president of the Upper Volta Economic and Social Council and first secretary of the president's office. Koboré's tomb bears an oval photo of the official, but someone had lifted the large oval picture that once illustrated the monument to functionary Winkoun Hienu (d. 1963), head of administrative services at the Upper Volta Foreign Office, appropriately buried among foreigners. What looked like a nicely cut stone Cross of Malta decorated a tomb which bore the only English inscription I found: "Faithful unto death John Eric Booth-Clibborn, born Aug. 23, 1895; died July 8, 1924; eternally loved."

Across the Atlantic, France's colonial ambitions gained a toehold, but not much more, in South America at jungly French Guiana on the northeast coast. French Guinea gained fame, or perhaps notoriety, as the home of Devil's Island, the penal colony where Paris sent incorrigible criminals, political pariahs, and other undesirable characters to perspire and perhaps to expire in the tropical sun. One of the most remote cemeteries I have ever visited occupies a small enclave on St. Joseph's, a speck of land which, along with tiny Devil's and Royal islands, comprised the prison complex in the Atlantic. Two lines of the Paris *metro* speed you to Père Lachaise, but getting to the little cemetery on St. Joseph's presents more of a challenge. From Cayenne, capital of French Guiana, you need to proceed up the coast to the town of Kourou where, if you are lucky, someone will show up to pilot the boat from the mainland out to the iles du Salut. After a voyage of about an hour and a half you dock at ile Royale just by the administration building where officials once processed arriving convicts. Although the building no longer serves that function, the history which lingers there to this day lends the nondescript yellow structure a certain sinister air. Once you reach ile Royale, St. Joseph's looms close at hand: only the boat-ride across a few hundred yards of shark-infested waters separates you from the tiny island.

Like Père Lachaise and other typical French cemeteries the grave markers were arranged in regular rows, forming an orderly pattern which contrasted with the surrounding jungle's vegetal chaos. A few of the markers bore gargoyle-like figures which recalled the sculpted images on Paris's Notre Dame cathedral, but most of the monuments, cracked and weather-worn, had suffered from time and the severe tropical climate. The simple slabs carried only brief inscriptions (all in French) which furnished basic information without embellishment. One marker, the deceased's name effaced, read ". . . the 21 October 1894 at the age of 28 years, victim of duty," while another stated the cause of death as yellow fever: if overwork or the climate did not get you a tropical disease would. The graves at this isolated burial ground held only prison guards and their families. The functionaries at Devil's Island disposed of the prisoners' bodies another way. After a brief church service the deceased convict would be thrown into the sea as food for the sharks, which learned to associate the ringing of the church bell with the imminent appearance of a fresh cadaver. Former convict Henri Charrière—confined for a time in a cage-like solitary cell whose rusting remnants I also visited on St. Joseph's— recalled the shark feast in *Papillon,* his book about life, and death, at the penal colony:

> The corpse was wrapped in flour sacks and a rock attached to his feet by a strong cord . . . The corpse never had time to sink much below the surface. It soon bobbed up again and the sharks would begin to fight for the choicest pieces. They say that to watch a man being eaten by sharks leaves a lasting impression.

Weeks, months, and perhaps even years must pass without anyone traveling to that little cemetery to read the inscriptions and momentarily recall those expatriate Frenchmen who left their native land to work at the Devil's Island penal colony, where they left their bones. Ever under threat from the encroaching equatorial greenery, it recalls the abandoned expatriate graveyard on the island of Taboga off the Panama coast, described by Graham Greene in *Getting to Know the General:* "Somewhere buried in the jungle—but we couldn't find the path—was an English cemetery; its inhabitants could now be regarded as buried twice over." In fact, interment on an island seems an especially deadly fate. No passing stranger can happen upon an island cemetery, the sort of place reached only by a determined traveler. Cemeteries on islands seem emblematic of the dead's estrangement from the earth. Although John Donne held that no man is an island, in death everyone becomes an island, separated from the mainstream and isolated, completely removed from the land of the living. In that way an island interment represents a truly expatriate death, for the deceased reposes not only remote from life but also disconnected from the greater world that lies across the water.

Some of the most evocative island graves lie alone in complete isolation. Splendid in their solitude and remote in their island location, these lone burial sites seem more impressive than the most elaborate tombs found crowded among other monuments in Paris's Père Lachaise, London's Kensal Green, Vienna's Zentralfriedhof, and other vast metropolitan necropolises. Under two plum trees in the yard by Palapala Hoomau Church, near the remote village of Hana on the Hawaiian island of Maui, lies the grave of Charles A. Lindbergh (d. 1974). A low border of volcanic rock surrounds the plot which overlooks the Pacific Ocean. Lindbergh, buried in khaki trousers and a plain shirt, ordered the simplest possible coffin, made of eucalyptus wood. On the grave marker appear only the deceased's name; the notation: "Born Michigan 1902 Died Maui 1974"; and an epitaph taken from Lindbergh's writings: "If I take the wings of morning and dwell in the uttermost parts of the sea." A similar sea view spreads before you from the ramparts west of Iraklion on the Mediterranean island of Crete, where a solitary tomb set in the Martinengo bastion houses the remains of Nikos Kazantzakis (d. 1957), author of *Zorba the Greek,* and other works. Kazantzakis, exiled from the Orthodox church, wrote his own starkly simple but powerful epitaph: "I hope for nothing. I fear nothing. I am free."

Other islands hold expatriate cemeteries that are more populated than the one-tombers for Lindbergh and Kazantzakis, and less isolated than the remote burial grounds at Devil's Island and in Panama. At Ocracoke, a small island off the North Carolina coast, repose four Englishmen, crew members of HMS *Bedfordshire* who died in 1942 when a German submarine torpedoed the ship. The sailors, two identified and two unknown, lie in a small plot leased in perpetuity to the United Kingdom in 1976, where the coast guard raises the British flag over the graves every morning. This must be the only place in the world where United States

forces hoist the Union Jack. A plaque at the cemetery bears
the famous lines by English poet Rupert Brooke:

If I should die, think only this of me:
That there's some corner of a foreign field
That is forever England.

English expatriate dead occupy more than just a corner of a
foreign field at the Upper Barracca Gardens in Valetta, capital
of the island of Malta. These gardens furnish a delightful
setting for people to spend their eternity. A splendid view
spreads out from that high point. Between the pale blue sky
and the darker azure sea stretch the city's beige limestone
structures—a small smudge of human presence between the
two impersonal blue hues. Birds laze through the sky, boats
slither along the water near the harbor, idlers stroll through
the park. The markers present a veritable history text of
English colonial exploits: Lieutenant Commander E. E. Walters and Chief Engineer A. Baker of the *Ardent* were
"drowned in Saloniki harbour on the night of the 8th October 1899. Erected by their messmates"; Rinaldo Sceberras,
a captain killed December 21, 1845, at the Battle of Fer-
ozeshah in India; fifteen men (eight bear the first name
William) on the destroyer *Orwell* killed 30 January 1903 "in
the collision between that ship and H.M. ship 'Pioneer' off
Cape Varlam"; Sir Thomas Francis Fremantly (d. 1819), "vice
admiral of the Blue," commander of the British navy in the
Mediterranean; twenty-seven soldiers "fallen during the siege
of Malta 1940–1943." At the end of an arcade rises the area's
most elaborate monument, a column to Clement Edwards,
Lieutenant Colonel of the First Ceylon Regiment, who died
in Valetta aged thirty-six in March 1816 "after a protracted
and severe illness." Edwards, who served as military secretary to Sir Thomas Maitland, inspired the unusual biographical reference of "First Commissioner of the board he had

originally projected for auditing colonial accounts." Epitaphs seldom honor deceased auditors, but Edwards' inscription serves as a reminder that not even the dead escape an accounting. Accountant Edwards further merited a gracious inscription of praise: "Few could vie with him in usefulness of talent and fewer still possessed a heart more benevolent or disposition more social. He died in the prime of life but lived long enough to know how fully he had secured the respect of all good men."

Located as it is in the middle of the Mediterranean, the island of Malta has served over the centuries as a way-station for any number of sea-faring adventurers and travelers. By way of contrast, Easter Island, in the remote reaches of the Pacific, lies as far from the mainstream as anywhere on earth. That tiny speck of lava land rises out of the ocean some twenty-seven hundred miles to the east of Tahiti, and about an equal distance west of the South American coast. Across that nearly fifty-five hundred mile stretch of empty sea only Easter Island, which boasts what must be the world's most remote burial ground, is inhabited. Two island residents, both European expatriates, lie buried there, about as far from their native lands as it is possible to get without going into orbit. German missionary Father Sebastian Englert, who died in 1969 at the age of eighty, after many years of ministering to the islanders, reposes in a simple grave next to the church at Easter Island's only hamlet. Below his epitaph—"E mutahiti inohoai irroto ia matou/He vanaya ito matou rea"— appears a Spanish translation which states: "He lived among us for 33 years. He spoke our language." For a foreigner buried halfway around the earth from his home this sentiment seems the ultimate accolade. "He spoke our language," taken literally or figuratively, indicates the deceased lived among these people with deep comprehension of his adopted society. The expatriate, in effect, had found a second home.

Next to Father Sebastian reposes Father Eugène Eyraud,

the first missionary to live on Easter Island. A mechanic by trade, the Frenchman emigrated to Argentina where he worked to pay for his brother's studies for the priesthood. After the brother left to serve as a missionary in China, Eyraud settled in Chile. Two French priests who came to his shop advised the mechanic that he could become a missionary without taking holy orders, so Eyraud left Chile in 1862 and, via Tahiti, made his way to Easter Island where he arrived in January 1864 with his carpenter's tools, a barrel of flour, tree cuttings, five sheep, and a bell. Eyraud found the natives unfriendly and justifiably so, for not long before six Peruvian ships had captured a thousand of their compatriots as slaves for the guano deposits on the Chincha Islands, off the coast of Peru. In time, however, Father Eyraud (d. 1868) won the people's confidence and now he remains among them, his Spanish epitaph a succinct summary of his history: "Easter Island/To Brother Eugène Eyraud/Who, from being a mechanic, a workman with machines,/Became a workman for God,/And won this land/For Jesus Christ."

The two priests, Eyraud from France and German native Englert, represented the religious element of the European infiltration of the Far East. Various motivations—among them God, gold, greed, and just plain curiosity—inspired Europeans to travel to Asia. One of the first men to venture to the Far East with a religious mission was St. Thomas, who traveled to India to introduce Christianity to that far land. There is something anomalous about Thomas in India, for early Christianity mainly spread around the Mediterranean, infiltrating North Africa and Europe. An ancient apocryphal manuscript entitled "Acts of Judas Thomas the Apostle" relates that the apostles "divided the countries among them, in order that each one of them might preach in the region which fell to him and in the place to which the Lord sent him. And India fell by lot and division to Judas Thomas the Apostle." There he paid court to King Gondophares, a Parthian who

ruled India from 19 A.D. to about 45 A.D., a late survivor of
the Greek influence introduced into the region by Alexander
the Great in the fourth century B.C. Some scholars suggest
that Gondophares was Gaspar, a name derived from its Armenian version, "Gathaspar," one of the three wise men who
journeyed from the East to worship Christ at the Nativity. St.
Thomas died in 68 A.D. in India, far from his native land in
the Holy Land. One version of his death states that a brahmin
speared the apostle with a lance on St. Thomas' Mount, a hill
eight miles southwest of Madras, while that early European
tourist Marco Polo relates that a passing tribesman "shot an
arrow at a peacock, which struck the apostle in the side.
Finding himself wounded, he had time only to thank the
Lord for all his mercies, and into His hands he resigned his
spirit." Thomas reposes in Madras at the San Thome cathedral, a narrow rectangular slot cut into the marble slab that
covers his tomb in the church crypt. Although the missionary himself, the original Doubting Thomas, might have been
skeptical, I took it on faith that the saint reposed there—the
first expatriate missionary to carry the gospel to the East.

St. Thomas arrived in India fifteen centuries after the first
great wave of west-to-east migration took place when Aryan
tribes, ancestors of northern Europeans, entered northern
India. A millenium later Alexander the Great's invading armies introduced Greek culture and customs into India, the
first substantial European influence to reach the sub-continent. The earliest modern Europeans to explore the East
were the Portuguese, whose probings began when Vasco da
Gama arrived in India in the spring of 1498. The explorer
returned to Lisbon with enthusiastic reports of the area, and
by 1502 the Portuguese had established themselves at Cochin
on the southwest coast. Eight years later they captured Goa,
further up the west coast, where Alfonso de Albuquerque,
appointed viceroy of India, set up his headquarters. Religion
motivated much of the Portuguese push into Asia. Both da

Gama and Albuquerque hated Muslims. In 1502 Vasco da Gama destroyed a Muslim fleet at Calicut, near Cochin, and then added injury to insult by cutting off the noses, ears, and hands of some eight hundred Muslims. The explorer sent the pieces of flesh ashore with the suggestion they be used to make curry. During the sixteenth century the Portuguese continued their advance into the East, eventually reaching the Moluccas, or Spice Islands, for years a bone—or condiment—of contention between European powers who sought to secure a monopoly of the clove and nutmeg supply. The Portuguese also gravitated to the pepper-producing islands of Sumatra and Java.

In 1511 Albuquerque sailed from Goa and in August that year his forces conquered Malacca on the Malaysian peninsula, demolishing tombs of the hated Muslims in order to obtain building materials for a fort. That installation, called A Famosa, stood for 130 years until the Dutch destroyed it in 1641. The Porta de Santiago, one of the four stone gates of the original wall, still survives as does the roofless shell of St. Paul's Church—called Nossa Senhora do Monte when Lisbon controlled Malacca—which rises on a hill just above the gate. At the sanctuary temporarily reposed St. Francis Xavier, the Jesuit misisonary who followed the footsteps of St. Thomas in attempting to convert the East to Christianity. In 1553, shortly after his death, the saint's body was removed to Goa for permanent burial, but within the walls of St. Paul's at Malacca still remains a mesh-covered rectangular hole furnished with slots through which the devout can drop coins onto a slab above the niche where the holy body apparently once reclined. Outside the church stands a statue of St. Francis Xavier, shown clad in a long robe, head slightly bowed, left hand clutching a crucifix to his chest, his right hand missing, amputated by time or theft.

Other less saintly Portuguese lie buried in Malacca in the Christian cemetery at the edge of town. Such names as de

Souza, Rodrigues, Pereira, and de Mello abound. The short and wistful inscription for Louzia Pereira (d. 1970) reads: "Memories are treasures no one can steal." She perhaps lived at the Portuguese Settlement, a fishing community just outside Malacca established in the 1930s, where some six hundred people of Portuguese descent reside. Recent history revives at the grave of the Reverend Alvaro Martins Coroado (d. 1944), vicar of St. Peter's Church, who "died in Singapore, a victim of the Japanese, on 8th March 1944." On the monument appears a photo of the victim, who sported a thick, twin-pointed white beard. The good pastor's polyglot name reflects the spirited (though not spiritual) competition between the Dutch and the Portuguese in the Far East.

The Dutch sailed into southeast Asia not far behind the wakes left in the uncharted seas by the early Portuguese expeditions. Unlike the Portuguese, the Hollanders ventured East to gain wealth rather than converts: the founding fathers of the Dutch empire in Asia were merchants, not fathers of the church. By 1598, a century after Vasco da Gama's arrival in India, the Dutch had sent five fleets, totaling twenty-two ships, out to Asia. In December 1601 Dutch forces clashed with the Portuguese at Bantam, a port in northwestern Java. The Hollanders prevailed and gained a foothold on that huge island. In 1602 the Dutch government granted a monopoly on all commerce in Asia to the newly established United East India Company, and within three years a dozen expeditions, comprised of sixty-five ships in all, reached Malacca, where in the end Holland prevailed, which contains more relics of the Dutch era than of the Portuguese. When the Dutch restored the Porta de Santiago in 1670 they added over the arch a stone carved with the coat of arms of the Dutch East India Company. A plaque embedded in the wall of the delightful and very Dutch seventeenth-century, salmon-colored *Stadthuys* on Malacca's main square, recalls that the Vereenigde Ooost Indie Companie served as "the servant and pioneer of Holland in the East, founded—1602, dissolved—1795." What history inheres in that laconic inscription. Behind and above the *Stadthuys* stands St. Paul's, renamed by the Dutch after they captured Malacca in 1641: the spoils of victory include rechristening religious buildings. Along the walls of the church some splendid seventeenth-century Dutch grave slabs, embellished with elaborately carved relief escutcheons, recall the presence of the merchants and military forces from Holland. On the ground, not far from St. Francis Xavier's crypt, a plain stone marks the "grave of Frau van Riebeck wife of John van Riebeck, founder of Cape Colony. The original grave stone was removed to Cape Town in 1905." But the Dutch colonization of South Africa is another story with other expatriate graves to revive the days of empire.

In the early seventeenth century the Dutch quickly spread over southeast Asia, mainly at Portuguese expense, finally sending their fleet based at Batavia (now Jakarta) in Java north to blockade the Straits of Malacca. Famine soon weakened the Portuguese outpost, and in January 1641 Malacca fell into the hands of the Dutch.

The fall of Malacca marked the end of any significant Portuguese presence in the Far East. Now the Dutch began to dominate the area, with Batavia serving in the seventeenth century as the nerve center of Holland's Asian empire. In Jakarta the Zion Church, still known as the Portuguese church, presents a picture out of old-time Holland, miles and years from the glorious days of Dutch empire. A graceful, reddish tile roof tops the whitewashed walls, punctured by large arched windows and smaller arched doorways, while a pair of picturesque lanterns flank the main entrance. When you enter the sanctuary you enter a completely Dutch enclave: from the ceiling hang four brass, Vermeer-ish chandeliers, dark wood chairs with carved cherub backs fill the nave, and below the elaborate pipe organ in the loft appears the phrase "Jesus Keristus Hidup!" Jesus Christ may not live right there, but Holland definitely does. A set of three splendid wooden markers on the wall beneath the organ loft recall the early Hollanders who ventured out to Batavia. These plaques, some eight feet high, bear inscriptions framed by escutcheon devices. One memorial commemorates Isaac Reynst (d. 1775), another recalls Louisa van Cotzhuisen (d. 1805), while the third, to Cristina Elisabet Marci, tells us her age with great specificity: "Obiit den 7 january anno 1805 oud 34 laaren 8 maanden 9 dagen." More old Dutch funeral markers, well-carved and richly crested gravestone slabs, line a corridor of the National Museum in Jakarta, not far from Zion Church. One such tombstone reads: "Hier Legt Begraven . . . Den Hoog Edelen Heere Gustaaff Willem Baron van Imhoff [1750] General Over de Infanteryi." (Here lies interred the most noble Gustav William Baron Van Imhoff, General of the Infantry.)

The Dutch-style Wolvendaal Church in Colombo, Sri Lanka (formerly Ceylon), which greatly resembles Jakarta's Zion Church, also houses memorials to the early settlers from Holland who established commercial connections with the Far East. It was Jan Pieterszoon Coen—appointed governor-general of the Dutch East Indies in 1618 and founder of Holland's naval and administrative capital for the region at Batavia—who transformed a scattering of trading posts into a chain of strongholds that greatly increased Dutch influence in the area. In 1658 Coen's successors expelled their Portuguese rivals from Ceylon, where they had gained a toehold in 1506 by exacting from the king of Kandy a tribute of cinnamon and ivory in exchange for protection against his enemies. A wooden memorial plaque of the type also found at Zion church in Jakarta hangs at Wolvendaal to commemorate Christiane Elisabeth van Angelbeek (d. 1792), wife of "Willem Jacob van de Graaff . . Gouveneur en Direkteur van Ceilon." In *De Wolvendaal Kerk,* published in 1957, R. L.

Brohien comments on these elaborate historic markers: "The story of those to be seen in the Wolvendaal Church alone would make an entrancing book. On the mass of these tombstones raised to the memory of the departed a great measure of skill was spent. The carving was obviously done in Holland or by specially trained craftsmen in Ceylon." After many bodies were removed in 1813 from the old Dutch church in the fort area of Colombo, Brohien recounts, "the tombstones pertaining to the distinguished persons whose remains were re-interred, were in due course also removed to the Wolvendaal and laid over the new vaults." Thus, more than three centuries of history lie under the artfully carved tombstones which pave the church floor.

A church called St. Peter's in the fort area of Colombo once formed part of the Dutch governor's residence where, perhaps, Jacob van de Graaff once lived. St. Peter's now functions as an Anglican church, reflecting the English succession to Dutch control in Ceylon, which began in the late eighteenth century. St. Peter's typifies the hundreds of monument-filled Anglican churches scattered throughout Asia, the sanctuaries themselves monuments to England's long-standing dominance in the region. Early English exploration companies, anticipating a high mortality rate among their personnel at remote outposts of empire, would ballast outgoing vessels with blank sandstone slabs which could eventually serve as grave markers. Perhaps stones such as those number among the markers which, along with wall memorial plaques, endow St. Peter's in Colombo with mini-histories of a few of the English settlers who served there. One marker recalls George Rivers Maltby (d. 1820) "whose life was unfortunately terminated in the 24th year of his age by a fall from his horse in the neighbourhood of Colombo." Violent death frequently lurked: William Wright (d. 1886) died "from injuries received on being thrown from his carriage ten days previously"; Charles Wallett (d. 1838) "was killed by an elephant." A fellow named William Tolfrey (d. 1817) was "called from his unfinished task" at age thirty-nine, the task of "rendering the Holy Scriptures into the Singhalese and Pali languages." And then there was the sad death of Lieutenant John Gore, "only son of Vice-Admiral Sir John Gore, K.C.B. who, during the voyage home in his Father's Flag-Ship 'the Melville' from their station, perished heroically in an unsuccessful attempt to save the life of a Brother Sailor, off Algoa Bay, on the 30th April, 1885." A poignant short story lies between the lines of that brief inscription: the admiral father watches from the bridge as his only boy drowns while trying to save his buddy. Funeral markers often present such vivid vignettes from life—necro-dramas.

The English took control of Sri Lanka, which they ruled for 133 years, after deposing the king of Kandy in 1815. Sweetly named Kandy nestles in a lovely verdant, hilly area in the center of the island not far from the highlands, terraced with tea plants. The pleasant town's most famous mausoleum, the Temple of the Tooth, houses a relic from the mouth of the Great Lord Buddha himself but even more relics from the English days survive in Kandy. One such throwback to colonial times is Kandy's creaky old Queen's Hotel, one of those imperial hostelries—like Raffles in Singapore, the Strand in Rangoon, Dean's in Peshawar, the Galle Face in Colombo—where you expect to see characters from Somerset Maugham lounging about the lobby or emerging from the antique, cage-like lift. Roads in Kandy named after the wives of former British governors and St. Paul's, an angular Anglican brick sanctuary that looks like an English village church, also lend touches of the home country. Memorial plaques inside St. Paul's, however, quickly reveal that the church stands not in England but in a far off outpost of the empire. Monuments to colonial functionaries and military personnel abound: Henry Templer, assistant government agent at Matelle, "cut off by disease incidental to the climate in 1851," whose marker was erected by "influential natives of the district"; Henry Simon Potyer, drowned at Trincomalie in 1886 "whilst returning home from duty"; Captain James Armar Butler (d. 1854) of the curiously named Half Pay Ceylon Rifle Regiment; Sergeant Peter Roland Strand (d. 1934), for thirty-two years a member of the more romantically named Ceylon Planters Rifle Corps; Lieutenant Colonel Thomas Fletcher, his marble relief monument showing a grieving figure kneeling beneath the curve of a bent palm tree: "After thirty-five years of civil and military duties in Ceylon, he retired, and died at Malta on the 8th March 1846, age 60, when returning to his native land"; and George Turnour (d. 1843), neither an administrator nor a soldier but a man of the mind whose "profound acquaintance with the ancient Pali language [combined] the accomplishments of a gentleman, the erudition of a scholar, and the piety of a Christian."

The Garrison Cemetery, another repository of the English presence in Kandy, lies not far from St. Paul's Church. The graveyard, hidden in an obscure corner of town, spreads across a gently rising bowl of land reached by a climbing, curving road overgrown with grass that dead-ends at a gate. The tombstones, which offered a great variety of shapes and designs, preserve stories of such offbeat deaths as those suffered by A. McGill (d. 1873) "who was killed by the falling of Mullegodde House, Kandy, August 18th 1861." The most famous name buried at the cemetery must be Christopher Wren (d. 1867), whose namesake—the famous London architect—might well have applied his professional skills to shore up Mullegodde House. The best-known grave houses Sir John D'Oyly, Bart. (d. 1824), "one of the members of His Majesty's Council of this island," supposedly the first British resident in Kandy, where he lived for twenty-two years. The Kandy museum, not far from the cemetery, displays Sir John's leather riding crop.

As I strolled around the cemetery keeper accompanied me and commented on some of the graves. Proud of his domain, Carl Gunatilaka complained about the vandals who had tumbled tombstones, ripped off brass plaques to sell as scrap metal, and stolen iron pickets from a fence. Warming to my interest in his burial ground, Carl disappeared into his cottage and soon returned with a survey plan of the cemetery prepared in May 1914. It platted the plots and listed the dead from #1, James Edwin McGlashan—who died in 1817, the first to be buried there—up to #163, George Sieble. Next to some of the names listed appeared the forlorn notation, "(not found)," a parenthetical aside that struck me as especially mournful—buried abroad and completely disappeared.

Carl showed me a guest book which contained only a dozen or so entries over about a two year period: as I had suspected from Carl's warm welcome, visitors were scarce at Garrison. Comments in the book reflected two different types of cemetery visitors: those who came for personal reasons and those rather curious kinds of characters drawn there by their interest in graveyards. An entry by a man from Armonk, New York, stated that "I came here to see my grandmother's grave." After commenting on the good condition of the cemetery the man concluded, "I did not find her grave." A girl with an English name from the Kodaikanal School in Tamil Nadu, India, wrote: "I enjoy wandering old cemeteries. Though no relatives of mine are buried here, I found it interesting." She took the words out of my pen.

All over the Far East I wandered through old cemeteries where expatriate English from the days of empire repose. You could write a history of the British colonization of Asia through monuments to the people buried in these graveyards. Here repose the pioneers who traveled "east of Suez" to serve the Crown. Back in those halcyon colonial days the English were everywhere, criss-crossing the globe. In *Eothen* A. W. Kinglake tells a delicious story about the time he was traveling across a remote corner of the Arabian desert when he espied approaching in the distance an English military man returning from a posting in India. As they drew closer "it became a question with me whether we should speak . . . I was quite ready to be as sociable and chatty as I could be according to my nature; but still I could not think of anything in particular that I had to say to him . . . and I felt no great wish to stop and talk like a morning visitor, in the midst of those broad solitudes. The traveller perhaps felt as I did, for, except that we lifted our hands to our caps, and waved our arms in courtesy, we passed each other quite as distantly as if we had passed in Pall Mall." Thus did Kinglake contradict in practice the view propounded by English essayist William Hazlitt in "On Going A Journey": "I should not feel confident in venturing on a journey in a foreign country without a companion. I should want at intervals to hear the sound of my own language . . . A person would almost feel stifled to find himself in the deserts of Arabia without friends and countrymen." Hazlitt concludes that he might well wish "to spend the whole of my life in traveling abroad if I could any—where borrow another life to spend afterwards at home." The English who settled in their nation's far-flung colonial possessions had but one life to give to their country, and thus—far from home—they lived and died. Although once upon a time the sun never set on the British Empire, these days it never rises on it. But the sun still never sets on the empire's cemeteries.

The English in a certain measure followed in the footsteps of the Dutch in the Far East. In once-Dutch Malacca, they converted the Hollanders' Christ Church, built in 1753, to an Anglican sanctuary which came to house English expatriate dead such as Mrs. Mary Betty (d. 1800), Norman Ken Bain, nicknamed Inky (d. 1955), and the Reverend William Milne (d. 1822): "the chief object of his labours . . . was the translation of the earliest Protestant version of the Holy Scriptures in Chinese." In the cemetery adjacent to the church repose such Englishmen as the well-traveled John Harrison (d. 1922), born in Barbados "the only son of Sir John and Lady Harrison of British Guiana." Even Jakarta in Indonesia, often thought to have been controlled only by the Dutch, boasts an English church, a small sanctuary in a pleasant garden where tombstones memorialize a number of British expatriates. Among them are James Bowen, Esq. (d. 1812) captain of the *Phoenix,* who died "in consequence of a Disease brought on by his exertions at an attack on a Powerfull Pirate at Sambasse"; Eleanor Hewitson, who expired in 1814 "after a Lingering Illness of 7 Months"; and William Barrett (d. 1814), whose epitaph concludes with the warning, "Reader reflect!!! Prepare to follow me/For the next grave that's made may be for thee." I briefly reflected, then left the peaceful churchyard behind. Outside whizzed Jakarta's lethal traffic which almost prepared me for the cemetery's next grave.

As Christ Church recalls, for a time the British ruled Indonesia, a somewhat forgotten interlude of Asian history. By the early nineteenth century the Dutch United East India Company's charter had expired, leaving England's East India Company free to acquire control of Indonesia. Dutch influence in the Far East faltered in the wake of their defeat by Robert Clive near Calcutta in 1759, virtually eliminating them from India; a British blockade in 1780 severed ship traffic between the East Indies and Holland, nearly bankrupting the United Dutch East India Company; and the English captured Dutch Malacca in 1795. These developments in colonial territories mirrored the situation in Europe, for continental rivalries frequently influenced events abroad. When Napoleon conquered Holland in 1806 and elevated his brother Louis to the Dutch throne, this defeat sapped the country's power in the Far East. Only in 1816, after Napoleon's defeat, did the Dutch regain control of Indonesia from the English, so provoking the disappointed British lieutenant governor in Java, Stamford Raffles, to search for another trading center and transshipment port for goods to and from China. Raffles proceeded to buy from the Sultan of Johore a barren island off the coast of Malaysia, and on 29 January 1819 the Union Jack rose over the new colony of Singapore, one of the last British settlements established in the East.

The English adventure in the East can be said to have begun nearly three-and-a-half centuries earlier in 1579, when Sir Francis Drake visited the Moluccas, the Spice Islands, on his voyage around the world. For years spice had enticed Europeans to the Moluccas, for each country wanted to monopolize the supply. In 1520 the Portuguese established outposts in the Spice Islands. In 1522 Magellan—Portuguese by birth, Spanish by profession—became the first to carry cloves directly from the islands to Europe when his *Victoria* put in at the Moluccas on the world's first circumnavigation. (Magellan thus managed to accomplish what his Spanish-sponsored predecessors had attempted, for the purpose of Columbus's 1492 expedition had been to discover a direct route to the Spice Islands.) In 1596 the Dutch traded at the Moluccas during their first expedition to the East.

In 1579, the year Drake showed the British flag in the Far East for the first time, the English began to infiltrate Portuguese territory when Thomas Stephens, the first of his countrymen to settle in India, became rector of the Jesuit college in Goa. The English incorporated the East India Company in 1600, two years before the Dutch United East India Company was founded. The British soon began to crowd the Dutch by establishing a trading post at Bantam on Java. In 1619 the Dutch, led by Jan Pieterszoon Coen, their able young governor-general, forced the English out and then proceeded to develop their fortress at Jacatra into the settlement of Batavia, later called Jakarta. Thwarted in Indonesia, the English turned their attentions to India where their efforts proved more successful. In 1639 Francis Day procured from a Hindu raja a small parcel of land where the Englishman constructed a fortified trading area which he named Fort St. George. Around this installation grew the city of Madras.

St. Mary's Church in Madras survives within the Fort St. George compound as a storehouse of British history in India. A notice states that the sanctuary was "built by the East India Company and consecrated in 1680. St. Mary's is the oldest Anglican church east of Suez." Memorials inside the building recall some of the perils faced by the early colonists: Captain Rochfort (d. 1847) died at the nominally optimistic Cape of Good Hope, while others succumbed to the rigors of an Indian summer: Josiah Webbe (d. 1804) "disdaining the little arts of private influence or vulgar popularity . . . he fell a martyr to an uncongenial climate"; Malcolm McNeill (d. 1852), who died in Rangoon "from the effect of a *coup-de-soleil*"; and the odd case of Lieutenant Colonel W. H. Atkinson (d. 1858), who found it impossible to adjust to another kind of heat, for "the change of climate required by a service of 32 years having been deferred till too late a season, he sank under the intense heat of the Red Sea, and died within a few days after his retirement, whilst on his passage to England." Another peculiar case involved the Reverend Christian William Gericke (d. 1803), who was "destined to labour in a peculiar vineyard (that of the conversions of the natives of India)."

Similarly evocative markers from the days of empire fill the St. Mary's churchyard, almost entirely paved with inscribed gravestones which offer history underfoot. Off to the right as you enter the side gate lie some thirty slabs, decorated with flourishing script, crests, skull and crossbone emblems, and other carved motifs. The years have caused many of the inscriptions to fade into obscurity, now but faint praises which survive only as vague curly designs on the time-worn stones, littered with leaves and stained by bird droppings. A typical inscription to a colonial functionary reads: "Here Lyeth William Warre Esqr who haveing serv'd the Honourable Company in severall stations, Dyed while he was Third of Council in Fort St. George on the 6th of May 1715." On the left side of the yard some sixty gravestones pave the ground. One commemorates Anne Fowke "who, after haveing lived with her husband Randall Fowke near Twenty one years: with a Character irreproachable, blameless and unspotted, departed this life on Saturday the 3d of August 1734." And whatever became of Randall, husband of that woman of unspotted character? I read on: "Likewise the body of Randall Fowke" reposes there, at rest (d. 1745) after forty years of toil for the East India Company and adjudged "An Honest Man." Another small stone, perhaps a fragment, bears two misshapen skull motifs, grotesquely and grimly grinning, along with three sets of crossbones and the legend: "The house appointed for all living."

The venerable gravestones at Madras recall the city's past as much by their own history as by their inscriptions. "Along the North side of the Church, and extending around part of the East and West sides, are a number of ancient gravestones which were taken from the old graveyard, and put in their present position about 1763," relates the guidebook for St. Mary's Church, published in 1967. In the original graveyard, situated where the High Court and law college now stand, reposes Elihu Yale's son David, who married Catherine Hinmers at St. Mary's. The British dismantled the old cemetery after the French siege of Madras in January and February 1759. Following the battle John Call, chief engineer, wrote to the authorities: "But above all I must beg leave to mention that we lately suffered great inconveniences from the tombs at the burying ground, which being large and arched structures, placed in a line almost close to each other, and opening into one another, not only protected the enemy from our shot, but afforded them a cover equally safe against our shells." The guidebook continues: "On the receipt of this letter, Government ordered the large tombs in the old burying place to be demolished, and in 1763 a new graveyard was opened on the Island [a small parcel of land behind Fort St. George formed by two branches of the river Cooum]. This is the St. Mary's graveyard which was used for burials until the year 1852. The slabs, or so many of them as could be removed, were brought to St. Mary's and formed into the pavement round the church. In 1782 during Hyder's [Hyder Ali, the ruler of Mysore] invasion, they were removed and used to mount the guns round the Fort. They were replaced in 1807, but many of them had been broken." What a functional cemetery this old Madras burial ground was. First moved and then removed to serve as gun emplacements, the graveyard participated in the area's history much as did the English colonists who repose there.

Although St. Mary's in Madras has managed to stay open for a few parishioners, the St. Mary's in Varanasi (Benares) seemed no longer to serve a congregation. That St. Mary's remained closed during my stay so I never saw the interior which likely contains memorials to the departed English, but the churchyard has a few forlorn grave markers. Near the wall across from Clark's Hotel rises a stubby Grecian column that indicates the grave of Major General James Alexander (d. 1847), "late in command of the Benares Division of the Bengal Army . . . [This] monument of his valued worth is raised by his afflicted son." On the opposite side of the yard, behind the church, stand five other markers including one to Ensign David Septimus Bech (d. 1855) "who was accidentally drowned near Mhaw"; a second to Major Francis Smalpage (d. 1838), also drowned; a third, which serves triple duty by commemorating Lieutenants John Stalker, Arch'd Scott, and Jeremiah Symes, "massacred at Sewalah on the 16th day of Aug'st 1781, Tho Erected by the Hand of Friendship Shall offer no praise which themselves might blush to read"; and another collective monument "erected over the remains of XII bodies removed from the Old City Burial Ground to this spot, the 10th January 1829 by James Prinsep."

Renowned as a cemetery city, Benares gains its funerary fame not from those few lonesome expatriate tombs at St. Mary's but, as mentioned at the end of the last chapter, for the Ganges. Into that sacred river Hindus cast the ashes of cremated bodies burned on funeral pyres at ghats along the water's edge. The cantonment, the old-time English enclave at Varanasi, seems a world apart from scenes down by the river. Log fires on the ghats burn fiercely, searing the already hot air and crumpling it into little warped nimbuses that surround the flames. On primitive stretchers nearby lie the corpses, covered with colorful cloths. Stacks of logs to fuel the fires rise by the bank. Large, woven-leaf umbrellas cast pools of round shade at irregular intervals. The ceremony begins when attendants take the body from the bier and immerse it in holy water before placing the corpse on the pyre where they smear it with ghee, clarified butter. Then the chief mourner, usually the deceased's oldest son, lights the pyre, at the head for a man or the foot for a woman. The mourners gaze in silence at the burning body as they watch and listen for the burst of the skull, a sign that the soul, trapped within, has been released. After the cremation, the family gathers at the ghat to collect the bones, which they cast into the sacred river to ensure the passage of the deceased into the next world.

Although the soul may flutter away from this earth, the bones would eventually float downstream to the swampy Ganges delta and on out to the Bay of Bengal near Calcutta, a major early outpost of the British Empire. A half-century after Francis Day acquired the first British territory in India at Madras in 1639, Job Charnock established a fortified base at Calcutta against the fading Moghul Empire. In the churchyard of St. John's Church in Calcutta stands an odd-looking eight-sided, cream yellow structure with a hint of Moorish influence, known as Job Charnock's Monument. This bears a marker to Calcutta's founder (d. 1692) as well as to such other early English expatriates as Martha Eyles (d. 1748) who "concluded this life with a becoming resignation," and William Hamilton (d. 1717) whose "Memory ought to be dear to this Nation for the Credit he gained ye English in curing Ffrrukseer the present King of Indostan, of a Malignant Distemper." A memorial plaque inside St. John's commemorates another medical practitioner, one Michael Cheese (d. 1816), a surgeon whose assistance to indigent patients is briefly summarized: "Mr. Cheese supplied the means." The unfortunate George Cracroft Aubert expired too suddenly for Cheese to provide the means: "On the evening of the 29th of April 1843, riding homeward from the residence of a friend, was overtaken by a sudden storm, and, with the horse which bore him, was struck dead by lightning." On the other hand, Henrietta Anderson (d. 1857) suffered no lightning-fast death but succumbed gradually "from the sheer want of proper nutriment during the siege of Lucknow."

St. John's, which stands in the spacious park that affords a pleasant oasis in the center of Calcutta, resembles Wren's great St. Stephen of Walbrook, in the City of London. Around the large yard which surrounds St. John's stand a scattering of graves. William Speke, son of the captain of the *Kent,* "left his leg and life in that Ship at the Capture of Fort Orleans the 24th of March Anno 1757" at age eighteen. Frances Johnson enjoyed a longer and fuller life from 1725 to 1812, surviving a series of spouses: in 1738 she married Parry Purple Templer; then, James Altham "who died of the Small Pox a few Days after the Marriage"; next, William Watts; then the Reverend William Johnson. Frances herself succumbed at the age of eighty-seven, "the oldest British resident in Bengal."

Back by the rear wall in St. John's churchyard stands a memorial recalling one of history's most famous mass entombments—the Black Hole of Calcutta. This live burial took place in an eighteen-square-foot prison room in Fort William where one hundred and forty-five Englishmen and one woman were jailed after surrendering to the nabob of Bengal's troops, who had marched on Calcutta in an effort to evict the British from the city. Fort William stood on a site now occupied in part by the Calcutta General Post Office building on Dalhousie Square. The memorial at St. John's, removed from the original site of the tragedy, includes an eight-sided pillar that rises above a base inscribed: "This Monument Has been erected by Lord Curzon, Viceroy and Governor-General of India, In the year 1902 Upon the site And in reproduction of the design Of the original monument To the memory of the 123 persons who perished in the Black Hole prison of old Fort William On the night of the 20th of June, 1756. The former memorial was raised by their surviving fellow sufferer, J. Z. Holwell, Governor of Fort William, On the spot where the bodies of the dead Had been thrown into the ditch of the ravelin. It was removed in 1821." Another plaque adds that the present monument was installed at St. John's in 1940 and that the names inscribed on the marker "are in Excess of the list recorded by Governor Holwell . . . [They] Have been recovered from oblivion by reference to contemporary documents." Of course, when all is said and done and time has worked its ways epitaphs "are cold consolations," for "the iniquity of oblivion scatterth her poppy and deals with the memory of men without distinction to merit of perpetuity," wrote Sir Thomas Browne in "Urne-Buriall," (1658) his great essay on the history of burial practices. All, all falls into oblivion—time's gravitational force that eventually pulls everything into its nothingness—but gravestones and funerary memorials, and perhaps even a cemetery book, can for a fleeting moment salvage a fragment of the past.

The most ghost-ridden corner of Calcutta's colonial past survives at the spooky South Park Street Cemetery, described by Geoffrey Moorehouse in *Calcutta* as a burial ground filled with "sad and heavily decayed relics which are now piebald with exposed brickwork and lingering cement." I spent a pleasant afternoon there, swishing through the overgrown weeds and roaming among the faded and broken stones, many discolored by the elements and seemingly suffering from a kind of lapidary impetigo. There used to be a North Park Street Cemetery as well, apparently located just across the street, where the father of novelist William Makepeace Thackeray was buried. "Never say die," is my motto when searching for a graveyard or a hard-to-find tomb, but North Park Street Cemetery was buried somewhere beneath contemporary Calcutta and I never found it: even entire cemeteries sooner or later fade into oblivion.

A sign at South Park Street Cemetery states that the burial ground was "Opened 1767 Closed 1790," a short lease on life for a graveyard but long enough to receive a large selection of illustrious English expatriates who lived in Calcutta, far from their little island homeland. The date of the graveyard's founding recalls that the very earliest modern European cemeteries—free-standing, unattached to churches, garnished with plantings, sporting individualized tombs and personalized epitaphs—originated not in nineteenth-century Europe but in European colonies: British India and French New Orleans.

The French established the first such graveyards in New Orleans in 1721. St. Louis Cemetery Number 1, which began receiving in 1789, still survives as a treasure trove of New Orleans history. Even earlier, Europeans had opened modern-style cemeteries in India. The tombstone for John Mildenhall (d. 1614) in the Christian cemetery at Agra is the oldest known English funerary monument in India. Mildenhall traveled through the Middle East to India where from 1603 to 1605 he attached himself to the court of the great Mogul, Akbar. From the ruler Mildenhall attempted to win trading concessions for England, an effort the Portuguese Jesuits opposed. When Mildenhall returned to London he found that both the East India Company and the king remained completely indifferent to his efforts on behalf of England, so in 1611 Mildenhall organized a private commercial venture in the East, where he fell sick at Lahore and died at Ajmere in 1614.

In the mid-1600s the English and other Europeans established outside Surat in India a cemetery with large mausoleums, some—such as the one for Christopher (d. 1659) and Sir George (d. 1669) Oxinder, the "most brotherly of brothers"—sporting domes and minaret-like towers, along with pointed windows and doorways that reflected the influence of India's Moghul funerary architecture. In the Dutch section at Surat rises a mausoleum to Henry Adriano Baron van Reede (d. 1691), a rather ponderous, many-columned construction with a cupola rising above an octagonal base. This and other late-seventeenth-century memorials replaced the monuments to early settlers levelled by the Dutch to make room for new and more imposing mausoleums, some put up by builders imported from the Netherlands.

In the seventeenth century Danes erected baroque tombs at their Tranquebar settlement, while as early as 1680 pyramids marked graves of other Europeans in India. Only more than half a century later, in 1742, did the first substantial solitary, free-standing tomb since the days of antiquity appear in the West—the huge, column-encircled mausoleum, designed by Nicholas Hawksmoor, at Castle Howard in Yorkshire.

The English founded the Park Street burial ground to receive casualties of the "sick season," the summer period when many Europeans succumbed to the oppressive Calcutta heat. Obelisks, pyramids, columns, mausoleums, and other constructions cram the venerable cemetery, a Père Lachaise or

Kensal Green of the East. Some in fact originated in England, for the expatriate community often ordered monuments from the home country. Gradually the cemetery grew into an English village of the dead. Kipling noted in *The City of Dreadful Night* that "the eye is ready to swear that it is as old as Herculaneum or Pompeii. The tombs are small houses. It is as though we walked down the streets of a town, so tall are they and so closely do they stand . . . strong man, weak woman, or somebody's infant son aged 15 months—it is all the same. For each the squat obelisk, the defaced classic temple . . . the candlestick of brickwork—the heavy slab, the rust-eaten railings, the whopper-jawed cherubs and apoplectic angels."

The most renowned figure buried at South Park Street Cemetery gained her fame as the idealized and idolized subject of Walter Savage Lander's well-known poem, "Rose Aylmer":

> Ah, what avails the sceptered race?
>   Ah, what the form divine?
> What every virtue, every grace?
>   Rose Alymer, all were thine.
> Rose Aylmer, whom these wakeful eyes
>   May weep, but never see,
> A night of memories and of sighs
>   I consecrate to thee.

Rose later died rather unromantically, from overeating on pineapples. A corkscrew-like pillar rises over a pedestal which bears the inscription: "In Memory of the Honorable [sic] Rose Whitworth Aylmer Who Departed This Life March The 2nd A.D. 1800 Age 20 years/What was her fate? Long, long before her hour, death called her tender soul, by break of bliss, from the first blossoms, from the buds of joy, those few our noxious fate unblasted leaves in this inclement clime of human life." Below those rather convoluted senti-

ments appear the remains of gold letters that form eerie
fragments of the stanza quoted above:

Wha—
  Ro—
A night—
  I con—

Beneath these ghostly remnants the poet's truncated name
forms an odd cluster: "—alter Savage—." Life is short and art
is long, so the ancient Romans held, but at Rose Aylmer's
tomb art, too, seems mortal: even poetry has begun to de-
compose.

Although cemeteries usually vitalize me, it made me melancholy to reflect on the nearly vanished poem. Not only was
Rose Aylmer gone, and Lander as well, but also the poet's
creation. The effaced stanza seemed to mock all efforts to
transcend oblivion. Nor did the cemetery's monuments offer
any hope, for all around—in that uncared-for and uncared-
about European cemetery in India—were decaying stones
which had been meant to memorialize the decaying dead. On
the branches of the trees perched ugly black crows which
picked through the garbage heaps that litter Calcutta's streets,
in competition with the women and children who also rum-
mage through the debris. Not far away reposed a few Indians, alive but deathly thin, who apparently inhabited the
old graveyard. Somehow the long-gone expatriates who lie at
Calcutta's unkempt English cemetery seemed to me more
dead than the departed who populate other less-melancholy
burial grounds. For at least a century the venerable graveyard
has been crumbling away. In *Echoes From Old Calcutta,* published there in 1897, H. E. Busteed remarked on "the passive
neglect which meets one at every step through the Christian
cemeteries of Calcutta." The deterioration seemed to make
the burial grounds all the more forlorn for "those who died in

exile, in a country where the European from his very arrival, looks and pines for the day when he may" return home. But there they remain, forever confined to that foreign terrain. Even the tombs seemed moribund. The South Park Street Cemetery boasts a truly world-class funereal atmosphere.

Just across from Rose Aylmer's pillar stands the so-called Juno Monument, an obelisk with relief anchors carved on three sides. Only those nautical motifs suggest the tale that lies behind, or under, the tomb for the small remaining piece of the slate plaque bears no more than the cryptic letters and numbers "ACKAY" and "04." These mysterious signs once related the name and death year of Captain William Mackay, who perished in 1804. At the end of May 1795 the freighter *Juno* left Rangoon for Madras with a load of timber and seventy-two people aboard, including Captain Mackay, the second mate. On leaving Rangoon the ship ran partly aground, springing a leak which grew worse when heavy gales hit. The vessel was finally submerged but, thanks to the cargo of buoyant timber, did not sink. For a time the passengers clung tenaciously to rigging and anything else that remained above water as the wrecked ship drifted along the Pegu coast, but one by one, they fell into the sea. The *Juno* drifted ashore on 13 July by which time there were some fourteen survivors, among them Captain Mackay, who two years later wrote an account of the shipwreck. Young Lord Byron, while still a student at Dr. Glennie's school in Dulwich, read the story and later drew on it to create the shipwreck scenes in the second canto of his epic poem "Don Juan." Thus did Byron transmute life into art, and so does this monument in a Calcutta cemetery bear faint echoes of his verse.

Unlike Rose Aylmer's memorial and the Juno Monument, with their echoes of English literature, most of the tombs at Park Street recall British history, especially the course of empire. Various members of the colonial cadre buried at

South Park encapsulate the British era in India: the businessman—William Beckford Gordon (d. 1817), "senior merchant" for the East India Company; the administrator—James Taylor (d. 1839), "assistant of the Secret and Political Department"; the jurist—John Hyde (1796), a puisne judge of the Supreme Court at Calcutta, "a firm and zealous friend . . . and a truly virtuous man"; the soldier—Edward Gordon (d. 1833), "for several years commandant of the military escort of His Highness the Nizam of Hyderabad." A steep, palm tree-high pyramid, a copy of Caius Cestius' pyramid by the Protestant Cemetery in Rome, marks the grave of "Elizabeth Jane Barwell ('The Celebrated Miss Sanderson') Married the 13th September 1776 to Richard Barwell Esqr. (The Friend of [India's first governor-general] Warren Hastings), Member of Council of the Hon. East India Co. Died the 9th November 1778, Aged About 23 Years."

Epitaphs of other exiles recall them for their personal rather than their colonial qualities: Lawrence Hall (d. 1806), "a very-very good son"; Elizabeth Ricketts (1794–1824): "Her short but eventful Life was passed in the strict performance of every Duty" as a child, wife, sister; and Mary Eliza Fagan (d. 1865), "Pause o'er the tomb of one whose untimely end, did not prevent her having discharged in a manner eminently exemplary, the duties of all those various relations of life." Major General Charles "Hindoo" Stuart (d. 1828), an Irishman captivated by Indian culture, reposes in a tomb resembling a mini-temple, with an onion-shaped dome and mask-like Oriental faces decorating it. A long eulogy to Charles Weston (d. 1809) includes among his many accomplishments the "wise and economical management of a Fortune far from enormous," and concludes: "READER This stone is no flatterer: Go, and do thou likewise." This admonition took on a sense of urgency when I came upon the inscription to Mrs. E. Hyde (d. 1817), whose "premature death . . . Holds out an awful example How uncertain [is] our tenure in this Vale of Tears." Just across from Mrs. Hyde's tomb stands a marker for Alexr. Gordon Caulfield, whose demise in 1818 seems an object lesson of those cautionary sentiments, for he "drowned in crossing the River Opposite this City In Company with his intimate Friend T. Abraham, Esq." who lies in the next grave, remembered for his "indefatigable zeal."

Also praised for that quality was John Angelo Savi (d. 1858) who was recalled as "indefatigable in business." Savi, seemingly savvy in business, reposes not in the English cemetery but in the French burial ground, Tiretta, a few blocks down Park Street. English settlements, remnants, and cemeteries greatly outnumber those of the French in Asia. The French failed to acquire an empire in the Far East, mainly because of political factors at home. Societé de l'Orient founded in 1642 managed to colonize only Madagascar. In 1664 Louis XIV and Colbert, his finance minister, incorporated the French East India Company, but it was ten years before François Martin established a French settlement at Pondicherry, eighty-five miles south of Madras. The French also pushed north into Bengal in 1690, building a trading post sixteen miles outside Calcutta, but when the Dutch captured Pondicherry in 1693 the French position in India weakened. Although they recovered the city in 1699, Pondicherry fell to the English in 1761, marking the end of any substantial French influence in India (although France later recovered Pondicherry, which it controlled from 1814 to 1954). The tenuous French presence in the East left few cemeteries behind. Two of them, the Calcutta burial ground and the one at Akaroa near Christchurch, New Zealand, are described earlier in this chapter.

The English and the Dutch, those commercially minded rival colonialists, settled some of their differences in the East in 1824 when they agreed by treaty that the British would evacuate their settlements in Indonesia in exchange for a free hand in Malacca, the Malay peninsula and in the new settlement of Singapore, a barren island acquired by Stamford Raffles in 1819. In Singapore today, not far from the famous hotel named after Raffles, stands St. Andrew's Cathedral, whose memorial plaques recall the days of empire on the island. Expatriate comings and goings echo from the past with the epitaphs of William Wilson Smith (d. 1847) "who died on his passage from Hamburgh to Singapore," and Ada Latham (d. 1898) "who died aboard the S.S. 'Sachen' between Aden and Suez" on the way home. Percy Gold left the colony and managed to return home, only to meet his end fighting for king and country in Europe where he "fell in action in Flanders on July 21, 1918 . . . This sounding board was erected by his friends in Singapore." Stokes C. F Anscombe also met his end in military service, "killed in action during the mutiny of the 5th Light Infantry, 16th February 1915. 'Ready, aye Ready.' " More succinct is the epitaph to John Harvey (d. 1879), whose inscription recalls no martial or colonial exploits but remembers him only as "a prominent resident here."

Near St. Andrew's lies the Foreigners' Cemetery, whose graves holding the departed from many nations indicate Singapore's role as a crossroads of Far Eastern cultures. Two of the many gravestones embedded in the low wall which surrounds the cemetery offer rare memorials of Americans buried in the Orient in the nineteenth century: William Stephenson of Boston, "born in Portland, Me. U.S.A.," died in Singapore (d. 1850), and William Lee, Jr., "born in the city of New York, United States of America . . . died at Singapore, March 1, 1856." Expatriates from many other nations repose in the cemetery: France—"Ci Git Le Comte de Thune," born in Paris, died in Singapore (d. 1863); Germany—"Hier ruhet William Andersen" (d. 1865); Russia—Wladimir Astafien (d. 1890), "late Lieutenant of the Imperial Russian Navy"; and the undescribed nationals of countries unspecified—John

Aroozoo (d. 1860); Harry Lambert Brabazon (d. 1842), "who died on this island where he came for a change of climate"; one "Mackertoom Galoost Mackertoom, Esqre" (d. 1864); and Leekhia Soon John (d. 1927), whose stone bears the prominent legend "Messr. Walton, Gooddy & Cripps Ltd. Marble Merchants & Sculptors, London–Carrara." This notice recalls the mother country's strong influence on expatriate burials. Perhaps this was especially true in Singapore which the English started from scratch, for no local practices existed already to influence burial procedures or cemeteries. Robert W. Habenstein and William M. Lamers note in *Funeral Customs the World Over* (1963) how "in Singapore the Christian community memorializes its dead with monuments built by monumental masons who look to England for inspiration in craftsmanship and design, and with services that would readily be understood anywhere among English-speaking peoples. In point of fact the Christian community in Malaya buries the dead along lines similar in many ways to burial in England."

Such English influence on postmortem practices appears in other cities on the Malaysian peninsula. At Kuala Lumpur, the capital of Malaysia, a small English cemetery contains tombstones set on a hillside in a manner that resembles the terraced rice paddies of the East. The graves there entomb the functionaries who made the wheels of empire turn. Lying in alien soil, now no longer even a colony, are David Prentice (d. 1889), who kept things moving as a locomotive superintendant; Archibald Douglas Waugh (d. 1920) of the Public Works Department; James Driver (d. 1903), federal inspector of schools; Harry Charles Syers (d. 1897), commissioner of police in the Federated Malay States, "killed by a sladang in Dahang"—a death with rhyme, if not reason, and as euphonious an inscription as the name of Daisy Fanny Labroody (d. 1955). At the burial ground's lowest level lies Charles Egerton Donaldson (d. 1917) "who was called to the grand lodge above," while near the top tier, closer to that celestial lodge, stand two prominent memorial statues, one to "Laurie"— Laurence Reynold Yzelman (d. 1912)—and a small angel to "our darling son," Heiman Laurence Yzelman (d. 1903). The Kuala Lumpur Foreigners' Cemetery claims one of the most curious gravestones I ever found, the memorial to Philip Pryce Smith. This life-sized figure of a little boy with a wistful expression, hands under his chin as if praying, bears the puzzling inscription: "Born Oct. 22nd 1920, Died Nov. 22d 1925, Reborn Feb. 23rd 1927."

Even small out-of-the-way towns in former colonies claim cemeteries for expatriates. At Kuala Kangson, north of Kuala Lumpur and not far from Ipoh, a Christian burial ground contains the remains of a few such foreigners remote from all connections with the home country. Near the entrance stands a whitewashed pillar "in memory of the officers and men who fell in the Perak War 1876 & 1877," while in the grave-yard reposes the "baby darling son of L. and D. Francke," born 1901 and died 1903. Others include Alexander Louis (d. 1957), who inspired the sentiment: "Memory is a golden chain that binds us till we meet again," and two departed souls with memorable names—Paraparathdimy Baylis (d. 1952) and Leonard William Money, Jr. (d. 1927): sometimes it pays to visit graveyards, for at the Kuala Kangson cemetery you can even find money. At All Saint's Anglican Church in the nearby town of Taiping repose Lizzie Nutt (d. 1898), Hubert Joseph Luigi Josa (d. 1907), and the venerable Janet Pasley "who died in Taiping on her 90th birthday December 20th 1908."

Old colonial burial grounds of the kind found in Malaysia, Indonesia, India, and other areas of Asia inspired Kipling to observe:

It is not good for the Christian Health
To hustle the Aryan brown.

For the Christian riles and the Aryan smiles
And he weareth the Christian down.
And the end of the fight is a tombstone white
With the name of the late deceased,
And an epitaph drear—A fool lies here—
Who tried to hustle the East.

Tombstones white with epitaphs drear fill foreigners'
cemeteries not only in former colonies but also in countries
that were never colonized, for Europeans hustled locals in
many lands. Commercial, diplomatic, and other relationships created the need for expatriate graveyards, but in
some cases the host country failed to meet that need until
foreigners forced the issue. In seventeenth-century Spain no
facilities existed for burying foreigners or non-Catholics, two
disfavored catagories of outsider and thus, of corpses.
Postmortem problems vexed not only expatriates and Protestants but also Jews, Hindus, unbaptized Spanish children, and
executed criminals. When the body of the English ambassador's secretary sank at sea in 1622 near Santander local
fishermen, fearing they would catch nothing while a heretic's
coffin remained in their waters, retrieved the casket and
brought the body onto land where predators devoured it. On
another occasion, a page to Charles I of England died in
Madrid during a royal visit to Spain and was buried under a
fig tree in the British embassy garden by special permission
of the Spanish court. A few years later, in 1650, Cromwell
concluded a treaty with Spain for the proper burial of Englishmen after he learned that the Spaniards had callously
stuffed the body of his assassinated ambassador, Ascham,
into a hole without any service or last rites. But until 1796,
when Lord Bute acquired a plot of ground for English burials
outside Alcalá gate in Madrid, British expatriates were buried
at night without ceremony in the Recoletos convent garden.
In November 1831 Ferdinand VII of Spain finally settled the

issue by granting permission for Protestant burial grounds in all cities where a British consul or agent resided. The British consul in Malaga opened the first such cemetery on terrain east of the city, another was later started up at Cadiz, and then other cities followed suit. However, burial problems of irregular characters lingered as late as the mid-twentieth century. In 1938, six years after the Spanish government had secularized the country's cemeteries, the Franco regime placed them under control of the church, which again excluded heretics and other undesirables from consecrated ground. In the early 1970s Spanish bishops authorized burial of Orthodox Christians, Protestants, and even divorcees in Catholic cemeteries, but as recently as 1974 the authorities required that a murderer executed by the *garrote vil* (an iron collar twisted to snap the victim's neck after a minute or two of gradual strangulation) be interred in an "English" cemetery. In Spain, murderers and foreigners enjoyed a similar status— at least posthumously.

You find these expatriate English burial grounds, also called Protestant or foreigners' cemeteries, all over the world. A deceased non-national, non-resident, non-believer, or any other sort of nonconformist to local routines, rituals, or religions usually ends up in one of those ill-defined graveyards, collecting points for misfits of all categories. In *Last Letters From Hav,* Jan Morris's fictional but realistic account of a foreigner in a remote land, she gently mocks the sometimes rather forced epitaphs found in these expatriate burial facilities. Somewhere by an old Anglican church—its steeple sheared off, its forecourt converted into a parking lot, the sanctuary now used to store oil drums—reclined the tombstone of an officer who "having recently achieved his Captaincy in the Royal Engineers, left this Station to Report to the Commander of a yet greater Corps." The decaying Russian burial ground at Hav typifies time- and weather-worn expatriate cemeteries everywhere: "The graveyard is forlornly neglected now, though its windbreak of dark cypresses makes it visible from far away, like a war cemetery . . . Often [the tombstones'] inscriptions have long been obliterated by the heat and the winds off the sea; everywhere the coarse grass grows, and here and there the scrub from the heath has broken through the surrounding wall. Soon it will have obliterated all but these obelisks, and an elevated angel or two." These crumbling old places where foreigners repose seem emblematic of the long vanished dead who represented long gone enterprises.

A sense of lost empire, of the once flourishing but now forlorn former colonial or commercial presence, haunts expatriate cemeteries. Elspeth Huxley in *Four Guineas* describes Bonny, a Nigerian palm oil center that had nearly become a ghost town: "The two-storey houses built there by European traders are flaking and crumbling away, and filled with the down-at-heel descendants of old house-chiefs. The last white trader left in 1921. The bones of his many forerunners lie in the neglected cemetery. Eight were buried there in one week—a yellow-fever epidemic, probably." A similar sense of a vanished world and a by-gone era overcame James Pope-Hennessy when he visited the English Cemetery at Macao. In *Half-Crown Colony,* a book on Hong Kong, he meditates on burial grounds containing the departed who once struggled to carry out the colonial endeavor: "These old English graveyards in the tropics—like, for example, that on Penang Island in Malaya—gave you a very sharp and melancholy vision of the hazards to which European lives lay open in the early colonial Empire. The youth, recorded on their tombstones, of many of those buried in such cemeteries seems to emphasize the transient quality of life in a community perpetually threatened by fever and the flu."

The epitaph for Mary Morrison, interred at the Macao cemetery, epitomizes such health hazards. Mary "suddenly, but with a pious resignation, departed this life after a short

illness, bearing with her to the grave her hoped-for child."
Beside her repose the day-old infant and her husband,
Robert, a missionary who "for seven years labored alone on a
Chinese version of the holy scriptures." The more than one
hundred and sixty gravestones at the neatly tended cemetery,
established in 1821 by the Portugese East Indian Trading
Company, encapsulate the history of Macao, a colonial outpost since 1557, the oldest in Asia. Two children of missionaries succumbed at early ages, two years and sixteen months,
to the rigors of the climate, while a Lieutenant Fitzgerald
perished "from the effects of a wound received while gal-
lantly storming the enemy's battery at Canton." Margaret
Hutchison suffered a less violent end, for she "at the age of 25
fell asleep in Jesus beside kind friends in Macao on June 19,
1848." The burial ground boasts the remains of the fifth duke
of Marlborough, an ancestor of Sir Winston Churchill, who
did "depart this life in the Macao Roads June 2, 1840" at age
forty-three, relatively old for that place and time. George
Chinnery, an artist, emigrated from London to end his days
in Macao, while poor Henry Margesson never made it back
to England either, for he drowned near Yokohama, Japan
"after a residence of 23 years in China and on the eve of his
return to Europe."

Some adventurers traveled to far lands for glory rather
than gain. In the remote tribal settlement of Chitambo near
Lake Bangweula in northwest Zambia repose the heart and
entrails of David Livingston, who died 1 May 1873. The last
white man to see Livingston alive, Henry M. Stanley of the
New York Herald, had greeted the explorer with the now
famous phrase, "Dr. Livingston, I presume." The rest of
Livingston's body was sent back to England for burial at
Westminster Abbey. Also in a remote corner of Africa lies the
founder of the Boy Scout movement, Lord Baden-Powell.
Buried in St. Peter's churchyard at Nyeri in Kenya, his
marker bears the Scout's circle-and-dot symbol indicating

"gone home." Another solitary European grave in Africa stands among the royal tombs in front of Trinity Church at Addis Ababa, Ethiopia, where Sylvia Pankhurst, a long time resident in that country and an expert on its culture, reposes. Below the inscription—"Born: Manchester 5 May 1882 Died: Addis Ababa 27 September 1960"—appears an open stone book.

In Gondar, north of Addis, another lone English tomb houses Walter J. Plowden, British representative of Queen Victoria to King Teodros. At Suez in 1843, while returning home from India where he had worked for a British trading firm, Plowden met a compatriot named John Bell. This adventurer enticed him along to explore opportunities in Ethiopia. Back in England, Plowden persuaded Lord Palmerston, the foreign secretary, of the merits of creating a British presence in Ethiopia, and in 1848 Palmerston appointed him consul for Abyssinia (the country's name at the time), based in Gondar. Plowden established a good relationship with the local rulers, especially Emperor Teodros II, an enlightened monarch who took the throne in 1855. Indeed, when bandits killed the Englishman in 1860, Teodros avenged his death by executing five hundred highwaymen. Plowden reposes by the low, round, Gemjia Mariam church which stands next to the castle compound in which half a dozen or so imposing, European-style, stone structures stand. On top of the Englishman's basalt rock tomb are a cross and a white stone on which Plowden's epitaph no doubt once appeared. On the right flank survives a barely legible inscription. Before long no one will be able to read any record of him on his tomb.

Plowden's violent death recalls the many hardships suffered by nineteenth century travelers who ventured abroad during the days of empire. In *The Mansions and the Shanties* Gilberto Freyre describes the burial grounds populated by

English tradesmen sent to exploit commercial opportunities in Brazil, where they were felled by yellow fever and epidemics: "Only today, visiting some of the old Protestant cemeteries—those of Recife or Salvador or Rio de Janeiro—which date from the beginning of the nineteenth century, and seeing the number of victims buried in those damp grounds, overgrown by rubber plants, shaded by huge palms, can one form an idea of the hardihood with which the English, to conquer the Brazilian market and establish a new zone of influence for their imperialism, risked death from the yellow fever."

Victims from another sort of hazard—war refugees—repose in the unusual expatriate cemetery in Brazil which contains the remains of disappointed American Southerners who emigrated in 1866 and settled in the area of Santa Bárbara, a town about eighty miles northwest of Sao Paulo. By the early 1870s some five hundred expatriate Confederate families inhabited a community known as Villa Americana. There they transplanted the South, crops and all. Cotton provided the principal cash crop, while a type of Georgia watermelon brought the settlement additional revenue. Major Robert Meriwether of South Carolina, one of the colonists wealthy enough to buy slaves, set up the first large-scale cotton plantation in the area. Although more than half of the settlers had returned to North America by the mid-1870s, the dead remained behind permanently. Just outside the burial ground, surrounded by a sugar cane plantation between the modern cities of Americana and Santa Bárbara d'Oeste, stands a monument to the original settlers—an obelisk which bears replicas of the Confederate flag flanked by the names of the first families. Inside the compound, weathered tombstones bear names such as MacKnight, Pyles, Steagall, Vaughn, and Whitaker. There is also a small church where Protestant members of the community worship and which houses the

July Fourth get-together when as many as one hundred and fifty people gather for the Society of the American Descendants' annual reunion.

The fortunes and misfortunes of war have scrambled many lives, and deaths. Thanks to the American Civil War, those wayward Southerners repose in a sugarcane field in far off Brazil. At the Christian cemetery which nestles under Bemura Hill in Kabul, Afghanistan, lie ten British soldiers killed in the second British-Afghan War, one of Britain's three unsuccessful attempts between 1838 and 1919 to colonize that land East of Suez. Located in Kabul's Sher Poor (place of lions) section, the cemetery also contains the graves of European and American hippies drawn to the Afghan capital in the early 1970s, as well as the tomb of Sir Aurel Stein, a noted western chronicler of Central Asia.

Graves of Englishmen who fell in imperial wars lie scattered all around the world. In a dispatch from Camp Omdurman in Sudan to *The Morning Post* in London on 8 September 1898 Winston Churchill, witnessing the casualties of an encounter between his countrymen and the Sudanese, reflected on the young men of England who "carry their brains and enthusiasm to the farthest corners of our wide Empire," adding remorsefully, "Their graves, too, are scattered." Fitzroy Maclean, in *Escape to Adventure,* recalled one such cluster of forlorn and forgotten British military graves that he came upon at Vis, an island off the Yugoslavia coast. There he saw "an old walled garden, long since overgrown and fallen into decay. In the middle stood a marble obelisk, with on it an inscription in English celebrating a British naval victory won in 1811 over the French off Vis. Then, looking more closely, I found, hidden in the high grass and among the shrubs and undergrowth, a dozen or so tombstones, commemorating British naval officers and seamen who had lost their lives in the battle, their names, good English names, almost obliterated by moss and weather." At the Greek Orthodox church off Roselle Street in Alexandria, Egypt, tombstones commemorate three British soldiers who died during the Napoleonic era. Colonel Arthur Brice (d. 1801) perished in the Battle of Alexandria, while Thomas Hamilton Scott and Henry Gosle, a military apothecary, both died in 1807 during General Frazer's expedition to Egypt, organized to determine if the English could create diversionary action there against the Turks. At Alexandria's main English burial ground, in the southern part of town, the foreign community interred Henry Salt, who first arrived in the area in 1809 on a mission to Abyssinia (Ethiopia). In 1815 Salt became the British consul-general in Egypt, where he excavated antiquities which he later offered at exorbitant prices to the British Museum which finally acquired his collection in 1823 after much Mideast bazaar-type haggling. Salt, who died near Alexandria in 1827, merited an evocative and original epitaph: "His ready genius explored and elucidated the Hieroglypics [sic] and other antiquities of this country. His faithful and rapid pencil and the nervous originality of his untutored senses conveyed to the world vivid ideas of the scenes that had delighted himself."

East of Suez, the British Empire encompassed India, Ceylon, Malaya, Burma, Hong Kong, and other territories in whose remote corners any number of English military personnel now lie. On a walk in the Burmese jungle Geoffrey Rawson (as he recounts in *Road to Mandalay*) stumbled over a large stone which proved to be a gravemarker inscribed: "In memory of Lieut. J. N. Roden R.N., H.M.S. Ranger. Killed in action with Dacoits at Shagwai 9 January 1887, aged 30 years." Roden was just one of the many who fell victim to the *dacoits*—robbers, highwaymen, and roving bands of maurauders—who infested northern Burma, an area the British tried to pacify in the late nineteenth century with thirty thousand troops.

A similar fate awaited Hans Markward Jensen, "Captain in

the Province Gendarmerie, born Denmark 1878, killed by Dacoits at Prayao on the 14 X 1902." I came across Jensen unexpectedly in the Foreigners' Cemetery in Chiang Mai in northern Thailand: what was a Dane doing in far off Siam? Although Thailand remained one of the few Asian countries never colonized, even there foreigners gathered in sufficient numbers to require their own burial ground. A few expatriates, like Jensen and "Edward Lainson Guilding, Major Essex Regiment, Died at Chiengmai, Siam, S. Valentine's Day 1900," were military types. Others came for commercial reasons: Eric Ramsey (d. 1916) and John Ewen Dalgliesh (d. 1917), both assistants in The Borneo Company, Ltd.; and David Fleming Macfie (d. 1945), "for many years forest manager of The Borneo Company, Ltd.," next to whom reposes his wife, Kam Mao Macfie (d. 1968). Still others gravitated to Thailand for reasons of religion: Reverend Daniel McGilvary, a stray American, founder of Christian missions in the north of the country, born in North Carolina; and Lilian Hamer (d. 1959), "missionary to the Lsu." The deceased at Chiang Mai cover the whole spectrum of nationalities, professions, and hues: Donald Blackchief (d. 1973), "Infant of H. White, d. 1919," and Forrest Brown (d. 1893, aged six months).

A military cemetery in the southwestern part of Thailand recalls the British presence during World War II. The burial ground lies at Kanchanaburi, not far from the famous bridge over the river Kwai. A cemetery for fallen expatriate warriors presents an especially poignant picture. Unlike the merchants or mariners or missionaries who ventured to far countries for possible gain—of wealth or converts—the soldiers were shipped overseas to face guns and bombs. Many of those who did lose their lives to the Japanese forces now repose in this distant Thai graveyard. With its unimaginative architecture, well kept but somewhat sterile appearance, and uniform rows of identical grave markers bearing only basic data about the deceased, the military cemetery at Kanchanaburi typifies such armed service burial grounds everywhere. An unattractive, small pavillion bears on its wall a long list of names and the notation: "The soldiers who are recorded here perished in captivity and their ashes are buried in two graves in Plot IX." In some cases the markers bear a pitifully brief sentiment, a fragment of an emotion recorded by a home-side loved one, half a world away: "Always in our thoughts. Mother, Father and Brother"; "He gave his today that we may have a tomorrow. A beautiful memory"; "Peace, perfect peace"; "At rest"; "Jesus, in his bosom wears, the flower that once was mine"; "A treasured memory of our darling. Mum and Toots."

Most striking, to my mind, were the names—those plain English names that designated the boys raised among the green fields and cozy villages and tidy towns at home, only to repose beneath the alien turf of a remote land in Asia. Flower, Day, Walker, Jones, Wentworth, Allen—these names parade before your eyes, simple syllables, plain and clear and soft, and dead. Some six thousand men lie there, half of them English and about a quarter Australian, for in the mid-twentieth century the former colonies joined with the colonists in a common effort. The Kanchanaburi cemetery, run by the Commonwealth War Graves Commission, thus seems a sort of echo of empire, with its ecumenical assortment of English, Australians, and New Zealanders.

As elsewhere in Asia, remnants of Britain's eastern colonial adventures survive at cemeteries in Australia and New Zealand. Memories of the early days of the home country's attempts to get a foothold in Australia appear on a monument at Melbourne General Cemetery, "erected by a few colonists to commemorate the noble act of the native chief Derrimut [1864] who by timely information given October 1835 to the first colonists Messrs. Fawkner, Lancey, Evans, Henry Batman, and their dependants, saved them from mas-

sacre, planned by some of the up-country tribes of aborig-
ines." In *Australian Sketches,* published in Melbourne in 1847,
Thomas McCombie encapsulates the difference between the
old country and the new with his comment about the
Melbourne burial ground: "I would rather be laid here, with
the free sky above and the open forest around, than be borne
in empty pomp and enclosed in the gloomy vault of some
ancient cathedral." Empty land rather than empty pomp
typified the new colony. No time-encrusted traditions or
ancient towns limited the newcomers who ventured to settle
in Australia.

Before long, however, "down under" came to resemble the
homeland up over, far across the seas. A corner of the old
country seems present at Melbourne General Cemetery, flat
and ordered, arranged in a rectangular space with neatly
sectioned units, the very epitome of an orderly, civilized land
tamed and settled and by now old enough to boast a certain
patina of age. More than a century has passed since Thomas
Valentine McFarland (d. 1874, aged nine) "was accidentally
killed by a dog passing over him in Millar St. West
Melbourne," and since Chandros Elliot (d. 1862) "was
drowned by the springing of a leak in a boat in Hobson's
Bay." Rather more recently, death snuffed out the mellow-
named Arno Glow (d. 1947) and also withered the Krokoss
family and a Plant (d. 1947), no longer perennials even
though they repose near William Rain (d. 1916). The poig-
nantly simple "I miss you"—a succinct but wonderfully evocative sentiment—furnishes the sole comment on the large
marble slab dedicated to Siegfried Mannheimer (d. 1961),
while the similarly laconic inscription "Our Dear Mother"
fails to include even the late lamented woman's name. On the
O'Neill family marker appears the statement, "Requested In
Peace"—this recalls the epitaph a wife put on her husband's
tomb: "Rest in peace—until we meet again"—while around

the cemetery signs warned that "approaching people and touting for work is strictly prohibited.

Perhaps the most famous decedent commemorated in Melbourne was English cricket. British military personnel introduced the game to Australia, and England and Australia played their first test match in Melbourne in 1877. The Aussies won that match and also gained a second victory five years later in England, so earning a trophy called the Ashes. On the trophy, a small black urn which holds the ashes of a burned wooden cricket stump, is engraved the inscription: "In affectionate remembrance of English cricket which died at the Oval 29th August 1882, lamented by a large circle of sorrowing friends and acquaintances. R.I.P. (N.B. The body will be cremated and the ashes taken to Australia.)."

In the mid-nineteenth century Melbourne residents worried about more than just Australia's cricket prowess. In 1851 a depression gripped the state of Victoria. As related by shop keeper William H. Hall in his 1852 *Practical Experiences at the Diggings of the Gold Fields of Victoria:* "In order to prevent this ruinous and daily-increasing evil . . . a meeting was held, at which it was resolved, to offer a reward of two hundred guineas for the discovery of gold, in sufficient quantities to pay for working, within one hundred and twenty miles of Melbourne. This had the desired effect; for shortly afterwards gold was found at Ballarat . . . The excitement it created in Melbourne was so intense, so all-absorbing, that men seemed bereft of their senses." The first sign of buried treasure at Ballarat, located seventy-five miles south of Melbourne, surfaced on 24 August 1851 when two prospectors scraped up two and a half pounds of gold, worth $600, at a sheep run. This proved to be the most fabulous single gold deposit ever discovered. Dozens of mining camps sprang up in Victoria at that time, with Ballarat alone yielding $300 million-worth of the precious metal, fully a quarter of the total amount of gold extracted in all of California during the gold boom of the 1800s. At Ballarat's Bakery Hill in 1858 a miner came upon the 2195-ounce Welcome nugget, second only to the 2284-ounce Welcome Stranger chunk of gold plucked from the earth the following year.

The almost treeless Ballarat cemetery enclosed by an unsightly, corrugated metal fence contains nuggets of information recalling the settlement's mining history. James Williams (d. 1861) "died on Ballarat," the *on* indicating that his demise occurred on the gold field itself rather than in the town. Richard Williams (d. 186?) was "killed in the Working Miners Claim," while yet another Williams—William Williams, buried near a Richard Richards—died in 1862 "from injuries received in the Bard & Albion" claim, and Robert Smurthwaite (d. 1868) was "accidentally killed" on another claim. In the cemetery's small Jewish section reposes Maurice Soloman, headmaster of the Ballarat Hebrew School, who died, we are told with great precision, on Thursday September 28, 1822. Others in that section include Hannah Tobias (d. 1892), who departed "at the ripe age of 94 years," and nearby, Edith Granat (d. 1900) who died "at the tender age of 14 years & 2 months." In another section at Ballarat lie Mr. and Mrs. Shoppee (d. 1925; d. 1912) beneath a marker "erected by Little Molly."

Those twentieth-century markers indicate that Ballarat, unlike so many other gold rush settlements, did not fade into a ghost town. The mining village of Arrowtown in southern New Zealand, however, disappeared into history. The now phantom settlement once yielded "Gold as yellow as Chinamen. Gold pollinated the whole town;/But the golden bees are gone," versified Kiwi poet Denis Glover, "Now paved with common clay/Are the roads of Arrowtown." One autumn day I made my way down those streets of clay to visit the Arrowtown graveyard. To my inquiry as to whether I was headed toward the old cemetery, a local replied, "Yup—new one, too," for the graveyard continues to serve the few men and women who cater to tourists visiting that relic of the Otago gold rush days. In the cemetery's old section, well overgrown with grass, weeds, and plants bearing red berries, repose such figures as Thomas Patchett (d. 1885): "He was a man, take him for all and all"; Maud Mary Gilmore (d. 1893, ten years old), "too gentle for this bustling world"; and next to each other, John Griffith Williams (d. 1878) and Lewis Robert Jones (d. 1878), both of whom "died at Franklin Hospital"—a rather omnious precedent for patients under care there. The newer section boasts neatly manicured grass and well kept graves, thus presenting a clear demarcation between the long gone and the more recent dead. The O'Fee family plot contains the remains of one Adam Smith, namesake of the famous British economist, an appropriate designation for one buried at a miners' camp where the gold standard once ruled.

Not far from Arrowtown lies Queenstown, whose cemetery holds one grave which recalls the region's gilded days of yore. The epitaph on that tomb, to Albert Scheib Born Gibbston who died in 1969 at age ninety-nine, is one of my favorite anywhere: "Mined for gold and coal in this district. Also the West Coast and Klondyke. 1898 Married Sophia Smith of Skippers. Farmed Wakatip district for many years. (He lived a full life.)" No one could wish for a more satisfying epitaph: only a full life can counterpoise an empty death. Nearby lies another venerable character, Nicholas Paul Baltasar von Tunzelmann (d. 1900, aged seventy-six), who arrived in Queenstown in February 1860 and "pioneered Fernhill Run in the West shore of Lake Wakatipu where Mt. Nicholas and the Von River record his presence." Only such early arrivals in a land can enjoy geographic commemorations as well as epitaphs. New Zealand's pioneers encountered a harsh nature: William Whyte of Oban, Scotland, "perished in the snow on Mount Gilbert while trying to save his flock 3 August 1867," while William Mackenzie "lost his life, in a snow slip in sight of his home, about noon on 8th August 1906." August was seemingly a dangerous month for the residents of Queenstown: Ervine John Daniel "died 22d August 1878 [aged ten] from the effects of a fall from his pony," and Lieutenant Walter Mackenzie perished "in action on Gallipoli, 9th August 1915. He fought to the end against odds uncounted. He fell with his face to the foe." It seemed strange to find a reference to the great European war in the pine-scent-permeated New Zealand burial ground overlooking the blue and serene waters of Queenstown Lake.

Another such echo of far off Europe lingers in an overgrown and under-cared-for cemetery on a ridge beneath Grafton Bridge in Auckland, in the far north of New Zealand. There lies Frederick Edward Maning, like Lieutenant Mackenzie repatriated from Europe. Maning, "known to colonial fame as the author of Old New Zealand," died in 1883 of "a painful malady . . . in the mother country . . . His last words were, let me be buried in the far off land I love so well." Better known to colonial fame was Captain William Hobson of the Royal Navy, who proclaimed British sovereignty over New Zealand in January 1840 and served as the colony's first governor. Hobson (d. 1842) reposes under a white marble slab at the cemetery's only well-kept grave: only a governor merits a gardener at that otherwise unkempt burial ground. Others interred there include James Poulter (d. 1888), bracketed by his two wives who repose together but died a half century apart, Catherine (d. 1865) and Mary (d. 1915); "E. M. A. J. T. H., six infants of J. & M. A. Gribble"; and William Hunter (d. 1896), "with Christ which is better"—no exaggeration, for just about anywhere would be better than that scruffy cemetery.

Much of New Zealand's history haunts St. Stephen's, a delightful little white chapel perched on a hill overlooking a small inlet in the Auckland harbor. Charlotte Kemp (d. 1860) "came to this colony 1819." Two nineteenth-century clergymen repose at St. Stephen's, one Vicesimus Lush (d. 1882), archdeacon of Waikato, and the more soberly named William Garden Cowie (d. 1902), primate of New Zealand. He lies next to his wife Eliza, who died two months after him, the pair recalled by a pleasantly poignant phrase: "They were lovely and pleasant in their lives and in their death they were not divided." Another pair of couples who repose together forge a chain of family history that links the generations: Georgina Lawford died in 1883, followed by her husband John in 1901, then Clement (presumably their son) in 1931, and finally his wife Beatrice in 1961. The years between Georgina's birth and Beatrice's death span virtually the entire history of New Zealand, from colony to dominion and in that way the two of them symbolize the advent and departure of the British Empire in the Far East. It is such little known families, modest in life and made obscure by death and time, which form the essential sinews of a society and a civilization.

It would be too Eurocentric a view of the Far East to leave the impression that only the English, Dutch, Portuguese, and French spread their influence throughout the region. While the expatriates of those European lands populate many graveyards scattered around Asia, another less distant country also contributed its fair share of nationals to the societies and cemeteries of the Far East. It was not simply a poetic conceit that inspired Denis Glover to refer to "gold as yellow as Chinamen," for workers from China comprised many of the early miners at the Otago fields in New Zealand and at Australia's Victoria gold camps. In the back of the Ballarat cemetery stretches the Chinese section, complete with a small furnace for the paper-burning mourning ritual. Expatriate Chinese buried there include the curiously named O'Cheong (d. 1865), not a Sino-Irishman, for the O was no doubt a corruption of Ah. Originally from Canton, O'Cheong served for nine years as an interpreter in Australia.

Although fortune cookies are quite unknown in China, fortune hunters abounded and literally thousands of Chinese swarmed to Australia in search of gold. The Chinese population in Victoria increased from fewer than two thousand in 1853 to some thirty-three thousand in 1858, even though the state government attempted to control the influx. In 1855 authorities instituted a poll tax of £10 on each Chinese immigrant and prohibited ships from carrying more than one Chinese passenger for every ten tons of the vessel's weight. But sea captains easily evaded these restrictions by landing in ports outside Victoria. The immigrants would then proceed overland to the goldfields, traveling in colorful processions such as that described by Alfred William Howitt in *Land, Labour and Gold; or Two Years In Victoria,* published in 1855:

> Near Ballarat, we met a company of Chinese removing to Creswick's Creek. It was quite a picture, and a curious one. The Chinese here, who have come lately in crowds, still continue their national costume in great measure, and their national custom of carrying everything on their necks on a long pole . . . At the end of a pole of some two inches thick, and six or eight feet long, they suspend weights astonishing, considering their slight physical structure. You would think the pole would cut their bare necks, if not their heads off.

But the Chinese kept their heads and their wits about them and settled into Ballarat, establishing there a lively if depraved corner of town, as described by English author Anthony Trollope when he visited the settlement one night in the early 1870s: "A more degraded life it is hardly possible to imagine. Gambling, opium-smoking, and horrid dissipation seemed to prevail among them constantly. They have no women of their own, and the lowest creatures of the streets congregate with them in their hovels."

This sort of scene, and other less seamy ones, were repeated in British colonies all around Asia, and even at the heart of the empire. Just as the English uprooted themselves to move to the Far East, so the Chinese migrated to England where cemeteries contain the remains of the Asian expatriates who lie half a world away from their homeland. In the Chinese section of the East London Cemetery at Plaistow repose such Sino-Anglo deceased as Yong Tack (d. 1960); Yung Ni (d. 1931), whose stone bears a Chinese inscription; Ho Ah Chow (Charles) (d. 1962) and next to him Egeta Rosina Lee Hin (d. 1961); nearby lie Wong Bing (d. 1962) and Mum Ivy Bing (d. 1973). A memorial cross bearing Chinese characters rises on a stand inscribed, "In memory of the Chinese who had died in England this memorial was presented by Mr. N. G. Fook of 33 Cavendish Road, Brondesbury, N.W. on the 7th day of Nov. 1927." In *The Chinese in London* Ng Kwee Choo tells of a ceremonial visit to the monument where "the caretaker poured some wine in oblation, lit the incense, and placed several flowers; then hurriedly and perfunctorily with the assistance of the two old men [who accompanied us] he planted one stick of incense and one flower in front of every Chinese tomb." What do the spirits of the Chinese departed there in London think of those traditional rituals? Someone once asked Confucius if a dead person knew what was happening in life. The great philosopher replied that if the deceased were aware, then pious descendants should kill themselves in honor of their ancestors, and if not then why perform elaborate rituals for vanished relatives?

In many Eastern countries Chinese expatriates remain a living presence and, in their overseas cemeteries, a dead one. In the former British colony of Singapore three-quarters of the people are Chinese, in Malaysia about a third, in Thailand more than one-tenth, in Indonesia and the Philippines a small fraction.

With thirty million expatriates in one hundred and nine countries (including nearly six million in Hong Kong), China abroad is one of Asia's most economically powerful nations. In many of the countries where they live the Chinese control a disproportionately large share of the local economy. And like the foreigners who established commercial settlements in the Far East, the Chinese have instituted their own cemeteries. Perhaps an inverse connection exists between pomp and power for Manila, where the Chinese comprise only a small part of the population, boasts one of the most grandiose Chinese cemeteries—or for that matter, of any type—anywhere. The necropolis, established more than a century ago, serves as a veritable Chinatown of the dead and lies near the Chinese General Hospital—perhaps too near for comfort, for from their rooms patients can gaze down on the graveyard. Many of the deceased repose in homey mausoleums that range from one-room structures to entire houses, varying in style from traditional pagoda-type buildings to modern mansions. The King Su clan resides in a Chinese temple-like dwelling with red roof tiles and a pair of ferocious looking, tri-humped, Meissen-green dragons that face each other. A little farther up the street the Lim family occupies a sleek structure built of poured concrete, aluminum-framed plate glass windows, a marble-bedecked facade, and spotlights to brighten the place up. A nearby residence, topped by dragons with splintery, green glass scales, houses not only a dead family but also (when I was there) a live one—the father reclined, buried in sleep, while the mother nursed their baby.

Some of the five thousand mausoleums at Manila's Chinese cemetery contain enough room for large clans, both departed and living members. Along so-called Millionaires' Row stand huge dwellings with air-conditioning, ornate furnishings, marble walls and floors, paintings and gold ornaments, elaborate wrought iron grillwork, stained glass windows, toilets, staircases, and other embellishments. Security guards patrol the cemetery to protect these mansions and their treasures from intruders. At least one mausoleum boasts a stocked bar where visiting relatives of the dead can imbide spirits while visiting others, while another sports mail slots on the door. (The mail box affixed to the expatriate tomb of Spanish poet Antonio Machado, buried in exile in Collioure, France, just across the border from Spain, receives more than four hundred pieces of mail a year.) At the intersection of Kiam Sian and Kong Tek Roads in Manila's Sino-city of the dead stands a collective mausoleum filled with niches, some bearing oval photos of the deceased, others decorated with flowers—plastic and bright or real and wilted—and still others with spent blobs of colorful candle wax. Just outside the mausoleum lies a small Chinese garden, complete with little stone pagodas and a pool where a sign warns, "Feeding Fishes and Littering Into the Pool Are Strictly Prohibited." Across the street is the Chinese temple, which seemed a direct transplant from mainland China. No Anglican church in the Far East recalled the home country more than did that expatriate sanctuary. Fierce-looking stone animals guarded the doorway of the pagoda, furnished with dragons, a Buddha-like gold statue, and other Chinese type motifs. I continued on to the less elegant part of town, leaving behind the mansion mausoleums and passing along a football field-length terrace crowded with identical grey tombs, below which ran a long, tall wall pocked with hundreds of small burial niches. In this section of the cemetery repose the Chinese who, in death, occupy quarters nearly as cramped as they most likely did in life.

The problem of overcrowding exists no less for the dead than for the living. Population pressure leads inexorably to a scarcity of cemetery space. In *Half-Crown Colony* James Pope-Hennessey relates how dying Chinese in Hong Kong used to be taken to death houses where their moribund bodies would be stored with those already dead. "It was only in the late eighteen sixties that the Surveyor-General discovered that the I Ts'z temple . . . was being used both as a death-house and as a morgue, 'the dead and dying huddled together indiscriminately in small filthy rooms.'" This led to the establishment in 1872 of the Tung Wah Hospital, financed partly by the sale of gambling licenses. In 1899 the Tung Wah built in Hong Kong a Coffin House, a way-station for dead people who preferred to repose in their ancestral homeland at a site possessing favorable *feng shui* (wind and water), symbols of the spiritual laws that govern *yin* and *yang,* nature's female-passive and male-active elements. Residents of the Coffin House, where caskets rest on planks a few feet above the floor, can choose between single rooms, doubles, and a dormitory hall. This is perhaps the world's only hotel for the dead. Most burials take place at a cemetery at Shenzhen, just across the border in China.

Those who choose to repose in land-short Hong Kong face early eviction. The following "Notice of Intention to Exhume" appeared in a Hong Kong newspaper when I was there:

> Notice is hereby given that the undermentioned 7-years periodical graves which were buried in the year 1960 will be exhumed by the end of six months duration from the date of this announcement. Descendants, ralatives [sic] and/or authorized persons of any grave listed below may claim for private exhumation within six months from the date of this notice through the undersigned for separate arrangement. The human remains of the grave unclaimed after the expiry of the notice will be exhumed and deposited in the ossarium of the same Cemetery by the Union. Full details of the graves such as the name, age, sex, date of burial, etc., can be seen at the Union office, Cemetery office and all Member-churches of our Union.

Below the notice appears a list of some two hundred four-digit numbers divided into two groups, adults and children.

Reduced to a number and their sleep disturbed after a mere seven years slumber—the seven-year pitch—these poor souls suffer a restless eternity.

Disposal of remains by burial is still disfavored in Red China. Graveyards and exhumed bodies in the mother country serve eminently practical purposes: bones salvaged from beehive-like necropolises around the cities are ground into fertilizer, while workmen bulldoze the cemetery areas into flatland for agriculture. In a break with traditional Chinese funeral practices, the regime encourages cremation—mandatory for Communist party members—rather than interment. The Funeral Administration Bureau in Beijing operates twelve crematoriums which ash about half of the capital's sixty thousand annual dead. In the mid-1980s the city replaced old, Czech incinerators with modern, computer-controlled, smokeless, Japanese equipment. At Babaoshan, the city's largest crematorium, rickety white funeral buses (in China white is the color of mourning) brightened with green stripes deliver the deceased and their mourners, who line up to await their turn for the memorial service. The proceedings cost the equivalent of about one month's salary, not including such extras as use of a special hall, paper flower wreaths, an urn, and a suit of funeral clothes blended with synthetics for a faster burn. This is a far cry from the elegant treatment accorded the Chinese dead who repose in the spacious mausoleums in Manila. Unlike the Europeans, the expatriate Chinese enjoy better post-mortem treatment than their countrymen at home.

The venerable and vast Bukit China burial ground in Malacca, covering more than one hundred acres, is one of the largest Chinese cemeteries outside the homeland, and thus a splendid specimen of China's overseas cities of the dead. In the middle of the seventeenth century Li Kup, alias Li Wei King, a fugitive who fled China during the Ming dynasty's downfall, gave the ground occupied by the cemetery to the

Chinese community at Malacca. In 1644 Li Kup founded the
Chengttoon Teng temple which houses a vivid portrait of Li
clad in a bulky, billowy, blue robe, a square black hat sporting
a white rectangular motif, and black slippers which perch on
the crossbar of his chair. A whispy white beard dangles from
his face, which bears a wistful expression. Roland Braddell,
in *The Lights of Singapore,* adjudged this magnificent portrait
"a perfectly wonderful Chinese painting . . . in Ming man-
darin robes, the blue of which is that heavenly shade which
. . . has never been approached anywhere else in the world,
and the secret of which died shortly after the Ming dynasty."
Li's legacy to his countrymen, Bukit China, occupies a large,
tomb-riddled hill on the outskirts of Malacca. In *The Tempta-
tion of the West* André Malraux has Ling, a Chinese in Europe,
write to a European traveling in China: "You have weighted
the universe with anguish. What a tragic countenance you
have given to death! A cemetery in a large European city fills
one with unpleasant thoughts. I think of the cemeteries you
are doubtless seeing even now, of the fields of the dead, where
some silent bird rules over the meditations of friendly
graves." There is something to this. The great European
burial grounds, and even some of their export versions—like
the European graveyards scattered about Asia—seem to make
too much of death. Too many statues, epitaphs, and frills fill
these cemeteries. Bukit China however, contains simpler
tombs, semi-circular niches set into the hillside, carefully
positioned by geomancers according to the tenets of *feng shui,*
a doctrine used to select the most auspicious place to construct a grave. Those unpretentious tombs blend into the
hillside as if natural repositories for the remains of those who
have experienced that phenomenon of nature which we call
death.

A short stroll up Serendit Road from Bukit China lies the
Christian cemetery, where a few Chinese, buried in the European style, repose. Ivy Ooi (d. 1935) lies there, as does Kenny

Lim Chin Keon, died aged five, whose monument includes a little, praying angel figure, a photo of a smiling boy, and the inscription: "We love him but God loves him best." And then there is the proverbial Chinese laundryman, Mah Wee Fah (d. 1946), late of the Shanghai Dry Cleaning Establishment. These Chinese buried in Malacca's Christian cemetery seem to synthesize the intermingling of East and West represented by the European expatriates who repose in the Asian burial grounds, repositories of history scattered around the Far East. There they lie, all those homesick-to-the-death wanderers, forever in a foreign land remote from their homeland, finally at peace after their travels and travails. This sentiment is echoed in the inscription on what is perhaps the single most striking and exemplary expatriate European grave in the Far East, the last resting place of a British wanderer buried far from home but, in the end, at rest at home. On a hilltop on the remote island of Samoa, a dot of land in the vastness of the Pacific, lies Robert Louis Stevenson, his monument inscribed:

Under the wide and starry sky,
Dig the grave and let me lie.
Glad did I live and gladly die,
    And I laid me down with a will.
This be the verse you grave for me:
"Here he lies where he longed to be;
Home is the sailor, home from the sea,
And the hunter home from the hill."

IV

The Melancholy of Anatomy

THE melancholy of anatomy is that it keeps disintegrating on us. Scattered around the earth lie all manner of mortal remains—bones, limbs, skulls, relics, skeletons, mummies, corpses, fleshy fragments—honored or coveted by families, the devout, collectors, antiquarians, curiosity seekers and other connoisseurs. Anatomy's residue surfaces in all sorts of places, some unexpected. Tomes as well as tombs hold bodily debris. An English medical man named Dr. Martin Lister recounted in *A Journey to Paris In the Year 1698* how he found among the books in St. Genevieve library "the leg of a

Mummi well preserv'd . . . I told the Father that this was still Flesh . . . [and] if that leg was kept a good while in a damp Cellar, it would yield and stink like very Carrion, tho' it was at least 3000 years old." Detached from its place, its time, its owner, the ancient leg became transmuted from subject to object—from part of an "I," to an "it." A wholesome life depends on remaining whole and on keeping your distance from all that is not us. "One of the main characteristics of life is discreteness," states Nabokov's Pnin. "Unless a film of flesh envelops us, we die. Man exists only insofar as he is separated from his surroundings. The cranium is a space-traveller's helmet. Stay inside or you perish. Death is divestment, death is communion. It may be wonderful to mix with the landscape, but to do so is the end of the tender ego."

Of all the disparate components of discarded human anatomy, the head exerts the most vivid impression on embodied souls who still reside in their cranium, that "space-traveller's helmet." A decedent's head demands less imagination on the part of the living to visualize the departed's nature than, say, a rib, a finger bone or vertebra. At the end of his stay in Rome in April, 1788, Goethe visited the Accademia di San Luca to pay homage to what he believed (incorrectly) to be Raphael's skull. Goethe rhapsodized on how "It was wonderful to look at—a brain-pan of beautiful proportions and perfectly smooth, without any of those protrubances and bumps which have been observed on other skulls." So taken by this remnant was Goethe—"I could hardly tear myself away"—that he obtained a cast of the skull "which I often look at and reflect upon."

An unknown admirer of the arts—or of skulls—coveted the head of another famous painter, Goya, for years ago the artist's cranium disappeared, perhaps into the hands of an aesthete as appreciative as Goethe. Between the time Goya died in exile at Bordeaux, France, in 1828 and the return of his body to Spain sixty years later the painter mysteriously lost his head, a bit of skullduggery which probably occurred when workers opened the Spaniard's coffin to resurrect him for repatriation. Goya's body, minus the head, returned to Madrid where it reposes in San Francisco church. Perhaps his skull decorates someone's abode: if you can't afford an original Goya the next best thing is the original Goya. Unlike head-poor San Francisco, the cathedral of Barcelona in Spain boasts a bodyless head, a cranium which dangles decoratively beneath the organ. This relic supposedly once topped al-Mansoor, "the Victorious," who in the tenth century destroyed Santiago de Campostela, sacked Barcelona, and devastated many other lesser Spanish settlements. During his military campaigns al-Mansoor collected from his armor dust which he directed should be put into his coffin as evidence to Allah that he had faithfully combatted the Christians. The hanging, severed head of the warrior who died at Medinaceli, 250 miles west of Barcelona, when returning from a campaign in Castile in 1002, exemplifies for the body's anatomy Benjamin Franklin's pronouncement in regard to the body politic—that we must all hang together or we will surely all hang separately.

Skulls haunt by evoking more than meets the eye. In a head can be read all sorts of things about its owner. Robert Burton in *The Anatomy of Melancholy*—that magnificent seventeenth-century compendium of marvels, oddities, facts, and fictions, strange and wonderful—maintained that beneath the superficial, or superfacial, covering the skull represented the underlying reality of a beloved: "Take her skin from her face, and thou shalt see all loathsomeness under it, that beauty is a superficial skin and bones, nerves, sinews." Because skulls seem to retain the essence of a decedent, posterity finds the craniums of famous departed worthy of contemplation. Such renowned heads, however, all too seldom surface for examination. The cranium of Oliver Cromwell (d. 1658), detached from his body in the late seventeenth century, has remained in private hands for nearly two centuries.

However, the skull of Mozart (whose body's last resting place in Vienna is described in Chapter II) happened to appear long after the composer had disappeared. In 1842 a grave-digger at St. Mark's cemetery, where Mozart was buried in 1791, gave the skull as a present to an artist, Jacob Hyrtl, whose brother, an anatomy professor, cut off the base of the cranium to examine the bony ear. In 1901 the skull, missing its base and lower jaw, came to rest in Salzburg where it remained in relative obscurity for nearly a century until, in 1990, a paleontologist at the local university examined the relic. The scientist found that the skull's structure resembled a portrait of Mozart painted by Dorothea Stock and that a faint fracture, with traces of bleeding just beneath the cranium, might have caused the dizziness and headaches which the composer mentioned in April and May 1790. Thus was Mozart's head examined fully two centuries after his death.

Back in 1835, a few years before the composer's skull surfaced, appeared the cranium of Jonathan Swift. Swift (d. 1745) reposes in Dublin's St. Patrick Cathedral, his grave designated by a modest brass plate in the floor next to an even smaller marker to his lady friend "Stella." Esther Johnson (d. 1728) also merits a wall plaque, topped by a stone skull, praising her as "a Person of Extraordinary Endowments and Accomplishments." (Another Swift memento is housed in the right transcept of the cathedral, where a simple white stone bears the inscription: "Here lieth the Body of Alexder McGee [d.1722], Servant to Dr. Swift Dean of St. Patrick's. His Grateful Master caused this Monument to be erected in memory of his Discretion, Fidelity and Diligence in that humble station.") After Swift's death he became an object of great curiosity due to his misanthropy and the mental instability that plagued him in later life. Eventually, in 1835 the opportunity arose to peek into Swift's mind. It happened that just at the time a group of phrenologists had gathered in Dublin for a conference, workers discovered water seeping into the crypt where Swift reposed. When church officials opened the grave to check possible damage the phrenologists flocked to examine the author's skull in great detail.

At Cornell University the Wilder Brain Collection, established in the 1890s by animal biologist Burt Green Wilder, includes the grey matter of more than one hundred departed, including the brain of Wilder himself, who died in 1925. Wilder assembled the collection, which once numbered some six hundred and fifty specimens—dissections destroyed many of them—by distributing brain bequest forms to people attending Cornell functions. In the medical seminar room at another university, in Padua, Italy, a glass case displays eight skulls willed by medical professors to the faculty. By each specimen appears the name of the cranium's one time owner/occupant. After a bean ball hit St. Louis Cardinal baseball great Dizzy Dean, the local newspaper carried the headline, "X-Ray of Dean's head reveals nothing." This suggests the possible embarassment awaiting a person who submits his brain to close scrutiny.

Brainy Jeremy Bentham, political thinker and founder of the utilitarian school of philosophy, decided to leave not only his brain but his entire body to posterity. Bentham pondered what he no doubt considered the ultimate utilitarian question—"Of what use is a dead man to the living?"—in an unpublished essay (the British Museum holds the manuscript) entitled "Auto-Icon, or Further Uses of the Dead to the Living." He proposed that preserved bodies be set up as monuments in a "Temple of Fame" which would come to contain "a population of illustrious Auto-Icons." The preserved body of Bentham (d. 1832) now practices what its former consciousness preached.

Jeremy's auto-icon occupies a glass display case at University College in London. The philosopher wears his normal attire: a wide-brimmed straw hat with a black ribbon tied in a bow, a black coat, a vest, brown leather trousers, woven leather slippers, brown gloves, a ruff-embellished shirt. The garments were cleaned in 1939—while the Department of Egyptology restored and restuffed the figure—and again in 1979. Bentham's skull resides in a small box, decorated with the college crest, stored over a nearby doorway. The surrogate head which now tops the philosopher's body consists of a puffy wax image molded into a mien that recalls Ben Franklin. After Bentham's demise technicians found his head difficult to embalm as the object exuded an unfreezable, oil-like substance which made the flesh intractable. When one observer suggested that the freeze-proof liquid might well serve to oil chronometers used in cold areas, a wit noted that this might lead to the killing of philosophers for their oil, much as bears are hunted to obtain their grease. Bentham's will contained detailed and explicit instructions for handling his corpse:

My body I give to my dear-friend Doctor Southwood Smith to be disposed of in manner hereinafter mentioned . . . The skeleton he will cause to be put together in such manner as that the whole figure may be seated in a chair usually occupied by me when living in the attitude in which I am sitting when engaged in thought in the course of the time employed in writing. I direct that the body thus prepared shall be transfered to my executor. He will cause the skeleton to be clad in one of the suits of black occasionally worn by me. The body so clothed together with the chair and the staff in my later years borne by me he will take charge of and for containing the whole apparatus he will cause to be prepared an appropriate box or case and will cause to be engraved in conspicuous characters on a plate to be affixed thereon and also on the labels of the glass case in which the preparations of the soft parts of my body shall be contained . . . my name . . . If it should so happen that my personal friends and other disciples should be disposed to meet together on some day or days of the year for the purpose of commemorating the Founder of the greatest happiness system of morals and legislation my executor will from time to time cause to be conveyed to the room in which they meet the said Box or case with the contents there to be stationed in such part of the room as to the assembled company shall seem meet.

So it is that twice a year the philospher's followers remove him from the case and seat their departed leader at the head of the table during the Bentham Society dinner, held in the main refectory of University College.

In this spirit, the most famous such auto-icons are the corpses of Lenin and Mao Zedong, which have served to inspire, amuse, fascinate, awe, repel or otherwise affect millions of gawkers who visit their show bodies in Moscow and in Beijing. The authorities carefully preserve and protect the great men. At Mao's mausoleum on Tiananmen Square in Beijing a mechanism lowers the chairman into a freezer every night. Lenin, who resides in a squat, granite mausoleum on Red Square in Moscow, was spirited away to Siberia for safekeeping—minus his brain—as the German army approached Moscow in 1941. Lenin's brain, pickled and sectioned, remained at the Soviet Academy of Sciences' Brain Institute, founded in 1926 to study the great man's grey matter. Since then the institute has probed many famous brains, including those of Stalin, writer Maxim Gorky and, most recently, physicist and dissident Andrei Sakharov. As for Mao's and Lenin's bodies, both fellows looked rather well—all things considered—when I stopped in to see them. Inside the drab, boxy mausoleum in Beijing, built in 1976 just after Mao's death, stands a statue of the leader with a benign expression on his face. In the display chamber reposed a similarly benign Mao, nestled under a red blanket bearing a hammer and sickle design. Mao's face looked rather waxy, with skin too smooth, and to his chin clung the wart which his "warts and all" portraits and photos show. Moscow's Lenin mausoleum—close to the ground, angular, sober— seemed a Russian version of Frank Lloyd Wright's prairie school architecture. At the entrance a stony faced guard "shhh-ed" everyone and directed women to form a line on the left, men on the right. The two files descended around to the left, of course, and entered the central chamber, there to see Lenin (d. 1924), also rather waxy looking, reposing on billowy red material. On his face appeared a few faint pock marks or blemishes. We walked around three sides of the body, viewing Lenin from different angles, then exited off to the right and filed past the Kremlin wall where tombs hold the remains of such Soviet leaders as Brezhnev, Andropov, and even Stalin himself. But none of them merited the posthumous privilege of serving as an auto-icon.

Public displays of human anatomy—especially religious relics—were once fairly common. Relics were to the Europe of half a millenium ago what baseball cards or antique beer cans are to America today. Impassioned collectors back then assembled exhibits of holy bones. Maybe the aficionados even attended conventions at which connoisseurs traded their specimens. In the fifteenth and early sixteen centuries Freder- ick the Great, the elector of Saxony at the time of Martin Luther, devoted a lifetime to making Wittenberg a depository of sacred relics. The prince traveled all over Europe to collect bones, religious objects and other ecclesiastical treasures, in- cluding such items as a thorn from Christ's crown, a tooth which once served St. Jerome, a quartet of pieces from St. Augustine's body, four of the Virgin Mary's hairs, a bit of gold and three pieces of myrrh brought by the Wise Men, and a twig from Moses' burning bush. In 1509 Frederick commissioned a catalog, illustrated by Lucas Cranach, which listed some five thousand items, and by 1520 the collection had expanded to include more than nineteen thousand holy bones alone. Although the displays enthralled many pious pilgrims, Martin Luther remained unimpressed, noting his skepticism in *Table Talk*—a compendium of six thousand five hundred and ninety-six of his pithy sayings and observations (one example: "The monks are the fleas on God Almighty's fur coat"): "What lies there are about relics! One claims to have a feather from the wing of the angel Gabriel, and the bishop of Mainz has a flame from Moses' burning bush. And how does it happen that eighteen Apostles are buried in Germany when Christ had only twelve?" Other religions also strain credulity by their excess of supposedly holy relics. Speaking of the many Buddha-related items boasted by various monasteries, Sir. J. G. Scott comments in *The Burman:* "Burma alone claims more personal remains than could possible have existed. The same thing is, I believe, true of Popish relics in Europe, where pieces of the true cross are as abundant as portions of the dress of the founder of Buddhism are in Burma."

Relics abound at one of Christendom's hotbeds of religious human remnants—Mount Athos, the Greek Orthodox monastic community tucked away on a narrow peninsula that extends into the Aegean from northern Greece. Reversby Sitwell, quoted in *Mt. Athos* by J. J. Norwich, holds that "in this unsavoury field, Mount Athos must stand supreme among all the shrines of Orthodox Christendom." Mount Athos is itself a relic from the distant past, for the venerable monasteries which dot that isolated strip of land survive as antiquated enclaves of the tenth, eleventh and twelfth centuries. Many of the monasteries boast bones that once comprised part of a saint, obscure long-gone holy men who survive only in a most fragmentary form: the head of St. Basil and left hand of Chilsostomos at Grand Lavra monastery; St. Nyphon's head and right hand, Prodromos's head at Dionysios; an unusually complete set of both legs as well as the right palm of St. Anastasia Romaia at St. Gregory; the left leg of St. Anna and the left palm of St. Gregory Theologos at Koutloumousiou, and his leg—whether right or left unspecified—at St. Paul; and dozens of other such pieces. An enterprising member of a local holy order possessed by a sense of order would induce the St. Paul monastery to trade its leg of St. Gregory Theologos with Koutloumousiou to be combined there with the saint's left hand so that gradually, after further such exchanges, the Athos monks might reassemble nearly complete skeletons of departed holy men for display and veneration. As things are now, if you want St. Gregory in all his glory you have to make the rounds of various monasteries and assemble him piecemeal in your mind, a definite challenge to people who are scatter-brained. In fact, the saintly remains are not displayed openly in the Mount Athos monasteries, nor do the monks show their treasures on simple demand, so only by chance did I manage to see some of the precious holy bones.

One morning as I was leaving the church at the Simon Petras monastery after an early service a sudden stir of priestly activity delayed me. The monks set up a long, low narrow table which they covered with a cloth. I looked on with anticipation: the bare table seemed full of possibility, and I tried to imagine what feast for the stomach, eyes or otherwise might soon materialize. Soon the monks returned with about six cigar box-sized silver and gold containers which they arranged on the cloth, then opened to reveal the treasured contents—bones or pieces of bone set into little niches and surrounded by jewels or designs worked into the precious metal that formed the frame. The robed monks filed by the open boxes, each worshiper bending down to kiss the contents, and after the procession had passed and the last kiss bestowed, I advanced to the table to inspect—not to buss— the relics, but without further ado the monks began to snap the lids shut. I managed to catch a quick look at a bony hand—whose I am not sure, for Simon Petras boasts the left hand of St. Magdalene and one belonging to St. Dionysious. But no matter, for at least I had glimpsed one of Athos's many relics and, when it comes to hands, I am sure that when you have seen one you have seen them all. The monks finished closing the boxes, which they quickly removed, then they folded the cloth, collapsed the table and the brief ceremony ended as abruptly as it had begun.

So quickly did that adoration of the relics transpire that I failed to check the color of the bones, whose hue seemingly determines their sanctity. As Maryse Choise—a French woman who disguised herself as a man to visit the all-male monastic community forbidden to females—recounted in *A Month Among the Men,* quoting a monk:

> We have no cemetery here, properly speaking . . . When a monk dies, he is buried without coffin, wrapped only in his cloak. Three years later his temporary tomb is opened. If his flesh has not been completely absorbed by the earth, that means he did not die free of sin. His soul has not been saved, and the whole monastery prays for the errant brother. If, on the other hand, the bones are found clean, dry, and honey-colored, this proves that the monk died a saint. The yellower the bones, the saintlier the monk.

While hiking around Mount Athos—the only way you can travel across the car-less peninsula—I found one of those burial grounds, a small plot by the sea next to St. Gregorio monastery. Curved mounds of dirt vaguely suggested the presence of bodies beneath—cloth-swathed monks planted in the field and gradually growing into the earth which devout survivors would later harvest for bones: on Mount Athos the monks grow their own religious relics.

Isolated religious communities such as Mount Athos generate, renovate and venerate their own home-grown, in-house relics. Santa Caterina, like Athos a Greek Orthodox enclave in a remote and hard-to-reach corner of the earth,

nestles in the valley below Mt. Sinai, occupying the site of a
fort built by Roman emperor Justinian in 530 to protect local
Christian anchorites from Arab attackers. In the early fourteenth century the retreat, originally called the monastery of
St. Mary, adopted its new name to honor the virgin martyr
beheaded early in the fourth century. Angels transported her
bones to the summit of Mt. Catherine, where monks at the
monastery discovered her remains some three centuries later.
The saintly bones exuded holy oil which the clerics collected.
About 1026 a monk named Simon accidentally detached
three of Catherine's fingers while he was extracting oil. When
Simon later visited Europe on one of the regular trips the
brothers took to collect offerings, he presented the fingers to
Duke Robert of Normandy, father of William the Conqueror, who deposited the relics in the Abbey of the Trinity,
soon renamed after St. Catherine, near Rouen and before
long the sanctuary became known as a place of miraculous
healings. The cult of Catherine rapidly spread throughout the
West—the voice of St. Catherine was one of those heard by
Joan of Arc in the early fifteenth century—and when pilgrims
from Europe began to arrive at Santa Caterina in the Sinai the
monks catered to the new interest by removing her bones
from the mountain and putting them in a chest displayed at
the monastery church. At least one latter-day man of religion, however, failed to appreciate the holy relics: complaining of "misplaced piety," American clergyman Harry
Emerson Fosdick referred to the treasures as "the horrid skull
and hand of Saint Catherine, decked with jewels and shrined
in a casket."

Although St. Catherine—with her jewel-covered cranium
and her left hand each reposing in a golden container at the
monastery's Byzantine Church of the Transfiguration—remains Santa Caterina's best known fragmentary personage,
the skulls and bones of some three thousand monks, most of
them anonymous, also inhabit the ancient religious settle-

ment. Because the monastery's graveyard contains room for only six souls at a time, when a monk goes to his reward his survivors disinter the remains of the longest buried predecessor and transfer his bones to the charnel house for permanent storage. A small white building outside the monastery's high, fortress-like walls houses the ossuary. In death, as in life, a hierarchy stratifies the inhabitants. The remnants of each new arrival receive treatment based on the rank of the man the bones once structured. The remains of archbishops and bishops, some clad in a *megaloschemos* (robe of angels), occupy small wooden caskets stored in reserved niches; priests reside in less elegant quarters; and mere monks end up with their heads tossed on a pile of skulls. Just inside the charnel house entrance, in the first compartment to the left, stand stacks of skulls piled high like interchangeable assembly-line products stored for later use. Along the right wall stretch nine rectangular alcoves filled with sets of bones that belonged to the higher ecclesiastics, and to the rear of the house stand four-foot-high stacks of mixed bones supplied by lesser mortals. A nearby cove holds a taller bank of bones taken from the extremities. Rotted skin of leathery feet and hands, some with their nails still vaguely visible, dangle at random to form a grisly pattern, while at the lower right of the bone stack, at the time of my visit—"awful yet pleasing," as colonial-era Yankee cemetery connoisseur Samuel Sewell described his 1696 Christmas visit to the family tomb—hung the sole of a stray foot as if the poor soul it belonged to was trying to step down from the pile of human residues. The departed Fromont brothers from Rennes, France, present the unusual spectacle of two skeletons linked by a chain. In the ninth century a bishop sentenced the brothers to undertake a penitential pilgrimage to Santa Caterina after they murdered their uncle. The pair spent the rest of their lives chained by fetters supposedly made from the murder weapon and designed so that whenever one of the penitents reposed the other was pulled up, a feature which ensured that one of them always remained awake to pray.

The most evocative resident of Santa Caterina's charnel house, St. Stephanos, sports on his seated skeleton a violet velvet cap and a *megaloschemos*. With his elegant attire, privileged position by the door, and well-connected bones St. Stephanos seems to preside over the ossuary. The black cape, far too large for his now fleshless frame, bears sewn crosses and other religious symbols, while a metal cross dangles from the figure's neck. All these enhancements lend the saint a lifelike appearance. In his more lively days Stephanos guarded the arched gateway which led to the stone stairway that climbs Mount Sinai. Only pilgrims who had confessed their sins could pass, so Stephanos either heard confession on the spot or accepted a certificate of confession issued elsewhere. According to legend the monk, who lived as a hermit, trained a panther cub to guard his cell against wild hyenas. Finally safe from hyenas and all other mortal hazards, Stephanos (d. 580) sits by the entrance to the charnel house but, now mute, no longer requests confession from visitors to the holy places there at Mount Sinai.

When John Lloyd Stephens, the famous nineteenth century American traveler, visited Santa Caterina he found the charnel house more disquieting than any of the many other ossuaries and catacombs he had previously seen. In *Incidents of Travel in Egypt, Arabia Petraea and the Holy Land* Stephens noted that none of the other such places struck "me so powerfully as the charnel-house at the Convent of Mount Sinai." Even the Capuchin catacomb at Palermo in Sicily, the most grotesque and gruesome burial area I have come across, failed to affect Stephens as strongly as did Santa Caterina and its bone piles. For me, however, the Palermo installation seemed much more mournful, both because it presents such a gloomy appearance and because the deceased figures, many of them not simply skeletons but dessicated bodies, wear clothes that make them especially macabre. Stephens described one such body, a once-dewy young thing who had embellished Palermo society, clad in death "in the same white dress which she had worn at the ball, complete even to the white slippers, the belt around her waist, and the jeweled mockery of a watch hanging at her side, as if she had not done with time." But no longer did the twenty-year-old beauty retain her charms, for now "her face was bare, the skin dry, black and shriveled, like burnt paper; the cheeks sunken; the rosy lips a piece of discolored parchment; the teeth horribly projecting; the nose gone . . . and a long tress of hair curling in each hollow eye." This strange subterranean enclave, where some eight thousand bodies moulder, originated in 1599 when Capuchin friars set aside a burial area for themselves. Later, prominent Palermo families sought permission to bury their dead in the holy catacomb, and over time the monks expanded the burial corridors to receive the increasing flow of bodies, many occupying open wooden boxes that line the underground passageways or hang along the white-washed walls. The Capuchins dehydrated the bodies by sealing them in chambers for six or seven months, then placing the corpses in a bath of aromatic herbs and vinegar, finally exposing them to the sun. The monks stuffed the shriveled bodies with straw, clothed them in their ordinary attire and installed the shrunken leathery figures in the catacomb. In times past, relatives of the deceased—which present an appearance only a mother could love—would visit their dear departed, dessicated family members to change the garments. Alfred Fabre-Luce described the mummies in *La mort à changé* as "large dolls": but what little girls would fancy playing with figures that grotesque and distorted?

Through the long corridors of this strange netherworld I wandered, passing quasi-people, their heads and hands with bits of leathery flesh clinging to them as if for dear life, the vaguely human skulls bearing slight patches of coarse skin that barely kept the bones at bay; hunched bodies and heads bowing as if in permanent prayer; oversized attire draped baggily over the shrunken forms. Skewed to the walls, the dead which dangle in Palermo's Capuchin catacomb comprise a bizarre collection of wasted corpses like mounted animal specimens on display in a natural history museum. It is the clothes worn by these gruesome figures which makes them so disquieting. Dressed in ordinary attire, the bodies somehow seem out of place—not quite dead but certainly not alive, lost in some sort of zombie-like limbo, a weird borderline existence. The mummies remain insufficiently removed from the world of the living to comfort us that we enjoy any essential advantage over those departed, but still human-like, beings: the grisly displays thus mirror our mortality.

Different areas of the catacomb include separate corridors for men, for women, for "professors" (doctors, lawyers and other professionals), for priests, and for the Capuchin friars, whose section contains the remains of the original forty monks who arrived in Palermo in the late sixteenth century. All manner of men, women and children occupy the corridors: in an alcove devoted to children sleeps a week-old baby, displayed high on the wall; one man sports a stovepipe hat worn at a jaunty angle; one alcove in the women's section houses virgins, their heads symbolically crowned with flowers; an Italian diplomat to the United States reposes in a cell near a carton bearing a crudely lettered sign, "baby girl sleeps in beauty," while the next to the ambassador lies Rosalia Lombardo (d. 1920), a perfectly preserved two-year-old girl sporting a satin ribbon in her still lustrous hair. Immediately after her demise, one Dr. Salafia injected the body with various secret fluids which have kept little Rosalia unblemished by the passage of time. Cosmetic companies would no doubt fork over a fortune to learn the doctor's formula, but unfortunately he died suddenly without recording the magic ingredients. Rosalia occupies her place in the Capuchin catacomb by special permission of the authorities, for a century or so ago the government prohibited burial of bodies outside cemeteries.

Very few burial chambers in the world boast life-like bodies as does Palermo's Capuchin catacomb. Most such installations contain only bones. In the early eighteenth century the Franciscan church in Toulouse, France, boasted a collection of mummies which the priests prepared by burying bodies in soil to consume their flesh, then exposing the remains to the air, after which they were put on display. The cloister at the famous Great St. Bernard hospice in the Swiss Alps houses mummies, as does the old castle at Quedlinburg in the foothills of the Harz Mountains in Prussia. Steps at the south transept of Bremen cathedral in northern Germany lead down into the *Bleikeller* (lead cellar)—so called because the room once held lead sheets used for the sanctuary's roof— where seven mummified bodies, the oldest dating from 1450, reside.

But Italy takes the prize as Europe's most mummified land. In a cave below the church of the little mountain village of San Stefano in Abruzzo province, east of Rome, once reposed bodies buried in their clothes and seated on cane chairs. In 1912 bricklayers working at the church fled with fright when they accidently broke into the cave. Later, when a school teacher threw a lit paper into the spooky room to illuminate it, the skeletons caught fire and burned to cinders. A similar fate befell the twenty or so mummies which once occupied San Michele chapel in the cathedral in Venzone, a town in the foothills of the Alps. Preserved by a special fungus that enabled the bodies to resist decomposition, or perhaps by special ventilation in the cathedral, the bodies became naturally mummified, and were only destroyed in 1976 by earthquakes. Alchemical experiments in the eighteenth century by the Duke of Sansevero preserved his servants' bodies, displayed at the Cappella Sansevero in the center of Naples. In "Labels," an account of a 1929 Mediterranean cruise, Evelyn Waugh tells of finding a pair of preserved bodies at the funerary chapel of the Sangro di Sansevero: "Two figures of death stood upright against the wall in rococo coffins, their arms folded across their chests. They were quite naked and dark brown in colour. They had some teeth and some hair. At first I thought they were statues of more than usual virtuosity. Then I realized that they were exhumed corpses, partially mummified by the aridity of the air, like the corpses at St. Michan's in Dublin."

St. Michan's indeed boasts "the Historic Old vaults in which Bodies may be seen in a wonderful state of preservation, though not embalmed," as the ticket of admission to the display promises. Open wooden caskets in stone cells beneath St. Michan's hold the leathery bodies, preserved—to a greater or lesser degree—by the even temperature and dryness supposedly facilitated by a layer of limestone beneath the vaults, first mentioned in the church's burial registers around 1670. Splendid lace-like webs woven by spiders which (along with, presumably, the insects they eat) comprise the only form of life in that underground realm, decorate the otherwise severe vault area. In the Leitram family chamber reposes the murdered Lord Leitram, so unpopular a land owner that a mob tried to prevent his corpse from interment when it arrived in Dublin. In another section twin caskets contain John and Henry Sheares, Irish patriots executed in 1798. On the centenary of their deaths an admirer put a wreath of fresh flowers into the vault. Before long dampness from the blooms caused the bodies to begin decomposing, and by 1940 the corpses had been reduced to bone. On a box at the rear of the chamber lie twigs, remnants of the fatal wreath. Toward the back of the vaults reposes a giant figure, some eight feet tall, known as the Crusader. His vertebrae, partly exposed, seemed about twice as big as those of an ordinary man. The guide told me it was supposed to be good luck to shake the Crusader's hand, but I opted instead to touch the skin of his chest, which felt smooth and supple like high quality leather. Adjacent lies a boy who still possesses perfect toe and fingernails, while at his ankles the blood vessels have barely deteriorated. The young man's left arm, however, remains less integrated, for nearly a century ago a thief detached the appendage, and it ended up in a private museum in County Down. In the early 1970s an eighty-eight-year-old woman, sister of the museum's owner, let it be known that she possessed the missing limb and intended to return it. Before long the relic—the arm, not the woman—arrived at St. Michan's, where it was restored to the original owner.

The so-called Pantheon in Guanajuato, Mexico, also houses a display of dessicated bodies, most of them unclad but a few wearing clothes and thus resembling the grotesque figures at the Capuchin catacomb in Palermo. Outside, above the Pantheon's subterranean mummy rooms, rises a large wall pocked with burial niches, while around the attractive little square near the wall stand stalls selling souvenirs, perhaps the world's most frivolous market located just by an interment area. Down in the darker precincts of the Pantheon thirteen glass cases line one wall of a long narrow hallway, each case holding about eight bodies, their skin yellowish and leather-like. One case contains only children, wearing diapers, while above another infant appears a sign: "The smallest mummy in the world," the figure's open mouth recalling Edward Munch's famous painting, "The Scream." A number of the women on display bear swollen bellies, as if they had died while pregnant. Through holes left by missing facial skin on one figure emerges the skull, its white bones contrasting with the yellow-orange fleshy remains. On the face of a body labelled Gabino Castro (d. 1904) remain well formed and fluffy looking hairs, never again to be shaved, while a woman wears a long braid of hair across her left breast in a permanent coquettish pose. One man, comically macabre, wears only a pair of underpants. Virtually every figure bears a mis-shapen head with grotesque expression which seems both vaguely human and distorted inanimate configurations. This odd combination lends the bodies a morbidly fascinating touch, for the objects retain warped traces of their former incarnation as people. Unlike mere bone piles or even a skeleton, which bear only sketchy resemblance to an actual human being, the mummies at Guanajuato—like the dessicated but well-preserved bodies at Palermos' Capuchin catacomb and those at St. Michan's in Dublin—combine the contradictory characteristics of temporality and eternity: in the figures one sees both the living and the departed, death with a human face and humanity with the skull beneath the skin.

Those three displays are, I believe, the world's only remaining major mummy depositories. Catacombs, crypts, ossuaries, charnel houses, *momento mori* chapels and other such funerary sites usually contain nothing more than bare bones. Some house only a skeletal sampler—just a few bony fragments or a scattering of skulls and other pieces of disused anatomy. Embedded in the floor of two rooms in the museum at Patzcuaro, Mexico, south of Guanajuato—in a building which housed what was supposedly the oldest school in the New World, established in 1540—lie vertebrae, a feature reminiscent of the era when haciendas had floors paved partly with bones used by ranch hands to scape mud from their shoes during the rainy season. Farther afield in Latin America, chambers beneath the San Francisco church in Lima, Peru, reached by passing a nineteenth-century funeral cart with four carved wooden skulls, bear decorations made of vertebrae and other gracefully curved bones, while around the burial niche of a Father Juan Gomez (d. 1631) runs a border of neatly arranged skulls. Farther along in the catacomb at San Francisco I passed a common grave filled with a chaos of dislocated bones, then more orderly, bathtub-sized pits where the remains rise in neat piles. At one point in this netherworld I gained a tomb's-eye view of the upper world, the land of the living, through a small grill set in the ceiling above me which afforded a look into the church where worshipers celebrated a mass. Another Lima church, San-Augustín, boasts a skeletal Death figure so sinister that its sculptor supposedly died of fright when he entered the vestry one evening and saw it lurking in the shadows grinning hideously. Like San Francisco in Lima, the church of that name in Cuzco in the Peruvian highlands houses bone displays. Bones from deceased Franciscans decorate a small cubicle just off the cloister, and from the ceiling hang cords formed by short, straight bones from which dangle pelvis lamps. Vertebrae pattern the ceiling and on two walls bones spell out messages from and about the grave. One partly deboned and skeletal phrase reads: "Hermana (m)ue(r)te es(p)e(r)a me" (sister death, wait for me). The other says, "Lo que eres tú, lo que soy seras" (As you are, so once was I).

Religious sanctuaries all around Europe house bones in various states of being—disconnected, attached, patterned, piled, displayed, littered, bejeweled. Such bones haunt hundreds of sacred precincts in obscure corners of the European continent. (The only catacomb in the United States burrows beneath the Ironbound section in Newark, New Jersey. Maintained by the Immaculate Heart of Mary church, the catacomb is open for tour.) In Brittany many churchyards include an ossuary, often topped by a "Calvary," an elaborate stone cross monument. Relatives of a deceased remove the skull and bones from the grave after a certain number of years. The wealthy enclose the skull in a small box in the form of a miniature church with a heart-shaped door through which the head can be seen. Survivors carry the skull boxes in processions or feasts of the dead. In the crypt of the Carmelite church in Paris (70 rue de Vaugiraud) lie the bones of 117 ecclesiastics beaten to death in 1792 and buried in a pit with manure and broken plates. A chapel at St. Peter's in Munich contains a macabre skeleton with a gold thread coverlet studded with pearls and with garish aqua, orange and blue stones, while in the eye sockets lie pads also decorated with stones. Not far from San Paolo in Ubeda, Spain— where the Heads of the Dead chapel bears over its entrance seventeen realistically carved relief skulls—lies the monastery chapel where the famous mystic poet San Juan de la Cruz lived his last days before attaining the death he so longed for: "I die because I do not die." A reproduction of the cell in which San Juan died in 1591 contains two bones from a finger of his right hand—perhaps the very same that once held the pen he used to write his poems—and other bones from his arm.

Not only church-connected locales but even secular sites house bones. The Hunterian Museum at London's Royal College of Surgeons by Lincoln's Inn Fields contains a splendid collection of skeletons as well as displays on various organs grouped into such categories as locomotion, digestion, sense. Exhibits of those soft, fleshy, perishable, non-bone components of human anatomy—extremely rare in their disembodied state—contrast markedly with angular, white, durable bones more commonly on display. So wonderous, graceful and artistic are these anatomical specimens— with amazing shapes, designs, whorls, configurations and convolutions—that they seem to have been engendered, by design or by chance, by a most talented creator. Elizabeth Barrett Browning wrote in *Aurora Leigh* how "Surgeons . . . spend raptures upon perfect specimens/Of indurated veins, distorted joints,/Or beautiful new cases of curved spine."

Nonmedical people seldom see such sights. In *Miss Lonelyhearts* Nathanael West describes the body's hidden innards, that abstract, painting-like organic cluster which surgeons "spend raptures upon": "Under the skin of man is a wonderous jungle where veins like lush tropical growths hang along over-ripe organs and weed-like entrails writhe in squirming tangles of red and yellow." Within this jungly system ebb and flow all manner of ideas, emotions, impressions, perceptions and feelings as well as juices, fluids, potions, liquids and secretions. These soft bodily components—so calibrated to support life, so colorful and artfully designed—epitomize the melancholy of anatomy, for the insubstantial organs soon wither and decay, leaving as residues only the colorless bony remains which evidence a decedent's former existence. Such bone remnants prevail at the Hunterian Museum. One exhibit consists of a series of tiny skeletons showing fetuses at various ages and stages: three months (two and a half inches), five months (seven inches), birth (eighteen inches). This must be the world's only bone display devoted to birth rather than death. These frail, bent, incipient beings resemble the hunched skeletal former beings on view at the catacombs in Palermo and Guanajuato. Similarly helpless, those pre-natal and postmortem curvy configurations bracket a brief interlude during which a being can stand up for himself. Upstairs at the College of Surgeons' museum stands a skeleton of William Cordes, executed in 1828 for the murder of Maria Marten. (The museum at Bury St. Edmunds contains an account of his trial bound in leather made from the killer's skin.)

Other skeletons at the Hunterian include the Sicilian Dwarf, Caroline Cracham, a 19.8-inch-high figure (1815–1824) exhibited at a show in England; and the Irish Giant, Charles Bryhe, some eight feet tall, shown with his glove—a substantial hunk of leather—and a shoe, a huge object compared with Caroline's dainty footwear which is also on display. Although the world's tallest man, nearly-nine-foot Robert Wadlow, failed to leave his bone frame behind for display—he reposes in Oakwood Cemetery, Alton, Illinois—the imposing skeleton of Siah Khan (d. 1940) occupies a glass case inside the main entrance of the medical school in Shiraz, Iran. Siah suffered from extreme gigantism and acromegaly (permanent enlargements of the head, thorax, hands and feet). Photos of him at ages twelve, eighteen, twenty-three and twenty-eight show Siah's terribly deformed face, like a partly melted wax mask, or putty moulded by an insane sculptor. To age six Siah appeared normal, but he then began to grow at a rapid rate and by the time he was nine, stood as tall as a person more than twice his age. The giant earned a living in Shiraz by putting himself on display. In return for the care he received while alive, Siah willed his skeleton to the medical school. After his death from pneumonia, his body occupied a metal coffin for five years until school personnel mounted Siah's huge bony infrastructure. Even as a skeleton Siah remains a strange and grotesque figure, one of the most frightening fellows of the postmortem world that I ever laid eyes on. Apart from the vast dimensions—a finger bone seemed about the size of a normal human foot—the deformities lend him an other-worldly, science fiction appearance: the cranium drops down over the eye cavities like a truncated hood, the teeth and cheeks sit deeply sunken in the skull. A half-century after his death the Shiraz giant still retains the power to disquiet on-lookers.

Much less disquieting than entire bodies—which resemble humans so closely that they remind us of our fate—are displays of disembodied anatomical parts. The millions of bones in the Paris catacombs seem almost abstract and disconnected from human existence. These objects were installed in the late eighteenth century after the French authorities began closing the ancient, festering burial grounds around the capital, respectfully exhuming the bones left by some nine centuries of departed Parisians and transferring the remains to the newly opened catacombs, installed in the Montrouge quarries, a labyrinth of cave-like chambers from which builders had taken stones to construct much of Paris. Gradually the caverns filled with bones disinterred from some thirty age-old graveyards, including Les Innocents, St. Roche, St. Eustache, and St. Sulpice. As bonfires cast eerie flickering shadows over the venerable cemeteries, workmen dug up the bones and—followed by priests who chanted the funeral service—carted them to the Montrouge quarries where the remnants were dumped through a shaft to the netherworld. The shaft still exists at number 21½ avenue du Parc-Montsouris. In 1786 the archbishop of Paris consecrated the new repository of old Parisian bones, comprising the residues of an estimated six million people, among them Mansart (original architect of Val-de-Grâce church, described below), Rabelais, Montesquieu, Lavoisier, Danton, Robespierre, Madame de Pompedour, and Saint Germain. Which particular bones belonged to those illustrious figures, however, remains unknown for of the millions of people in the catacombs not a single soul can be identified. In 1830 authorities granted and then withdrew permission for visitors to the subterranean burial ground, concluding "that it would be a sort of profanation to exhibit the bone piles arranged with a completely unseemly symmetry and that it would perhaps be immoral to offer to the curiosity of the public a display unworthy of a civilized people." By then the French must have felt rather put down: Voltaire, arguing in the 1780s that Les Innocents should be closed, stated that the "cemetery is still a witness to a barbarity of a sort which puts the French well below the Hottentots," and now the prefect of the Seine implied that his compatriots might not be altogether civilized in wanting to visit the catacombs. But in 1874 the officials again opened the ossuary, which over the years had attracted such distinguished, and now extinguished, visitors as Bismarck, Napoleon III, Emperor Francis I of Austria, two regiments of Russian troops bivouacked on the nearby Montsouris plains in 1914, and Crown Prince (later king) Oscar of Sweden who, during his tour in May 1867 (the caverns were specially opened for the royal review of bones) scratched graffiti which can still be seen: "Toute vie a sa mort/Toute mort a sa vie" (All life has its death/All death has its life).

The moribund catacombs occasionally get a new lease on life. Once a year in early November on the day after All Saints Day a chorus sings a requiem mass in the bone-lined corridors. The most famous musical performance there, however, echoed through the ossuary between midnight and 2 a.m. on 2 April 1897 when some hundred people gathered to attend a recital in the Rotonde des Tibias featuring such selections as Chopin's "Marche Funébre," Saint-Saëns "Danse Macabre" and the "Marche Funèbre" from Beethoven's *Eroica*. Nor have the visual arts been ignored in the subterranean burial ground. A man named Decure, a former soldier who worked as a laborer in the catacombs between 1777 and 1782, idled away his spare time by carving from the stone a small replica of the Balearic Island fortress of Port-Mahon where he had been imprisoned in 1757. Even as a cave-in at the catacombs killed Decure, he held the chisel with which he had sculpted his creation. Other workmen in the caverns entertained themselves by experimenting with fish in a subterranean pool called the Fountain of the Samaritan. In 1813 they put four goldfish into the water but the new arrivals failed to reproduce and, lacking light, they became blind. In April 1885 workers added two carp and a tench to the pond, but they survived only until December 1886. At one time, at least, some animal life enlivened the catacombs, for according to the nineteenth-century travel writer Augustus Hare, any visitor left behind in the labyrinth of tunnels would soon be eaten alive by rats.

A visit to the Paris catacombs is not a spur-of-the-moment diversion. The city opens the subterranean burial area only two Saturdays a month (once a week in July, August and September). The May day I chose for a visit glowed with the warmth and brightness of a Paris spring. Winter's grey had given way to the newly coloring city, and the recently activated fountains that hissed through the warm air succeeded winter's dismal drizzle. I was surprised to see a long line of people waiting to leave the attractions of that Paris spring for the dark underworld which lay below: perhaps more cemetery collectors exist than I ever imagined. The entrance to the catacombs hides inside a pavillion near the Lion of Belfort statue in place Denfort-Rochereau. The French underground resistance movement literally went underground during the August 1944 uprising by establishing its command post beneath the opposite pavillion. Operating what must be the best concession in all of Paris, a stand by the entrance sold small candles which, as visitors descended the narrow stairway, burned with kinetic flames that cast eerie patterns on the walls. At the bottom, some sixty feet down, you continue on a short distance through the tunnels to arrive at the ossuary entrance where a line from the poet Delille welcomes you: "Arrête, c'est ici l'Empire de la Mort" (Stop, here lies the Kingdom of Death). But no one stops, for even a notice so solemn as this is not sufficiently arresting to halt the living from their progress through life. Ignoring the admonition, the visitors hurry on, candles flickering, anxious to see the underworld where death reigns.

Here, beyond the entryway, begins the kingdom of Death. Neatly stacked bones and skulls line the passageways. On they stretch, pile after pile along the walls of tunnel after tunnel—thousands, millions of bones, all anonymous and each of them quite useless now. Seen in such huge quantities the bones somehow seem detached from all human meaning, disconnected from life, like man-made artifacts rather than man-making anatomical components. The relics resemble building materials, stored down there in warehouses for future use in new structures, and why not? They once structured frames for people, so perhaps they could serve the same function for constructions. Dr. Gordon Seagrave, the famous Burma surgeon, told of finding "a long row of skulls to be used as stepping-stones along the Refugee Trail" in western China; outside Lhasa in Tibet a macabre village contains huts built of skulls and bones occupied by workers who prepare corpses for the vultures; and in the Ottoman Empire the Turks often constructed skull towers to terrorize their enemies. One well-known example, which stood from 1560 until the middle of the nineteenth century, was a pyramid at Houmt Souk, capital of the Tunisian island of Djerba, built with craniums supplied by Philip II's massacred Spanish garrison.

The skull is man's final claim to individuality. After the fleshy features have disintegrated and each skeleton separated into anonymous bones only the cranium remains to distinguish one individual from another. Even in death, every head remains different: the three squiggly lines that mark where the cranium's sections join trace varying patterns, no two exactly alike. In the Paris catacombs I stepped from the slowly advancing line of visitors to examine a few of the skulls. Light cast by the moving candle flames mottled the heads with strange, sallow shapes. The skulls gazed at me with a grin, or chagrin, and I stared back and touched flesh to bone, following with my index finger a jagged cranial seam. In my imagination I tried to clothe the bare bones with flesh, an exercise quite the opposite of Flaubert, who looked through living beings—with a kind of morbid x-ray vision— to their ultimate fate: "I never saw a child without visualizing a tomb. The contemplation of a naked woman makes me imagine her skeleton." I took care not to disturb the dead heads. In *The Silent Traveller in Paris* Chiang Yee recalls his visit to the Paris catacombs where he watched some youngsters hold candles under skulls to see if the bone would burn. True to his belief in ancestor worship, he adjudges this mischief "a bad joke. Who knew whether those very skulls did not belong to the youngsters' own long-deceased ancestors?"

After a time I rejoined the long line of visitors and continued on past the thousands of tibias and fibulas, the clavicles and sternums, the false and the floating ribs, and all sorts of other bone specimens, as well as a series of signs, inscriptions, proscriptions and admonitions that form on the catacomb walls an anthology of death. One line from Horace summarizes the theme espoused by all the others: "Believe that each day will be your last." Hard to believe, even rubbing shoulders sixty feet underground with the bones of those who had already lived their last day. And such a sentiment became yet less credible as I emerged from the shadowy kingdom of Death into the bright warm daylight that caressed Paris that May afternoon. Can't imagine a day without a tomorrow, a dawn without a dusk, a night without a morning. No way another day will not come my way. Hard to believe otherwise, even for a cemetery collector—especially for a cemetery collector: all those graves out there, under there, always and ever belong to someone else, for I'm simply a graveyard visitor, just passing through.

Although the word *catacomb* most commonly denotes ancient subterranean ossuaries used by Christians to dispose of their dead, the secular Paris catacombs bear no intrinsic connection with Christianity. They do, however, conform to the etymology of the word: in Greek *kata* means "below" and *tumba* denotes "tomb." Similarly, the lesser-known Kom al-Shuqafa catacombs in Alexandria, Egypt, seemingly house non-religious remains, unconnected with the church. In 1858 archeologists did discover underground Christian ossuaries in the area, formerly Alexandria's cemetery quarter, but now only the burial chambers at Kom al-Shuqafa (hill of potsherds), discovered in 1900 and apparently containing secular graves, survive. These tomb areas, which date from the second century B.C., occupy three tiers of niches carved in the rock a hundred feet below the ground. Sculpted portrayals of vicious looking, bearded serpents, coiled beneath a round shield-like object, flank the doorway which leads into the main burial chamber. Each of the three niches in the now boneless tomb room contains a large sarchophagus confectioned out of the rock, while on the wall appear bas-reliefs carved in mixed styles. The central scene shows an Egyptian-style jackel-faced person—or is it a human-bodied jackal?—holding the deceased's heart in its left hand, while the figures that flank the doorway seem to reflect Egyptian, Greek and Roman art. On the left there is a spear-carrying, dog-headed demon with a reptile-like body dressed in military costume, and on the right lurks an Anubis-like creature, also dog-headed, clad in a Roman soldier's uniform. In his guidebook to Alexandria E.M. Forster calls the Kom al-Shuqafa catacombs "unique any where: nothing quite like them has been discovered. They are unique both for their plan and for their decorations which so curiously blend classical and Egyptian designs; only in Alexandria could such a blend occur." Although Forster adjudged Kom al-Shuqafa unique, the carved catacomb in a vague way recalls the nearly forty-five-hundred-year-old Maltese Hal-Saflieni Hypogeum, discovered about the same time (1902). In effect a three-level temple hollowed out below the ground, the hypogeum also served as a burial area, as evidenced by the remains of some seven thousand people which archeologists found there. During World War II that resting place for the dead became a refuge for the living when the Maltese used the hypogeum as an air raid shelter.

Those subterranean catacombs hollowed-out from the rock recall certain above-ground burial caverns cut into cliff faces. High on the red rock face at Petra, the two-thousand-year-old town hidden away in a valley in the southern Jordanian desert, open tomb rooms once held the ancient settlement's deceased. Here, unlike at most cemeteries, the departed rose above their place in life and looked down on their survivors. Over the years following my visit to Petra I have only occasionally come across other elevated burial areas carved from the rock. Just as the Petra tombs lie above the amphitheater, so at Syracuse on Sicily the so-called Street of Tombs runs above and behind the famous amphitheater where the ancient Greeks performed their plays. At Syracuse, however, the whitish rock face lacks the pleasant rose red hue which tinctures Petra, where the tomb facades bear carved decor not found at Syracuse. High above the valley at Bandiagara in Mali's remote Dogon country are partly walled openings, still used to house the remains of departed tribespeople. This elevated cemetery and a similar one in central Yemen at Shibam—whose pre-Islamic tombs pock the red stone cliff above the town very much as at Petra—recall Chateaubriand's romantic and dramatic description in *The Genius of Christianity:* "In Switzerland the cemeteries are sometimes placed on rocks, where they overlook lakes, precipices and valleys. The chamois and the eagle take up residence there, and death grows on those precipitous sites, like those alpine plants whose roots are plunged into eternal ice."

In contrast to the above-described secular underground ossuaries at Paris and Alexandria, Rome boasts the first catacombs to house the remains of persecuted Christians. The term *catacomb* as now used originated in reference to the *catacumbas* beneath San Sebastiano church on the Via Appia, while the idea of mass subterranean burial grounds began with the Roman Jews who, in the first century A.D., dug catacombs (described in Chapter VI) to create an area where their dead could repose apart from gentiles. Perhaps Jews took the concept of separate burial from the rich Christians who erected private tombs in their villa gardens as places of interment removed from pagan cemeteries. Christians soon adopted the practice of common underground graves, and up to the fifth century they dug in the soft yet stable tufa subsoil more than seven hundred and fifty miles of galleries at five levels to a depth of eighty feet, excavating below Rome a total of some forty catacombs which held an estimated 194,000 deceased devout. The Roman government at first chose not to oppose the Christians' excavated cemeteries, and indeed protected them from vandalism. To the catacombs Christians transferred for safekeeping such treasures as relics of the apostles Peter and Paul, with St. Peter's remains again hidden away at San Sebastiano a second time—after reposing in a sarcophagus accessible to pilgrims—during the reign of the tyrannical emperor Heliogabalus (d. 222). Christians used the catacombs not only for burials but also as places of worship. Their first churches thus originated in such underground venues of the dead, which were also dug at Naples, and in Sicily at Syracuse, Catania, Agrigento and Palermo. As a visit to the catacombs reveals, these earliest sanctuaries lack cross symbols, an emblem rare until the fourth century. Early Christians preferred other religious representations, such as a fish, anchor, dove, lamp, lighthouse, ship or palm. Crosses only began to appear in the thirteenth century in connection with the dead, and not until the seventeenth and especially the eighteenth centuries did the devout place crosses over individual graves in cemeteries. When the Roman government realized Christians were also using the catacombs as gathering places and to worship, Emperor Valerian issued a decree in 253 prohibiting the sect "either to hold assemblies or to enter those places, which they called their cemeteries." After the persecutions ended at the close of the fourth century, the Christians resurfaced. Open air interments soon became fashionable, and by the time of Pope John III (d. 575) most burials in Rome took place within the city walls. The Roman catacombs fell into disuse and remained hidden for a millenium until the ancient ossuaries were rediscovered in the fifteenth century.

Rome now boasts a scattering of those ancient subterranean burial grounds. San Callisto out on the Via Appia was adjuged by no less an authority than Pope John XXIII to be "the most impressive and most renowned" of the Roman catacombs. At the stairs leading down into the depths appears a sign, "silenzio," both a description and a request. Gravestone fragments decorate the walls on the way into the first chamber, the Cappella dei Papi (third century), supposedly Rome's most holy catacomb room. Wall niches house large stones bearing Greek inscriptions, while beneath the altar lies the original stone slab floor. My tour group moved on to the tomb of Cecelia, featuring a recumbant marble statue and seventh century Byzantine frescoes, then continued through narrow passageways past a small display of gravestone pieces bearing such devices as the fish, the anchor and the dove. We passed a few small vaults and chapels, some with sketchy colored frescoes, and then came to a display of small clay lamps used by visitors in bygone times. When John Evelyn visited the catacombs in May 1645 he noted: "We ever and anon came into pretty square roomes, that seem'd to be Chapells with altars, and some adorn'd with very ordinary ancient painting. Many skeletons and bodies are plac'd in the sides one above the other in degrees like shelves . . . Many of the bodies, or rather bones (for there appear'd nothing else) lay so intire as if plac'd by the art of the chirurgeon, but being only touched fell all to dust." Perhaps visitors over the years touched all the bones, for the nearly boneless catacombs now lack almost all traces of human postmortem presence that formerly filled the caverns. One room contains a pair of caskets with leathery shreds and bone fragments. All the rest is gone.

Rome's lesser known catacombs are quiet enclaves where the centuries seem to linger, hidden beneath the busy city. Out at Santa Constanza and Sant-Agnese, nestled within a pleasant garden removed from the noise of the Via Nomentana, lie three-mile-long catacombs dating from the second to the fifth centuries. According to the guide, these survive as Rome's best preserved catacombs but they, too, for the most part lack bones. In one of the long niches cut into the volcanic rock repose a few crumbling bones gradually mingling with the dust. Some of the grave signs symbolize the deceased's profession: a ham motif marks a sausage maker's tomb; a trowel designates a mason; a pick and shovel indicates a grave digger. The catacomb of Priscilla on the Via Salaria outside the center of Rome offers an example of how the practice of subterranean burial in excavated caverns originated. In the earliest days of Christianity the pious would bury their dead privately on family property. These burial areas gradually expanded as land owners allowed poorer Christians to repose in the villa cemetery. To accommodate the increasing number of dead, wealthy Christian families would add underground galleries to their burial chambers. Such new extensions formed the nuclei of the original Roman catacombs, which date from the beginning of the second century. The Priscilla catacomb, supposedly Rome's oldest, takes its name from a noble Roman lady whose family developed a private sepulchral hypogeum on its country estate. During the third and fourth centuries the burial area grew to become one of the largest catacombs in Rome. A visitor receives a rather spooky introduction to that netherworld: after you press a button at the entranceway, a remote-controlled door automatically swings open. A long curving passage descends to a chapel, then you proceed through a corridor lined by empty burial niches. The smaller compartments once held children. The Cappella Greca bears a Greek funeral inscription, frescoes of the three Wise Men, and of Moses striking the rock for water, as well as terra cotta reliefs reminiscent of the decor found in Etruscan tombs. Elsewhere lies a cistern, dug in the fourth century to supply water for funeral banquets held in the outdoor cemetery above.

Murals, reliefs, niches, grave markers, cisterns and other features are housed in the catacombs of Rome, but the ossuaries lack the one object most associated with them—bones. For bones in Rome one needs to visit the curious burial chambers of the Capuchins installed in Santa Maria della Concezione on the Via Veneto near the Piazza Barberini. As mentioned in the previous chapter, Pope Urban VIII directed the devout to bring sanctified soil from Jerusalem in the Holy Land to the church cemetery, a project similar to that which brought holy earth to the Campo Santo cemetery in Pisa. In the burial ground at Santa Maria della Concezione repose the remains of some four thousand Capuchins, interred there between 1528 and 1870. Their flesh has by now melted away, but the monks' bones survive to serve as components of artful designs that decorate the corridor and a series of compartments. The Capuchins seem inordinantly fond of this sort of macabre, bone-based necro-art. Sacheverell Sitwell recalls in *Journey to the Ends of Time* how "the Capuchins had their catacombs of old bones; four thousand dead friars at the Capuchins in Rome, decorating the walls and ceiling of four [in fact six] vaults with their skulls and bones; and eight thousand corpses of priests and citizens of Palermo in the subterranean corridors of the Cappuccini, either mummified or reduced to bones"—a "morbid drama," Sitwell elsewhere describes such bony exhibitionism. These odd displays seem to exert a strange fascination on most visitors. When Tolitha Wingo, grandmother of the narrator of Pat Conroy's novel *The Prince of Tides,* toured the bone-embellished grottos in Rome "she sent us a postcard picturing the macabre arrangement of monks' skulls stacked like artillery ordnance in a side altar at the Capuchin catacombs." A friend of mine once threatened to send such a postcard, inscribed with the message, "Wish you were here." Tibiae, vertebrae and other skeleton components decorate the walls and ceiling in elaborate designs and fantasies, including wreaths formed by skulls, arabesques of arm and leg bones, arches, angular patterns, a hand and foot bone chandelier above a rib cage altar, while in bone-built alcoves nestle skeletal figures clothed in baggy brown monks robes, all much as Nathaniel Hawthorne described in *The Marble Faun:*

> The knobs and embossed ornaments of this strange architecture are represented by the joints of the spine, and the more delicate tracery by the smaller bones of the human frame. The summits of the arches are adorned with entire skeletons, looking as if they were wrought most skillfully in bas-relief. There is no possibility of describing how ugly and grotesque is the effect, combined with a certain artistic merit; nor how much perverted ingenuity has been shown in this queer way; nor what a multitude of dead monks, through how many hundred years, must have contributed their bony frame-work to build up these great arches of mortality!

Hawthorne comments on the robe-clad figures, whose skulls "look out from beneath their hoods, grinning hideously repulsive. One reverend Father has his mouth wide open, as if he had died in the midst of a howl of terror and remorse, which perhaps is even now screeching through eternity." Repulsed as he was by the macabre scene, the author finally finds in the bone rooms one saving grace: "There is no disagreeable scent. . . . The same number of living monks would not smell half so unexceptionably!"

A more obscure but no less macabre corner of Rome occupies a forbidding dungeon-like chamber in the lower reaches of the ominously named Santa Maria dell' Orazione e Morte (St. Mary of the Oration and Death) on the Via Giulia, a lovely and quiet street dripping with leafy vines (the church entrance is on Lungotevere along the Tiber River). Stone skulls adorn the door of the church, founded by a religious confraternity established in 1551 to collect bodies of the unknown dead and give them a Christian burial. On its annual feast day the organization would present religious skits, with the scene that represented purgatory peopled by real cadavers enlisted from Santa Maria's own inventory. The nun who admitted me to the establishment led the way down to the gloomy tomb room. At one end of the long narrow chamber a cross made of skulls decorates the wall, flanked by skull and crossbone motifs. From the ceiling hang three chandeliers and two candelabra, all fabricated from bones, and along the length of the room two glass cases hold 140 skulls, many with the name and death date of the cranium's former occupant scratched on the forehead. On niches at the center of the lateral walls stand skeletons, one with a large hour glass nearby and the other with a scythe. On the former skeleton appears a sign: "Deh! Teche qui venisti/Un requiem non scordar/Le mie copiose lacrime/Deterei col pregar!" (Oh, please! Those who come here/Don't forget a requiem/My many tears/Require a prayer!) Apart from the infrequent visitors to this lugubrious venue, once a year a service held on the Day of the Dead in early November enlivens the tomb-like and deathly still ossuary. Leaving the dark, bone-bedecked tomb room behind and below, I for once found Rome's noise, dust, heat, dazzling sunlight and commotion pleasurable: the Eternal City is better than that eternal resting place any day.

Bone-decorated funerary halls such as those at the two Santa Marias—della Concezione and dell'Orazione—in Rome remain relatively rare. An ossuary in a church at Kutna Hora, Czechoslovakia, sports a bone chandelier with candles atop skulls and bones hanging from the ceiling. At Sedlec, also in Czechoslovakia, a medieval cathedral bears bone decorations mounted by the parishioners to replace valuable ornaments taken when Mongols ransacked the sanctuary. São Francisco at Evora, Portugal, houses a bone-bedecked chapel with wall areas formed by arm parts, ribs and arms decorating six pillars, skulls along the ceiling, and a stubby rough-textured section created by the ends of stacked bones. In sharp contrast to the curvy white bones above, an incongruous, brightly colored tiled frieze runs along the lower walls by the floor. St. Ursula church in Cologne boasts a *Goldene Kammer,* a seventeenth-century chapel with reliquaries and figures of saints on shelves above which, on three walls, rise nine rows of bones arranged in rosettes, flowery shapes, fan-like motifs, parallels, herring-bone patterns and various other designs. The versatile vertebrae, seemingly the most servicable—for artistic purposes—of the bone family, form more refined designs, with two large sections of one wall comprised of such pieces. Arm, leg and other straight bones structure less-elaborate panels. Over the main altar words formed by bones salvaged from some of the eleven thousand martyrs at an ancient Roman cemetery spell out the message, "Maria, S. Ursula pro nobis ora, si etheri ora pro nobis, Jesus corona martyrium." Lewis Carroll visited Cologne in July 1867 on his way to Russia and he noted in his *Russian Journal* how he had made the rounds of various churches in the city, "the effect of which was that I have no very definite idea of any one of them," but Carroll did recall the unusual sights at St. Ursula where "bones are stored away in cases with fronts of glass."

In contrast to the elaborate and often gaudy displays of bones which fill catacombs and chapels around Europe, hearts are hidden away in obscure, hard-to-find corners, as if the heart is a more private and personal part of a human's being than are the more numerous and less symbolic bones. As cities go, Paris is definitely the queen of hearts. Three years after Voltaire died (1788) officials brought his coffin to the Panthéon where through the years the great philosopher's fellow countrymen came to pay him homage. When the tomb was opened in the 1860s, however, Voltaire was no longer there: some fanatics had pillaged his grave and thrown the remains onto a rubbish heap, and the great man had

disappeared virtually without a trace. Only two parts of
Voltaire survived—his brain, kept in a jar and sold at auction
to an unknown buyer; and his heart, bequeathed by the third
marquis de Villette to the bishop of Orléans who sold it to
Napoleon III, who in turn gave it to the National Library in
Paris where—along with the products of his brain—it still
resides. In a chapel at St. Jacques des Haut-Pas reposes the
heart of the dutchess of Longueville (d. 1679), benefactor of
the church and of the famous abbey of Port-Royal. In the
"obituarie," a hand-written necrology maintained by the sisters of Port-Royal, appears an entry (15 April 1679) noting
that "she left us six thousand pounds by her will. Her heart is
buried near the grill in our choir." When Port-Royal was
demolished in 1710 the church removed her heart to St.
Jacques. On a stone column at sharp bend in the Paris catacombs, described above, appears the following notice:
"Within this pillar is a small alcove cut to receive the heart of
General Campi found 28 June 1893 in an excavation at avenue
Niel and removed to the catacombs. This heart was enclosed
in a lead box with a parchment bearing the following inscription: 'Heart of Division General Baron Campi, died at Lyon
14 October 1832, embalmed by M. Jourdan, pharmacist.'"
Although the Panthéon lacks Voltaire and his heart, in a niche
by the door leading to the crypt the famous mausoleum
boasts the heart of Léon Gambetta (d. 1882), the French
Republican leader, brought there on November 11, 1920,
second anniversary of the World War I armistice.

Some two centuries ago Paris was truly not just another
heartless big city. The Reverend William Cole, who wrote *A
Journal of my Journey to Paris in the year 1765,* came across
hearts all over town. On Tuesday 2 November ("Very fine
Day," Cole notes, with an Englishman's attention to the
weather) at St. Germain des Prés church he found "a Marble
with an Inscription on it for a natural Son of Henry 4th,
Lewis de Bourbon, Duke de Verheuil, who had been Com-

mendatory Abbat here and Bp of Metz, but afterwards married: at his Death in 1682 he ordered his Heart to be buried in this Place." A week later (12 November, "Foggy Weather") Cole visited the convent of Celestine monks on the Right Bank where he discovered "one of the most elegant & well-fancied Monuments I ever saw: it is a beautiful Pillar, consisting of 3 Figures of Women in White Marble representing the Graces, who with uplifted Hands support a conjoyned Heart of gilt Copper in which are those of King Henry 2 & his Queen, Catherine de Medicis . . . Close to its stands another of much the same Design . . . in which is enclosed the Heart of King Francis, 2d Husband to Mary Queen of Scots." And on Thursday 21 November ("Fine, day, frosty & cold") Cole visited the Maison Professe des Jesuits on rue St. Antoine to find that "the Heart of the Prince of Condé is in an Urn, held by Angels, under the Arch which Communicates with the Side Chapel where Lewis 13 his Heart is preserved." Louis XIII's heart must have later been removed to the crypt at St. Denis, while the aspe of the mausoleum chapel at Chantilly, near Paris, houses a *cippus* which contains the hearts of several other members of the Condé clan.

Not all separately interred Paris hearts belong to exalted blue-bloods, such as kings, queens and princes. As mentioned earlier, General Campi's heart occupies a niche in the Paris catacombs, while the heart of Marshal Cannes, duke of Montebello, resides in the family vault at Montmartre cemetery (the rest of the marshal reposes in the Panthéon). In July 1793 admirers of Marat displayed the revolutionary's embalmed body, and the bathtub in which he died, at the former chapel of the Cordeliers. Two days after his burial in the garden there on 16 July Marat's heart was put into an urn, centerpiece of a 28 July celebration in Marat's honor at the Luxembourg Gardens. Following the demise of the duke of Orléans in 1723 attendants put his heart in a box for transport to Paris's Val-de-Grâce church, but the duke's great dane pounced on the morsel and gobbled up a good chunk of the heart before anyone could intervene. No doubt more disembodied hearts reposed at Val-de-Grâce—which boasted some fifty-five such organs—than at any other single site in the world. The custom of depositing the hearts of princes and princesses there started with the death of Anne of Austria in 1666, about the same time Jesuits began to propagate their cult of the Sacred Heart. During the seventeenth and eighteenth centuries the St. Anne chapel at Val-de-Grâce became a repository for hearts of deceased members of the French royal family. Anne initiated the practice after the death (1662) of her granddaughter Anne-Elizabeth, daughter of Louis XIV. When the old lady, then in residence at Val-de-Grâce, told the abbess, Mother Dufour de St. Bernard, that Anne-Elizabeth was dying the nun asked the queen to obtain from Louis XIV his daughter's heart. In due course Anne delivered the little heart to the abbess, stating, "My mother, here is a heart I bring to you in order to join it to mine soon," and on 22 January 1666, two days after Anne's own death, her heart did come together with that of her granddaughter. At first the hearts reposed in the St. Scholastic chapel, but a few years later the nuns moved the relics to the St. Anne funerary chapel. In January 1696 Louis XIV, displeased by such prominently displayed reminders of death, ordered that all but three specimens of the growing heart collection be removed to a marble-decorated chamber below the St. Anne chapel, its ceiling painted black with silver tears. Between 1662 and 1789 a total of forty-five hearts were deposited at Val-de-Grâce. The hearts occupied niches draped with thick black curtains. Linen containers with black velvet or white satin, depending on the deceased's age, held lead boxes enclosed in silver-gilt enamel mini-coffins, topped by a silver crown and placed on black velvet squares or silvery cloth.

The last royal heart buried at Val-de-Grâce belonged to Louis-Joseph-Xavier-François de France, the dauphin, who died 4 June 1789. After that came the deluge, which washed the blue-blooded hearts away from their privileged places in the sanctuary and into the clutches of revolutionary mobs. Like so much else in France during the revolution, the hearts disappeared. Revolutionaries desecrated the St. Anne chapel, grabbed the royal hearts and offered them for sale. One was fed to a dog, while another—poorly embalmed—burst under the rough handling. The heart boxes made of precious metal, the intruders carried off to the mint. The most gruesome fate, however, befell the royal hearts—perhaps including the oldest one, that of Anne herself—which the revolutionaries who sacked the church in 1793 crushed and ground up to produce a powder which a genre painter and Sèvres porcelain decorator named Martin Drolling (1752–1817) used to make paint. At the Louvre hangs the artist's portrait of L. C. Maigret, a bourgeois, done the same year and thus perhaps partly painted with the red hearts of French blue-bloods. The Louvre also houses Drolling's *Interior of a Kitchen,* painted in 1817, which includes a woman sewing a blood-red garment, while the Musée des Beaux-Arts in Orléans contains a number of the artist's works, including a self-portrait showing him with a squarish head, thick features, lumpy nose, heavy eyelids, fuzzy eyebrows, shaggy brown hair and a stare—hardly a regal countenance, but perhaps powder ground from kingly hearts comprises some of the painter's features. Only one heart is known to have survived the years of turmoil—that of the dauphin, Louis XVI's oldest son. After a certain Legoy, an official at the observatory, came across a box with the boy's name inscribed on it, in 1817 the mayor of the twelfth arrondisement presented the container to the royal family who took it to the royal mausoleum at St. Denis for interment.

As late as about 1880 relics from the heart collection's earliest days resurfaced when the heirs of a Dr. Dabon sold off his furniture and curiosity collection. Among the objects on offer was a small package bearing the description; "Skin of Anne of Austria's right arm, taken from her coffin in the underground area of Val-de-Grâce 12 May 1800 by me, Dabon, physician of Val-de-Grâce." The church continues to house the heart of Mary Damby, an English woman not otherwise identified whose relic reposes in a narrow lead container bearing her name; and that of Baron J.D. Larrey, chief surgeon of the imperial guard, whose name is inscribed on the Arc de Triomphe. After Larrey died at Lyon in July 1842 his family embalmed the body and removed the heart, kept at Saint-Germain-l'Auxerrois church in Paris until his son delivered it to Val-de-Grâce a few years later. In November 1924 when a physician removed the heart from its container to repair the organ he found that decay had eaten half of it away, so the doctor made truly a half-hearted attempt to salvage the relic. It is now preserved in a glass case with a death mask of Larrey and other mementos of his life.

Apart from Paris, a few other places in France boast detached, buried hearts. A marble monument at the cathedral in Orléans bears the inscription: "Here lies the heart of Adele-Felix-Françoise d'Astorg, countess of Choiseul Daillecourt" (d. 1818), while the gothic basilica of Cléry near Blois houses an urn which contains Charles VIII's heart. Elsewhere in Europe, by the door of the chapter house of the church in Santo Domingo, Spain, appears a monument to the buried heart of Enrique de Trastamava (d. 1379). At Goslar, Germany, the *Kaiserpfalz,* the country's largest surviving Romanesque palace, built during the reign of Emperor Henry III (1039–56), contains the monarch's remains, installed at St. Ulrich's chapel where his sarcophagus holds a separate casket for the heart. Vienna's Augustiner church holds the heart of Emperor Franz Josef (d. 1916), whose embalmed body reposes at the Capuchin church, and viscera in St. Stephen's Cathedral. In Warsaw's Church of the Holy Cross lies Chopin's heart, brought from Père Lachaise. St. Peter's chapel at the Church of the Transfiguration was erected in the city in 1693 by John Sobieski in gratitude for his victory over the Turks near Vienna. His heart reposes there, as well as that of King Stanislaus Augustus Poniatowski. Lying in wait at Arlington National Cemetery is the body of pianist and first premier of the Polish republic, Ignace Paderewski (d. 1941), one of the graveyard's few foreigners. He requested interment there "temporarily" until his homeland became a free country, at which time he specified that the body should be shipped to Poland but the heart retained in the United States.

Americans seem not to have adopted the practice of heart burial, but the tombstone of movie actress Jayne Mansfield (d. 1967) at Fairview Cemetery, Pen Argyl, Pennsylvania, is heart shaped, as was the swimming pool at her former residence. San Lorenzo Monastery in Mexico houses the heart of Don Carlos Bermudez (d. 1729), a Mexican who in 1725 became archbishop of Manila. After the prelate died in the Philippines his heart returned home to San Lorenzo "where it was the subject of solemn honors."

Members of the Saxon royal family supposedly still observe the tradition of separate burial of the heart (and entrails). During the burial service the heart, placed in a small container, reposes on a white satin cushion. The heart box is then put into a small coffin which, along with a jar covered in white satin that contains the entrails, occupies a place in the family vault. At Dashwood mausoleum in West Wycombe, England, reposed the heart of a poet named Paul Whitehead, until someone stole the relic in 1839. When Thomas Hardy died in 1928 his literary friends managed to obtain a place for him at Westminster Abbey, the first novelist buried there since Charles Dickens (d. 1870) and the first poet since Tennyson (d. 1892). Although his ashes occupy a place in Poets' Corner at the famous abbey in London, Hardy's heart—removed by a surgeon and stored in a cookie can—was buried

at Stinsford churchyard, so symbolizing that the writer belonged to the nation but the private man to Dorset.

Such is the pull exerted by one's native terrain that when
Jose Tarradellas returned in 1977 after nearly thirty years of
exile in France to his Catalan homeland, the politician
brought with him to Barcelona a glass vial containing the
heart of Francesco Macia, who in 1931 proclaimed a Catalan
republic. The heart of African explorer David Livingstone,
however, remains far from his native land. Livingstone's
body was carried for months through the African back country to the coast and then shipped to London for burial at
Westminster Abbey. The heart remained at Old Chitambo, a
tiny settlement in northern Zambia, where a squat obelisk
topped by a cross marks the site where Susi and Chuma, two
of the explorer's bearers, buried the heart beneath a tree on 1
May 1873 while an African named Jacob Wainwright read the
service. Residents of Chitambo eventually moved the village
elsewhere and in 1902 the rotting tree was cut down. Now
the monument to Livingstone's heart stands at the ghost
town of Old Chitambo in the middle of nowhere.

Another expatriate heart, buried far from its owner's
homeland and his remains, belonged to Daniel O'Connell, a
nineteenth-century Irish nationalist, whose body reposes in
Dublin's Glasnevin cemetery. O'Connell, who died in
Genoa, left his heart in Italy: "He's at rest . . . in the middle of
his people, old Dan O'," says Joyce's Mr. Power to Mr.
Dedalus at Dignam's funeral in Glasnevin, "But his heart is
buried in Rome." Indeed, the wall of O'Connell's crypt—to
which he was transferred from his original grave at Glasnevin
in May 1869—contains the inscription: "My heart to Rome,
my body to Ireland, my soul to heaven." Dublin, however, is
not heartless. The cemetery contains the heart of a Surgeon-
Major Clarke (d. 1829) and that of a Miss Longmore, while a
chapel at Christ Church Cathedral in the Irish capital houses

the heart of Lorcan Ua Tuathail, or Lawrence O'Toole, the city's patron saint, consecrated in 1162 as archbishop of Dublin. The body of O'Toole, who died in Normandy (1180), reposes at Eu, but in 1230 Dubliners returned the heart to the church where it remains, enclosed in a heart-shaped metal container, housed in a birdcage-like device hanging in the chapel.

The well-traveled heart which belonged to Robert the Bruce, king of Scotland, finally came to rest but not, as he wished, in far off Jerusalem. Before he died on 7 November 1329 the monarch summoned a courtier, Lord James Douglas, as recounted in Froissart's *Chronicles,* to announce that he would not live long enough to fulfill his vow "to make war against the enemies of our Lord Jesus Christ, and the adversaries of the Christian faith. To this point my heart has always leaned." Afflicted with leprosy, the king stated that "since my body cannot accomplish what my heart wishes, I will send my heart in the stead of my body to fulfill my vow." Robert requested that after his death Douglas "take my heart from my body, and have it well embalmed . . . [and] you will then deposit your charge at the Holy Sepulchre of Our Lord [in Jerusalem]." Douglas promised to carry out this charge, and when the king died his followers buried him in the monastery at Dunfermline, delivering his embalmed heart to Douglas who departed for the Holy Land in the spring of 1330. The Scotsman, who carried the king's heart in a silver enamelled case worn around his neck, first made his way to Spain where in August he participated in a battle near Cordoba, pitting the forces of King Alphonso of Castile against the Saracens. After the encounter, during which Muslim soldiers killed Douglas and his Scottish knights traveling with him, his body and the heart box were recovered and returned to Scotland, Lord James for burial in the church at Douglas and Robert's heart for deposit at Melrose Abbey. But Robert the Bruce's wish was not entirely forgotten, for a marker set in the altar floor at St. Andrew's Presbyterian Church in Jerusalem reads: "In remembrance of the pious wish of King Robert the Bruce that his heart should be buried in Jerusalem." At the bottom of the plaque appears a thistle-flanked, heart-shaped device, while around the edge of the marker an inscription states: "Given by citizens of Dumfermline and Melrose in celebration of the sixth century of his death . . . 1329 7 June 1929."

In a few isolated cases heart burial has survived to modern times. In Athens the Benaki Museum occupies the mansion once owned by Antony Benaki, who in his will stated that "my wish is that even after my death something of myself should remain in the museum which I created with such enthusiasm and love. I therefore direct that my heart shall be immured in the entrance." As he desired, there among the collection of art objects assembled by Benaki over thirty-five years reposes his heart, enclosed in a wall at the top of the stairs near the side entrance and commemorated by a shiny plaque bearing a replica of the family seal. Also in Greece lies the heart of Baron Pierre de Coubertin, who founded the modern Olympic games. In March 1938 Greek Prince Paul carried a small padded, wooden box containing Coubertin's heart to Olympia. There a monument to the deceased now stands near the new stadium, not far from the ancient ruins where the original Olympic games took place.

The most notable disembodied heart in sports, however, belonged not to the father of the modern Olympics but to one Phar Lap, the great Australian race horse. After Phar Lap died in 1932 a necropsy, as animal autopsies are called, revealed that his heart weighed thirteen pounds, more than twice that of an ordinary horse. Devotees of the famous racer put the heart on display in Canberra, and a man named Dr. W. A. Stewart McKay wrote a book dedicated to Phar Lap, expounding the theory that the size of a horse's heart determined the animal's racing prowess. Like some of the human bodies mentioned in this chapter, Phar Lap's cadaver was divided up, the atomised anatomy parceled out, skin and bones, among his admirers. As noted in the next chapter, the museum in Wellington, New Zealand, houses the skeleton, the white bones pieced together into a static structure that belies the energy and motion which once flowed through the fleet-footed animal's body, while in the museum at Melbourne, Australia, stands the "great mountain of a horse," as someone once described him, the skin mounted on a hollow frame.

Just as Phar Lap, in death, was scattered to the four winds, ending up distributed over two countries, so too were the remains of his fellow Australian Ned Kelly dispersed. Born in 1855, Kelly became a bandit with a heart and bank account of gold, a rogue who combined the qualities of Robin Hood, Jesse James and Wild Bill Cody, to whom he was distantly related through his paternal grandmother, Mary Cody, of Tipperary, Ireland. Kelly roamed the roads of Australia's Wild East, raiding banks and adventuring in Victoria and New South Wales until authorities arrested him in 1880. As the executioner slipped the noose over Kelly's head at Melbourne gaol on 11 November 1880 the condemned man exclaimed, "Ah, well, it has come to this." And just before the trap was sprung Kelly murmured, "Such is life." After the hanging, attendants cut off Kelly's head, which later served—so an attendant at the gaol, now a museum, told me—to decorate a prison official's office. The head now resides at the Australian Institute of Anatomy in Canberra. As for the rest of the deceased, he was buried on the spot, reposing in peace until 1921 when Melbourne demolished the old gaol and workers uncovered a coffin marked "Edward Kelly." Students from the nearby Working Men's College swarmed to the site to salvage the folk hero's remains, cannibalizing his skeleton for souvenir bones. So great did the rush to dismember dead Ned become, that the wrecking crew had to close off the area so that they could continue the demolition. But by then Ned Kelly had been demolished, and now his bones are scattered around Melbourne, and perhaps elsewhere, lying in untold numbers of attics, boxes, garages, basements, drawers, bags and other obscure corners, never again to fit together in the pattern that once formed a man by the name of Ned Kelly.

That is the way things go. After a time, nothing coheres, nothing holds together. Anatomy becomes dismembered, scattered, disremembered. Samuel Beckett's Murphy, who died after the explosion of a gas heater in the mental hospital where he worked as an orderly, requested in his will: "With regard to the disposal of these my body, mind and soul, I desire that they be burnt and placed in a paper bag and brought to the Abbey Theatre, Lr. Abbey Street, Dublin, and without pause in what the great and good Lord Chesterfield calls the necessary house, where their happiest hours have been spent, on the right as one goes down into the pit, and I desire that the chain be pulled upon them, if possible during the performance of a piece, the whole to be executed without ceremony or show of grief." On the way to carry out Murphy's request his friend Cooper, lugging the four-pound parcel of ash, stops off at a pub where he drinks for "some hours" and then, in a fit of anger, hurls the package at another man. The bag bursts, the ashes scatter, and "by closing time the body, mind and soul of Murphy were freely distributed over the floor of the saloon; and before another dayspring greyened the earth had been swept away with the sand, the beer, the butts, the glass, the matches, the spits, the vomit." So scattered Murphy, the melancholy of anatomy personified—or depersonified—and such is the melancholy of anatomy.

V.

Dear Dumb Beasts

PHAR Lap, the great Australian racing horse, sported many human qualities. Like Ned Kelly—the famous Aussie highwayman hanged on Melbourne Cup Day exactly a half century before Phar Lap's three-length victory in the race of 1930—the horse became an Australian hero. "Such is life," intoned young Kelly, aged twenty-six, as the noose slipped over his neck. Phar Lap, too, almost suffered from an early death—by murder. A few days before Melbourne Cup Day a gunman, supposedly hired by disgruntled bookmakers who had lost a bundle betting against the nearly unbeatable runner—thirty-seven wins, three places, and two shows in fifty-one starts—stalked Phar Lap, hoping to assassinate him. But Phar survived, won the race, and ran on to greater victories.

In early 1932 Phar Lap—Thai for "sky blink," or lightning—travelled across the Pacific to compete in North America in an attempt to establish a new world record for career earnings. Three weeks before the Agua Caliente Handicap in Mexico a stone jammed between Phar's shoe and hoof, splitting the hoof. A veterinarian put a bell boot over the injured foot, and in late March the handicapped Phar not only won the race but also set a new track record. Now at the top of his form, Phar Lap was poised to conquer all comers. But then, suddenly—on 5 April 1932—Phar Lap died in Menlo Park, California. Such was his fame that the horse's demise made the front page of the *New York Times,* which reported that the steed had expired of colic, a common cause of death in thoroughbreds, who often suffer from delicate digestive system. Phar Lap no longer circulated, but rumors did: that the champion had in fact been poisoned by gambling figures annoyed that such a lightning-fast horse upset the betting system. Perfection was too predictable.

Whatever the reason, the runner was gone, taken away—like the brigand Ned Kelly—in the prime of his career. Both robber and runner, each in his time, caught the fancy of the Aussies. Australians mourned the passing of their famous four-legged compatriot. P. F. Collins of Sydney composed a poem in memory of Phar Lap, "some say he was possessed/of Human Intellect," who "closed his eyes in Yankee-land":

> Five hundred years may come and go
>   Before another's bred
> To equal that swift noble steed
> Now numbered with the dead.
> But if a man did poison him
> May his flesh and blood decline,
> May his grave be made on a mountain-side
> Where the sun will never shine.

Like the holy remains of a venerated saint, Phar Lap's flesh, blood, and bones were distributed among his admirers. Museums are his mausoleums. The gelding's skeleton graces the Wellington Museum in New Zealand, land of his birth, while the (stuffed) hide reposes in a museum at Melbourne, scene of one of the runner's greatest triumphs. The huge heart—at thirteen pounds it weighed twice as much as most horses' pumpers—resides in Canberra, capital of the nation which lauded him as a folk hero. So ended Phar Lap, his last race won—dismantled, divided, scattered, and properly honored by his countrymen.

Unlike Phar Lap, most animals pass from the scene without such elaborate praise or posthumous commemoration. To "honor the thousands of animals who never received a final resting place"—unnamed, unknown beasts which die in the wild, family pets disposed of without ceremony or burial, other furry, finny or feathery beings—in 1990 the Rosa Bonheur Memorial Park in Elkridge, Maryland, erected a Tomb of the Unknown Pet. Some beasts, however, are afforded burials and monuments as elaborate as those enjoyed by humankind.

Mankind's view of its relationship to the animal kingdom has always been touched with a certain ambiguity. Gobineau, the French thinker, affirmed that man was indeed related to the apes, but he refused to specify which species descended from the other. Similarly, Montaigne blurred the contrast between man and beast with his observation: "When I play with my cat, who knows if she amuses herself with me more than I with her? We entertain each other with mutual apish tricks." In *Italian Journey* Goethe tells of seeing horses and mules, their manes and tails braided with ribbons, being brought to church during the Feast of St. Anthony, patron saint of animals, to be sprinkled by the priest with holy water. Are the animals parishioners or are the parishoners animals?

In France up to the eighteenth century animals accused of causing a human's death faced legal proceedings and execution. The French hanged such types as horses and pigs for their misdeeds. As recently as 1906 Swiss courts tried dogs which participated in a robbery or murder. Mens' perceptions of animal mortality reveals more about people than it does about the Phar Laps, lap dogs, or other beasts humankind mourns. But what does an anthropomorphic treatment of deceased beasts imply? Do we, by lionizing dead animals, raise them to man's supposedly more elevated state, or does such fawning diminish humans to a brutish level of being? Perhaps mankind is more brutish and beastial than the animal kingdom. In the 1952 movie *Forbidden Games* animals enjoyed a funereal status far above that accorded to humans. While adults toss corpses into unmarked graves during the German invasion of France in June 1940, two children establish an animal cemetery where pets receive a decent burial.

A few years ago a suburban weekly in Kansas City, Missouri, started publishing pet obituaries. The "Pet Passing" column included not only dogs and cats but also lesser mortals. One obituary noted the demise of Riley, a pet mouse who died at the age of two: "Riley was a member of the sacred runners of the wheel and enjoyed eating oatmeal and cheese," the notice said. "He leaves Mr. and Mrs. Roberts, two guinea pigs and a cat." More recently, the *Daily Local News* in West Chester, Pennsylvania, began running pet obituaries in a weekly feature entitled "Pause to Remember." Animals mentioned in the first weeks included the usual cats and dogs along with a Rhode Island red rooster named Henry, a manx cat called Butch, and Chipper, a guinea pig mourned by his cagemate, Oreo.

From very early days the death of an animal occasioned special treatment or ceremonies. Herodotus tells of burial customs for animals in ancient Egypt:

> If a cat dies in a private house by a natural death, all the inmates of the house shave their eyebrows; on the death of a

dog they shave the head and the whole of the body. The cats on their decease are taken to the city of Bubastis, where they are embalmed, after which they are buried in certain sacred repositories. The dogs are interred in the cities to which they belong, also in sacred burial-places. The same practice obtains with respect to the ichneumous; the hawks and shrew-mice, on the contrary, are conveyed to the city of Buto for burial, and the ibises to Hermopolis. The bears, which are scarce in Egypt, and the wolves, which are not much bigger than foxes, they bury wherever they happen to find them lying.

At the end of the last century archeologists came across a large cemetery with cat mummies at Benihassan in Egypt. Felines sacred to Pekhet, patron goddess of the region, reposed there. Modern peasants used the remains as manure, thus forging a dust-to-dirt-to-food-to-flesh-to-dust chain. Other ancient Egyptian animal cemeteries which have been discovered include a monkey burial ground at Thebes, a crocodile graveyard at Monfabut south of Crocodilopolis, stork tombs at Thoth (Hermopolis), and the Serapeum, the famous necropolis for the sacred bull, Apis, discovered at Saqqara in 1851 after being buried in the sand for almost four thousand years, by the French archeologist Auguste Mariette. Also at Saqqara, by the entrance to the tomb of Queen Her-nit, reposed a dog, apparently her pet. Excavations by Professor W. B. Emery at North Saqqara between 1967 and 1971 revealed a whole series of subterranean, rock-cut galleries lined with niches containing hundreds of mummified baboons and ibises, sacred to the gods Toth and Imhotep. Some of the baboon mummies are on display at the Ashmolean museum in Oxford. In 1987 archeologists excavating at Ashkelon, a seaside city thirty miles south of Tel Aviv, occupied between 1800 B.C. and about 1200 A.D., unearthed a twenty-five-hundred-year-old dog cemetery. One of only three known ancient dog cemeteries (the others are in Iraq and Turkey), it contained the graves of several hundred greyhounds, thought to be corpses from a kennel which raised the animals for hunting.

Ancient animal burial involved ritualistic and sacrificial ceremonies, in contrast to the sentimental interments of today. In *De Legibus* Cicero states that under Roman law a grave was not considered a burial site until a pig had been sacrificed there. At the funeral of a Viking chief witnessed by an early Arab traveler named ibn-Fadlan in 922 A.D. near the modern town of Bulgar on the Volga River, a dog, two horses, two cows, a rooster, and a hen were sacrificed. A fifteen-grave Viking cemetery on Westray in the Orkney Islands contained human remains accompanied by skeletons of dogs and horses.

Horse burial dates from ancient times. The Mycenaeans (about 1600 B.C.–1200 B.C.) interred horses, while later Greek cultures occasionally accorded an honorable burial to chariot teams. At Acragas in Sicily marble pyramids mark the graves of horse favorites buried there. Post-World War II excavations at Salamis in Cyprus unearthed a human cemetery which included animals from the eighth and seventh century B.C.. Through a *dromos* (passageway) a chariot-hearse drawn by two horses (if a royal burial) or donkeys (if a commoner) rode to the tombs. As one animal was bludgeoned to death the other twisted away in fright and was choked by the yoke, falling in the opposite direction where its remains reposed for some twenty-six centuries. In the *Iliad* Homer recounts a funeral of heroic proportions—the interment of Patroclus, his body smeared with the fat of sheep and cattle whose carcasses were placed around the bier, along with those of four newly slain horses, and two of the deceased's nine dogs. The Scythians, who dominated the area north of the Black Sea around the seventh century B.C., used to inter horses—and much else—when their kings died. A year after one monarch's demise, so Herodotus relates, fifty of his attendants and fifty of the finest horses were strangled to death. Around the tomb, workers erected fifty pairs of stakes onto which the horses were placed. Then, with the help of an additional stake, the cadavers were mounted on the horses. Another royal tomb contained the skeletons of four hundred horses. The Romans, too, sometimes memorialized their horses, one surviving tombstone bearing a verse commemorating an African mare named Speudusa (hasty) perhaps the Phar Lap of his time: "Sired on Gaetulian sands by a Gaetulian stallion, speedy as the wind, in thy life unmated, now, Speudusa, thou dwellest in Lethe."

Horses of famous men have on occasion received special treatment. In the Samarkand mausoleum of the conqueror Tamerlane (d. 1405) once hung what was purported to be the tail of his horse. After Alexander crossed the Indus River to invade India in the spring of 326 B.C. his loyal steed, Bucephalus, died. In commemoration Alexander built a settlement named Bucephala. The site is now a mound opposite Jhelum, a city in present-day Pakistan, a hundred miles north of Lahore. Near the Baths of Fasiladas at the edge of Gondar in Ethiopia stands a crumbling rotunda, a mausoleum for Suviel, the horse of the emperor Yohannes. Under a canopy tucked among the cypress trees of the vast cemetery at Uskudar, across the Bosporus from Istanbul, reposes the favorite horse of Sultan Mahmud I, a rather rare example (in post-classical times) of an animal buried in a human graveyard.

J. Pinkerton, in his *Recollections of Paris in the years 1802-3-4-5* mentions an unusual sort of horse burial that he discovered in an exhibit at the National Library in Paris: "In one case are contained the curious fragments that were found in the tomb of Childeric near Tournay. Among these, it is well known, are many golden figures of bees, about the size of life. No reflecting antiquary even doubted that these bees decorated the leathern trappings of his horse at that time buried with his owner, as is still practiced in some parts of

Tartary." Paris's most famous horse remnant is no doubt the one on display near the main entrance of the Army Museum where the skeleton of Napoleon's favorite charger stands. Ridden by Napoleon at the Battle of Marengo (1800) and named after that encounter, the horse is believed to have carried the emperor at Waterloo as well. Another famous European military leader whose horse has been memorialized is Albrecht von Wallenstein, a renowned seventeenth-century adventurer, soldier, and mystic who helped drive the Swedes out of Prague. Wallenstein built a palace in Prague on land the emperor confiscated from executed or exiled Bohemian nobles. Buried on the palace grounds is the horse killed under Wallenstein in the Battle of Luetzen (1632), during which the famous Swedish general Gustavus Adolphus was killed. As for Wallenstein, the emperor, fearing he was plotting with the Swedes, assassinated him in 1634.

Horse memorials also dot the New World. Perhaps the first mount honored here was that of Cortez, the sixteenth-century conqueror of Mexico. Cortez left his horse at Peten Itza in the care of the Mayas, who believed that the Spanish steeds were supernatural. When the horse died, the frightened natives carved a stone image of the animal in an effort to appease the Mayan gods. The image, which became the object of veneration, the natives called Itzmin Chac, "Thunder-and-Lightning"—a precursor of Phar Lap.

In Yankee-land, as the Aussie poet-mourner of Phar Lap dubbed the States, horse legends and lore galore gallop through the Wild West's history. That quintessential cowboy figure, Buffalo Bill Cody, liked to give his horses special burials. One of Bill's favorites was Old Charlie, a half-breed Kentucky steed which starred in the cowboy's Wild West traveling show. Old Charlie was perhaps the most famous horse of his time. Buffalo Bill considered him "an animal of almost human intelligence." In the spring of 1888, when the company was returning to New York on the chartered ship

Persian Monarch after a triumphant engagement in London, Old Charlie died. Colonel Cody at first wanted to take the carcass home and bury it at his ranch in North Platte, Nebraska, but he then decided to give his beloved horse a burial at sea. They wrapped Old Charlie in canvas and covered the corpse with the American flag. Buffalo Bill delivered the eulogy:

> Old fellow, your journeys are over . . . Obedient to my call, gladly you bore your burden on, little knowing, little reckoning what the day might bring, shared sorrows and pleasures alike. Willing speed, tireless courage . . . you have never failed me. Ah, Charlie, old fellow, I have had many friends, but few of whom I could say that . . I loved you as you loved me. Men tell me you have no soul, but if there is a heaven and scouts can enter there, I'll wait at the gate for you, old friend.

Another of Buffalo Bill favorites was a horse named Buckskin Joe. In 1869 Colonel Cody encountered at Fort McPherson a Pawnee scout, member of an Indian band who had helped the United States forces against the Cheyenne. Taking a fancy to a big, yellow horse the Pawnee owned, Bill traded various items for the animal. As might be expected, Cody had a good eye for horse flesh, and Buckskin Joe turned out to be one of the greatest long distance horses of the day. Buffalo Bill relied on the steed for all his scouting and hunting expeditions. At times he would start off on another mount but take Buckskin Joe along in case the trek became difficult or dangerous. After a grueling 195-mile ride the animal went blind, so Cody retired the horse to his ranch. When the faithful steed finally died his master buried him with a tombstone that read, "Old Buckskin Joe, the horse that on several occasions saved the life of Buffalo Bill by carrying him safely out of range of Indian battles, died of old age, 1882."

The Indian wars brought fame to horses as well as to men.

One of the most famous was Comanche, a mustang which served with the United States Seventh Cavalry. The horse joined the unit at the age of six or seven after being purchased for ninety dollars from commercial traders in St. Louis, Missouri, in the summer of 1867. The new trooper supposedly received his name when he replaced a mount shot out from under Captain Myles W. Keogh during a skirmish between the newly-formed Seventh Cavalry and a small band of Comanches near Ellis, Kansas. Nine years later Captain Keogh rode Comanche in the ill-fated Battle of Little Big Horn, "Custer's Last Stand." On 27 June, two days after the encounter, General Alfred Terry arrived there to find some two hundred dead soldiers and a scattering of carcasses of cavalry horses and Indian ponies. Custer himself lay near the crest of a knoll surrounded by a ring of dead horses and forty or so officers and men. Not a single living creature relieved the scene. But near an Indian village not far from the site of the massacre wandered a badly wounded horse—Comanche. On 29 June the horse, along with the few wounded men who managed to escape, began the slow march back to the junction of the Little Big Horn and Big Horn rivers where the steamer *Far West* took them on to Fort Lincoln. Seventh Cavalry personnel there nursed Comanche back to health. The horse enjoyed an elegant stall and special privileges which he exploited by grazing on the lawns and flowerbeds of the base. On Saturday nights the men supplied the old trooper with ample quantities of beer, a treat Comanche supposedly eagerly looked forward to every week. Beer, plus a daily massage, tenderizes the flesh of Japanese cattle slaughtered to produce the famous Kobe beef, but even with all the beer he imbibed crusty old Comanche, battle-scarred and world weary, was by then beyond tenderness.

Comanche's final post was Fort Riley, Kansas, where he died 7 November 1894 at the age of thirty-one. Farrier Samuel J. Winchester, Comanche's handler during the horse's last year, described how he died "while I had my hand on his pulse and looking him in the eye." Captain Henry J. Nowlan, who had discovered the horse near the Little Big Horn battlefield, arranged with L. L. Dyche of the University of Kansas at nearby Lawrence for Comanche to be preserved. Dyche performed the taxidermy: clay was applied to a wooden frame to model the animals' body over which was placed the skin, preserved and treated with arsenic to protect the coat from insects. After being displayed at the 1893 Chicago Exposition Comanche returned to the University of Kansas where he occupies a glass case at Dyche Hall, the Museum of Natural History. Underneath the saddle lies a blue blanket bearing a yellow "7" to indicate that the steed served with the Seventh Cavalry. Admirers of Comanche have mounted various efforts to rustle the horse hero from his comfortable glass stall at Dyche Hall. In 1947 the United States Army—through no less a personage than General Jonathan M. Wainwright—tried to acquire the cavalry veteran, while in 1953 the Lewistown, Montana, Kiwanis club attempted to remove Comanche to the museum at the Custer Battlefield National Monument.

Although the army failed to retrieve its beloved beast, Fort Riley, site of Comanche's last stand, does boast its own horse grave and monument. Chief, a bay gelding foaled in 1932, entered military service in 1940 at Fort Robinson, Nebraska. In 1941 he moved to Fort Riley to join the Tenth Cavalry. In the winter of 1949/50 the army sold off its horses sixteen years or younger, while older mounts were put out to pasture. Some 220 steeds thus went off duty. By the time Chief died in 1968 he was the very last cavalry mount on the rolls of the United States Army. His death marked the end of an era: the army once boasted thousands of cavalry mounts; now there were none. Chief's Fort Riley colleagues buried him with full military honors including a color guard ceremony, remarks by the commanding general, and a band which blared such numbers as "Hit the Leather," "Black Horse Troop," and "Sabre and Spurs." Buried standing up, Chief reposes near the Cavalry Museum at Fort Riley beneath a statue of a mounted rider, based on a painting by Frederick Remington in 1898 entitled *The Cavalryman.*

Other military horses—like Comanche and Chief—have also been memorialized. At the Virginia Military Institute Museum in Lexington, Virginia, stands stuffed Little Sorrel, war horse of Thomas J. "Stonewell" Jackson, who taught at V.M.I. until called to arms in 1861. Also in Virginia, Confederate General Robert E. Lee's horse Traveler (d. 1872) lies on the grounds of the chapel at Washington and Lee University not far from his master's crypt. As for Lee, when the general died in 1870 flood waters cut the town of Lexington off from the outside world and the undertaker finally located a small casket, so short that Lee's shoes had to be removed before he could fit into the box.

When Captain Simon Smith returned from the French and Indian War in 1760 he contracted a mysterious illness. On the way home to New London, Connecticut, he fell from his horse and died in Andover, Connecticut. Fearing smallpox, the alarmed town fathers ordered man, beast, and gear buried on the spot. A worn marker reads: "Loved yet unattended. All alone. Sweetly repose beneath this humble stone ye last remains." In 1779 General John Sullivan buried the pack horses which had faithfully served him during his campaign against the Iroquois in up-state New York. Ten years later the valley's first white settlers found the bleached skulls and called the settlement Horseheads, a name the town still bears. Across the continent, Apache chief Cochise lurked in his stronghold in the mountainous Chiticahua area of southeastern Arizona. According to legend, when Cochise died in 1874 his braves buried his body—along with his horse, dog, and rifle—in a deep crevice at some lonely, manzanita-filled canyon where the bones of the leader and his animals moulder away, still undiscovered. The skin and skull of Kidron (d. 1942), a twentieth-century military horse that belonged to American general John J. Pershing, resides at the Smithsonian Museum of Natural History in Washington. Pershing himself (d. 1948) lies nearby in Arlington National Cemetery. The general wrote out his funeral instructions, which the army kept in a Pentagon file marked "Top Secret." In addition to General Pershing's horse the Smithsonian museum also houses a horse named Lexington (d. 1875). Lexington, a champion race horse and sire of champions, once reposed by the Kentucky stables which sheltered the brood mares he "covered," as horse people so vividly call it. Later his skeleton was mounted and presented to the Smithsonian where the bones now comprise an exhibit in Osteology Hall.

Lexington—not the horse but the equine city in Kentucky—has consecrated some of its blue grass terrain to memorialize horse heroes. The most renowned is Man O'War, winner in all but one of his twenty-one races, who lies under his life-size statue in the Kentucky Horse Park in Lexington. Next to the grave of Man O'War—said to be the only horse ever embalmed—stands a small grave marker to Isaac Burns Murphy (d. 1896), "Famous Negro Jockey."

In another corner of Lexington, just to the south of Winchester Pike, nestles the horse cemetery of Hamburg Place, a horse farm which produced a stableful of winners. In the middle of the small enclave, enclosed by a limestone wall, stands a four-tier stone monument with a plaque to "Nancy Hanks Record 2:04 1886–1915." This refers to the trotter's record run for the mile in 1892. She later retired undefeated. Around the center section of the cemetery stand thirteen low stone markers, each with a metal plaque. These memorialize Sir Martin (d. 1930), two-year-old American champion in 1908; Siliwo (d. 1926), Kentucky Futurity winner in 1906; Hamburg Belle (d. 1929), "for 16 years holder of the world's record"; Major Delmar (d. 1912), "missed world record by a fraction. For years the world's Speediest Gelding"; Plaudit (d. 1919), "the Kentucky Derby 1898"; Star Shoot (d. 1919), "America Leading Sire 1911–12–16–16–17–18–19"; Ogden (d. 1925), "winner of 2 races in one day"; Lady Sterling (d. 1920), "one time world's champion mare"; Imp (d. 1909), "'The Black Whirlwind' stakes winner of 65 races"; Ida Pickwick (d. 1908), "the Queen of the West"; Miss Kearney (d. 1925), "the dam of Zex"; Princess Mary (d. 1926), "dam of Flying Ebony Kentucky Derby 1925." A few yards beyond stand two larger, more recent, monuments to Pink Pigeon (d. 1976), a thoroughbred that set world records for 1⅛ and 1¼ miles, and T. V. Lark (d. 1975), the country's leading sire in 1974. By the outer walls rises a marker to the polo pony "Springtime [died] On the Polo Field September 10th 1933."

In contrast to the hidden corner of Kentucky where the Hamburg Place steeds lie buried, a filly named Ruffian rests in full view of thousands of horse fans at the Belmont Park race track in New York. After Ruffian broke a leg during a race in 1975 officials destroyed her, watched by television viewers across the country. The horse was later buried just past the finish line, beneath a flag pole in the infield. A horseshoe-shaped floral piece of 1,362 white carnations garnished Ruffian's funeral. Another unusual horse grave is as obscure as Ruffian's burial place is prominent. During and just after World War I a horse named Palmer De Forest beat all comers in harness races at county fairs in southern Illinois. His owner, Otto Snider, earned enough money from the horse to put two sons through medical school. When Palmer De Forest retired from competition his owner brought him back to the family's thirty-eight-hundred-acre farm near Royalton, Illinois. One day, while standing in the middle of his pasture, a bolt of lightning struck and killed the retiree. Snider buried the horse on the spot where the animal had died, erecting there a tombstone which proclaims that Palmer De Forest was "never defeated in his class." Another champion, Rex McDonald, reposes on the front lawn of the American Saddle Horse Museum in Mexico, Missouri. Rex was said to be the greatest five-gaited horse ever shown. The New Bern, North Carolina, Fireman's Museum houses the mounted head of Fred, an old fire horse who died in his traces while answering an alarm.

Occasionally American political figures would memorialize their horses. President John Tyler's epitaph for The General, a horse he rode for twenty years when traveling the circuit as an attorney recalls that "in all that time he [The General] never made a blunder. Would that his master could say the same." Horse gravestones grace the grounds of another president, Rutherford B. Hayes, whose Fremont, Ohio, estate, Spiegel Grove, contains markers to such favorites as Old Whitey, Piddig, and Black Yanco. Daniel Webster also honored his horses. On his Marshfield, Massachusetts, property he buried his steeds in a standing position, complete with saddle and halter.

In the world, and underworld, of cemeteries, funerals, and burials, horses are unique for they alone, of all the animals, play an active role. In Belgium black horses were bred especially for the funeral trade. If, as occasionally happened, the animal's coat turned out to be rust-colored, it was dyed black. Attendant's blackened the hooves, and if the tail seemed too skimpy they strapped on flowing hairpieces, the better to impress mourners. Similarly, if an animal's mane was not thick enough, black velvet caparisons over the neck concealed the defect. Until made illegal shortly before World War I, bunches of black ostrich plumes decorated its forehead. The Turks added a special touch to the horse which accompanied its master's funeral procession: they inserted into its nostrils mustard seed so that the animal, its eyes irritated, would shed what observers supposed were tears of grief. In *Martin Chuzzlewit* Dickens describes a funeral staged by the evocatively named undertaker, Mr. Mould: "The four hearse-horses, especially, reared and pranced, and showed their highest action, as if they knew a man was dead, and triumphed in it. 'They break us, drive us, ride us; ill-treat, abuse and maim us for their pleasure—But they die; Hurrah, they die!' "

A triumph of horse over man such as Dickens described appears in A.E. Houseman's poem "A Shropshire Lad." A dead farmer wonders if the team he used to drive still ploughs, and is told that the horses now trample the ground under which he lies. Dickens' hearse-horses lacked that great advantage over man which animals enjoy—ignorance of death. When Ulysses, on the island of Circe, asks one of his men who has been turned into an animal why he does not want to be turned back into a human, he replies that knowledge of death is too great a burden to bear.

A Pirandello short story entitled "Black Horses" delves more deeply than did Dickens into the psychology of funeral horses. It seems that a nag named Nero has been sold out of the stables of a modern-minded prince who took a fancy to a new-fangled machine called a motor car. Since the machine moves without horse power, the prince disposes of some of his steeds, Nero included. Nero and his new stall-mate Fofo exchange gossip and small talk about the love lives of their colleagues. Chatting in the stable where Nero has recently arrived, Fofo also explains to the newcomer what his duties will entail: working for an undertaker "means that your job is to pull a strange-looking black carriage that has four pillars supporting the roof and is all decked out grand with gilding and a curtain and fringes—in fact a handsome carriage de luxe. But it's a sheer waste—you'd hardly believe it—sheer waste, 'cause no one ever comes and sits inside it." With his horse-eye view of the funeral cortege, Fofo is somewhat puzzled by the fact "that human beings seem to look upon it as an object of peculiar reverence." Fofo also observes that they haul their cargo to "some fine, green meadows full of luscious grass; but that's all sheer waste, too, for one's not allowed to eat it." Fofo speculates on the contents of the boxes that the horses haul. The goods seem to be valuable, for a number of people accompany the procession and the crowd pays much solemn attention to the box. On the morning of the discussion between Nero and Fofo the undertaker calls them to duty. He hitches the two stablemates together, then the procession proceeds to a certain palace where Nero suddenly becomes agitated. An old man in livery emerges from the mansion and shouts a cry of recognition—Nero, a recent resident of the establishment, is none other than the favorite horse of the late princess, whose body he must now haul to the cemetery. "You still remember her, don't you?" says the old coachman soothingly. "They've shut her up in the big box." Meanwhile, the garrulous Fofo continues to chatter, observing, "Yes, now I know all about it . . . That's why our job is such a soft one! It's only when men must weep that we horses can be happy and have a restful time."

This horse-sense view of human mortality tends to put into perspective the solemnity associated with death, burial and funerals. To the horses, a funeral is just another day's work—and even a happy time—and a cemetery simply a grassy area where it would be pleasant to graze. A country parson's grave supposedly bears the epitaph:

> The horse bit the parson,
> How came that to pass?
> The horse heard the parson say,
> All flesh is grass.

In the end, then, man and beast assume the same lowly status—pushing daisies, enriching grass, nourishing worms. So why, wonders Kholstomer (strider), the piebald gelding who narrates Tolstoy's short story of that name, is a distinction made between horses and people even in death? Al-

though the man, according to the horse, is useless—"Neither
his skin nor his flesh nor his bones could be used for anything"—his corpse would be dressed up in a fancy outfit and
placed in an expensive lead coffin. After the horse dies,
however, the nag's carcass would be unceremonially cast
away and devoured by a she-wolf and her cubs. Mens' remains are coddled but dead horse flesh is waste. This is
unfair, maintains Kholstomer, for by that point in time—post
mortem—are not man and beast truly equal?

Kholstomer's pragmatic view of the relative usefulness of
man and horse—a grading of different species—seems to
echo Thorstein Veblen's analysis of the difference between the
utility of various kinds of animals. In the chapter on "Pecuniary Canons of Taste" in *The Theory of the Leisure Class* Veblen
distinguishes between "productive goods," such as barnyard
fowl, hogs, cattle, sheep and goats, and pets, which he labels
"items of conspicuous consumption." In the latter category
he includes pigeons, parrots, cats, dogs and "fast horses . . .
[which are] on the whole expensive, or wasteful and useless."
Thus Veblen's opinion of the Phar Laps of the world. Cats,
Veblen allows, may be less objectionable than the other kinds
of pets for felines "may even serve a useful end." Dogs,
however, are useless, their main function being the frivolous
one of playing "to our propensity for mastery." He calls dogs
the "filthiest" and the "nastiest" of the domestic animals, thus
scoring at least half on the character test proposed by W. C.
Fields, who said that anyone who hated dogs and children
could not be all bad.

Viewed economically, dogs, it seems, are the low man on
the totem pole. In Ronald Blythe's *Akenfield: Portrait of an
English Village* a country veterinarian observes: "There are
lots of dogs in the village. The pet population of England is
fantastic. Of course, it's different in the country. All our
village animals are economic, with the exception of the dog."
The vet wryly observes that in the city pets "have become

members of human families, lovers, partners—anything you like—so when they are sick you can charge their owners anything you like. . . In the village you only treat an animal up to the economic level." This practical view of dogs, which relegates them to a lowly status, is quite the opposite of the way most people see their puppies, pooches, and doggies. Perhaps more than any other animal, dogs are fawned over and made part of the family. And when the pet's final hour comes those little darlings are treated in death with an attitude almost human in its rituals and sentiments.

Perhaps the most elaborate rites for a dead dog took place after the shooting of Jim Kelly's hound in a Dodge City saloon. Dog Kelly, as the animal lover was sometimes called, owned about a hundred dogs which he employed to chase rabbits and coyotes. One hound happened to stray into a saloon where he took an ill-timed nap from which he never awoke, for when Mysterious Dave Mather, the Dodge City marshal, shot a tinhorn in an argument over a card game, the bullet whizzed on to kill the dozing dog. No one bothered about the dead man, but the dog's death caused quite a stir in town. Jim Kelly went after Dave Mather with a shot gun, but when the boys at the saloon promised to bury the dog with military honors and hold an inquest, Kelly calmed down. The coroner, one Joyful Brown, was summoned, a jury impaneled, and witnesses called. They testified they had never seen the dog order a drink in the saloon, so he probably had no business being there. Furthermore, it was argued, the hound should have known better than to take a nap in a Dodge City saloon, a high hazard corner of town. The jury absolved Dave Mather and then—further to mollify Dog Kelly—the locals hired a hearse and organized a funeral procession which, accompanied by the Dodge City Cowboy Band, proceeded to Boot Hill where the animal was put to rest, complete with sermon and a chorus of "The Cowboy's Lament."

Another sentimental Wild West dog burial took place with less musical and liturgical fanfare when a miner interred his beloved pet with a private ceremony in a remote corner of Nevada. In 1891 diggers discovered gold near Las Vegas and the town of Johnnie Mine sprung up around the lodes. After the deposits petered out the mine closed, only to be reactivated in 1945. An unknown miner staked a small claim in the area and, accompanied by his dog Paddy, worked the vein a time before moving on. When Paddy died his master felt that the most appropriate place for burial would be in the claim near Johnnie Mine, so he wrapped the animal in a blanket, carried the body back, and put it into a coffin which he buried where the two of them had tried to scratch out a living. Above the grave the miner erected a rather surrealistic monument built of rocks, bits of glass, wooden ornaments, all topped by a carved replica of Paddy.

All manner of dogs are commemorated around the United States, canines famous in their own right and those remembered for having belonged to a well-known master, as well as thousands of just plain mutts. A brass plate embedded in the sidewalk at the corner of Limestone and Main Streets in Lexington, Kentucky, memorializes Smiley Pete (d. 1957), the "town dog." (This recalls the granite marker on the Natchez, Mississippi City Hall lawn: "Tripod Oct. 9, 1983 'The City's Kitty.'") One of the most publicized dog-master combinations in American history was Richard Nixon's Checkers. Checkers became famous in 1952 when Nixon referred to the dog on television in his "I am not a crook" speech. Checkers, who died in 1964, lies buried in the Bide-a-Wee Cemetery at Wantagh, Long Island. The pet dogs of another Washington figure, the FBI's J. Edgar Hoover, repose in Aspen Hill Pet Cemetery in Silver Spring, Maryland. The cemetery director there once observed: "A man buries his wife because he has to, but he buries his dog because he wants to." Eight of Hoover's dead doggies rest at Aspen Hill.

One of the grave stones bears the inscription: "In memory of Spee De Bozo. Born July 3, 1922. Died may 24, 1934. Our best friend." Another Maryland dog marker commemorates Tessie, H. L. Mencken's pet, at 1524 Hollins Street, Baltimore, where the author spent virtually his entire life. In 1920 Mencken walled in the backyard, laying the bricks himself. When Tessie died the next year he inserted in one wall a bronze plaque to her memory.

In Pine Ridge Cemetery for Small Animals at Dedham, Massachusetts, polar explorer Richard E. Byrd's dog Igloo lies under a granite iceberg marked with the phrase: "More than a friend." Another stone monument portrays a dog poking its head out of a briefcase. Also in Massachusetts three and a half miles outside Sheffield is a burial ground with the name Bow Wow Cemetery, but the grave yard contains no "bow wows" as it is not a pet cemetery. Another polar dog awarded a special monument was a malamite named Balto. Balto lead a team of huskies which carried diptheria serum to the relief of Nome, Alaska, in 1925. A bronze statue of the hero—New York City's only monument to a dog—stands in Central Park near Fifth Avenue at the Sixty-sixth Street level. Sculpted in 1926 the figure, perched atop a rough-hewn boulder, shows Balto with his tail curled over his back and his ears pricked up, his face looking alertly at the passing scene. The commemorative plaque reads: "Dedicated to the indomitable spirit of The Sled Dogs that relayed antitoxin six hundred miles over rough ice across the treacherous waters through arctic blizzards from Nenana to the relief of stricken Nome in the winter of 1925. Endurance Fidelity Intelligence."

Work dogs, such as Igloo and Balto, are often fondly remembered for the services they have rendered. The Coon Dog Memorial Graveyard near Cherokee in northwest Alabama, founded in 1937, began when Key Underwood buried there his favorite hunting hound, Troop. More than a hundred coon dogs repose at the ten-acre burial ground, embellished with a large limestone memorial built in 1960 portraying two dogs treeing a raccoon. Another hunting dog is remembered, though not interred, at the grave of Ethal Barrett (d. 1941) in Woodstock Hill Cemetery, Woodstock, Vermont. On Barrett's stone appears a fox, a dog, a gun, and the notation: "This is Fanny, my favorite fox hound. I have shot over two hundred foxes with the gun that I hold." Back in the 1920s and 1930s smugglers used dogs to carry tobacco across the border from Erquennes in Belgium into Hon in France. Every week frontier guards would shoot some fifty dogs trained by French smugglers to transport two baskets, each filled with five pounds of tobacco. The dogs were buried by a road with a sign in French and Flemish: "Here lies a canine smuggler. Human smugglers take warning." Another trained French dog was the watchman's pet at the Cimetière Marin at Sète where poet Paul Valéry reposes. The dog was taught to lead visitors to the writer's grave. (In his *Memoirs* Chilean poet Pablo Neruda tells of Rango, an orangutan at the botanical gardens in Medan, Indonesia, who was trained to open the garden gate, for which the attendant rewarded him with a pitcher of beer, a treat also given to the above-mentioned Comanche, the horse which survived Custer's Last Stand.)

Back in France, the prefect of police in Paris ceremoniously buried the dogs Léo and Papillon, killed in the line of duty by criminals, while soldiers in World War I interred the dog Pax and a cat named X, employed in the trenches to warn of poison gas. The Smithsonian Institution in Washington houses the stuffed body of a terrier mutt named Owney, adopted as an unofficial post office mascot. After postal workers found him as a puppy among mailbags in Albany, New York, in 1888, Owney was sent all around the country in postal rail cars. In 1895 the mutt traveled overseas, visiting China and Japan and sailing on around the world as a "registered dog package." Owney eventually retired in Albany, but one day he slipped onto a train bound for Toledo where—in an incident never clarified—he died of a gunshot wound on 11 June 1897.

Dogs which mimic men by displaying human traits or talents merit memorials. In Pine Forest Cemetery, Wilmington, North Carolina, a statue of a small pooch named Jip (d. 1904) bears a description of him as "the only dog we ever knew that attended church every Sunday." Hopefully, the sermons Jip heard were not too dogmatic. But an even more remarkable dog named Jim outdid Jip in human-like behavior. Jim first saw the light of day on 10 March 1925 when he turned out to be the runt of a litter of setters born in Louisiana. His siblings brought the dog breeder twenty-five dollars each, but Jim sold for only five. Sam Van Arsdale, owner of the Hotel Ruff in Marshall, Missouri—a small town in the west-central part of the state—eventually came into possession of Jim, who soon began to exhibit his extraordinary talents. It seems that Jim possessed almost human powers of reasoning and intelligence. Asked to pick out a certain car, the dog would proceed directly to the vehicle; ordered to fetch a copy of the *Saturday Evening Post,* Jim would trot to the drug store and pick out the magazine; presented with a list of Kentucky Derby entries, the animal predicted the winner—seven years in a row. People from all over traveled to Marshall to observe the Wonder Dog, as he was called, go through his paces. He predicted election winners, accurately forecast the gender of babies, obeyed commands in five or six different languages. A. J. Durant, dean emeritus of the University of Missouri School of Veterinary Medicine, believed that the animal "possessed some occult power that may never again come to a dog in many, many generations," while a psychiatrist suggested that Jim was telepathic, receiving whatever his master was thinking. In 1933 Jim performed his feats for members of the Missouri

General Assembly at the state capitol in Jefferson City. Hundreds of people witnessed Jim's amazing performance, but no one ever learned his secret. The famous setter died on March 19, 1937, and reposes in Marshall's Ridge Park Cemetery—a burial ground for humankind—where a pink granite stone marks his grave. A well-worn path from the cemetery's iron gates attests that Jim the Wonder Dog is better remembered than the people buried at Ridge Park. Shops in Marshall sell Jim's official biography, and the dog's portrait hangs in the banquet room of the Marshall Inn.

At Warrensburg, not far from Marshall, another renowned dog is commemorated. On the Johnson County courthouse lawn stands a bronze of Old Drum, a black and tan hound whose death in 1859 occasioned a famous trial. It seems that Leonidas Hornsby, upset by all the sheep he had lost to dogs, vowed to kill the next hound that ventured onto his property. One night Old Drum wandered onto the farm and, true to his threat, Hornsby ordered the animal shot. Charles Burden, the dog's owner and Hornsby's brother-in-law, sued for damages. George Graham Vest—who served in the Missouri House, the Confederate States Senate and for twenty-four years in the United States Senate—represented the plaintiff. The final trial took place in Warrensburg on 23 September 1870. During the proceedings Vest delivered his now famous "Eulogy to A Dog":

> The one absolutely unselfish friend that a man can have in this selfish world, the one that never deserts him and the one that never proves ungrateful or treacherous is his dog . . . If fortune drives the master forth an outcast in the world, friendless and homeless, the faithful dog asks no higher privilege than that of accompanying him to guard against danger, to fight against his enemies, and when the last scene of all comes, and death takes the master in its embrace and his body is laid away in the cold ground, no matter if all other friends pursue their way, there by his graveside will the noble dog be found, his

head between his paws, his eyes sad but open in alert watchfulness, faithful and true even to death.

This oration naturally brought tears to the eyes of the jury members, and money to Charles Burden's pocket: the jury delivered a verdict awarding Old Drum's owner fifty dollars.

But a dog need not be famous, like Old Drum, or sport special talents, like Jim the Wonder Dog, to be adored and remembered by its owner. In a remote area of Wisconsin, near Couderay I came across a grove called the "Tubby Forest," a memorial wood dedicted to one Tubby, a brown and white springer spaniel described by a sign as "loyal comrade, constant companion for fourteen years, and a friend to all mankind." So deep is the devotion between master (or mistress) and pet (or pette) that some people will go to any length not to be separated from their dogs. In 1978 a woman named Lillian Kopp was buried in Paw Print Gardens, the first person to be interred in the pet cemetery in Chicago's west side. She lies near her German shepherd, Rinty, who died in 1972, aged fifteen. A similar postmortem reunion took place at the grave of Pulitzer Prize-winning author Ellen Glasgow (d. 1945) at Hollywood Cemetery in Richmond, Virginia. As a child the author liked to visit the cemetery. Glasgow, a dog lover, never married: her dogs were her family. When one of them, a Sealyham named Jeremy, died in 1929 the *Richmond Times-Dispatch* ran a lengthy obituary. Glasgow buried some of her dogs in Richmond's Pet Memorial Park, others in her garden. The author left instructions that on her death the dogs in the garden should be exhumed and put in her casket. When Glasgow died, Jeremy and also Billy, a French poodle, were disinterred and reburied with their mistress.

New Yorker magazine cartoonist Charles Addams and his bride so adored her dead pets that the couple chose to get married in the dog cemetery at Toad Hall, the new Mrs.

Addams' Long Island estate. Five dogs and a turtle lie there, interred beneath stone figures of themselves. The macabre cartoonist once noted that he enjoyed playing in cemeteries as child: "I like them still. I find them rather cozy. It's where we'll all be someday."

Few humans get buried or married with their dead dogs. But dogs will do nearly anything with and for humans. A monument at Oakdale Cemetery in Wilmington, North Carolina, recalls the time a dog named Caesar tried to rescue fire captain William A. Ellerbrook from a burning building where he was pinned by a fallen rafter. Both died in the flames and man and dog now lie together in the same casket. Dog loyalty delights by its constancy, a quality little known to humans. Dog fidelity knows no boundaries—emotional or geographical. By the Shibuya subway station in central Tokyo stands a bronze statue of a dog named Hachiko. For twelve years Hachiko used to meet his master at the station every evening. One day the man was killed, but for ten years afterwards the faithful animal still came daily to wait at the same place. On the other side of the earth, the elaborate, black marble tomb of Cardinal Mazarin at the Institute de France in Paris includes the figure of a spaniel-like dog—a symbol of loyalty—looking up with a tender expression. In Plein Square, near the Mauritshaus in The Hague, stands a bronze statue of William I of Orange shown companioned by his dog, ears cocked and gazing up at his master with a longing look. William (d. 1584) lies buried in New Church in Delft, his mausoleum decorated with a life-size, regally clad figure of the deceased reclining on a marble mattress. By his feet lies his dog, which refused to eat after its master's death and presumably died of hunger. The dog's head rests on its left paw and bears an immensely sad expression. Although imposing figures of Justice, Liberty, Religion, Valor, and Fame embellish the tomb, and columns, carvings, and other ornaments add decorations, it is the melancholy expression of

William's faithful dog which humanizes—so to speak—the cold marble and metal sculpture. Of what importance are such abstractions as Justice and Liberty, and such ephemera as Valor and Fame, when compared to a dog's enduring loyalty to his master?

In his *Brief Lives* Aubrey relates how, when the Earl of Pembroke died in 1570, his dog—"a little reddish picked nosed Cur-dog: none of the Prittiest"—refused to "goe from his Master's dead body, but pined away, and dyed under the hearse; the picture of which Dog is under his picture in the Gallery at Wilton." A more recent case in England involved the 1865 funeral of Tom Sayers, a well-known pugilist from London's East End. Londoners observed an unofficial public holiday for the popular boxer's funeral. Crowds lined the streets as the hearse passed by on the way to Highgate Cemetery. The chief mourner, riding by himself in a mail phaeton and dressed in a mourning outfit with black crepe around the neck, was a large brown dog.

An even more poignant example of canine loyalty in Britain featured a Skye terrier named Greyfriars Bobby. Originally a stray, Bobby eventually found a home in Edinburgh with an impoverished shepherd named Jock Gray. Man and dog were inseparable, until death carried Gray off in 1858. But even then, Bobby refused to abandon his master. For the next fourteen years the terrier never left Gray's grave in Greyfriars churchyard, apart from a daily visit to Traill's Dining Rooms—where the twosome had often lunched together—to eat a meal. Nine years after Gray's death, Bobby was summoned to court on charges of vagrancy and trespassing in the churchyard. By then an Edinburgh legend, the dog attracted powerful support: the city officially adopted him and Lord Provost William Chambers paid Bobby's license fee every year. He also presented the dog with a brass-plated collar inscribed: "Greyfriars Bobby, from the Lord Provost, 1867, Licensed." Bobby's fellow Edinburghers built him a shelter and made certain he was always well fed. Over the years the terrier doggedly continued his vigil at Jock Gray's graveside. After the animal finally died in 1872 his admirers put him to rest near where Gray lay. On cobblestoned Candlemaker Row, across from the two graves, stands a small statue of Greyfriars Bobby, now forever—in his frozen metallic pose—watching over his beloved master's final resting place, and his own.

Although such dogged loyalty can be heart-warming, in some cases animals—like humans—can exaggerate their affection. In a passage in *The Anatomy of Melancholy,* Burton tells of various animals which became unusually attached to humans:

> [W]hat strange fury is that, when a Beast shall dote upon a man! Saxo Grammaticus hath a story of a Bear that loved a woman, kept her in his den a long time, and begot a son of her, out of whose loins proceeded many Northern kings . . . A Peacock in Leucadia loved a maid, and when she died the Peacock pined. A Dolphin loved a boy called Hernias, and when he died, the fish came on land, and so perished . . . [A certain writer tells of having seen] a lynx, which [he] had from Assyria, so affected towards one of [his] men, that it cannot be derived but that he was in love with him . . . Such another story he hath of a Crane of Majorca, that loved a Spaniard, that would walk any way with him, and in his absence seek about for him, make a noise that he might hear her, and knock at his door, and when he took his last farewell, famished himself.

Of course, loyalty with animals works both ways. The English exemplify that kind of fawning pet love which occasionally degenerates into sentimentality. Two rather maudlin tombs at London's Highgate Cemetery honor canines. In an oval niche at the pink granite obelisk which marks the tomb of Ann Jewson Crisp (d. 1884) stands a marble relief of a dog with cocked ears and a slight double chin, recalled by the inscription: "Her Faithful Dog Emperor." The nearby black stone monument to Theresa Augusta Pierssene (d. 1927) includes a white relief of "her Faithful Pet 'Jack' " placed in a featured position at the top of the marker, with the deceased's husband Harry (d. 1949) relegated to a lower place.

At the turn of the century a canine cause-célèbre agitated the country when grisly medical experiments on a little brown terrier became known. In the name of science, researchers slit open the dog's abdomen, tied its pancreatic duct and attached electrodes to a neck nerve. The terrier, not unexpectedly, died and in 1906 mourning Londoners collected a fund to erect a bronze statue—later stolen from Battersea Park—of the victim with the inscription; "In Memory of the Brown Terrier Dog done to death in the laboratories of University College in February 1903, after having endured vivisection extending over more than Two Months and having been handed from one vivisector to another Till death came to his release."

A particularly precious—in the English sense of the world—dog encomium is Virginia Woolf's biography of Flush, Elizabeth Barrett Browning's red cocker spaniel. Although biographical data was scarce—"all researchers have failed to fix with any certainty the exact year of Flush's birth, let alone the month or day"—Woolf managed to flesh out Flush's life in sufficient detail to write an entire book about him. The volume truly tells us more than we ever wanted to know. Flush's every move and mood are described. He enters Elizabeth's bedroom, Woolf writes, as if going into a tomb:

> Only a scholar who has descended step by step into a mausoleum and there finds himself in a crypt, crusted with fungus, slimy with mould, exuding sour smells of decay and antiquity, while half-obliterated marble busts gleam in mid-air . . . —only the sensations of such an explorer into the

burial vaults of a ruined city can compare with the riot of emotions that flooded Flush's nerves as he stood for the first time in an invalid's bedroom, in Wimpole Street, and smelt eau-de-cologne.

In the end Flush, as must all good dogs, died "but the date and manner of his death are unknown." The precious pet is interred in the burial vaults at Casa Guidi, in Florence, Italy.

Perhaps only in England could there have been published a book—combining the English fascination with spiritualism with their love for pets—devoted to the posthumous spiritual life of animals. In *When Your Animal Dies,* first published by the Spiritualist Press in 1940, Sylvia Barbanell maintains that "there is enough evidence to prove conclusively that the higher animals survive 'death' as individual personalities because of their association with man." Perhaps animals have souls as well. Descartes held that animals are nothing but machines, but most eighteenth-century sages disagreed and argued that dumb beasts did possess a sort of soul. Some thinkers toyed with the doctrine—taken from Eastern religions—that the transmigration of souls included animals in the cycle of transformations. One observer responded to this theory by stating that the concept appealed to him, provided that in his next incarnation he could return as a pampered dog. In his *Philosophical Dictionary* Voltaire pondered the question "of the soul of animals." After noting that some philosophers maintained that animals enjoyed life and sensations but nothing more, while other savants held that even toads and insects possessed a soul, Voltaire concluded: "I confess my ignorance," adding that four thousand tomes of metaphysics would not suffice to enlighten one on the question.

As for *When Your Animal Dies,* chapter titles suggest the book's rather eccentric themes: "Animals Who Reason," "Pets Who Like Séances," "Psychic Animals," "They All Come

Back," "Proofs by Spirit Photography," "Life In the Next World." In Chapter II, "Dogs Who Think," the author recounts the story of one Kurwenal, owned by Mathilde, baroness von Freytag-Loringhoven. Reminiscent of Jim the Wonder Dog von Missouri, the dachshund—a "most celebrated" educated dog—would sometimes "adopt a rather 'cheeky' manner with learned men. A young neurologist and animal psychologist at the University at Berne wanted to test him. Kurwenal, who thought he had been investigated quite enough for that day, exclaimed, 'I answer no doubters. Bother the asses.' "

The English were not always compassionate or considerate about their dogs. At one time, Londoners pitched dead dogs into a ditch without sentiment or monument. John Stow noted in his 1598 *Survey of London:* "From Aldgate northwest to Bishopgate lieth the ditch of the City called Houndsditch, for that in old time, when the same lay open, much filth (conveyed from the City), especially dead dogs, were there laid or cast." (At an annual memorial service in St. Andrew Undershaft Church, London's lord mayor puts a fresh quill pen in the hand of the historian's statue.) Long after the days when Houndsditch brimmed with hound carcasses an elaborate ring of dog thieves operated in London, blackmailing animal owners for the return of their beloved pets. Even Queen Victoria was not immune: they abducted her pet when it was undergoing treatment from a veterinarian.

But by and large the English have honored their dogs, dead and alive. Fully two centuries before London's Houndsditch became clogged with discarded dogs at least one English canine lover expressed her sentiments. Beneath the tomb of Lady Cassy (d. 1400) in Deerhurst church, Gloucestershire appears the word "Terri," presumably a reference to the lady's pet which reposes there. Evidence of English devotion to dogs abounds. One curious example are the kennels nestling beneath the raised pews on the south side of St. Mary Abchurch, near the city of London, where worshipers would install their dogs during services. Another London church, St. Mary-at-Lambeth, contains what may be the world's only commemorative window to a dog. According to popular tradition, in the sixteenth century a street vendor bequeathed to the parish a plot of land known as the Pedlar's Acre, on condition that his portrait and that of his dog be represented on a window of the church.

No window but a more obscure and modest memorial marks the last resting place of what might be the world's best known dog, and possibly the only one registered at the United States patent office. Under a mulberry tree in the backyard of a house on Eden Street in Kingston-on-Thames, outside London, lies Nipper, a fox terrier adopted when he was a puppy by an English artist named Francis Barraud. Nipper became fascinated with voices emanating from an early Edison phonograph, and Barraud painted a picture of his listening pet entitled *His Master's Voice*. For a decade the painting gathered dust. When a friend suggested that Barraud update the work, the artist visited the showroom of the Gramophone Company on Maiden Lane in London to sketch late-model phonographs. A suspicious employee, fearful that Barraud was collecting information for a competitor, took him to the company's president, William Barry Owen, who asked to see the painting. Owen immediately purchased the work, and shortly thereafter Eldridge Johnson of the Victor Talking Machine Company, an American firm, saw the picture and adopted it as Victor's trademark. Affiliates elsewhere also began using the portrayal of the terrier, his head cocked quizzically at the large horn of the talking machine, and Nipper's image soon became world famous. But, alas, the dog had predeceased his fame, having died in 1895 at age eleven, five years before his likeness came into use. Following

World War II, more than a half-century after the dog's death, nostalgic Nipper lovers erected a small marker on his grave.

Out in the English countryside, at Ilford in Essex, lies a pet cemetery with various accomplished animals, among them a rescue dog, and a boxer employed against terrorists in Jerusalem. Other tombs hold such lamented departed as a mascot goat named Lewis; and Prince, a dog whose tomb bears a rubber ball device and the following inscription: "Rescued 18th December 1963. Went byes 18th October 1964, age 13 years. Guard-dog, comrade, a perfect gentleman."

Britain boasts many other canine tombs, contradicting the complaint versified by Lord Byron to his dog Boatswain (d. 1808). At the poet's home in Newstead Abbey, Nottinghamshire, an inscription on the octagonal monument to the pet laments that "the poor dog, in life the firmest friend"

> Unhonour'd falls unnoticed all his worth—
> Denied in heaven the soul he held on earth.

Byron praised his beloved Newfoundland with a graceful epitaph which recalls that "near this spot are deposited the remains of one who possessed Beauty without Vanity, Strength without Insolence, Courage without Ferocity, and all the virtues of Man, without his Vices. This Praise, which would be unmeaning Flattery if inscribed over human ashes, is but a just tribute to the Memory of Boatswain, a Dog." At Abbotsford in Melrose, Scotland, home of another famous English writer, Sir Walter Scott, stands an effigy of his deerhound, Maida, whose epitaph reads: "Beneath the sculptured form which late you wore,/Sleep soundly Maida, at your master's door." Edinburgh Castle, and Powerscourt Desmene near Dublin both boast dog cemeteries. In Ireland an inspirational verse enlivens the tomb of Master McGrath, a champion Irish greyhound racer buried at the crossroad in

Collingan, County Waterford. The triple Waterloo Cup winner (in 1868, 1869, and 1871) inspired the lines:

> Though thrice victorious on Altcar's Plain,
> McGrath's fleet limbs will never run again.
> Stay man thy course, the dog's memorial view;
> Then run thy course as honest and as true.

In Wales two especially affecting monuments recall dogs. By a relief head of the deceased, who was poisoned in 1937, an inscription in Swansea states: "Erected to the Memory of Swansea Jack, the brave retriever who saved 27 human and 2 canine lives from drowning, loved and mourned by all dog lovers." In the village of Bedd-Gelert near Portmadoc in south Caernarvonshire lies the grave of the dog Gelert. The inscription recites that in the thirteenth century Llewelyn, prince of North Wales, returned home to find his infant son gone and blood everywhere. Shortly after the prince had put Gelert to death for the supposed misdeed he found nearby a wolf which the dog had slain. "The Prince, filled with remorse, is said never to have smiled again. He buried Gelert here—the spot is called 'Beddgelert.'" That word means "Gelert's grave," and thus did a remote Welch village take its name from a dog wrongfully killed seven centuries ago.

One nineteenth-century stately home in England which definitely went to the dogs was Oatlands, a country estate nestled in the pine woods at Weybridge. Oatland's mistress was Frederica, duchess of York, niece of King Frederick of Prussia, and wife of George III's favorite son. On the estate lived not only a hundred dogs but also monkeys, kangaroos, ostriches, and—in an aviary—eagles and macaws. Frederica so adored her animals that her servants at Oatlands tended to ignore guests in favor of the pets. One visitor, Charles Greville, complained that although horses filled the stables he could never get a steed to ride, and that the servants were too busy caring for the animals to answer a bell. When one of her favorites died, the duchess would erect a monument over its grave. The markers stood grouped around a fountain in front of a grotto where, in the summer Frederica would retire to read, meditate, and grieve among the tombs of her late pets. Another English court figure, Henrietta Howard, managed to persuade two of England's greatest writers to compose works about her dog. Henrietta was the mistress of George Augustus (later George II), both when he was prince and later when he became king. Swift wrote an epistle to her lapdog, Fop, and Pope wrote the animal's epitaph.

Thomas Hardy's bitter poem "Ah, Are You Digging on My Grave?" rather brutally destroys the image of the mistress–pet relationship idealized by Henrietta and her beloved doggie. The hound Hardy describes does not pine away and whine in grief over his departed owner, as the pampered little Fop might have. A dead girl, Hardy writes, wonders who might be digging in her grave. Not her loved one, she decides, for he has married someone else, nor her kinfolk who are disinterested. Finally the deceased realizes with a thrill that her dog is the one who loyally paws her grave:

> That one true heart was left behind!
> What feeling do we ever find
> To equal among human kind
> A dog's fidelity!

But then, in the last stanza, Hardy reveals the awful truth:

> Mistress, I dug upon your grave
>   To bury a bone, in case
> I should be hungry near this spot
> When passing on my daily trot.
> I am sorry, but I quite forgot
>   It was your resting place.

Some English dogs were so beloved they merited not only a memorial marker but also a portrait. In a small basement court called Monk's Yard at Soane's Museum near Lincoln's Inn Fields in London stands an elaborate stone monument whose base bears the inscription, "alas—Poor Fanny." Fanny was Mrs. Soane's dark-haired terrier, a dog which rather resembled a rabbit, as can be seen in John Jackson's painting of the pet perched on her mistress's lap. By the fireplace in the front parlor of Thomas Carlyle's London house hangs Robert Tait's *A Chelsea Interior,* in which Nero, a white terrier with black patches sits in a privileged position on a couch. Jane Carlyle, not fond of the painting, said that "the dog is the only member of the family who has reason to be pleased with his likeness," adding that the "dog looked like a wooley sheep." Nero lies buried at the rear corner of the garden under an uninscribed, jagged white rock which replaced the original marker stolen about 1885 when the house was restored. A later dog, Tiny, may have brought about Jane Carlyle's death, so the curator at the house told me. One day in 1866 when Tiny jumped out of a carriage Mrs. Carlyle pursued the animal. Shortly thereafter she suffered a heart attack, and was taken to St. George's Hospital where she died the same day. An especially poignant 1837 painting by Edwin Landseer at the Victoria and Albert Museum, *The Old Shepherd's Chief Mourner,* shows the grieving dog, its head resting on a cloth that covers the coffin of its departed master. On the floor nearby lies the shepherd's abandoned walking stick.

Pet deaths are no less provided for in London than the passage of people. Under the category "Pet Services" in the *London Shopping Guide* by Elsie Burch Donald appears a listing for the firm of J. H. Kenyon, 45 Edgeware Road, an establishment of "funeral directors who will undertake pets. Kenyon will supply a coffin relative to the size of the pet, a hearse for transport to the pet cemetery if required, and will make arrangements with the cemetery for a grave and headstone. (Petticists seeking a more tangible immortality are advised to see a taxidermist.)"

Although less renowned than the legendary Paris pet cemetery on the ile des Ravageurs in the Seine (see below), the animal burial ground in London displays an array of heart-felt pet epitaphs and memorials. Located in a garden behind the gatekeeper's lodge at Victoria Gate in Hyde Park, the cemetery began in 1880 when the duke of Cambridge received permission to bury his wife's dog there. Other dog burials followed and by 1915 some three hundred tombstones marked the graves of deceased animals, all dogs but for a few cats and birds. After that, no further burials were allowed, but additions could be made to existing graves.

Enclosed in the tennis court-sized corner of Hyde Park by a metal picket fence are neat rows of headstones, each about two feet high. One marker which illustrates additional burials in an existing plot memorializes "My Wee Pet Monte 6–13–17. My Sweet Baby Anita 11–2–1936. Also Darling Tsing 9–5–15." Other epitaphs fondly recall the dear departed ones—"My Ruby Heart died Sept. 14, 1897. For seven years we were such friends"; "Dear Little 'Lord Quex'" (d. 1900); "Jack the Dandy A Sportsman & A Pal" (no date); "Dolly My sunbeam. My consolation. My joy" (d. 1898); "A notre cher 'Bob' 1894." The animals' names present a catalog of their masters' whimsey: Girlie (d. 1898); Quiz (d. 1899); Smut; Pickles (d. 1914); Danger, "born city of Mexico" (d. 1901); Yum-Yum (d. 1895); Fattie (d. 1899); Fi-Fi (d. 1922); Zulu (d. 1895); Sir Isaac; Scum; Dolly (d. 1898); Curio (d. 1899); Bow-wow Ralli (d. 1899); Snap Ralli (d. 1900); Freeky (d. 1894); Bogey Church (d. 1894); Impy (d. 1886); Titsy; Puppy (d. 1895); Little Doggie (d. 1898); Darling Pinchie (d. 1895); Pomme de Terre (d. 1899). Then there are a few felines: Peter "the faithful cat" (d. 1902); "In loving memory of Ginger Blyth of Westbourne Terrace 'A king of Pussies' who passed peacefully away March 29th 1946 aged 24 years and 7 months 'His little life was rounded with a sleep' Shake-speare"; and finally, the most recent marker I found, to one Kim, a blue persian (d. 1953). Mourned little loved ones also repose at an annex of the London pet cemetery in Hunt-ingdonshire.

Compared to the London pet cemetery the one in Paris offers more folklore and history as well as a surprisingly wide variety of interred amimals. Not only do the usual dogs and cats repose on the ile des Ravageurs but also a lion, a tiger, a boa, carrier pigeons, a horse (Troytown, who fell at Auteuil race track while competing in the Grand Prix de Diane con-course), and—at one time—a man. As Eugène Sue told the tale in *Mysteries of Paris*—a mid-nineteenth-century narrative which vividly describes the crime and misery that disfigured the city prior to Baron Haussmann's improvements—certain shady characters used to frequent the ile du Ravageur (as it was known then), a desolate island in the Seine near Asnières on the west side of Paris. Explaining how the island was named, Sue relates that a group of "freshwater pirates" who dwelled there, the Martial clan, earned their living as *rav-ageurs*—river scavengers. Often, Sue recounts, they "find in the sand fragments of gold and silver jewelry, brought into the Seine either by the sewers which are washed by the stream, or by the masses of snow or ice collected on the streets, and which are cast into the river." But François, the youngest Martial son, finds something else. Sent by his mother to the wood pile to fetch some logs, the boy ex-claims, "I saw in a dark corner near the wood-pile a dead man's bone; it was sticking a little way out of the ground . . . it was a dead person's bones—a dead man's bones. I saw quite plainly a foot that stuck out of the ground." Such was per-haps the first burial on ile des Ravageurs. And it was no doubt the last human interment on that remote piece of Parisian terrain, for in 1899 the island became Paris's pet cemetery where more than forty thousand animals have been buried.

One of the most famous animals entombed there is a St. Bernard named Barry. The inscription on his monument (all inscriptions are in French) relates how Barry "saved the lives of forty persons and was killed by the forty-first." During a snowstorm near the St. Bernard monastery in the Alps the good samaritan ran to help a stranded traveler who mistook the dog for a bear and killed him. A monument to Barry stands at the St. Bernard Pass, and his mounted skin is on display at the Natural History Museum in Berne, Switzerland.

Barry is not the only talented dog who reposes on the ile des Ravageurs. Dalmote, who guarded the French embassy in Washington, D.C., during World War II, lies there (he died in France in 1945). So does show dog Rin-Tin-Tin, as well as two other performing canines—Poilu, who acted in *Mon Curé Chez Les Riches,* and "Prince of Wales, called Poulot Pidot, who appeared four hundred and six times on the stage of the Theatre du Gymnase in 'Mademoiselle Josette, Ma Femme,' 1905–1906."

In addition to famous dogs, dogs of the famous repose on the ile des Ravageurs. Among them are Drac (1941–1953), "loyal companion in exile" to the queen of Romania, and the pets of creative types such as Edmond Rostand, Léon Daudet, Sacha Guitry, Renée Franceois Sully-Prudhomme, and Camille Saint-Saëns. Some of the tombstones which mark dogs that belonged to nobility bear the coats of arms of the family but most of the bereaved owners, mere commoners, memorialized their pets with less regal expressions of grief. One poignant inscription reads: "To our dear doggies . . . Your affection consoled us against human ingratitude." Another quotes Pascal's epigram echoing that sentiment: "The more I see of men the more I like my dogs."

A less bitter but even more melancholy epitaph says, "To our little Marquis so loyal, died 24 July 1923 at the age of nine years. Our only friend." Only nine years: surely one of life's true tragedies is that the span of time allocated to dogs is so much less than that granted to men. We lose six or seven dogs for every dog that loses us. In at least that way, dogs are luckier.

All at the ile des Ravageurs is not gloom. Happy memories also enliven the gravestones. Remembered fondly are "Jerky 1963 My friend for good and bad days," and "Dora You who asked so little but who gave us so much." More inspired, and inspirational, is the paean to a certain nameless pet (dog, cat, hamster, flea, or whatever)—"My humble friend may you be for me a great example/O you who have loved me as a saint loves his God." But my favorite epitaph at the Paris pet cemetery is the simple, succinct, sweet: "To my so gentle and so loyal Sexy 1955–1963."

Unlike the London Pet Cemetery, the animal burial ground in Paris contains monuments to a goodly number of cats. This, I think, somehow typifies the two cities: London seems a dog town, whereas Paris is a feline sort of place. London barks, Paris purrs; London growls, Paris meows. Paris is sensuous, sinuous, slinking, while London seems as earthy and as straight-forward as a hunting setter's pose. Cats which belonged to writers François Coppée and Barbey d'Aurevilly lie side by side on the Ile des Ravegeurs, while those beloved by less renowned Parisians stare at you from photos which decorate their tombs. The loyal-looking, little faces (but are cats truly loyal?) tug at your imagination, if not your heart strings, and in your mind's eye you envision the frisky antics or devoted lap-sitting which so pleased their adoring masters or mistresses. During my visit to the cemetery I observed a bereaved old lady offering her respects at the grave of her late cat. The woman kneeled, then removed from her purse a clean cloth which she used to polish to a crystal purity the glass over her dead pet's picture. She stayed down a good while, perhaps praying, then rose and shuffled away, leaving her shining cat to rest in peace. Héloise mourning her beloved Abélard it was not but, still and all, that vignette of devotion—humankind's love for a fellow creature of flesh and blood—was one of the most touching scenes I have come across in any cemetery.

At least one Parisian cat enjoyed a sepulcher much more elegant than any of the burial plots found on the ile des Ravageurs. In *A Journal of my Journey to Paris in the year 1765* the Reverend William Cole tells of coming upon an elaborate cat tomb in the garden of Les Diguieres on the Rue de la Cerisaye:

> But before I left the Garden, in an obscure Parterre I saw the Tomb of a Cat, viz. a Black Cat Couchant upon a White Marble Cushion, fringed with Gold, and Gold Tassels hanging at the Corners upon a square Black Marble Pedestal. On one of the sides of that Marble is writ in letters of Gold,
>
> Here lies Menine, the most loveable and the
> Most loved of all cats.
>
> On the other side
>
> Here lies a pretty cat:
> Its mistress, who loved nothing,
> Loved it madly
>
> But why say so! You can easily tell
>
> This is not the first instance of this kind of Folly; I have seen something of it in England; and have read much more in History. If you blame me for transcribing this Epitaph, I will submit.

Well might I echo the last sentence of Cole's comments. Similarly, I would not deny a reader's charge that I have frivolously and even uselessly spent all too much time visiting cemeteries. But, dear reader, pray tell—have you spent your days and years any better? Where have they gone, and what do you have to show for them?

Dead cats in Paris were not always memorialized as elegantly as Menine, she with the gold-tasseled tomb. In 1896 excavators uncovered a pit near the Odéon into which thousands of cat heads had been pitched. A restaurant that specialized in jugged hare formerly occupied the site. Not to be outdone, London, too, has its catsditch, the feline equivalent of Houndsditch. Back in the early twentieth century when Londoners coveted cat fur, an alley behind the Borough Road contained an enclave called Cat-Skinners Court where, presumably, the executions took place. An eccentric picture labelled "The Funeral" in *Death, Heaven and the Victorians* by John Morley shows a line of cats marching in a funeral procession behind a trio of caskets. Below the picture—an illustration from *Death and Burial of the Three Little Kittens,* one of Dean's New Series of Large Toy Books (1860)—appears the verse:

> In the morn, full of pride—in the evening they died;
> How sudden and shocking their fate!
> The three little kittens, who still wore their mittens,
> Were buried next morning in state.
> Meow ow! meow ow! meow ow! meow ow!

Probably the most curious cat casket in history was an organ in Dublin's Christ Church Cathedral. Displayed in the cathedral crypt are the corpses of a rat and a cat. The church beadle told me that workers dismantling an organ found the bodies in 1846 after they had reposed unnoticed for about 150 years. It seems that the cat was literally caught in the act of pursuing the rat when its hip became wedged inside the organ mechanism. The trapped cat could not advance and the rat, finding its escape route blocked by the cat, retreated to a far corner out of reach. In that state of suspended animation those eternal enemies died. The cat, although leathery-looking, appears well preserved and at least as healthy as the human skins displayed in nearby St. Michan's vault (discussed in Chapter IV). Its body stretches in pursuit, tail flying and legs fairly flaying, as if charging toward the intended victim in preparation for a pounce. The rat, however, scrunched up into a near ball-shaped position, has fared less well.

Although many poems, paeans, tributes, and effusive epitaphs honor dogs, only a few truly eloquent admirations to dead cats exist. Is that because cats have less distinctive personalities than dogs? Or because the type of person which favors felines boasts less creative temperaments than canine owners? Perhaps the ultimate expression of sentiment for a lost cat appeared in a lengthy article by Matthew Flinders, the early-nineteenth-century explorer who sailed the coasts of the huge, southern continent which he named: "I call the whole island Australia," Flinders wrote in a letter in 1804. Flinders published a narrative entitled *A Biography and Tribute to the Memory of Trim, Isle of France—1809,* which he ends by promising to erect a monument to perpetuate the memory of the cat, "And this shall be thy epitaph":

To the memory of TRIM. The best and most illustrious of his Race, the most affectionate of friends, faithful of servants, and best of creatures. He made the Tour of the Globe, and a voyage to Australia, which he circumnavigated, and was ever the delight and pleasure of his fellow voyagers. Returning to Europe in 1803, he was shipwrecked in the Great Equinoxial Ocean. This danger escaped, he sought refuge and assistance at the Isle of France, where he was made prisoner, contrary to the laws of Justice, of Humanity, and of French National Faith; and where, alas! he terminated his useful career, by an untimely death, being devoured by the calophagi of that island. Many a time have I beheld his little merriments with delight, and his superior intelligence with surprise. Never will his like be seen again! Trim was born in the Southern Indian Ocean in the Year 1799, and perished as above at the Isle of France in 1804. Peace be to his shade and Honour to his memory.

No man, let alone beast, could wish for a more fulsome epitaph.

But as for a visible, tangible display of cat love, perhaps nothing exceeds the eccentricities at a place called Red Cat Farm near Blairstown in northwestern New Jersey. A German couple—Baron Rupprecht von Boecklin of Baden, Germany, and his wife Mary—lived on the estate, which they embellished with statues and figurines of cats as well as cat signs setting forth the farm's name. In the late sixties, at Cedar Ridge Cemetery in Blairstown, the baron installed for himself and his wife a red granite tombstone decorated with a carved crouching cat at the top, and a bas relief mouse below. Over the years the von Boecklins buried several cats in the family plots, which thus became a catacomb, so to speak. Then in early June 1978, the seventy-four-year-old baron shot and killed both his wife and their pet cat, then killed himself, and the couple finally joined their beloved felines interred at the cat-tomb, in death.

The Australia that Matthew Flinders (and Trim) circumnavigated and named boasts a complete set of institutions adopted from the mother country including, of course, pet cemeteries. In Sydney, for example, there are two such graveyards. One occupies space on the grounds of a convalescent home attached to the Royal Prince Alfred Hospital at Yaralla, Concord. Dame Edith Walker, whose deceased favorites are memorialized by fourteen small marble tablets bearing the animal's name and death date, donated the property for use as a pet cemetery. In Sydney's general pet cemetery located at Berkshire Park near the suburb of Windsor, repose the usual dogs and cats—Nuggy, Biddy, Scamp, Cuddles, Peaches, Buttons ("Butt's Our Pal, Sadly Missed"). None, however, possesses an epitaph so delicious as the one said to appear on the grave of an Aussie dog buried at Brible Island, Queensland: "In memory of Ranger. Died May 8, 1936. If there be an afterworld for such as thou, May the juiciest of bones be thy reward." Also in Sydney lie the remains of such rarities as a sheep (Horrie, by name), a macaw (Charlie), a kangaroo and—shades of the old days on the ile des Ravageurs—even humans, for the ashes of six people have been interred in the graves of their pets.

Formal animal burial exists in countries other than France, England, and Australia. But elsewhere, so it seems, royal purses often subsidize pet interments. When John Evelyn visited the seaside estate of Prince d'Orias in Genoa in 1644, the English diarist noticed in the garden under a large statue of Jupiter "the sepulchre of a beloved dog, for the care of which one of this family receiv'd of the K. of Spaine 500 crownes a yeare during the life of that faithfull animal." The famous Renaissance artist of about the same time, Giulio Romano—the only painter mentioned in any of Shakespeare's plays—made his reputation at the Mantuan court of Federico II Gonzaga, where Romano's first project was a tomb for the duke's favorite dog, a long-legged bitch that died while giving birth. In Holland, a few miles north of Utrecht, stands the House of Doorp, the last residence of the Kaiser (d. 1941), who now reposes in a brick mausoleum there. Nearby lie five of his dogs, his companions in exile: Wai-Wai, Arno, Senta, Topsy, and Bambi. Similarly, near the chateau of Sans-Souci in France repose Charles V's pet greyhounds, their graves marked by eleven square stone markers. In Tangier, as Ted

Morgan recounts in *On Becoming American,* a certain entrepreneur once bought some land in order to build on it. The authorities, however, rejected his construction permit. The developer later learned that the proposed building would have blocked the view enjoyed by King Hassan II's aunt, Princess Lala Fatima Zora, of the dog cemetery where one of her favorite poodles was buried. Farther afield, one of the thirty-two colored panels portraying Ethiopian history in Africa Hall at Addis Ababa, Ethiopia's capital, shows a tearful Emperor Haile Selassie mourning by his dog's grave, on which appears the pet's portrait.

An especially unusual pet cemetery and crematorium operates at Fuchu, near Tokyo, run by a Zen Buddhist couple named Nagata. Under the belief that animals possess a soul, the Nagatas offer bereaved pet owners a storage niche for their animal's ashes in a temple. Memorial sticks mark the remains, to which the family brings offerings on the day prescribed by Buddhist ritual for visiting the dead. The enterprising Nagatas also offer a plan by which both human and animal ashes can be stored together in fancy lacquer cabinets. As might be expected, Japan has a high-tech pet disposal service as well. A firm called Jippo operates a fleet of mobile crematoria for deceased pets. The jippomobile will come to the bereaved home, conduct a funeral service, then cremate the corpse. The firm's trucks bear the slogan "Pet Angel Service." With some eight thousand pets dying in Japan each day, Jippo's business could be the biggest thing to hit Japan since *sushi*.

The Swiss—great hoteliers and paragons of efficiency as they are—once offered, at the famous old hotel in Ouchy on Lake Geneva, perhaps the ultimate guest amenity: an animal cemetery. Amid tulips, pines, and cedars of Lebanon on the hotel grounds nestled a burial area for guests' pets. Among the favorites interred there were Tosca, Poupette, Toots, Micky, "Ma Petite Parfaite," "Taffy, my beloved friend," and

"Darling Topsy" born 1921 in Philadelphia and died 1934 in Lausanne. But of all lands and eras, surely it is in contemporary America that pet cemeteries have reached their most elaborate and business-like incarnation. For pet cemeteries, as with all other commercial ventures, American ingenuity knows no bounds. One cemetery in Pennsylvania devised the idea of selling gift certificates for animal burial services, while the Bonheur Memorial Park Cemetery in Elkridge, Maryland, came up with a combination plan, a marketing ploy which offered burials (in the pet cemetery) for humans in plots next to their beloved animals. A creative midwestern graveyard entrepreneur introduced both pre-need plans (plots sold before the pet's death) and a so-called farm burial program in which animals' bodies collected from vets' freezers are mass buried for especially low charges.

Although six out of every ten households in the United States own pets, (sixty million felines versus fifty million canines) only 1–2 percent of these animals find their final resting place in one of the country's 300 or so pet cemeteries, the first of which, the Hartsdale Canine Cemetery at Hartsdale, New York, was established in 1896. The economics and operation of the business were revealed in the following classified ad for an Arizona pet cemetery published in the *Wall Street Journal* for 22 March 1974:

ESTABLISHED BUSINESS FOR SALE
PET CEMETERY

Only pet memorial park operation in Tucson, Arizona. Established 5 years. Approx, 8 acres, 2½ acres fully plotted, landscaped (Lawn-Turf, Magnolia and Italian Stone Pine trees), concrete walkways, automatic (time-controlled) underground Sprinkler System, center section with exclusive Columbarium section and Matthews Bronze St. Frances [sic] Statue Feature (Garden of St. Assisi). Architectural designed 1,365 sq. ft. Masonry Bldg. containing Offices fully furnished, Chapel, Casket and Marker Display Room, Mortuary and Storage Areas. 5 Acres of 8 Acres graded for expansion. Power maintenance equipment including Toro Mowers, Trimmers etc. plus Datsun Ambulance. Operated on like basis of Human Cemetery except NO TRANSFER of Title to Real Property (Interment Privilege only). Requires only one full time Maintenance-Man. Average Interment $150.00 including Trust-Care Maintenance Fee. Projected on number of standard Interment Sites each acre, return per acre excluding Trust-Care Maintenance Fees in excess of $600,000. Current MIA Appraisal reflects Land Value $80,000. Owner-Broker liquidating investments offers FOR SALE: $145,000. ($55,000 down and Terms). With exclusion of 5 Acre expansion parcel $95,000. ($55,000 down and Terms).

The nation's busiest pet cemetery, Bide-a-Wee Pet Memorial Park in Wantagh, Long Island, New York (where, as mentioned above, Richard Nixon's beloved Checkers reposes) buries some hundred animals a month. The fifty thousand dead there include horses, monkeys, parrots, and a grasshopper named Gary. At Paw Print Gardens on Chicago's west side lie more than four thousand animals, mostly dogs and cats but also horses, a Shetland pony, a spider monkey, a duck, a guinea pig, two lovebirds, and a parakeet. The cemetery offers a round-the-clock dead pet pick-up service, as well as counseling sessions for grieving survivors. "Marble-Hill Crematory For Pet Animals," as the sign over the Gothic doorway puts it, provides funerals for bereaved New York City animal lovers. Founded in 1939, the upper Manhattan establishment mounts a dignified service in a vine-covered chapel, then cremates the deceased (on one occasion, a kangaroo) in a retort—a kind of oven—which reduces the late pet to a pure white ash. Some owners take the remains home and scatter them on the terrain where the pet once frolicked; others put the ashes in urns installed in the chapel wall. At five-acre Memorial Park Pet Cemetery near St. Louis, Missouri, founded in 1960 and designed to resemble a human cemetery, repose some fifteen hundred animals, including a monkey, a skunk, baseball star Stan Musial's poodle, and a dog with the epitaph, "Born a mutt, died a prince." The thirty-acre AAA Pet Service Center—the supermarket of the industry—in Taylor, Michigan, includes not only an animal cemetery but also a dog and cat motel, a canine college, and a canine beauty shop (no catty gossip there). The seven-acre Pet Haven in Syracuse, New York, permanent home to more than five thousand deceased aninmals, offers cheap, plastic-bag burials. A firm called Jeff's Preservation Specialities in Pinellas Park, Florida, uses a freeze-dry chamber to remove moisture from dead pets, so mummifing them in a perfectly preserved state.

For pet cemeteries—as for so many other somewhat curious features of contemporary American culture—California seems to rank as the leader. The opening scene of *Sunset Boulevard,* set in Los Angeles, sets the tone: an aging Hollywood screen goddess stages an elaborate funeral for her dead pet monkey. The Los Angeles Pet Cemetery, founded in 1929, claims the remains of celebrities such as Hopalong Cassidy's horse, the MGM lion, and Rin-Tin-Tin (one of several such star dogs; another, as noted above, reposes in Paris's ile des Ravageurs animal cemetery). Near San Francisco operate such establishments as the Contra Costa Pet Memorial Cemetery, and Pet's Rest Cemetery (one marker there reads: "Penny: She never knew she was a rabbit") in Colma, that vast necropolis town where five hundred living beings oversee some two-and-a-half million dead souls (human and animal) interred in seventeen cemeteries. On a hill overlooking Napa Valley perches fifty-acre Bubbling Well Pet Memorial Park, by area the nation's largest pet cemetery. Established in 1972, the burial ground holds more than forty thousand animals which lie in such sections as the Garden of Honor (for police dogs killed in the line of duty), the Garden of Gentle Giants (for great danes and St. Bernards), the Garden of Companionship, Kitten Corner and—the most elegant and expensive area—the Garden of Devotion. Bubbling Well was the cemetery featured in *Gates of Heaven,* a documentary about pet death. The movie begins by relating the story of Floyd McClure, a paraplegic whose dream is to run a pet cemetery. He established Foothill Memorial Gardens in Los Altos, south of San Francisco, but lost the business when the owners of the land decided to put up a housing development on the property. The four hundred and fifty pets at Foothills were disinterred and reburied at Bubbling Well, where the grave marker for Nimo and Fred reads: "God is love—Backward it's dog."

The classic send-up of American pet cemeteries appears in Evelyn Waugh's *The Loved One,* which satirizes both the follies and foibles of humankind's funeral practices and the customs prevailing for animal burials. The Los Angeles pet cemetery called the Happier Hunting Ground offers interment or incineration—"Buried or burned?" the staff asks owners of deceased pets. Dennis Barlow, a twenty-eight-year-old expatriate English poet who runs the cremation oven, observes that "an open casket is all right for dogs and cats who lie down and curl up naturally. But parrots don't. They look absurd with a head on a pillow." The well-run cemetery sends to the human survivors a remembrance card on the anniversary of a pet's passing: "Your little Arthur is thinking of you in heaven today and wagging his tail." A particularly impressive funeral was mounted for a beloved Alsatian, with a "non-secterian clergyman" delivering to dozens of mourners a sermon with the thought; "Dog that is born of bitch hath but a short time to live."

Waugh's mockery notwithstanding, most United States pet cemeteries epitomize not strange and garish American funeral customs but the universal characteristic of mourning for and remembering a loved one. That the beloved happens to be a beast rather than a fellow human in no way diminishes the heart-felt sentiments. On the grounds of Tao House, Eugene O'Neill's estate in Las Trampas Hills at Danville, near San Francisco, is the grave of the playwright's dalmation Blemie with a marker that reads: "Born Sept. 20, 1927 England Died Dec. 17, 1940 Tao House Sleep In Peace Faithful Friend." To have your epitaph written by a winner of the Nobel Prize for literature is quite up-scale. Even hard-bitten military professionals honor their animal dead. At the Marine Corps' basic training camp on Parris Island, South Carolina, I came across neatly tended graves of various mascots—Baron (d. 1977), Paul Bunyan (d. 1975), Klinker, Herbert the Valiant (d. 1967), and a metal plate for Mike (d. 1916) "Honest and Faithful." Between rusted cannon mounts on the rampart walls surrounding the moat at Fort Monroe, Virginia, nestles another military cemetery with some six hundred service animals, memorialized by about three hundred tombstones. Pets of active and retired military personnel from all the services can be buried at Fort Monroe. The post's maintenance crew tends the cemetery, but the bereaved families are required to supply the grave marker and coffin. One family provided a three-limousine cortege from Washington for a dog's funeral. The Presidio in San Francisco boasts a similar such military pet cemetery.

More typical than the exotic Californian burial grounds or the relatively rare military graveyards are the ordinary civilian pet cemeteries one comes across in obscure corners around the country. Let a few of the animal cemeteries in Tennessee—to pick a state at random—serve to give the flavor of your ordinary, run-of-the-mill, garden-variety pet memorial parks in the United States. Pinecrest Pet Cemetery in Memphis (on Hacks Cross Road near the Mississippi state line) lies in a secluded grove of pines whose brown needles carpet the ground. Buried there are Poochie (d. 1974), Bubbles (d. 1976), Bad (d. 1977), Spunkey (d. 1967) and Skippy

(d. 1975)—"He loved dog biscuits." Others include Tiny Baby (d. 1973)—"We miss you so much"—as well as Little Ho Bo (d. 1967), Dr. Miller (d. 1967), a dachshund named Wiggles (d. 1971), Bobo (d. 1975), Bee Bee (d. 1975) who "took so little but gave so much," and at least one feline named simply "The Kitty" (d. 1974). The cemetery charges by the inch: in a recent year animals under thirty inches long, measured from nose to tail root, cost about $145 including the plot and a satin-lined pine casket. Headstones start at about $150. At Cheekwood Mansion, now an art museum and show house in Nashville, repose pets of the family which once owned the property—Poor Little Sue Spring (d. 1950), Alice in Wonderland (d. 1948), Laddie (d. 1951), Sappho (d. 1940), Sambo (d. 1954), Aristotle (d. 1937), Huldah's Hero (d. 1938), Emmie (d. 1938), Daniel the Spaniel (d. 1952).

South of Nashville, on the west side of Highway 51 between Spring Hill and Columbia, the Cedar Hill Pet Cemetery, established in 1972, occupies gently sloping terrain bright with plastic flowers. On the front of the mortuary and chapel plaques recall Dirt'e Joe (d. 1973), a parrot memorialized "for making us happy"; Chip (d. 1969), "Our Pal"; Little Bit (d. 1978), "Our Little Boy"; Nosey (d. 1962), "Sweet Memories Dear"; and a mournful tribute recalling one

> . . . so small, so precious, so soon,
> Oh for the sound of a vanished bark,
> And the touch of a paw which is still,
> Our little son now rest in the arms
> Of St. Francis Assisi in heaven.

Stones embedded in the ground commemorate Little Pudgy (d. 1973), "One of us"; Penny Lunn (d. 1975), "A four legged little angel"; Bitsy (d. 1977), "Our little girl"; Tom Purr Purr (d. 1973; a cat); Spot (d. 1973), "A true friend"; Cheesecake (d. 1978); Frisky (d. 1978); Snoopy (d. 1977); and two hounds which merit photos—Tookie Marie (d. 1976) and Nena (d. 1978), "She was our baby." By a low hedge on a grey granite base stands a pillar with reliefs of dogs' heads marking the Garden of Love, "dedicated to all pets resting in this hallowed garden. Their memory and love lingers soft and warm in our hearts." Toward the back of the cemetery rises the only standing grave marker, a stone decorated with the head of a German shepherd and an oval K-9 Corps device to indicate the final resting place of dogs which once worked for the Nashville Metropolitan Police Department. "My eyes are your eyes . . . My ears are your ears . . . My nose is your nose," reads the inscription in honor of such police canines as Officer Max (d. 1975), "Bomb dog fearless and loyal"; Devil (d. 1977); and Mr. Blue (d. 1978), "Narcotics Dog."

A veritable menagerie of animals has been interred in pet cemeteries. One need only consult a book entitled *Epitaphs of Some Dear Dumb Beasts* "by Their Mistress" Isabel Vallé (published in 1916) to see the range of animals awarded epitaphs by adoring survivors: a toad, a cottontail, a canary, a swan, a bantam cock, a stray pussy, a goldfish, plus—as always—a generous selection of dogs. Perhaps the most poetic epitaph is the one composed for Jacqueline, a pig:

> If only sweet pig babies
> Need not grow up at all!
> Oh, butcher mills grind swiftly
> And they grind exceedingly small!

I will refrain from reproducing any other samples.

The varied array of creatures is by no means a fanciful list, for all manner of beings—furred, feathered, finned, freckled, wild and tame—have been ceremoniously put to rest by the hand of man. On Route 146 east of Anna, Illinois, stands the tomb of King Neptune, a naval mascot pig auctioned off for nineteen million dollars in war bonds. In 1902 at Smithfield,

Virginia—no hog heaven but a porker hell, for the town is a ham producing center—P. D. Gwaltney cured a large Smithfield ham, never refrigerated and believed to be the oldest chunk of cured meat in existence. Around the delicacy circles a brass collar labelled "Mr. Gwaltney's Pet Ham." Also honored was another distinguished porker, whose epitaph at Cock Inn, Walkden Road in Wonsley, England, reads: "In Memory of Polly, Mother of 200 Pigs, Died Dec 23rd 1904, Aged 15½ Years." A marker at the Dr. Joseph Johnson House in Charleston, South Carolina, memorializes "Simon Langley Hall, Died Sept. 7, 1963, Age 6 years and 5 Months, Sleep peacefully under your white rose of Sharon." Simon was a guinea pig. The City Cemetery in Key West, Florida, includes a statue of a key deer—a diminutive deer about the size of a large dog—which marks the grave of someone's pet. On the grounds of Tom Mann's Fish World in Florida, supposedly the world's largest freshwater aquarium facility, with ten fourteen-hundred-gallon tanks, stands a monument to Leroy Brown, a large-mouth bass that for more than six years was featured as a leading Fish World attraction. When Leroy expired owner Tom Mann erected a memorial: "Most bass are just fish, but—Leroy Brown was something special."

Back in the 1920s a goldfish received a special interment. It seems that that Gabriele D'Annunzio, the Italian writer, kept in a crystal bowl at his quarters in the Hotel Trianon in Paris a goldfish he adored. On one occasion, when D'Annunzio returned to Italy for a visit, he instructed the staff at the hotel to care for the fish. While away, the anxious fish fancier frequently telegraphed, asking about his pet's well-being. It happened that one day Adolphus, as D'Annuzio called his beloved treasure, died. A hotel employee disposed of the remains by tossing the corpse out the window. When the writer next inquired after Adolphus he was duly informed of the pet's passing. He wired back: "Bury him in the garden. Arrange his grave." By then, however, Adolphus's body had disappeared—perhaps into the stomach of a cat—so a hotel employee wrapped a sardine in silver paper and buried the package in the garden beneath a cross inscribed: "Here lies Adolphus." When D'Annunzio returned he immediately asked to see the goldfish's grave. Someone at the hotel took him to the memorial where the writer, shedding a generous flow of tears, mourned his departed pet.

Confusion of human with beast burial transpired in a case involving Richard Burton, the famous nineteenth-century explorer. In 1842, when Burton was stationed with the Eighteenth Regiment of Bombay Native Infantry in Baroda, 244 miles north of Bombay, he took a fancy to cockfighting. Burton's favorite bird—Bhujang (dragon)—enjoyed its greatest triumph over a thoroughbred cock owned by a rich Indian. When Bhujang died the Englishman gave him an elaborate funeral, burying the bird in a special grave near Burton's bungalow. This immediately gave rise to a rumor that Burton had buried a baby there. A less controversial bird burial by an Englishman was the interment at Chartwell, Winston Churchill's country estate, of a Bali dove that Clementine Churchill had acquired during her round-the-world trip in 1935. The expatriate dove died after a few years at Chartwell and was buried under a sundial in the walled garden with the epitaph (from a poem by W. P. Ker):

Here lies the Bali Dove
It does not do to wander
Too far from sober men,
But there's an island yonder,
I think of it again.

Next to the grave of two-time Kentucky governor James B. McCreary at Richmond, Kentucky, reposes his pet parrot, which merits its own tiny tombstone.

At the English country estate Twyford, near Winchester,

home of Bishop Jonathan Shipley, a squirrel received a special burial and epitaph. In June 1771 Benjamin Franklin went for a week's visit to Twyford where he began writing what would become his famous *Autobiography*. As a present for Shipley's five daughters, Franklin obtained from his wife a grey squirrel from Philadelphia. The animal came to be called Skugg, a common name for pet squirrels in England. One day Skugg wandered away and fell victim to a dog. After the girls buried the squirrel in the garden at Twyford one of them, Georgiana, asked Franklin to compose an epitaph. In a letter dated 26 September 1772 he responded: "I lament with you most sincerely the unfortunate end of poor [Skugg]. Few squirrels were better accomplished; for he had had a good education, travelled far, and seen much of the world. As he had the honour of being, for his virtues, your favourite, he should not go, like common skuggs, without an elegy or an epitaph. Let us give him one in the monumental style and measure, which, being neither prose nor verse, is perhaps the properest for grief; since to use common language would look as if we were not affected, and to make rhymes would seem trifling in sorrow." After proposing a flowery epitaph which parodied the pompous style often found on tombstones, Franklin concluded: "You see, my dear Miss, how much more decent and proper this broken style is than if we were to say, by way of epitaph:

Here Skugg
Lies snug
As a bug
In a rug.

Thus did Franklin create a phrase which has become proverbial.

On another occasion Franklin contributed not just an animal epitaph but an entire animal—his deceased Angora cat—

to a collection of dead specimens. In the summer of 1786 Charles Willson Peale opened part of his house in Philadelphia as "a repository for natural curiosities, the wonderful works of nature." Peale, who taught himself taxidermy and mounted most of the animals himself, installed at the new display—which he named Peale's Museum, although the public called it the American Museum—a veritable Noah's Ark of wildlife, including turtles, frogs, toads, lizards, snakes, fish, birds, bear, deer, a leopard, tiger, wildcat, fox, raccoon, rabbit and squirrel. One item destined for the museum was Franklin's cat, but when Peale botched the preparation he discarded the feline. Undeterred, Peale turned to George Washington, writing the general at Mount Vernon to request that any pheasants which might die be sent to Philadelphia for display in the new museum. Washington replied, "I cannot say that I shall be happy to have it in my power to comply with your request by sending you the bodies of my pheasants; but I am afraid it will not be long before they will compose a part of your museum as they all appear to be drooping." Washington's fears soon became reality, for a few weeks later he wrote to Peale advising, "Sir, you will receive by the stage the body of my gold pheasant packed in wool. He made his exit yesterday, which enables me to comply with your request sooner than I wished to do. I am afraid the others will follow him but too soon."

Perhaps no higher tribute is paid to a deceased animal as when a renowned author, or a famous figure such as Franklin, composes a pet epitaph or encomium. "On the Death of the Giraffe" by English poet Thomas Hood runs: "They say, Got wout!/She died upon the spot:/But then in spots she was so rich,—/I wonder which?" And that renowned wordsman Samuel Johnson in 1772 composed a Latin couplet to be engraved on the collar of a goat. Naturalist Joseph Banks, who had accompanied Captain Cook on the *Endeavour*'s round-the-world journey, asked Johnson for a few lines to honor the goat, which "had been on two of his adventurous expeditions with him," as Johnson explained to his friend Mrs. Thrale, and was then "by the humanity of his amiable master, turned out to graze in Kent, as a recompense for her utility and faithful service." Johnson here referred to the practice, common at the time, of keeping aboard ship a she-goat to provide fresh milk for the officers' coffee.

Another well-appreciated milk-giver, a prolific Holstein-Friesian, lies buried at Highfield Farm in Lee, Massachusetts, her grave marked with a marble slab recalling that the cow "held the world record for lifetime milk production." A marble memorial to Elisha Cady (d. 1880) at Evergreen Cemetery in Central Village, Connecticut, bears a relief portrait of a cow with the inscription; "Rosa, my first Jersey cow/Record 2 lbs. 15 ozs. Butter/from 18 qrts. 1 day milk."

A less domestic but more renowned animal reposes in a remote corner of the Wild West. In 1950 a seventeen-thousand-acre fire in Lincoln National Forest, near Capitan, New Mexico, severely burned a four-month-old black bear cub. After rescuing the infant, a district game warden took him to Santa Fe where he was nursed back to health. Some creative officials proposed that the cub be made the living symbol of the United States Forest Service's five-year-old fire prevention program. Thus was born Smokey the Bear. Smokey, who earned more than one million dollars in royalties on products bearing his name, received so much mail that he had his own zip code. In May 1975 Smokey, crippled by age, moved to a retirement cage at Washington's National Zoo where he died in his sleep, aged twenty-six, in November 1976. The forest service flew the body to New Mexico for interment at the Smokey Bear Historical State Park near Capitan. A plaque on a stone in the corner of the park marks the grave.

At another unusual grave in the American West reposes Haiji Ali, a Syrian camel driver brought to the United States in the 1850s. Secretary of War Jefferson Davis imported seventy-four camels in an effort to improve military transport across the southwestern desert. By 1863 the government had lost interest in the camels and they were turned loose to roam free in the area of Quartzsite, a desolate corner of the Arizona desert off U.S. Highway 100. Hi Jolly, as the Syrian came to be called, remained in the area near his flock. He died 16 November 1902 and reposes in a sandy cemetery at Quartzsite, his tomb marked by a stone pyramid built of black lava, white quartzite rock, and petrified wood, all topped with a two-foot-high camel figure which looks like an enlargement of the Camel cigarette logo. The last descendant of this herd died in a Los Angeles zoo in 1934. The animal's undertaker probably failed to follow the custom practiced by devout Muslims, who buried camels which died on caravan treks through the desert with the beasts' heads turned toward Mecca.

When it comes to the death of dear dumb beasts, something awe-inspiring surrounds the disposition of larger creatures, such as whales or elephants. Unlike goldfish, birds, or mice, or even cats and dogs, you cannot just pitch into a ditch such mammoth beasts, or lay them to rest in a small hole in the ground. A whale or elephant demands special handling. Arrian, a Roman historian who wrote in the second century A.D., tells how the troops of Alexander the Great came across some whales stranded on a beach below the Persian Gulf. The huge beasts were rotting away, "leaving their bones for men to use for their houses. The larger ribs make the beams for their dwellings; the smaller ones, the rafters, while the jawbones serve as doorframes." In more recent times, a whale which washed ashore near Provincetown, Massachusetts, was also put to good use. When the whale arrived on the beach the locals notified Louis Agassiz, a Harvard professor and famous naturalist. Assisted by some students the professor salvaged the beast's skeleton, which he loaded on a flat car. In the meantime, Dr. Cope of the Academy of Natural Sciences in Philadelphia had arrived on the scene and he managed to persuade the station agent to send the car and its cargo to Philadelphia, rather than to Cambridge. So—in what was perhaps the largest heist on record—the whole skeleton ended up at the academy, where the relic is still preserved. By way of contrast, no one spirited away an eighty-ton, seventy-two-foot long, blue whale—the largest living species on earth—washed up on the shore of Golden Gate National Recreation Area in San Francisco in 1988. The great beast reposed there on its back, slowly decaying as all efforts to remove it failed. The coast guard craft was too frail to tow the carcass to sea, and bulldozers spun in the sand in a vain effort to pull the carcass from the beach. Authorities finally decided to dissect the body and bury the pieces one by one.

Another jumbo-sized museum exhibit was—well, the original Jumbo. In 1885 P. T. Barnum's star attraction, a twelve-foot, six-and-a-half-ton elephant named Jumbo, was killed instantly when it was hit by a locomotive. The showman mounted Jumbo's skin on frames. Weighing one thousand five hundred and thirty-eight pounds, the elephant's epidermis was exhibited as part of the "Greatest Show On Earth," and then displayed at Tufts University until a fire eventually destroyed the relic. As for Barnum, the death-defying feat the great showman pulled off was perhaps his greatest show on earth, and his last one. Lying on his death bed, the circus impresario took to wondering what his obituaries would say about him, so Barnum asked the *New York Evening News* to publish the death notice in advance. His curiosity was satisfied on 24 March 1891 when the paper headlined "Great and Only Barnum. He Wanted to Read His Obituary; Here It Is." Two weeks later he died and was buried at Bridgeport, Connecticut's Mountain Grove Cemetery across the road from where he had erected a memorial to

Tom Thumb, a forty-foot-high marble shaft topped by a pint-sized, life-size statue of the midget circus attraction, who died in 1883.

Another circus elephant which, like Jumbo, suffered sudden death was a pachyderm named Norma Jean. In the summer of 1972 the Clark and Walters Circus stopped at Oquawka, a western Illinois hamlet on the Mississippi River. After her handlers tethered Norma Jean to a tree, a storm blew up and lightning struck the tree. The charge ran along the chain that fettered the elephant's leg, instantly killing the animal. A circus crew brought in a backhoe to excavate a jumbo-sized grave, over which rises a monument topped by an elephant statue and bearing the inscription: "Norma Jean Elephant Aug. 10, 1942–July 17, 1972."

In the West elephants function merely as amusements—circus performers or zoo exhibits—but the Oriental world takes the animals more seriously. In Asia elephants serve as transportation, as religious or royal symbols, as important gifts. In the early sixteenth century an Indian prince, seeking to please Leo X, the Medici pope from 1513 to 1521, presented him with an elephant. The animal, which lived in the Vatican gardens, was taught to kneel before the pope. Persons it did not care for, the elephant sprayed with water. The pope's pet died of poisoning from paint used to gild it for a holiday appearance and was buried in the Belvedere courtyard behind the Vatican library.

At Fatepur Sikri in India reposes the favorite elephant of Akbar, the seventeenth-century Moghul emperor. Akbar's tusker—as elephants are often called in the Far East—lies under a seventy-foot-high tower named Hiran Minar, from which the emperor used to shoot driven antelope and other game. The round tower, which stands below the city and outside its walls, bristles from top to bottom with replicas of elephant tusks, pointed reminders of the great beast buried beneath.

Another elephant memorial in Asia rises at Chiang Mai in northern Thailand. A tusker may lie beneath or near the statue there but, in any event, a tale lies behind the monument. A less-than-life-size elephant likeness stands near the entrance to the hilltop temple, Doi Sutep, to commemorate the animal which chose the sanctuary's site. The story begins in 1332 when a monk of Sukhothai, a kingdom in central Thailand, dreamed of an angel who advised that the monk would find some relics of the Buddha under a horse-shaped bush and should take them to Chiang Mai. After locating the treasures, the monk put them into a crystal container which he then placed in a series of bronze, silver, and gold boxes, one within the other. The king of Sukhothai promised to build a golden temple to house the find if it was kept in his kingdom, but the monk carried the relics to Chiang Mai and deposited half of them at the Wat Suan Dork, a temple rebuilt in 1383 to receive them. The other half—or perhaps a whole, for the parts were said to have each grown to the size of the original find—was bound to the back of a white elephant which King Kuna of Chiang Mai used to choose the location of the new temple he decided to build for the relics. The animal wandered about, finally reaching a thirty-five-hundred-foot-high hill on the outskirts of town. After climbing to the top, the elephant refused to budge until attendants removed the relics from its back, and there the king constructed Doi Sutep temple. Perhaps the white elephant which selected the site lies somewhere up there near his statue.

Wat Suan Dork, the sanctuary where the first half of the Buddha relics were deposited, is noteworthy as the mausoleum of Chiang Mai's royal family. Princess Dararasmai, born in 1872, grew up to become a celebrated beauty, with ankle-length black hair that was cut at the traditional ceremony which marked her coming of age. One guest at the festivities, an envoy sent from Bangkok by King Chulalongkorn, proposed marriage on behalf of the monarch. This was a political rather than a romantic proposal, for Chulalongkorn hoped to keep the princess from concluding a marriage alliance with a prince in the Shan states of Burma. Princess Dararasmai accepted the offer and at age fifteen became one of the king's wives. But before long she grew unhappy in Bangkok and longed to return to Chiang Mai. Fearing her departure, the king placed the princess under house—or palace—arrest, but Chulalongkorn soon died and his successor, Vachiravat, allowed her to return home. At Chiang Mai, Dararasmai became a patron of the arts. Among her projects was organizing a dance troupe whose members she prodded in the rear with a fork to encourage them to learn the correct positions. But the princess's greatest accomplishment was turning Suan Dork into a kind of Westminster Abbey, as one observer has put it, for the structure holds the remains of many of Chiang Mai's royal figures. Dararasmai—who died in 1933, aged sixty-one, the last princess of Chiang Mai's royal family—collected the ashes of assorted northern princes from various temples and interred the remains in tombs at Suan Dork. The cemetery nestles in a small compound near the temple, a long wood-roofed pavillion which, curiously, resembles the wooden church I once visited on the other side of the world at Yigoran in Paraguay. In the burial compound rise almost identical angular, white-washed cement markers, contrasting with the individualized grave stones found in Chiang Mai's foreigners cemetery, discussed in Chapter III. This difference is perhaps emblematic of the contrast between the Western view—starting with the Renaissance—of man as an individual, and the Eastern emphasis on non-self.

The white elephant which King Kuna used to locate a spot for a temple to house the Buddha relics recalls another difference between East and West. In the East a white elephant is a living talisman. Prior to becoming the Buddha, the Gautama's last incarnation was a white elephant. It is curious that what in the East is a venerated beast signifies to an English-speaking person an undesirable possession—a "white elephant." Alas, white elephants and golden retrievers must—to paraphrase the refrain—like chimney sweeps all come to dust. Such was the archetypical fate of Bendicò, the dog which belonged to Sicilian Prince Don Fabrizio in Giuseppe di Lampedusa's novel *The Leopard*. On the verge of death at age seventy-three, Don Fabrizio draws up "a general balance sheet of his whole life, trying to sort out of the immense ash-heap of liabilities the golden flecks of happy moments," some of which "Bendicò's delicious nonsense" provided. In July 1888, twenty-two years after Don Fabrizio's death, Bendicò's remains are found among "an inferno of mummified memories" in the family villa at Palermo. All the past—all of it—has, it seems, become forgettable and disposable. Bendicò, dead for forty-five years, is now a heap of moth-eaten fur. A descendant of the prince decides to throw away the mouldy remains:

> As the carcass was dragged off, the glass eyes stared at her with the humble reproach of things that are being annulled. A few minutes later what remained of Bendicò was flung into a corner of the courtyard visited every day by the garbage collector. During the flight down from the window his form recomposed itself for an instant; in the air one could have seen dancing a quadruped with long whiskers, and its right foreleg seemed to be raised in imprecation. Then all found peace in a heap of livid dust.

So disappeared the "straw dog," the name given in the Tao classic *Lao Tzu* to effigies thrown out as trash after being used in sacrificial ceremonies: to heaven and earth "all things are but as straw dogs."

VI.

Diasporadic Conclusions

IN an obscure corner of lower Manhattan, miles and millenia from the original Promised Land, nestles a little-remembered and less noticed burial ground called the First Shearith Israel Graveyard. In that tiny patch of green at St. James Place, just south of Chinatown's Chatham Square, repose eighteen members of the first Jewish congregation established in the United States. The history of that congregation, which arrived in New York in 1654, typifies the great disapora, the scattering of Jews from the Holy Land to the globe's far corners where Hebrew cemeteries serve to recall Jewish tribulations and migrations over the centuries.

When Spain and Portugal expelled the Jews in 1492 some of the outcasts took refuge in Holland. A few of the exiles later settled in Brazil, but when Portugal recovered that

South American land in 1654 the Jews there returned to Holland. A Spanish pirate captured one ship carrying twenty-three refugees, whom the French captain of the *Saint Charles* proceeded to rescue. The Frenchman brought the exiles to Nieuw Amsterdam (now New York), whose Dutch governor, Peter Stuyvesant, opposed the immigration of the Jews. But the Dutch West India Company, which had a number of Jewish stockholders, over-ruled the governor's objections and on 12 September 1654 the new arrivals celebrated a New Year service. Before long the Sephardic community rented a room in a windmill where they held their religious services. A bronze plaque erected in 1954 in tiny Peter Minuit Plaza, east of Battery Park, memorializes those twenty-three pioneers. Two years after the immigrants arrived the city allocated them a plot of land for use as a burial ground. The precise location of this cemetery—described at the time as "outside the city"—remains unknown, but by 1682 New Amsterdam's Jewish community acquired a tract of land near today's Chatham Square. The First (actually the second) Shearith Israel Graveyard still survives on that site.

The venerable cemetery, the oldest existing artifact on Manhattan Island, contains eighteen graves of Jews who fought in the Revolutionary War, during which General Charles Lee mounted two cannon batteries in the burial ground to defend against a British invasion. Those interred at Shearith Israel include Solomon Myers Cohen, a spermaceti oil merchant; Myer Myers, a silversmith; Jacob Hart, who lent two thousand pounds to General Lafayette; and Gershom Mendes Seixas (d. 1816), supposedly the first American-born rabbi, a trustee of King's College (later Columbia University), and one of the thirteen clergymen present at George Washington's inauguration. Seixas's brother Benjamin, also buried in the graveyard, served as a lieutenant in the New York militia and was a founder of the New York Stock Exchange. The epitaph of Walter J. Judah, who died at age twenty, recalls him as a "student of physic, who worn down by his exertions to alleviate the sufferings of his fellow citizens in that dreadful contagion that visited the city of New York in 1798 fell a victim in the cause of humanity." The cemetery also contains the oldest grave marker in New York City, that of Bueno de Mezquita (d. 1683). The original congregation's descendants, who now worship at a synagogue located at 8 West 70th Street in Manhattan, still maintain the historic Shearith Israel Graveyard although it was closed in 1831.

Shearith Israel means "remnant of Israel." Such remnants of Israel surface at many remote and distant places. Henry Wadsworth Longfellow's poem "The Jewish Cemetery at Newport"—a well-known Rhode Island cemetery established on land acquired in 1677 by members of fifteen Dutch families who arrived in America in 1658—captures the exotic flavor of Jewish burial grounds in foreign countries far from the Promised Land:

How strange it seems! These Hebrews in their graves . . .
The very names recorded here are strange,
Of Foreign accent, and of different climes.

Far from the old Jewish Cemetery at Newport in the east is an unusual funeral monument commemorating early Jewish settlers in the Wild West town of Tombstone, Arizona. The memorial seems somewhat incongruous amid markers to desperados and other rough-neck figures. At the Boothill Graveyard just outside the Arizona town rises a curious hybrid memorial, erected in 1984, "dedicated to the Jewish pioneers and their Indian friends." A container inside the monument holds a yarmulke, a menorah, a Kaddish cup and an Israeli bowl filled with dirt from Jerusalem. In 1881, a few years after the town was founded, a sufficient number of Jews lived in Tombstone for them to organize a local Hebrew

Association. A Jewish mine superintendant named Abraham Hyman Emanuel served as the town's mayor from 1896 to 1900, while Josephine Sarah Marcus, a Jewish dance-hall girl, became the third wife (or, some say, lover) of Wyatt Earp. On the marker, which stands in a small plot outlined by a crumbling adobe brick foundation, appear a star of David and Indian symbols, an odd synthesis of two wandering tribes.

Other wanderers who made their way to Tombstone repose on the sloping hillside above the monument. There stretches the old cemetery, a rocky, cactus-filled graveyard established in 1878, perhaps the world's most appropriately named burial ground. The city received its unusual designation from the warning given to early prospector Ed Schieffelin, who discovered the area's first mine, that all he would find in the desolate land would be his tombstone. A wide variety of colorful Wild West characters who "died with their boots on" repose at Boothill, their markers—not tombstones but metal markers which replace the time-worn original round-topped, wooden slabs—relating in epitaph form the story of the town's wild early days. Frank and Tom McLaury (d. 1881), killed at the famous shoot-out at the O.K. Corral lie there, as do John Beather, "hanged" (d. 1881); John King, "suicide" (d. 1881); a teamster, "killed by Apaches" (d. 1881); "unknown found in abandoned mine"; John Heath "taken from county jail and lynched" (d. 1884); Daniel Dwyer, "drowned" (d. 1881); smallpox victim John Blair, who arrived at his final place after a "cowboy threw a rope over feet and dragged him to his grave"; Glenn Will, whose "ashes arrived collect on delivery" (sent by his son for burial in Tombstone in 1953); and the famous epitaph, "Here lies Lester Moore/Four Slugs/From a 44/No Les/No more." This, like so many other grave inscriptions around the world, may be more poetic than precise, more entertaining than enlightening: the name of the town's newspaper, the *Tombstone Epitaph,* encapsulates a wit's cynical comment that epitaphs and newspapers are mankind's most lying institutions. At Boothill's upper rear section repose expatriates as remote from their homeland as Tombstone's Jews were from the Promised Land: "Mrs. Ah Lum (China Mary) born in China, died in Tombstone Dec 16, 1906"; "Two Chinese died of leprosy"; "Chink Smiley shot 1884"; and others who ventured from the Far East to the Wild West, such as Sing Wan, Foo Kee and Hop Lung. In the east, in the cemetery of the gold-mining town of Ballarat, Australia, the small Jewish section holds a few "down under" pioneers, among them Maurice Solomon, headmaster of the Ballarat Hebrew School, and others as noted in Chapter III. Also in the Far East, at a Queensland, New Zealand, graveyard, two markers isolated beneath fragrant pines on a hill above other tombs commemorate Aaron Walde (d. 1885) and, with inscriptions in Hebrew, English, and German, Louis D. Beer (d. 1887).

One of the most remote Jewish cemeteries in the world occupies a rather scruffy compound enclosed by a concrete block wall in the Amazon River city of Manaus, Brazil. This jungle cemetery truly lies in "different climes." In the nineteenth century Jews from the ghettos of Spanish and French Morocco emigrated to Brazil where prosperous Jewish merchants in Belém, at the mouth of the Amazon, hired the newcomers to man trading posts up-river. The Amazon outposts bartered tobacco, medicine, clothes, and other such products of civilization for rubber, nuts, skins, fish, and oil supplied by the natives. Many of the immigrants eventually intermarried with local Indians and became assimilated into the native culture, but around two thousand of Brazil's hundred and twenty thousand Jews still live in Amazon River towns. Manaus is the home of some seven hundred Jews. The graveyard there contains the body of Rabbi Salom Moyal (d. 1910), who traveled along the Amazon to collect contributions from Jewish settlers for his theological school in Jerusalem. Moyal died in Brazil, where he became a kind of saintly figure after his demise. Messages and offerings left by natives in gratitude for miracles attributed to the rabbi adorn his grave for his remains are believed to possess supernatural powers. These spontaneous offerings represent a curious parallel to the practice followed by the early Hebrews, who regarded burial places as sacred, offering to the dead such presents as spices, incense, and food.

Although Jewish cemeteries—or at least interment sections reserved for Jews within non-sectarian graveyards—exist all around the world, the Hebrew burial grounds in Europe boast especially evocative markers and inscriptions. Much history reposes in these cemeteries, but some of it is hidden in obscure corners of the continent and must be ferreted out by the dedicated cemetery collector. The old Jewish Cemetery in Dublin, used from 1717 to 1899 (with a few breaks) occupies the backyard of a nondescript grey stucco house at 67 Fairview Strand Road in Drumcondra near the Ballybough Bridge. On the facade of the house, built to protect the cemetery which lies behind it, appears the date of construction: 5618 (1858). A Jew who once visited a residence in the neighborhood happened to notice that Jewish gravestones formed its fireplace. To prevent people from further pilfering Jewish funeral monuments for building material, the Jewish community constructed the house which now stands in front of the cemetery. The caretakers—who occupy the residence for free in exchange for maintaining the burial ground, their back yard—told me that, apart from two visits by the Jewish community's graveyard committee, I was the first person in six months to ask to see the site. From her kitchen the lady of the house enjoys a view of the cemetery, a spooky sight which, she said, dissuades her from doing the dishes at night.

The graveyard contains some 130 stones, most inscribed in both Hebrew and English and many of them simple, unadorned slabs. I failed to find the graves of characters said to be buried there such as Barnaby "Pencil" Cohen, a lead pencil pioneer; Chocolate Phillips, an early chocolate manufacturer in Ireland; and Benjamin d'Israeli, not related to the British Prime Minister of that name but a sheriff in County Carlow. Other graves, however, were well-marked. Toward the rear wall stretches a Harris plot, which boasts the latest marker I found, for Maude Jeanette Harris (d. 1958), while nearby sleeps the well-praised Herbert Wormser Harris (d. 1880): "He was an exemplary son, an affectionate brother, an erudite scholar, and a truly religious and virtuous Jew." Elsewhere repose Sarah Jordan (d. 1884) "who departed this life at Philadelphia, U.S.A."; Fritz Rothschild, "a native of Altona [Germany]. He settled in Dublin at an early age where he died on the 11th of Nisan 5636"; Marinus de Groot "of Rotterdam, for 26 years President of the Dublin Hebrew Congregation, who died April 16, 1910." One of the most decorative stones, embellished with relief flower clusters, commemorates Florence Louisa Davis (d. 1890), while near the back door of the house lies Esther Landau (d. 1891), her final resting place sporting a freshly painted metal fence at the time of my visit.

The oldest Jewish burial ground in Britain today opened in London in 1656, half a century before Dublin's Jewish cemetery. Back in medieval times London's Jewish community lived in a ghetto which still retains the name Old Jewry, a corner of the metropolis located a block west of the Bank of England. To this quarter, noted the famous historian Holinshed, prior to the reign of Henry I (1100–1135) the Jews in England were "constrained to bring all their dead corpses from all parts of the realm," for Old Jewry offered Britain's only official Jewish burial ground. Before Edward I expelled the Jews in 1290, a synagogue also stood in the area. In 1656, Cromwell allocated the Jewish community land for a cemetery at present-day 253 Mile End Road—an appropriate street name for a graveyard—in East London, not far from Bethnal Green. Since my visit the graves, so I have read, have been transferred to a cemetery in Brentwood, Essex, to free the ground for the medical school of Queen Mary's College, so the following account describes the old burial ground as it used to be. London has now swallowed the cemetery's open fields. Across the street rises a block of modern flats, and nearby stretch the Mile End Hospital's buildings, by which stands a small, graceful, red brick Georgian structure built in 1913 as an old folks home. Behind this house—on whose site a hospital for the poor opened in 1665—stretches the old cemetery, where members of the Spanish-Portuguese Jewish community repose.

Clumps of ferns and thick grass green the graveyard, where a scattering of boxy tombs and some simple slabs recall the London Jews of a hundred and more years ago. Many of the stones, which largely date from the seventeenth century, suffer from cracks and other wear, and most of the inscriptions are now effaced or illegible. On a few markers a fragment of Hebrew, or some stray Spanish or Portuguese phrase—"su alma goze la Gloria"—appears, rather ghost-like. In 1924 descendants of one lucky decedent restored his tomb, which recalls: "Here lies buried Don Isaac Lindo . . . a gentleman of Campo Mayor in Spain who, being driven from his native land because of his faith found, about the year 1663, a new home in this congregation of London where he became a leader of the Synagogue. He died the 18th March 1712, at an advanced age, and left a family whose members for generations have borne the vessels of the Lord." Nathan Rothschild (d. 1836), of the famous banking family, also supposedly reposes in the cemetery, but his grave remains obscure.

A Rothschild mausoleum, however, stands in the new Jewish burial ground near Stratford New Town in West Ham. A well-kept, eleven-acre spread on Cemetery Road, this cemetery was opened in 1858 to replace the Mile End Road graveyard. The frieze-decorated Rothschild mausoleum houses the remains of such family members as Evelina de Rothschild (d. 1866), recalled as "My Darling Wife" by Ferdinand James Anselm de Rothschild (d. 1898). The art nouveau grillwork over the grave has the name "Eva" worked into the design, while the capitals of the mausoleum's columns contain an "R" motif. To the right of the cemetery's center aisle a box tomb painted a pallid beige contains David Salomons (d. 1873), member of Parliament for Greenwich, lord mayor of London 1855–6, barrister, whose inscription notes: "In the year 1869 Sir David Solomons, Bart, presented a memorial window to the Corporation of the City of London in commemoration of the removal of those civil disabilities under which the Jews in Great Britain had previously laboured." (The window referred to was installed in the Guildhall.) Such disabilities the inscription on the tomb of Charles Mosley, originally from Jamaica, recalls: he interred his wife and child at the Old Burial Ground, North Street, Whitechapel Road "where he had also purchased adjoining ground for his own remains of which he was deprived by the act of the legislature." The graveyard also numbers among its inhabitants a man named Mordecai Million (d. 1972), who reposes near a corrugated metal chapel. The bare rear section, comprised of a grassless, rock-surfaced area, the stones black from soot, contains late-nineteenth-century remains removed from Hoxton Cemetery on Hoxton Street, a displacement necessitated when the London City Council acquired the site.

As in England, and elsewhere, the Jews in France suffered from restrictions on the disposal of their dead. For centuries Jews—and Protestants as well—could claim no legal identity under French law. No openly operated Jewish cemeteries existed, but a police ordinance allowed Jews to bury bodies in gardens or cellars. The earliest Jewish burial area in Paris, located on the rue Galande, dates from 1198 while in 1223 another Jewish graveyard started up at the intersection of the Boulevard St. Michel and the rue Hautefeuille. In the 1690s an inn called L'Étoile stood at today's 46 rue de Flandres, then located outside Paris. Behind the stables stretched a garden where the inn-keeper, a man named Camot, surreptitiously buried Paris' Sephardic Jews (from Spain, Portugal, North Africa, and the Middle East). For this service Camot charged fifty francs per adult and thirty francs for children. After Camot's widow died in 1773 the site passed to François Matard, a tanner, who began burying in the garden horses and cattle that he had skinned. The Jewish community, offended by the mingling of beasts' bones with those of the Hebrew dead, tried to buy the property but Matard asked an unreasonably high price. The Jews then acquired an adjacent site at 44 rue de Flandre, with those participating in the purchase entitled to free burial. The first interment took place in 1780, making this burial ground one of Paris' oldest cemeteries. The last burial occurred in 1810 and today the forlorn cemetery occupies an obscure plot behind a huge modern apartment building.

Except for two box tombs which rise above the ground, the other thirty or so markers lie flat on the weedy, stony terrain over which tower the adjacent high-rises. Time has dealt harshly with many of the gravestones, whose effaced inscriptions leave the deceased mostly nameless and praiseless. But a few phrases remain to evidence the vanished Portuguese Jewish community. Twin slabs recall Abraham Lopes Laguna (d. 1807) and his wife Rachel Silva-Lopes Laguna (d. 1806), while another stone memorializes Joseph Cavaillon, died aged ninety-eight "in the year 5557 of the Creation of the World which corresponds to the 8th Thermidor of the 4th [?] year of the French Republic." Judith del Valle (d. 1798) lies there; a stone gracefully shaped like a keyhole, but broken across the middle, honors Mardochee Leon (d. 1803); and one of the box tombs holds Moïse Salom (d. 1796). Near the lone tree at one end of the cemetery reposes Solomon Perpignan (d. 1781), instrumental in acquiring the ground for the graveyard. Perpignan was under treatment for hypochondria in his residence on the Rue de Seine when he jumped out a window to his death. His epitaph notes that he was "one of the founders of the Free Royal School of Design established in 1767, during the glorious reign of Louis XV in the city of Paris, for the perfection of art, and named by Monseigneur Le Noir, lieutenant general of the police, trustee for Jews originating in Avignon."

At about the same time that the rue de Flandre Sephardic burial ground was functioning another Jewish cemetery, for Ashkenazis (from Germany and eastern Europe), operated in the Montrouge area of Paris. In 1785 a man named Cerf Berr, a junk dealer, bought a plot of ground and opened a graveyard: perhaps he viewed disused human anatomy as junk no less than other discarded items. Berr charged for burials until 1792 when he gave the cemetery to the Jewish community. The French authorities did not object to those two late-eighteenth-century Jewish cemeteries, provided burials took place only at night, without any ceremonial activities. Remnants from the Montrouge cemetery, where the last interment occurred in September 1809, are on display in a curious compound at 90 rue Gabriel Pau. Here a prefab-type building houses a simple synagogue in a *shetl*-like area occupied by some five hundred Jewish families. Community members salvaged the tombstones when the remains of the dead were removed from the old cemetery in the mid-1960s and transferred to a common grave. Along the walls in the square, tree-shaded yard surrounding the synagogue stand forty-two Hebrew-inscribed gravestones—some embellished with engraved designs, such as a rosette, flower sprigs, an hour glass, a pair of hands—along with sixteen fragments of monuments. In this Jewish Parisian enclave scenes for the movie *The Dreyfus Affair* were filmed.

No modern Jewish cemeteries exist in Paris, for in 1881 a law gave all French citizens the right to be buried without regard to religious affiliations or other previously disabling characteristics—among them, having comitted suicide or not having undergone baptism—to a normal interment. This law seems not to have applied to Muslims, who had been given a special section at Père Lachaise by Napoleon III during the Crimean War (1854–56) to please his Turkish allies. (Separate Muslim areas also exist in the cemeteries of Bobigny and Thiais.)

These little-known and seldom visited Jewish cemeteries in the western European capital cities—Dublin, London, Paris—lack both magnitude and atmosphere. They survive as mere shadows of their former selves, tiny areas which contain only a few monuments, many illegible, on unattractive bits of terrain lost in the vast cities that surround them. These poor little cemeteries, forlorn and forgotten, hardly compare to the evocative Jewish burial grounds in central Europe, where substantial Jewish cultures existed for so many centuries. In Poland alone more than three hundred and fifty Jewish cemeteries survive, several dozen of them dating before 1800. The oldest known grave is at Wroclaw in southwestern Poland. One of the largest and most picturesque old Jewish cemeteries occupies a history-haunted area in the German Rhine River town of Worms. (Worms—what better name for a cemetery town! In *The Devil's Dictionary* Ambrose Bierce defines *worms'-meat* as "the finished product of which we are the raw material. The contents of the Taj Mahal, the Tombeau Napoleon and the Grantarium. Worms'-meat is usually outlasted by the structure that houses it.") Written in the dust and ashes at Worms are the traditions and heritage of the vanished German Jewish community, crushed like a worm underfoot by the Nazi boot. The old graveyard at Worms inspired atavistic feelings in philosopher Martin Buber during a visit in the early 1930s:

I stood there and was one with the ashes and unified through
the ashes with my forefathers . . . I stood there and experienced it all myself—all the death, all the ashes, all the frag-
mentation, all the silent grief is mine. And that feeling of
kinship comforts me. I lie upon the earth, tumbled like these
gravestones. And I feel comforted.

Miraculously, this splendid, nearly one-thousand-year-old
cemetery which so moved Buber has survived virtually unscathed by the many turmoils which have afflicted Germany.
The oldest known marker, still well-preserved, bears the
inscription: "This is the gravestone of Jakob ha-Bachur, who
in the year 1076 paid his debt to time. His soul now rests in
harmony with life." Seven other eleventh-century gravestones survive, while about fifty date from the twelfth century. In the printing museum at Safed, Israel hangs a photograph labeled: "Tomb stone of Worms, Germany (1183).
The characters are very popular and show a certain lack of
skill." Although this sounds like a book review, the comment
sets forth an accurate view of the eight-hundred-year-old
inscriptions at Worms, for the lettering on Jakob ha-Bachur's
stone indeed presents a rough-hewn appearance. Not long
afterwards, however, the carvers improved their technique
for monuments at the cemetery. Inscriptions became less
crude, and by the turn of the fourteenth century such markers as those for Rabbi Meir von Rothenburg and Alexander
Wimpfen, referred to in the next paragraph, boasted sharply
incised, clearly cut texts. In the middle of the thirteenth
century the Jews of Worms built a wall around the burial
ground, an addition perhaps instigated by a local Christian
demand for protection money, on threat of destroying the
cemetery. Even after receiving payment the Christians in
Worms used the graveyard as a quarry for construction mate-

rials. Six centuries later, workers discovered a number of Jewish gravestones embedded as building blocks in Worms' city wall. In 1911 the Jewish community opened a new cemetery and closed the old one to all but those who inherited the right to repose there. During World War II the old cemetery escaped damage except for a few gravestones destroyed in 1945 by a stray allied bomb. Finally, nine centuries after its founding, the old burial ground, under the care and protection of the city of Worms, rests in peace—for now.

Many of the one thousand graves in the old section sport well embellished markers and contain storied occupants. One pair of artfully inscribed, rectangular stones stand side by side a few inches apart, as if facing pages of a book. Indeed, they recount a story about the two men who repose beneath the open volume. The tale explains why Rabbi Meir von Rothenburg (d. 1293) and Alexander ben Salomo Wimpfen (d. 1307), a Frankfurt businessman, lie so close together. In 1286 Rabbi von Rothenburg, along with many other Jews of the time, wanted to emigrate from Germany to Palestine. Rudolf of Hapsburg, who feared reduction of the royal revenues if the Jews were allowed to leave, imprisoned the rabbi to prevent the religious leader from taking his followers to the Promised Land. Although the Jews offered Rudolf a large sum of money to release the rabbi, von Rothenburg refused to buy his freedom and he died in prison on 27 April 1293. But even his death afforded no release, for the ruler retained the rabbi's body in custody until finally, in 1307, Alexander ben Salomo Wimpfen purchased the corpse which, in accordance with von Rothenburg's wishes, he buried in the Worms cemetery. In return for his payment, Wimpfen requested only that he be interred next to von Rothenburg. Shortly after the rabbi's long-delayed burial the Frankfurt merchant died and was laid to rest in an adjacent grave.

Many other rabbis repose at Worms. The stone of Rabbi

Jakob Molin (d. 1427) stands out by standing apart, aligned at a right angle to the other nearby markers in the so-called Glen of the Rabbis section. While all the other rabbinical gravestones face in the direction of the synagogue, Molin's marker is oriented toward Jerusalem. The top part of his stone has been sheared off, but on the lower section appears a fragmentary inscription: ". . . the world darkened, as the homeward journey, comparable to a well-ripened fruit because of its great. . . ." The row of adjacent gravestones extends chronologically from the marker for Rabbi Naphtali Hirsch Spitz (d. 1712), decorated with a leaping deer *(Hirsch)* to one for Isaak Adler (d. 1823), not a rabbi himself but father of Samuel Adler who in 1857 became a rabbi in New York. And so, suddenly, surfaces a reference to the New World, there at the age-old Old World burial ground. Some cemeteries, like the Jewish graveyard in Worms, suggest continuation and continuity: the story goes on, the old stones seem to say.

The only other major European cemetery which stirs such a feeling of Jewish culture and traditions spanning the centuries is the ancient Jewish burial ground at Prague, whose atmsophere David Philipson vividly captured in 1894 in *Old European Jewries:*

> As one wanders among the graves, most of them old, centuries old, thought cannot but revert to the past and the checkered history of the Jews. Everything is quiet and peaceful now in this home of the dead, the troubled are at rest; but as we read the names chiseled in the tombstones, some of celebrities who shed glory upon the Jewish community of Prague, most of them unknown or forgotten, we see pass before us the changing views of the panorama of bygone days, depicting scenes in which those resting here, the great and the small, the rich and the poor, the learned and the ignorant, were the actors.

For three hundred years Jews of Prague's Josefov quarter, officially established by order of the city administrators in the thirteenth century, were interred in the crowded burial ground wedged into the ghetto. Up to twelve layers of graves lend the little enclave true historical depth. The oldest tombstone, dated 25 April 1439, memorializes the poet Abigdor Karo, who wrote a dirge about the 1389 massacre of the Jews which he witnessed. About twelve thousand weather-worn, sinking or sunken stones commemorate some of the seventy-two thousand dead interred there up until 1787 when Emperor Joseph II banned burials in residential sections of Prague. In 1903 the city took part of the cemetery grounds for roads and a museum. Albert Camus' Mersault in *A Happy Death* glimpses, but does not enter, the old graveyard: How could Mersault resist visiting this picturesque corner which survives from medieval Europe? A pleasant chaos of tumbled markers—square, round, pointed—fills the densely populated graveyard which Geoffrey Moorehouse compares to Calcutta's Park Street cemetery, described in Chapter III: "The old Jewish Cemetery in Prague is probably the only one in the world more congested with corpses than Park Street, for there the grave slabs slope sometimes one on top of the other." Many of the markers bear representations which illustrate the deceased's name: bear, wolf, rose, a bird *(Vogel)*, a pigeon *(Taube)*, a flower *(Blum)*, a lion *(Löwe)*, and similar such visual puns.

Among the illustrious figures buried in Prague are Mordecai Meisel (d. 1601), a philanthropist who paved the Jewish quarter and built two synagogues as well as an almshouse, a school, and a bath house; the historian David Gans (d. 1613), who wrote a chronicle of Jewish events; Rabbi David Oppenheim (d. 1736), whose collection of Hebrew books and manuscripts, the "Bibliotheca Oppenheim," resides at Oxford's Bodelian Library, and who was also great-grandfather of J. Robert Oppenheimer, father of the atomic bomb; and

Joseph del Medigo (d. 1655), a physician, mathematician, and philosopher who studied with Galileo. The cemetery's most famous grave houses the remains of Rabbi Judah Lowe, whose large monument includes four slabs of Hebrew text, three few-foot-high columns, and a bas-relief lion to represent the deceased's name. A native of Worms, Germany—site of that other historic and atmospheric Jewish cemetery—Rabbi Lowe became famous around 1570 as the inventor of the Golem, a figure something between a robot and a human. When Christians in Prague mounted an intensive campaign to convert the Jews in the late sixteenth century Rabbi Lowe petitioned the heavens for a method to combat them. He was told to proceed to the river and with the clay there to mould a figure which, by certain rites and recitations, could be brought alive. Thus was born the Golem. The Golem (in Hebrew the word means "formless" or "mindless") resembled a man but it, or he, could hardly speak and lacked the power to reproduce. When the Golem was not busy helping Lowe defend the faith the rabbi kept it busy sweeping the floor and running errands. Eventually the Golem became a problem child, unruly and hard to handle, so Rabbi Lowe decided to get rid of his invention. One version of the Golem's end holds that the rabbi decided to destroy the robot by effacing the first two letters of *aemaeth* (truth) on the figure's forehead to leave the word *maeth* (he is dead). The Golem, however, had grown too tall for its master to reach up to the forehead, so Lowe ordered it to remove its boots, and when the robot bent to obey, the rabbi rubbed out the crucial letters. But then the clay man fell over and crushed its creator to death. A more whimsical version of Lowe's demise tells how even Death feared a direct confrontation with the miracle-working rabbi, so in order to approach him by surprise Death hid in a rose which a young girl gave Lowe to smell. When the ninety-six-year-old rabbi sniffed the bloom, Death leaped from the flower and claimed him.

After the old Prague cemetery closed in 1787 the Jewish community interred its dead in the more spacious burial ground located on the Zizkoo heights. Family members of writers Rainer Maria Rilke and Franz Werfel repose there, as do Franz Kafka and his parents. An arrow sign which points the way to Kafka's grave seems to be passing a literary judgment: "Franze Kafky odd. 21." The three Kafkas lie under a short, six-sided, pointed stone pillar bearing Hebrew inscriptions and their names and dates: "Dr. Franz Kafka 1883–1924 . . . Hermann Kafka 1854–1931 . . . Julie Kafka 1856–1934." These mute dates tell that the son predeceased his parents, as though the boy carried out the desire that he had expressed in "Letter to His Father": "If I was to escape from you, I had to escape from the family as well, even from Mother." Other renowned Czech cultural figures populate Prague's Vysehrad cemetery, where the composers Bedrich Smetana (d. 1884) and Anton Dvorak (d. 1904) repose. Also there lies Czech writer Jan Neruda (d. 1891), whose name one Ricardo Eliezer Neftalí Reyes y Basoalto adopted as a pseudonym: the Nobel Prize-winning poet Pablo Neruda of Chile. Vysehrad, however, does boast a world famous writer—Karel Capek (d. 1938), his marker (if not his life) an open book. Capek's 1921 play *R.U.R.,* an acronym for Rossum's Universal Robots, coined the word *robot.* The word derives from the Czech verb *robotiti,* which means to work in a drudging sort of way, like Rabbi Lowe's Golem.

Viewing the venerable Jewish graves in the ancient cemeteries of Prague and Worms, one cannot help but meditate on the events of the twentieth century which these Jews escaped. A cemetery visitor enjoys an odd perspective on the past. Whereas his present life continues on into the unknown future, he can clearly see all the years that have elapsed since the deaths of those buried in the graveyard. This retrospective view clarifies what to the deceased represented their unknown future, a knowledge of which gives the tomb visitor a sense of omniscience. This experience of transcending time seems especially vivid at cemeteries. Cemetery collector Elias Canetti—"The attraction of cemeteries and graveyards is so strong that people visit them even if no one belonging to them is buried there," he notes in *Crowds and Power*—observes that "the time that separates [the cemetery visitor] from their death is somehow reassuring and exhilarating: he has known the world for that much longer . . . All the centuries he knows are his. The man in the grave knows nothing of the man who stands beside it, reflecting on the span of the completed life." When Zeitblom (*Zeitblum:* "timeflower"), the narrator in Thomas Mann's *Dr. Faustus,* writes in April 1944 about the autumn of 1912, he notes that the present interacts with the past in "a quite extraordinary interweaving of time-units, destined, moreover, to include even a third; namely, the time which one day the courteous reader will take for the reading of what has been written; at which point he will be dealing with a threefold ordering of time: his own, that of the chronicler, and historic time." In just the same way, a cemetery visitor participates in a temporal triad: his own, that of the deceased, and all the time which existed and which will exist beyond his and the departed's existences. Reading gravestones—those capsule summaries of individual lives—makes vivid the time before one's own life began.

Zeitblom observed in 1944 of Adrian Leverkühn, the fictional composer whose life the book describes: "Adrian is safe from the days we dwell in," much as were the Jews interred in the Prague and Worms cemeteries secure in death and immune to the turmoil of the 1930s and 1940s. Our knowledge of what came after the demise of the dead lets us perceive an additional dimension of time—that which unfolded after their day and (to a certain extent) before ours.

The non-being of the deceased and our own pre-being over-lap. This cemetery-inspired viewpoint enriches our awareness of all the time which has existed, and will exist, without us.

Prague's Orloj—the great late-fifteenth-century astronom-ical clock on the old town hall—includes an animated scene in which Death tolls a tiny bell, whereupon an old man shakes his head to express his unwillingness to die, and then Death reverses the hourglass enabling the man, at least for a time, to escape death. The Orloj runs on, but the hourglass reverses and death recedes, as if time were running backwards, just as it seemed to D. H. Lawrence when, in 1924, he wrote his remarkably precient "Letter From Germany," holding that German society was reverting to the past and displayed "the old, bristling, savage spirit." Lawrence claimed that "it looks as if the years were wheeling swiftly backwards, no more onwards. Like a spring that is broken, and whirls swiftly back, so time seems to be whirling with mysterious swiftness to a sort of death." Such backward, atavistic recoiling of time failed to disturb the departed Jews of Prague and Worms, an advantage of their death unknown to them but vividly appar-ent to us. Such after-knowledge somehow seems to extend their existence into the context of later eras and also serves to wheel backward our time to connect with theirs. Thus link lives lived and living lives.

Being dead is a part of life. In *Atala* Chateaubriand main-tained that a person who returned from the dead would be unwelcome, even by those who had genuinely grieved his or her demise, as survivors quickly adjust to the loss and form new relationships. But by visiting the dead we can return to them, befriend them, and in a way revive, at least in our imagination, eras which existed without us. This sort of retrospective perspective can help to reassure us that our non-existence—both prenatal and postmortem—holds fewer ter-rors than we sometimes fear.

In his *Philosophical Dictionary* Voltaire posed the question:

"Why, as we are so miserable, have we imagined that not to be is a great ill, when it is clear that it was not an ill not to be before we were born?" Elaborating on this concept, Mark Twain observed that "annihilation has no terrors for me, because I have already tried it before I was born—a hundred million years—and I have suffered more in an hour, in this life, than I remember to have suffered in the whole hundred million years put together." Twain looked back on his non-existence "with a tender longing and with a grateful desire to resume" that carefree state of being or, rather, non-being, much as young Lucius Priest, in Faulkner's *The Reivers,* longs "to be home, not just to retrace but to retract, obliterate . . . in reverse if necessary, travelling backward to unwind, ravel back into No-being, Never-being." Of all human constructs, cemeteries best allow us to visualize time from various perspectives; to imagine our non-being during past times when other beings thrived, and during future years when new beings will live and look down on us in our graves; and to reconcile ourselves to not being. Others are not; we, too, can be not. The late-nineteenth-century German writer Wilhelm Raabe summarizes this intermingling of past and present, life and death, is-m and was-m in a scene from his short story "The Elderflower," set in Prague's Jewish cemetery:

> I saw the countless intermingled layers of stone tablets and the ancient elders whose gnarled branches spread and entwined with one another. I wandered through the narrow paths and saw the ablution vases of the Levis, the hands of the Aarons and the grapes of the tribe of Israel. As a sign of my respect, I, like the other visitors, placed a stone on the grave of the great Rabbi Jehuda Löw bar Bezalel. Then I sat sat down on a black 14th century stone and, feeling the significance of the place, a shiver came over me in full force. For a thousand years the dead of God's people had been assembled here, just as they, living, had been enclosed within the confining walls of the Ghetto.

The ghetto cemeteries which once abounded throughout Europe have for the most part disappeared along with their thriving Jewish communities. The term *ghetto*—derived from the Italian verb *gettare:* "to cast in metal"—originated in 1516 when the city of Venice set aside a district for Jews among the foundries. In this quarter Venice's Jews lived until 1797 when Napoleon ordered the ghetto gates removed. Before the second Jewish cemetery opened in Via Cipro, at the Lido, about two-and-a-half centuries ago, the old Jewish cemetery of the ghetto community was established in 1386 at Riveria San Nicolo 2 on the corner of Via Cipro, at the Lido. It was here that Goethe's servant picked up and then dropped a man's skull whose bones split along their sutures, thus suggesting to the great man his theory that all animal anatomy was based on a single structural schema. (On another occasion Goethe was also inspired upon seeing Jacob van Ruisdael's painting "The Jewish Graveyard," now at the Dresden State Picture Gallery, and prompted to compose his essay "Ruisdael as Thinker.")

pose his essay "Ruisdael as Thinker.")

In Rome, at 6 Via di Valle Murcia on the lower part of the Aventine hill near the Mazzini statue, lies a small rose garden overlooking the Circo Massimo. A white stone plaque there bears a Hebrew inscription which I assume recalls that until a century or so ago a Jewish cemetery occupied the site. As recently as 1925 there was another Jewish cemetery in Rome—described in rather disparaging terms by Augustus Hare in *Walks In Rome:*

> A lane on the left leads to the Jewish Burial-Ground, used as a place of sepulture for the Ghetto for many centuries. A curious instance of the cupidity attributed to the Jewish race may be seen in the fact that they have, for a remuneration of four baiocchi, habitually given leave to their neighbours to discharge the contents of a rubbish-cart into their cemetery, a

permission of which the Romans have so abundantly availed themselves, that the level of the soil has been raised by many yards, and whole sets of older monuments have been completely swallowed up, and new ones erected over their heads.

Even older Jewish burial areas came to light in Rome in the 1970s, when a pair of two-thousand-year-old Jewish catacombs were restored.

Beneath Rome, as described in Chapter IV, once burrowed more than forty Christian catacombs comprised of 35 miles of burial chambers. During the first and second centuries A.D., when Rome's population of one million included an estimated fifty thousand Jews (more than live in all of Italy today), the Jewish community established seven catacombs, which preceded the Christian subterranean burial chambers by several centuries. Based on God's statement to Adam (Gen. 3:19), that "dust thou art, and unto dust shalt thou return," Jews customarily favored interment in the earth. Even though burial in underground niches violated that tradition, between the first and the fourth centuries Rome's Jews laid to rest in the black volcanic rock thousands of their coreligionists. Perhaps the Jews—also contrary to their usual practice—used the burial chambers to hold religious services, as did the Christians their catacombs. Colorful traditional representations, including scrolls, shofars (ram's horns), menorahs, and Torahs decorate a few of the tombs. Inscriptions are for the most part written not in Hebrew—reserved for religious rites and not generally used to mark gravestones until the eighth or ninth centuries—but in the classical languages. Of the six hundred inscriptions found in the Jewish catacombs, only twelve appear in Hebrew, one in Aramaic, and all the others in Latin, Greek, or a mixture of the two. This evidences a rather high degree of assimilation with the local population. Over the centuries all the catacombs in Rome, even the Jewish ones, fell under the jurisdiction of the

Vatican. Although the Jews—unlike the Christians, Egyptians, Etruscans, and other early cultures—did not bury precious objects with their dead, grave robbers vandalized their catacombs such that at the end of the twelfth century Popes Gregory VIII and Clement III issued directives to prohibit "the plunder and digging up of Jewish graves and cemeteries."

In 1984 the Vatican ceded control of the two surviving Jewish catacombs to Rome's Jewish community. One lies on the Via Appia Pignatelli off the Appian Way, south of the city; the other, in the center of Rome on the grounds of the Villa Torlonia, a thirteen-acre estate on the Via Nomentana where Mussolini once lived. The Via Appia necropolis, used for wealthier decedents, boasts a small, mosaic-paved courtyard above ground, while below a six-foot-wide passageway branches off into narrower tunnels where brightly colored frescoes decorate the burial vaults. Workers excavating the foundations of stables at Villa Torlonia in 1918 discovered the catacomb there. This subterranean graveyard, which housed poorer members of the Jewish community, contains a corridor lined with crude burial slots about a foot deep, two feet wide, and of varying lengths for children and adults. Some 150 memorial stones carved with Greek or Latin inscriptions—"Here lies Pegaianos, the scribe and lover of the law"; "Here lies Phillip, known for the love of his brother, who lived thirty-three years"—remain in the catacombs.

All around the Mediterranean basin Jewish communities of the Disapora established catacombs for their dead. Such subterranean burial areas existed in Carthage, Cyrene (modern Libya), Sicily, Sardinia, Phrygia (Asia Minor), near Alexandria in Egypt, and at Venosa and Prata in lower Italy. Israel itself, however, boasts the best-preserved of the ancient Jewish catacombs. At Beth She'arim, ten miles southeast of Haifa on the road to Nazareth, a hillock contains twenty-six catacombs dug in the third and fourth centuries, after the

Jews were barred from burying their dead at the Mount of
Olives cemetery in Jerusalem as a result of their revolt in the
second century A.D. Beth She'arim, which had been the most
important religious community when the center of Jewish
culture shifted from Judea to Galilee in the second century,
soon became the Jews most hallowed burial site. At Beth
She'arim functioned the Sanhedrin, the supreme council of
the Jews, while Rabbi Yehudah Ha'Nasi (d. 220), who codified the Jewish oral laws known as the Mishnah, lived and
died at the settlement. The necropolis served as a central
cemetery not only for area Jews but also for those in *eretz*
(Greater) Israel and in the Diaspora. In a kind of reversal of
this scattering, Jews from such settlements around the Middle East as Antioch, Palmyra, Byblos, Tyre, Sidon, and
Beirut returned to the homeland for burial. Into the rock hill
at Beth She'arim workers cut open courtyards from which
hinged stone doors lead into corridors and burial chambers.
Some of the original doors still swing on their seventeen-
centuries-old hinges. In contrast to the rock-face tombs at
Petra in southern Jordan, whose artfully decorated facades
front unembellished chambers, here elaborately decorated
interiors lie beyond bare facades.

Archeologists who conducted excavations at Beth
She'arim from 1936 to 1956, discovered more than one hundred limestone sarchophagi, some three hundred burial inscriptions in Hebrew, Greek, Aramaic, and Palmyrene, and
decorations both religious (menorahs, shofars, Torahs) and
secular (animals, ships, geometric designs). In one representative chamber, the Catacomb of the Sarcophagi, stands
an assortment of stone caskets set in niches, while on the
walls appear a number of inscriptions and religious symbols.
Just inside the entrance the cover of a sarcophagus bears the
rather piquant epitaph: "Here they lie, Atio, the daughter of
Rabbi Gamliel, son of Nehemia, who died a virgin at the age
of twenty two years and Ation, the daughter of Rabbi Judah,

the son of Rabbi Gamliel, who died at the age of nine years and six months, may their resurrection be with the worthy." The chastity of Rabbi Judah's daughter is left undefined. The Israel Museum in Jerusalem houses a more solemn inscription (in Greek) on a third-century marble tombstone from the site: "I, Justus, the son of the late Leontius, son of Sappho, am lying dead, after having picked the fruit of all wisdom, and relinquished the light, the wretched parents who ever mourn, and the brothers, woe, at my Beth She'arim, and after having gone to Hades, I, Justus, am lying here with many of my folk, because such was the will of the prevailing Fate. Take courage, Justus, no man is immortal." An epitaph (in Aramaic) at the catacombs reads: "He who is buried here is Simeon, the son of Yohanan, and on oath, whoever shall open upon him shall die of an evil end." This admonition predates by a millenium-and-a-half the similar cautionary epitaph on Shakespeare's grave (d. 1616) at Stratford-upon-Avon:

> Good frend for Jesus' sake forbeare,
> To digg the dust enclosed here.
> Blese be ye man [who] spares these stones,
> And curst be he [who] moves my bones.

So do similar sentiments surface in cemeteries and tombs across the years and miles.

The wall decorations at Beth She'arim include human figures portraing Biblical scenes—among them Daniel in the lion's den and Noah in the ark—mythology, and vignettes of such subjects as Roman soldiers or gladiators. At least one sarchophagus pictures a bearded face. All these human representations violate the Mosaic law (Deut. 4:16), prohibiting the "making of a graven image, the similitude of any figure and the likeness of male and female." This law many of the grave markers I came across in the Jewish cemetery on Rue

Damas (Damsacus street) in Beirut, Lebanon, also violated. A fairly elaborate monument to Selim Saad Levy (d. 1956) bore his photograph, while the album-like grave of Henriette Dana (d. 1954) sports not just one but two photos, an oval one picturing her in a formal pose and a candid, rectangular one showing Henriette casually perched on the edge of a cot, her expression jaunty, her legs insouciantly crossed. On the monument of Abramino Picciotto (d. 1953), who died "following a tragic horse accident," appears his picture along with the verse; "How green was the valley/The valley of the one who is no more." Was Picciotto of Italian extraction? It is Italians, more than any other nationality, who favor the use of photos on tombs. Visiting such an Italian postmortem photo gallery is a rather spooky experience. The pictures somehow seem to violate a departed's privacy. In *American Notebooks* Nathaniel Hawthorne mentioned that "a tombstone-maker, whom Miss B———y knew, used to cut cherubs on the top of the tombstones, and had the art of carving the cherubs' faces in the likeness of the deceased." This sort of stone image seems less intrusive than a photographic likeness, which exposes the dead to continued grave-side scrutiny. Commenting on an epitaph he found "an artless expression of intimate personal grief," John Sparrow in *Line Upon Line: An Epigraphical Anthology* compares the inscription to "the photographic portraits set incongruously in the marbles of an Italian *camposanto*." The pictures which adorn the graves at the Beirut cemetery make it a Jewish *camposanto*, perhaps the only such burial ground, for at no other Jewish graveyard have I seen photos of the deceased on tombs. Mosaics at the fourth century Hammath Temple near Tiberias include portrayals of human images—heads and full figures in and around a Zodiac circle. In Tiberias at the grave of Maimonides (d. 1204), the famous medieval Jewish scholar, a wall bears the titles of two of his works, *Guide to the Perplexed* and *The Strong Hand*, the latter symbolized by an artfully drawn hand, its knuckles carefully delineated, the pointing index finger realistically lined with wrinkles and, for good measure, one final touch: a button on the shirt cuff.

Seven centuries after Maimonides expressed in his will his desire to be buried in the Holy Land, at Tiberias, Vladimir Jabotinsky (d. 1940), the radical Zionist leader, stated in his handwritten will in 1930, eighteen years before Israel was founded: "I want to be buried, or cremated (it is all the same to me) just wherever I happen to die; and my remains (should they be buried outside of Palestine) may not be transported to Palestine unless by order of that country's eventual Jewish Government." That government, indeed, eventually came into being and Jabotinsky's remains now repose in Herzl Park on the outskirts of Jerusalem. Near his grave lies Theodor Herzl (d. 1904) himself, removed to Israel—as he wished—from Döbling cemetery in Eisenstadt, Austria, in August 1949.

Some of the other political and cultural pioneers of Israel lie in the main Tel Aviv cemetery on Trumpledor Street. A cluster of graves off to the left of the entrance includes the poet Bialik, commemorated by a cube-shaped marker; Prime Minister Moshe Sharett, recalled by a simple, shiny black stone; Meir Dizengoff, the first mayor of Tel Aviv, memorialized by a modest monument; and Max Nordau, an early-twentieth-century Zionist leader, who occupies a small mausoleum.

Holy graves abound in the ancient Holy Land. Many biblical figures repose in the earth of the terra sancta. In and around Jerusalem alone lie such burial sites as Rachel's Tomb; Mary's Tomb; the rock-hewn Tombs of the Sanhedrin ("the Judges"), not unlike Beth She'arim's excavated burial chambers; the Tombs of the Prophets; the last resting places of Absalom, of Zacharius, and of Jehosophat, cut from the stone cliff of the Valley of Jehosophat ("God will judge"); as well as such more recent graveyards as the Jewish Military

Cemetery on Mt. Herzl and the British Military Cemetery on Mt. Scopus. Overlooking the valley perches the Mount of Olives, perhaps the ultimate cemetery for there history will end. On the mount repose Jews who will, so the Lord states in Joel 3:10–11, be called to final judgment and resurrection. Jordanian soldiers dismantled much of the ancient cemetery in the 1950s and 1960s when they used tombstones to construct camps and strategic emplacements. At the end of Jehosophat Valley, where it meets Hinnom Valley, lies Haceldama ("the field of blood"). The site was purchased with the blood money Judas received for his betrayal of Christ. Repenting, Judas returned the thirty pieces of silver which the priests used to buy "the potter's field, to bury strangers in. Wherefore that field was called, the field of blood, unto this day." (Matt. 27:7–8.) I found only a few pitiful, rotting bones scattered in the chambers carved from the rocky cliffs there at the world's first potter's field cemetery.

The most renowned Jewish tomb in the Holy Land, of course, is that of Jesus. His crucifixion and interment took place at the site where the Church of the Holy Sepulchre now stands or, according to another version, at the so-called Garden Tomb, north of Jerusalem's Damascus Gate. Unwilling to risk leaving Jerusalem without adding Jesus' grave to my cemetery collection, I visited both of his tombs. I can therefore affirm that I have seen Jesus' final resting place, but I am unable to say exactly where it is. When I saw the church, late one afternoon during Easter week, most of the pilgrims had already come and gone for the day, and the sanctuary was dark and still. A priest and I entered the small alcove which houses the holy sepulchre. Candles flickered; the priest prayed; I gazed. Below me stretched the white marble slab which covers the famous tomb. The tapers' dancing light played across the stone. I remained there as the candle wax melted away. Finally I took a last glance around the spooky chamber, then left and started through the gloomy and nearly empty church. Suddenly a Coptic priest darted from the tiny chapel just behind the holy sepulchre. He clamped his fingers around my arm, drew me into his little alcove, pushed me to my knees, guided my right hand to the edge of a rock while ordering me "please to touch the sacred rock, the holy sepulchre," sprinkled me (and my guide book) with a pleasantly scented dose of rose water—"Holy water for luck," he explained—murmured a few prayers, helped me to my feet, extended his hand—"Please to give an offering"—and then, offering given and received, proceeded to usher me out of the cubicle, his eyes already scanning the dark church for his next client. All this took about half a minute: a model of assembly-line efficiency Honda or Toyota would envy.

A short distance on, another priest emerged from the shadows. I retreated but he waved me forward and, ever curious, I cautiously approached the man. After hestitating another moment, I ventured into his chapel domain. Without further ado the priest pointed to an opening off to the left, handed me a thin candle and whispered, "Joseph of Arimathea's tomb." So practiced was his routine that I had the distinct impression that I was not the first tourist to visit the chapel. Sucker for tombs that I am, I risked a second fleecing by taking the candle and entering the alcove. The thin flame barely lit the area. I advanced slowly. Although I could see nothing, at least I was adding yet another burial place to my collection. I shuffled forward in the darkness. Still no tomb. I wondered where the grave was. Then, suddenly, I tumbled into the tomb, a hole some three feet deep. The candle died immediately but fortunately I did not, even though I found myself in the grave. The priest looked in as I resurrected myself from the tomb. I limped away, slightly shaken but, still and all, quite pleased for Joseph's final resting place had unexpectedly provided me with a unique specimen for my cemetery collection—I had both feet in the grave and lived to tell the tale.

Compared to the Church of the Holy Sepulchre, the Garden Tomb seemed harmless. But it also lacked interest, for Jesus' tomb there consists of a small empty chamber carved into the side of a rock face. General Gordon of Khartoum suggested that this rocky knoll which resembled a skull was the Calvary or Golgotha (*calva* in Latin and *gulgoleth* in Hebrew mean "skull") where Jesus' crucifixion and burial took place. So perhaps this ground was the very spot described in John 19:41–42: "Now in the place where he was crucified there was a garden; and in the garden a new sepulchre . . . There laid they Jesus."

Although many pilgrims visit one or the other or both of Jesus' tombs, few travelers find their way to the supposed grave, much more difficult of access, where that other biblical leader, Moses, supposedly reposes. The patriarch expired on the heights of Mt. Nebo, now in Jordanian territory. From the summit I enjoyed a splendid view of the land promised to some and holy to many. In the middle distance undulated stony hills and ridged terrain, beyond which spread the gracefully curved Dead Sea, an embryo-shaped body of water from which its umbilical cord, the river Jordan, dangles. The river winds along the valley to the plains of Jericho, and in the far distance rises the vague smudge of clustered structures which is Jerusalem. It seemed as if this biblical landscape had remained unchanged from the day Moses stood just there to survey the Promised Land. Why is it said that such places are timeless? Rather, they are time-full, rich with the past, permeated with history and evocative of the centuries. The Bible (Deut. 34) recounts that "Moses went up from the plains of Moab to Mount Nebo . . . And the Lord showed him all the land . . . [and] Moses died there in the land of Moab, according to the word of the Lord, and he buried him in the valley in the land of Moab opposite Beth-peor; but no man knows the place of his burial to this day." However, Franciscan monks who excavated the remains of a basilica on Mt. Nebo claim they know where Moses reposes. In the central nave of the ruined church I saw some square holes that open into subterranean tombs, in one of which Moses was supposedly interred, there in that remote corner of the Holy Land overlooking the Promised Land.

What to some souls was the Promised Land became to others a foreign land. By the Zion Gate in Jerusalem stands a fifteenth-century Armenian church whose floor is paved with splendid old gravestones decorated with artfully incised relief designs that include scepters, sashes, crowns, keys, and other heraldry emblematic of the church patriarchs interred there. Next to the church stretches a large burial ground where lesser mortals—sub-patriarchial—who died in the Holy Land far from their homeland repose. Like the Jews, the Armenians possess a long religious tradition, the Armenian Ortho-dox Christian church, that acts as a binding ethnic force; they suffered a holocaust at the hands of the Turks who massacred more than half-a-million Armenians between 1915 and 1923; they have been forced to settle all over the world and look to the mother country as the homeland; and, like the Jews, deceased members of the Armenian diaspora repose in ceme-teries scattered around the world. In California, far from his homeland and from Jerusalem, Armenian-American author William Saroyan found Ararat, the Armenian cemetery in his town of Fresno, "most deeply satisfying as a place for a summer afternoon visit." Saroyan, a true cemetery lover, noted in *Obituaries* that "I enjoy visiting graveyards, for they are the truly peaceful places of our country and our world, and they provide the nicest moments of our lives."

Far-flung Armenian burial grounds around the world pro-vided me with some nice moments as I added those grave-yards to my cemetery collection. On the grounds of Singapore's St. Gregory the Illuminator Church, named after the patriarch who in 301 made Armenia the world's first Christian nation, a few graves recall the local Armenian community. One marker memorializes "the widow of the late Parsick Joaquium" (d. 1905), remembered not in her own right but only as a spouse, while another reads: "In loving memory of our darling Rosie Sarkies" (d. 1906), probably a member of the Sarkies clan that founded Singapore's famous Raffles Hotel. In Calcutta I visited the secluded Armenian church, its yard formed by hundreds of flat tombstones as if the dead were paving the way for the living. The pudgy, grey-bearded priest at the church—supposedly Calcutta's oldest Christian sanctuary (c. 1621)—accompanied me around the enclave as I searched for the slab memorializing one Esahac Abrahamian, who supposedly perished from lion wounds suffered in a gladiatorial contest. We could not find this marker but during our amble the priest informed me about various local curiosities, such as that Calcutta's beggars belong to a union and that the city exacts a fine of five rupees for killing crows, valued as they help clear away refuse by scavenging. One always learns interesting things when visiting a cemetery.

In some remote regions, far from the centers of Christendom, Armenian churches served as burial areas not only for congregants but also for other Europeans who happened to expire there. Such cemeteries therefore serve to epitomize the diaspora suffered by all families, nationalities, religions, sects, clans, things, bodies, organs, peoples, and people, for in time, they and all that which inhabits the earth scatter, fragment, disperse, decay, disappear. Cemeteries, which collect the random scatterings of chance and time, are sort of diasporeceptacles. Graveyards accumulate in one place the most unlikely tombfellows: some people who, while alive, would not be caught dead socializing with one another. The Armenian church in Shiraz, Iran, contains a varied group.

Many of the epitaphs commemorate Englishmen who died far from home. The Royal Engineers serving in Persia (Iran) erected a plaque "in memory of Sergeant Robert Collins, R. E. who was murdered near this city on the 23rd July 1872," while another marker recalls "Captain David Ruddell of the Bengal Army, who, while proceeding from Tehran to Calcutta with dispatches from His Britannic Majesty's Ambassador at the court of Persia, was cut off by fever, in this city, on the 16th Dec 1835." The earliest inscription expresses "the last tribute of a friend to the memory of departed worth in the person of Thomas Henry Sheridan, late public Secretary to Sir Harford Jones's Mission" (d. 1812, aged twenty-six). Outside in the churchyard stand a few grave slabs bearing Armenian inscriptions.

Another Armenian church in Iran, at Ishfahan, also houses slabs with Armenian epitaphs as well as monuments to such varied European types as Catherine Mary Ironside (d. 1921), "Medical missionary in Persia from 1904"; George Malcolm "of the Bombay civil service" (d. 1826); and Andrew Jukes (d. 1821), political agent "in the Persian Gulph." The large graveyard nearby, a rather forbidding, treeless, rocky field, contains the graves of a wide selection of nationalities. In the Polish section repose Joanna Rozanska (d. 1945), Jan Mazur (d. 1944), Izabela Stefanska (d. 1942). How did they get there? On the plain grey stone slabs, all identical, appeared only the names, dates, and "R.I.P." Nearby lies Amy Florence Hemming (d. 1954), "May she rest in peace," and Pastor Ernst J. Christoffel (d. 1955), a missionary, who on his marker avows "I fought the good fight," in German, Farsi, and Armenian. Farther on, in the cemetery's higher section, repose other stray Europeans: Leonard Douglas Keith (d. 1937) "of the Imperial Bank of Iran"; Georg Hemmer (d. 1940), with a swastika on his stone; Albert Simler (d. 1907) of Zurich, "Gone but not forgotten"; the evocative and appropriately named Hilda Nightingale (1943), "C.M.S. Missionary Nursing Sister in Yezd & Isfahan for 15 years . . . Well done good and faithful servant"; next to her "Leslie G. Griffiths of Melbourne, Australia, medical missionary of the C.M.S. for 9 years in Egypt and Iran . . . Also his son Ian Neal Aged 10 years, who died together in Luristan August 3, 1942 . . . They were lovely and pleasant in their lives, and in their death they were not divided," a sentiment from the Bible. Others from varying eras and scattered points around the globe, now rather incongruously united there in Iran in death, include James L. Garland (d. 1933), archdeacon of Ishfahan; John Hall Paxton (d. 1952); Lydia Tomatro (d. 1965) from Russia; Edward Pagett (d. 1702), whose stone bears a worn Latin inscription; Mrs. Sambar Glover (d. 1912) and E. H. P. Glover (d. 1898), next to Tommy Glover (d. 1975), the most recent decedant I found; Ernest Charles Haycock (d. 1927), "British Vice Consul in Isfahan"; Gysbert Willemboon (d. 1848) from The Hague; Isabel Hoernic (d. 1886), with the epitaph: "He brought me to the banqueting house and his banner over me was love."

What a mixture of names, nationalities, dates, places, professions, epitaphs—not only at that foreigners' burial ground in Iran but at all the cemeteries I have visited around the world, over long years of travel. Always and everywhere have I, ever the cemetery collector, found those grave confusions, a chaos of cast-off bodies. So often did Bela Lugosi (d. 1956, buried at Holy Cross cemetery in Los Angeles) die in horror movies that a guest at the actor's funeral service observed that seeing him reposing in a coffin had become a familiar sight. Similarly, I have spent so much time in so many cemeteries that by now I consider myself an honorary decedant. Here and there and everywhere I came across the dead—long-gone, just gone, young, old, hardly started, ripe departed, Christian and Jew, Muslim and Mormon, saints and sinners, losers and winners, outlaws and in-laws, black and white and red all over, rich and poor, top dogs and fat cats, big shots and small fry, the once healthy and wealthy and wise and foolish and poor, the dead in all their rich variety, scattered about the earth in capital cities, small towns, remote corners, crowded burial grounds, empty fields, lying in the earth remembered, forgotten, adored, ignored, commemorated, nameless, all, all claimed by the great democracy of death.

How I have enjoyed visiting cemeteries and then arranging my impressions into words which ordered these experiences. Of course, one's final encounter with a cemetery provides the only ultimate order. That encounter draws ever closer: as time moves on, one begins to see dark at the end of the tunnel. But this is no way vexes me. I am of the same mind as Horace Walpole: "As mine is a pretty cheerful kind of philosophy, I think the best way is to think of dying, but to talk and act as if one was not to die; or else one tires other people, and dies before one's time." A famous ancient Roman epitaph known as "On the Tomb of a Happy Man" reads: "No tears for me, for my urn knows only spring. Death I've known not, for I've only changed my state." Visiting cemeteries brought no tears for me but, in the spirit of that happy man, only pleasantly provocative diversions. For me graveyards yielded a rich mixture of history, art, biography, nature, humor—delights which, hopefully, you, faithful reader, have enjoyed as you patiently paged your way through this book of cemeteries I have patiently collected from here and there, near and far.

In his "Epistle to the Reader" at the beginning of *Ancient Funerall Monuments,* John Weever cautioned: "So many burials, Reader, in one booke/Warne thee, that one day, thou for death must looke." To be sure, many dead lie emtombed in the pages of this tome, but—in contrast to Weever—my hope is that in this cemetery book you see life rather than death. For such is what I found during my visits to all those graveyards. You do not need to haunt or to read about dozens of cemeteries to realize that, as phrased in *Romeo and Juliet,* "all things that we ordained festival,/Turn from their office to black funeral." One cemetery—or even none: simply life itself—suffices to reveal that truth. But cemetery visits also serve a more positive purpose: they denote vitality. The epitaphs and the histories of the departed recall so many efforts, so much energy, such a wide range of accomplishments. This is extremely inspiring. For it was no secret to the now dead— as it is no secret to us—that black funeral awaited them in the end. Yet in spite of that end they did things. It is amazing how much humankind which came, and went, before us accomplished. Missionaries, moneymen, mercenaries, magnates, moguls, merchants, military, mariners—what tales the epitaphs tell of these adventurers and achievers, what stories about the wonderful busyness of the world, the motions and emotions, the to-ing and fro-ing, the coming and going, the creations and recreations and procreations, all recalled by monuments to people who lived and thrived in the face of their ever-approaching black funeral. Some of them even wrote books. All those cemeteries, those precincts of death, I visited made me marvel at the vitality of human life.

And now, dear reader, our cemetery visits are over and the time has come for us to part. Perhaps you are reading these words long after my time, just as I read the epitaphs of so many dead long after their day. May all the departed souls remembered in these pages vitalize you: I hope that so many graves in this book remind thee that thou for life must look. It only remains for me to take my leave, and you yours. Every end deserves an epitaph, and so—at the end of our brief time together—I leave you with one final epitaph which seems to me best to summarize my cemetery-filled years among the living. On a New Year's Day of a year now old I came across this inscription from a land far away and a time long ago—ancient Greece—on one of the Elgin Marbles at the British Museum in London: "After many pleasant sports with my companions I, who sprang from the earth, am earth once more. I am Aristokles of Piraeus, son of Menon." Reader: Farewell.

Last Writes: Tomb Tomes

THE following list of more than 150 works on cemeteries, burial areas and related matters will hopefully be useful to readers who wish to pursue a subject which for so many years has intrigued, entertained, and delighted me. I include this rather extensive compilation of sources because—as became apparent to me during my research for this book—few complete, non-specialized bibliographies on cemeteries exist. Omitted, for the most part, are more general works which happen to contain information on cemeteries, and also narrowly focused or highly specialized books. Although I consulted other books in addition to those mentioned, the list is restricted to material directly related to the subjects covered in this book. Two especially useful organizations which specialize in graveyard literature are the Center for Thanatology

Research, 391 Atlantic Avenue, Brooklyn, New York 11217, and the Association for Gravestone Studies, 46 Plymouth Road, Needham, Massachusetts 02192. The Center for Thanatology offers for sale books and articles on cemeteries and related subjects, while the Association for Gravestone Studies publishes annually *Markers* and also a quarterly newsletter. Two professional groups publish monthly trade journals: *Stone in America,* issued by the American Monument Association, and *American Cemetery,* put out by the American Cemetery Association.

A Collection of Epitaphs and Monumental Inscriptions, Historical, Biographical, Literary, and Miscellaneous, with an Essay on Epitaphs by Dr. Samuel Johnson. 2 volumes. London: Lackington Allen, & Co., 1806.

Aloi, Roberto. *Architettura funeraria moderna.* Milan: Editore Ulrico Hoepli, 1948.

Andrews, William. *Curious Epitaphs.* London: W. Andrews & Co., 1899.

Annual Report 1986. Office of Chief Medical Examiner, The City of New York.

Arbeiter, Jean, and Linda D. Cirino. *Permanent Addresses: A Guide to the Resting Places of Famous Americans.* New York: M. Evans and Company, 1983.

Ariès, Philippe. *Western Attitudes Toward Death from the Middle Ages to the Present.* Translated by Patricia M. Ranum. Baltimore: Johns Hopkins University Press, 1975.

————. *The Hour of Our Death.* Translated by Helen Weaver. New York: Alfred A. Knopf, 1981.

————. *Images of Man and Death.* Translated by Janet Lloyd. Cambridge: Harvard University Press, 1985.

Bailey, Conrad. *Harrap's Guide to Famous London Graves.* London: George G. Harrap & Co., 1975.

Ball, James Moores. *The Body Snatchers: Doctors, Grave Robbers and the Law.* New York: Dorset Press, 1989 (original edition 1928).

Barbanell, Sylvia. *When Your Animal Dies*. London: Spiritualist Press, 1969.

Barker, Felix. *Highgate Cemetery*. Salem, N. H.: Salem House, 1984.

Batsford, Herbert. *English Mural Monuments and Tombstones*. London: B. T. Batsford, 1960.

Beable, W. H. *Epitaphs: Graveyard Humour and Eulogy*. London: Simpkin, Marshall, Hamilton, Kent & Co., 1925.

Beagle, Peter S. *A Fine and Private Place*. New York: Viking Press, 1960.

Beck-Friss, Johan. *The Protestant Cemetery in Rome*. Malmö, Sweden: Allhems Förlag Publishing House, n.d.

Bendann, E. *Death Customs: An Analytical Study of Burial Rites*. New York: Alfred A. Knopf, 1930.

Boase, T. S. R. *Death in the Middle Ages*. London: Thames & Hudson, 1972.

Böcher, Otto. *Der alte Judenfriedhof in Worms*. Worms, Germany: 1968.

Bowman, Leroy. *The American Funeral*. New York: Paperback Library, 1964.

Bradford, Charles A. *Heart Burial*. London: George Allen & Unwin, 1933.

Braet, Herman, and Werner Verbeke. eds. *Death in the Middle Ages*. Leuven, Belgium: Leuven University Press, 1983.

Brown, Frederick. *Père Lachaise: Elysium as Real Estate*. New York: Viking Press, 1973.

Browne, Sir Thomas. *Hydriotaphia: Urne Buriall or a Discourse of the Sepulchrall Urnes Lately Found in Norfolk*. London: 1658.

Bunnen, Lucinda and Virginia Warren Smith. *Scoring in Heaven: Gravestones and Cemetery Art of the American*

Sunbelt States. New York: Aparture, 1991.

Burgess, Frederick. *English Churchyard Memorials.* London: Lutterworth Press, 1963.

Burgess, Pamela. *Churchyards.* London: SPCK, 1980.

Byers, Laura. *'Till Death Do Us Part: Design Sources of Eighteenth-Century New England Tombstones.* New Haven: Yale Center for American Art and Material Culture, 1978.

Cacciu, Angelo M. *The Basilica of SS. John and Paul in Venice.* 5th ed. Venice: Edizioni Zanipolo, 1969.

Chaunu, Pierre. *La mort à Paris.* Paris: Fayard, 1978.

Coffin, Margaret M. *Death in Early America.* New York: Elsevier/Nelson Books, 1976.

Cohen, Kathleen. *Metamorphosis of a Death Symbol: The Transi Tombs in the Late Middle Ages and the Renaissance.* Berkeley and Los Angeles: University of California Press, 1973.

Combs, Diann Williams. *Early Gravestone Art in Georgia and South Carolina.* Athens, Georgia: University of Georgia Press, 1986.

Coriolis [pseud.]. *Death Here Is Thy Sting.* Toronto and Montreal: McClelland and Stewart, 1967.

Crossley, Fred H. *English Church Monuments, A.D. 1150–1550: An Introduction to the Study of Tombs and Effigies of the Mediaeval Period.* London: B. T. Batsford, 1921.

Culbertson, Judi, and Tom Randall. *Permanent Parisians: An Illustrated Guide to the Cemeteries of Paris.* Chelsea, Vt.: Chelsea Green Publishing Company, 1986.

———. *Permanent New Yorkers: A Biographical Guide to the Cemeteries of New York.* Chelsea, Vt.: Chelsea Green Publishing Company, 1987.

Curl, James Stevens. *The Victorian Celebration of Death.* Detroit: Partridge Press, 1972.

———. *A Celebration of Death: An Introduction to Some of the Buildings, Monuments, and Settings of Funerary Architecture in the Western European Tradition.* London: Constable, 1980.

Dansel, Michel. *Au Père-Lachaise: son histoire, ses secrets, ses promenades.* Paris: Fayard, 1973.

de Brunhoff, Anne. *Souls in Stone: European Graveyard Sculpture.* New York: Alfred A. Knopf, 1978.

Deetz, James, and Edwin S. Dethlefsen. "Death's Head, Cherub, Urn and Willow." *Natural History* 76 (March 1967).

Dennis, George. *The Cities and Cemeteries of Etruria.* London: John Murray, 1878.

Desfayes, Mlle. "Les tombeaux de coeur et d'entrailles en France." *Bulletins des Museés de France* 12, no. 8 (Sept.– Oct. 1947).

Dethlefsen, Edwin S., and Kenneth Jensen. "Social Commentary from the Cemetery." *Natural History* 86 (June 1977).

Dewhurst, C. Kurt, Betty MacDowell and Marsha Mac-Dowell. *Religious Folk Art in America: Reflections of Faith.* New York: E. P. Dutton, 1983.

Dickerson, Robert B., Jr. *Final Placement: A Guide to the Deaths, Funerals and Burials of Notable Americans.* Algonac, Mich.: Reference Publications, 1982.

Dingley, Thomas. *History From Marble.* London: Camden Society, 1867.

Duval, Francis Y., and Ivan B. Rigby. *Early American Gravestone Art in Photographs.* New York: Dover Publications, 1978.

El dia de los muertos: The Life of the Dead in Mexican Folk Art. The Fort Worth Art Museum, 1987.

Eliade, Mircea. *Death, Afterlife and Eschatology.* New York: Harper & Row, 1974.

Ellis, Nancy and Parker Hayden. *Here Lies America: A Collection of Notable Graves.* New York: Hawthorn Books, 1978.

Enright, D. J., ed. *The Oxford Book of Death*. Oxford and New York: Oxford University Press, 1983.

Esdaile, Katherine. *English Church Monuments, 1510–1840*. Oxford: Oxford University Press, 1946.

Etlin, Richard A. *The Architecture of Death: The Transformation of the Cemetery in Eighteenth-Century Paris*. Cambridge: MIT Press, 1984.

Fabre–Luce, Alfred. *La mort à changé*. Paris: Gallimard, 1966.

Farrell, James J. *Inventing the American Way of Death, 1830–1920*. Philadelphia: Temple University Press, 1980.

Fisher, Major Payne. *The Catalogue of Most of the Memorable Tombes, Gravestones, Plates, Escutcheons, or Atchievements in the Demolisht or yet Extant Churches of London*. London, 1668. Reprint. Revised and edited by G. Blacker Morgan. n.p. 1885.

Florin, Lambert. *Boot Hill: Historic Graves of the Old West*. New York: Bonanza Books, 1966.

———. *Tales the Western Tombstones Tell*. Seattle: Superior Publishing Company, 1967.

Forbes, Harriette Merrifield. *Gravestones of Early New England and the Men Who Made Them, 1653–1800*. Boston: Houghton Mifflin, 1927.

Garland, Robert. *The Greek Way of Death*. Ithaca: Cornell University Press, 1985.

Georgakas, Dan. *The Methuselah Factor*. New York: Simon & Schuster, 1980.

Giesey, Ralph E. *The Royal Funeral Ceremony in Renaissance France*. Geneva: Librarie E. Droz, 1960.

Gillon, Edmund Vincent, Jr. *Early New England Gravestone Rubbings*. New York: Dover Publications, Inc. 1966.

———. *Victorian Cemetery Art*. New York: Dover Publications, Inc. 1972.

Gittings, Clare. *Death, Burial and the Individual in Early*

Modern England. London and Sydney: Croom Helm, 1984.

Gould, Richard, and M. Schiffero. *The Archeology of the U.S.: The Cemetery and Cultural Change*. New York: Academic Press, 1981.

Gravestone Designs: Rubbings and Photos from Early New York and New Jersey. New York: Dover Publications, 1972.

Grigson, Geoffrey. *The Faber Book of Epigrams and Epitaphs*. London: Faber & Faber, 1977.

Grinsell, Leslie V. *Barrow, Pyramid and Tomb: Ancient Burial Customs in Egypt, the Mediterranean and the British Isles*. Boulder, Col.: Westview Press, 1975.

Habenstein, Robert W., and William M. Lamers. *Funeral Customs the World Over*. Rev. ed. The National Funeral Directors Association of the United States, Inc., 1963.

————. *The History of American Funeral Directing*. Rev. ed. The National Funeral Directors Association of the United States, Inc., 1963.

Halporn, Roberta. *New York Is A Rubber's Paradise: A Guide to Cemeteries of Interest in the Five Boroughs*. Brooklyn: Center for Thanatology Research, 1984.

Harmer, Ruth Mulvey. *The High Cost of Dying*. New York: Collier Books, 1963.

Harris, James E., and Kent R. Weeks. *X-Raying the Pharoahs*. New York: Charles Scribner's Sons, 1973.

Hillairet, Jacques. *Les 200 cimetières de vieux Paris*. Paris: Éditions de Minuit, 1958.

Howe, W. H. *Here Lies: Being a Collection of Ancient and Modern, Humorous and Queer Inscriptions from Tombstones*. New York: A. L. Burt Co., n.d.

Huntington, Richard, and Peter Metcalf. *Celebrations of Death: The Anthropology of Mortuary Ritual*. Cambridge: Cambridge University Press, 1979.

Hurtig, Judith W. *The Armored Gisant Before 1400*. New York: Garland Press, 1979.

Irion, Paul E. *Funeral Customs the World Over*, Bulfin Press, 1966.

Jackson, Charles O., ed. *Passing: The Vision of Death in America*. Westport, Conn.: Greenwood Press, 1977.

Jackson, Kenneth, and Camilo Vergara. *American Cemeteries*. Princeton: Princeton Architectural Press, 1988.

s'Jacob, Henriette. *Idealism and Realism: A Study of Sepulchral Symbolism*. Leiden: E. J. Brill, 1954.

Jacobs, G. W. *Stranger Stop and Cast An Eye*. Brattleboro, Vt.: Stephen Greene Press, 1973.

Jones, Barbara. *Design for Death*. Indianapolis: Bobbs–Merrill Company, 1967.

Jones, James. *Sepulchrorum Inscriptiones: Curious Collection of the Most Remarkable Epitaphs in the Kingdoms of Great Britain, Ireland, &c. In English Verse*. Westminster, 1726.

Julian, Philippe. *Le cirque du Père-Lachaise*. Paris: Fasquelle, 1957.

Kemp, B. *English Church Monuments*. London: B. T. Batsford, 1980.

Kirsch, G. P. *The Catacombs of Priscilla*. Rome: Friends of the Catacombs, 1971.

Koykka, Arthur S. *Project Remember: A National Index of Gravesites of Notable Americans*. Algonac, Mich.: Reference Publications, 1986.

Kull, Andrew. *New England Cemeteries*. Brattleboro, Vt.: Stephen Greene Press, 1975.

Kurtz, Donna C., and John Boardman. *Greek Burial Customs*. Ithaca: Cornell University Press, 1971.

Lai, T. C. *To the Yellow Springs: The Chinese View of Death*. Hong Kong: Joint Publishing Co. and Kelly & Walsh, 1983.

La Mort au Moyen Âge. Association of French Medieval Historians. Strasbourg: Librarie Istra, 1975.

Le Clere, Marcel. *Cimetières et Sépultures de Paris.* Paris: Hachette, 1978.

"Le Meilleiur Commerce du Monde: Les Pompes Funèbres." *Crapouillot* 69 (Juin–Juillet 1966).

Lesy, Michael. *The Forbidden Zone.* New York: Farrar, Straus & Giroux, 1987.

Letronne, M. *Examen critique de la decouverte du pretendu coeur de Saint Louis, faite à la Sainte-Chapelle, le 15 mai 1843.* Paris: Firmin Didot Frères, 1844.

Lewis, R. A. *Edwin Chadwick and the Public Health Movement, 1832–1854.* London: Longmans, Green & Co., 1952.

Lewnfohn, Dr. L. *Sechzig Epitaphien von Grabsteinen des Israelitifshen Friedhofes zu Worms.* Frankfurt, 1855.

Linden-Ward, Blanche. *Silent City on a Hill: Landscapes of Memory and Boston's Mount Auburn Cemetery.* Columbus: Ohio State University Press, 1988.

Lindley, Kenneth. *Of Graves and Epitaphs.* London: Hutchison, 1965.

———. *Graves and Graveyards.* London: Routledge & Kegan Paul, 1972.

Loaring, H. J. *Epitaphs Quaint, Curious and Elegant.* London: W. Tegg, 1873 (?).

Ludwig, Allan I. *Graven Images: New England Stone Carving and Its Symbols, 1650–1815.* Middletown, Conn.: Wesleyan University Press, 1966.

Mann, Thomas C., and Janet Greene. *Over Their Dead Bodies.* Brattleboro, Vt.: Stephen Greene Press, 1962.

———. *Sudden and Awful: American Epitaphs and the Finger of God.* Brattleboro, Vt.: Stephen Greene Press, 1968.

Marion, John Francis. *Famous and Curious Cemeteries.* New York: Crown Publishers, 1977.

McManners, John. *Death and the Enlightenment.* Oxford: Oxford University Press, 1981.

Meller, Hugh. *London Cemeteries: An Illustrated Guide and*

Gazetteer. Amersham, England: Avebury Publishing Company, 1981.

Meyer, Richard E., ed. *Cemeteries and Gravemarkers: Voices of American Culture.* Ann Arbor: UMI Research Press, 1989.

Mitford, Jessica. *The American Way of Death.* New York: Simon & Schuster, 1963.

Morley, John. *Death, Heaven and the Victorians.* Pittsburgh: University of Pittsburgh Press, 1971.

Mucklow, Walter. *Cemetery Accounts.* New York: American Institute Publishing Co., 1935.

Munby, Arthur J. *Faithful Servants: Being Epitaphs and Obituaries Recording their Names and Services.* London: Reeves & Turner, 1891.

Naples, Joshua. *Diary of a Resurrectionist.* Edited by James Blake Bailey. London: Swan Sonnenschein, 1896.

Neal, Avon, and Ann Parker. "Graven Images: Sermons in Stone." *American Heritage* 21 (August 1970).

Ovando, Roberto Jiménez. *La capilla mortuoria del exconvento del Carmen, San Angel, D.F.* Mexico City: Instituto Nacional de Antropologia e Historia, 1980.

Panofsky, Erwin. *Tomb Sculpture.* New York: Harry N. Abrams, 1964.

Paul–Albert, N. *Histoire du cimetière du Père-Lachaise.* Paris: Gallimard, 1937.

Penny, Nicholas. *Church Monuments in Romantic England.* New Haven: Yale University Press, 1977.

———. *Mourning.* London: Her Majesty's Stationary Office, 1981.

Peters, James Edward. *Arlington National Cemetery: Shrine to America's Heroes.* Kensington, Md.: Woodbine House, 1986.

Pettigrew, T. J. *Chronicles of the Tombs.* London: H. G. Bohn, 1857.

Pini, G. *Cremation in Italy and Abroad from 1774 to Our Day.* Milan, 1885.

Puckle, Bertram S. *Funeral Customs: Their Origin and Development.* London: T. Werner Laurie, 1926.

Ragon, Michel. *The Space of Death: A Study of Funerary Architecture, Decoration and Urbanism.* Charlottesville: University Press of Virginia, 1983.

Ronan, Margaret, and Eve Ronan. *Death Around the World.* New York: Scholastic Book Services, 1978.

Sabatier, Robert. *Dictionnaire De La Mort.* Paris: Éditions Albin Michel, 1967.

Sparrow, John. *Line Upon Line: An Epigraphical Anthology.* Cambridge: University Printing House, 1967.

Spiegl, Fritz, ed. *A Small Book of Grave Humour.* London: Pan Books, 1971.

Stannard, David E., ed. *Death In America.* Philadelphia: University of Pennsylvania Press, 1975.

————. *The Puritan Way of Death: A Study in Religion, Culture, and Social Change.* New York: Oxford University Press, 1977.

————. "Calm Dwellings: The Brief, Sentimental Age of the Rural Cemetery." *American Heritage,* 30 (August 1979).

Tashjian, Dickran, and Ann Tashjian. *Memorials for Children of Change: The Art of Early New England Stonecarving.* Middletown, Conn.: Wesleyan University Press, 1974.

Toynbee, J. M. C. *Death and Burial in the Roman World.* Ithaca: Cornell University Press, 1971.

Vallé, Isabel. *Epitaphs of Some Dear Dumb Beasts.* Boston: Gorham Press, 1916.

Vincent, W. T. *In Search of Gravestones Old and Curious.* London: Mitchell & Hughes, 1896.

Walker, George Alfred. *Gatherings From Graveyards.*

London: Longman & Company, 1839.

Wallis, Charles L. *Stories on Stone: A Book of American Epitaphs.* New York: Oxford University Press, 1954.

———. *American Epitaphs Grave and Humorous.* New York: Dover Publications, 1973.

Waugh, Evelyn. *The Loved One.* Harmondsworth, England: Penguin Books, 1951.

Weever, John. *Ancient Funerall Monuments With In the United Monarchie of Great Britaine, Ireland, and the Ilands Adjacent.* London: Thomas Harper, 1631.

Whaley, J., ed. *Mirrors of Mortality: Studies in the Social History of Death.* London: Europa, 1981.

Williams, Gwilym M. *The Nation's Tribute: An International Illustrated Guide to Animal Memorials.* Bala, North Wales: Animal Lovers Anonymous, 1969.

Willshire, Betty, and Doreen Hunter. *Stones: A Guide to Some Remarkable Eighteenth Century Gravestones.* New York: Taplinger Publishing Company, 1978.

Wilson, Samuel, Jr., and Leonard V. Huber. *The St. Louis Cemeteries of New Orleans.* New Orleans: St. Louis Cathedral, 1963.

Young, Melvin A. *Where They Lie,* Lanham, Md: University Press of America, 1991.

Zelinsky, Wilbur. "Unearthly Delights: Cemetery Names and the Map of the Changing American Underworld." Chapter 7 of *Geographies of the Mind,* edited by David Lowenthal and Martyn J. Bowden. New York: Oxford University Press, 1976.

Index